THE RING
OF THE
SLAVE
PRINCE

X
Let's Stop Here

1

'Physician, fuck thyself,' Sutty grumbled, pulling on to Oxford Road. It was his first day back on active duty and he'd insisted on driving. Insisted on sharing every thought that went through his head. The night shift had passed without incident. It was 6 a.m. and they were rewarded with a spectral pink dawn, turning the city from one thing into another.

'Can you drop me somewhere round Piccadilly?' said Naomi, changing the subject.

Sutty glanced over at the girl, the *woman*, as she'd insisted he call her. She was buried somewhere inside a brand-new black parka jacket, with one knee up against the dash, reading the story about Chase's promotion to the role of Chief Constable. Sutty had read it earlier, noting that Alistair Parrs would step into the vacated position of Chief Superintendent. He'd given it a second's thought.

Naomi ripped the page out and screwed it up.

She'd seemed preoccupied all night but Sutty didn't ask why. Better to watch, wait and work it out for himself. When he pulled on to Portland Street and she opened the door to get out, he turned.

'Same time tomorrow?'

'It's a date, Sutts.'

She climbed out without looking back, hands in her pockets against the morning chill, and he watched her for a minute. Walking in the direction of the Northern Quarter. Sutty nodded to himself. Mystery solved.

Naomi couldn't explain why exactly she kept coming back.

Sometimes it was a good feeling and sometimes it was a bad one, but it never came to much. She turned on to Aidan's road and was surprised to see the light on inside his flat. She stood there for a moment and then laughed, crossing the road and pressing the intercom. A moment passed and she was buzzed inside, walking through the small hallway and up the stairs. The door was ajar and when she pushed it open she saw packing materials. Boxes and bin bags.

'You should have told me,' she said. 'I'd have helped.'

Anne turned to her and smiled.

'I've had a lot of practice lately, and I thought it might be a chance to feel close to him. What brings you here?'

'Sometimes I just find myself walking by,' said Naomi, going to the kitchenette. 'I hope you haven't packed the kettle.'

'Help yourself.'

Naomi found two mugs and busied herself with the tea, talking about her first shift with Sutty. She concluded the story to no answer and turned to check Anne was OK. Aidan's sister was standing at the bookcase, her back to the room. Naomi gave her a minute and then went over, touched her shoulder and handed her a cup of tea.

'Everything OK?'

Anne accepted the drink with one hand. The other was resting on the bookcase, shaking, and she was frowning, confused. The shelf was packed full except for this one spot between Charles Dickens and Geoff Dyer, where it looked like a book the size of a house brick had been removed. Naomi tried to read the complicated expression on Anne's face and was surprised to see her break into a smile. Then she looked from Aidan's sister to the shelf, trying to sound casual and keep it light.

'Are you missing something?'

About the Author

Joseph Knox was born and raised in and around Stoke and Manchester, where he worked in bars and bookshops before moving to London. He runs, writes and reads compulsively. His debut novel *Sirens* was a bestseller and has been translated into eighteen languages.

The Sleepwalker is a Detective Aidan Waits novel.

THE RING OF THE SLAVE PRINCE

BJARNE REUTER

Translated by Tiina Nunnally

Andersen Press · London

Published in 2004 by
Andersen Press Limited,
20 Vauxhall Bridge Road, London SW1V 2SA
www.andersenpress.co.uk

Published by arrangement with Dutton Children's Books,
a member of Penguin Group (USA) Inc.

CIP Data available.

ISBN 1 84270 370 6

Originally published in 2000 by Gyldendal, Copenhagen, Denmark, under the title
Prins Faisal's Ring.

Designed by Irene Vandervoort

Printed and bound in Great Britain by
Mackays of Chatham plc, Chatham, Kent

To Filip, Anders, Anna Sophie, and Max

B.R.

Contents

PART I

1. *Tom O'Connor* 5
2. *Feodora Dolores Vasgues* 15
3. *Ramón the Pious* 28
4. *Father Innocent* 36
5. *Bibido* 52

PART II

6. *Nicolaus Copernicus* 67
7. *Lucifer's Boot* 82
8. *Joop van den Arle* 101
9. *Master Briggs* 113
10. *Sugar George* 126
11. *Sarah Briggs* 137
12. *Sunday Morning* 150
13. *Ina* 161
14. *Kanuno* 170

PART III

15. *El Casto Josephine* 181
16. *Viva España* 196
17. *Caballito del Diablo* 204

18. *Nyo Boto* 214

19. *Island* 232

20. *Gráinne Ni Mháille* 245

PART IV

21. *The Devil's Pate* 265

22. *C. W. Bull* 286

23. *Indigo Moon* 303

24. *Orion's Belt* 316

25. *Gianlucca from Portofino* 332

26. *São Miguel* 341

27. *Prince Abebe's Ring* 355

EPILOGUE 373

THE RING
OF THE
SLAVE PRINCE

Part I

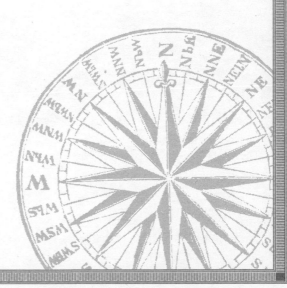

1 Tom O'Connor

IN THE YEAR OF OUR LORD 1639, a Portuguese full-rigger capsized off the coast of Saint Kitts and sank, with all hands lost. On its way from Africa to Brazil, in the New World, the galleon had run into a hurricane and then fallen prey to mutiny, whereupon it had changed course. What else the crew and the four hundred slaves on board might have endured is unknown, but rumors of the shipwreck spread like wildfire across the small islands of the Caribbean. Night after night, men and women, young and old, could be seen putting out to sea in their little skiffs, lanterns glittering like thousands of fireflies, as they searched for the valuable wreckage.

The three-masted galleon had been a magnificent ship, with yards on all the masts, incomparable in size and beauty. Now nothing remained but a ripple on the sea, a figurehead that was still afloat, and two miserable souls, whom this story is about. And it's also about Tom O'Connor, of course, a boy of about fourteen, who was born and raised on the island of Nevis, known for its dense rain forests and the ancient dormant volcano that stands in the middle of the island with a narrow white rim around its top.

The O'Connor family consisted of three members: Tom; his mother; and his half sister, Feodora, who was three years older than Tom. They earned their keep as servants at a small inn near one of the island harbors. The owner, Señor López, had taken the family in when Feodora's father, a Spaniard, was killed in a duel. Later the widow remarried, this time to an Irishman, who succumbed to fever two years after Tom was born.

The widow was then left to the whims of Señor López and to the diligence of her children. They lived at the inn, receiving their daily meals and the clothes on their backs. But ever since Tom could walk, he had combed the waters along the shore in hopes of finding treasure that with one stroke would free his family from the brutal López.

The story began one dark and stormy night in September. Tom had just finished wiping down the tables and shut the door to the back room, where Señor López was arguing with Tom's mother about the accounts. Tom knew that his mother would never dream of cheating anyone, and especially not Señor López. Once a week she and Feodora had to bathe the innkeeper's feet, clean his nails, trim his beard, delouse his hair, and scrub his back. They gave him tansy against intestinal worms, marjoram for his digestion, and red wine to counter his gloomy spirit.

"I know about your craving for money," whined the innkeeper. "I know about the eternal flame that burns for mammon in the sick hearts of men; you're not one iota better than anyone else. And your impudent daughter with her sharp tongue and haughty manner has been scaring off so many customers that soon I'll have to lock the doors and look around for some other means of making a living. And then God only knows what will become of Widow O'Connor and her two fatherless brats."

"But your establishment is a little gold mine," protested Tom's mother, who stood behind the innkeeper, combing out his black hair.

Señor López was seated in an overstuffed armchair that had to be expanded three times a year in order to make room for his ever-more enormous rear end, which Tom and Feodora had nicknamed the Far Beyond. "Gold mine?" sniveled the Spaniard, unbuttoning his collar. "What do you know about the expenses and risks that an innkeeper must endure? And then to be endowed with a pliable temperament, which you and your offspring exploit like ticks."

Tom shook his head and started setting the chairs on top of the tables so he could wash the floor.

"And your daughter has the nerve to talk back to me," continued López. "To me, the widow's only protection against poverty and disease. To me, as I hold my hand over the widow's head, just as I hold my hand over the head of her daughter and her son, that devil of an Irish boy. There's a real demon in his sickly eyes. He breathes through gills, that he does. Spends so much time underwater that his countenance has turned green and abominable. A man nurtures a viper in his midst, tossing and turning all night at the thought of what that boy might do to him as he lies in his sheets."

"Señor López can rest easy," said Tom's mother.

"But I do *not* rest easy. Worst of all are the stories he makes up. Lies through and through. They pour out of him the moment he opens his mouth."

"Tom's a good boy. You know that quite well, Señor. He has a lively imagination, but that's not the same thing as lying."

"He's a rogue, and his sister is haughty, brazen, and snide, and she makes fun of a person. As if a man could be his own creator."

"I'll talk to Feo, Señor López." The widow's calm, deep voice usually soothed the temper of the stout innkeeper.

The conversation intensified around his favorite topic, which was Feodora's sharp tongue, a topic Tom also favored. The thought that his half sister would be subjected to yet another reprimand that very night put him in a better mood and brought a little smile to his lips as he went over to bolt the door.

"It's hard to believe the girl's father was a Spaniard," López went on.

"That's precisely the problem," muttered Tom. He was about to snuff out the candle on the counter when he heard a knock at the door. He sighed and looked at the strip of light dividing the tavern from the back room, where two huge candlesticks always burned because the innkeeper was afraid of the dark. At night Señor López slept with a corner of his nightshirt in his mouth. Tom went over to the door and said softly but firmly that the inn was closed.

There was another knock.

"I said, we're closed. Come back tomorrow."

At that moment light from the back room flooded the tavern. Tom glanced over his shoulder and saw his mother in the process of washing the innkeeper's feet. The fat man was sitting there, pointing his silver-studded cane at Tom. "You Irish cur," he croaked. "Open the door if a customer wants a drink. What do you think we live on, boy?"

Tom shrugged and opened the door. Even though the figure was partially disguised by a snug-fitting cowl, and even though there was no light in the pitch-black night except what came from the sea, he recognized the wanderer Zamora at once. People said that she was two hundred years old.

She herself claimed she had witnessed the oceans as they emerged from the mouth of the frog—the frog that was the origin of everything and that had bestowed on Zamora her great wisdom and her milky eye, which could peer into people's futures. Otherwise she lived off the peculiar salves she concocted to heal people's wounds and rid them of constipation. Countless boatswains had offered her a bottle of the best wine in the house, only to discover before long that they were about to find romance and misfortune in one and the same person. Yet it was common knowledge that in her younger days Zamora had been an excellent and reliable midwife, as she had been for Elinore O'Connor when Tom was born.

Zamora sat down at the front table and asked for a tankard of water.

"Make sure to get the money first," the innkeeper called out.

Tom went behind the counter to the bucket he had used for wiping the tables. He wasn't about to give away fresh drinking water free of charge, and especially not to Zamora, who seldom could pay and who just now was preventing him from putting out to sea before the other treasure-hunters headed out at dawn. He poured the filthy water into an earthenware mug and set it in front of the old woman.

With a weary gesture, she pushed back her hood. There wasn't much hair left on her small sunburned head. One of her eyes was always closed. The other, the milky one, looked at Tom with an inscrutable expression. Her hands trembling, she emptied the mug and wiped her mouth on the back of her sleeve. "Tom O'Connor," she said, sighing, "your father owed me money."

Zamora was known for those sorts of remarks. No one paid them any mind.

"But we won't let that come between us, my boy. Where's your mother?"

"My mother is with Señor López, and the inn is closed."

"Your mother usually doesn't refuse me a glass of wine from the dregs cask. But perhaps you've drunk it all yourself? How like your father you are. Do you still fight with your half sister? Yes, you do, Tom. You hate Spaniards, and she despises your Irish blood. I can read it in your green eyes. So, pour me a glass, and let's talk about your father. He could certainly hold his own. To hell with the fever that took him. Hail Hippocrates the Wise, for superstition is still the best friend of disease. Take heed of that, young Tom. God's will has nothing to do with fever, and the plague is something that people get from rats. But let's set some wine on the table."

Tom crossed his arms. "If you want wine, you'll have to pay."

"Oh, but of course I'll pay, Tom."

"With what?"

Zamora looked around, a little smile playing on her liver-colored lips.

Tom cast a glance at her stunted shadow slanting across the ceiling.

"It's a peculiar wind we have tonight," Zamora sniffed, "first from the east, then from the west, drifting over the sea but leaving not even a ripple. Do you know what that kind of wind is called? It's called the breeze of the will. It comes from the great maw of fate, and whoever knows how to listen will learn a great deal. It's on a night like this that a person meets his destiny." Zamora's milky eye gazed at Tom appraisingly. "But as always, Fate travels with clenched fists, holding in his hand the path you should take. Now the question is: which hand will you choose, dear Tom?"

Tom sighed and shook his head.

"Give me your hand, young O'Connor."

"I'd rather not."

"I know it takes courage to have your palm read, but I assume you are man enough to hear what's in store for you. Your father was a man of courage. Fiery and hot-tempered, but brave."

"I know."

"There's not much left for someone like me who has witnessed the birth of the oceans and seen the Earth turn to fire. But it occurs to me that *your* destiny in particular is different from anyone else's."

"It is?"

With a sudden movement and surprising strength, Zamora grabbed hold of Tom's wrist. The milky eye pierced him like a thorn. "For a glass of wine, just one glass, I will offer you the rest of your life."

"Let go of my arm, Zamora."

"Just one glass from the dregs cask, which your sister pours through a red cloth to filter out scraps of food, tobacco, and contagion. Oh, I know about life in a tavern. You see, Tom, I've been everywhere. I've seen men die of drink and sailors get rolled and end up hanged by the same rope they used as a lifeline when they crossed the Atlantic Ocean. Your path, Tom O'Connor, is strewn with flint and stones, and it will take you farther out than you care to go. But there's a remedy for that, and if one day you reach the ends of the Earth, then mark my words. Because in Jamaica there's a so-called public house named Lucifer's Boot. That's where you should go when all other possibilities are used up, for the Boot is the graveyard of lost souls. But even there they have a dregs cask and wouldn't refuse a thirsty soul the wine that was once in someone else's mouth. But I'm not choosy and will make do with the dross. Give me your right hand. The left isn't suited for palm reading since it clasps the sword, the instrument of death. Because you're left-handed, aren't you, Tom O'Connor? I noticed it the minute you emerged from your mother's womb, just as red-haired as you are today. But perhaps you can't bear to hear more about the life that awaits you?"

Tom didn't reply but backed up to the counter and found a clean tankard, which he lowered into the dregs cask as he glanced toward the back room.

Zamora downed the wine just as quickly as she had gulped the water. Her milky eye suddenly acquired a glow, as if rings were spreading from the black pupil into the sickly iris, which shifted so that the eye became as dark as the sky above the roof of the inn. "Put your hand on the table, Tom. Put it there, clenched tight. Clench it until the blood fades from your fingers and you can feel the pain all the way up to your armpit."

Tom stared at his clenched fist, which grew whiter and whiter, and he felt the pain settle into his arm, which shook so hard that the table rattled.

"Harder, Tom, even harder."

"I can't . . . do it anymore."

"Yes, you can."

Everything went black before his eyes. He gasped for air and raised his fist, as if to strike the old hag on the brow.

"All right, Tom," whispered the fortune-teller. "Open your hand and put it on the table."

Tom fell back in his chair, exhausted.

"Your hand, Tom, is a sea chart of your future," whispered Zamora. "You can set your course by it. If you know its possibilities, its dangers and short-cuts, you can take stock and become your own captain. Tonight I will grant you perfect recall so that you will remember every word I say. You will forget nothing."

Tom cleared his throat. "Tell me what you see."

"You're a stubborn fellow, Tom."

"Yes, that's what people say. What else?"

"And an ambitious one. You want to be rich, terribly rich. But your greed is not solely for your own benefit. You want to buy your mother's way out of this house."

"Everyone knows that."

"Deep inside," said Zamora, "deep inside you also want to buy your half sister's way out."

"You don't know what you're talking about," grumbled Tom. "Spanish dogs have to look out for themselves."

Zamora leaned across the table. "What do you get if you mix a drink from the noblest wine, the strongest rum, and the purest springwater?"

Tom rolled his eyes and shook his head. "Something totally undrinkable."

The remark seemed to amuse the fortune-teller. "You've just described yourself, Tom O'Connor." She laughed hoarsely.

"Myself? Is that supposed to be a riddle or a bad joke?"

"Neither. In your hand I see the oblique line for nobility, and the triangle for purity, along with the parallel line for villainy. You have blue blood, springwater, and a raging pirate all mixed up inside you. As you said yourself, quite an undrinkable brew."

"I'd be hard-pressed to find the likes of such foolishness," grumbled Tom, who knew his ancestors, none of whom were blue, noble, or had tendencies toward piracy. Although pure springwater he could certainly accept.

Zamora smiled. "Tell me what your plans are for tonight."

"I thought you were the one who was supposed to tell me. But since you ask, my plans are the same as they've been for the past five nights."

Zamora nodded encouragement. Tom lowered his voice and told her about his searches in his skiff. About his long, dizzying dives and about his hope of finding the treasure that with one stroke would change his family's fortunes. Whenever he dreamed, it was always about that: paying López off and at the same time giving him such a hard kick in the Far Beyond that he could never sit down again.

"Wreckage," jeered the fortune-teller, "deck planks, candlesticks, and cannonballs. The ocean is filled with dead people's belongings. Porcelain so smooth you can't even imagine, jewels so sparkling that they must have come straight from the starry skies, shoes with buckles of gold, and gemstones that gleam like the eyetooth in the pirate's mouth."

Tom cleared his throat. "What pirate?" he murmured.

The fortune-teller grinned. "The only one worth mentioning: C. W. Bull."

"Have you seen him?" whispered Tom.

"I've seen everything, Tom, and the sight turned one of my eyes white and made my life on this Earth a heavy burden. Yet it should be said that his eyetooth isn't a gemstone at all; it's rotten and painful."

"Do you mean the real C. W. Bull?"

"Does he interest you, Tom?"

"Did you or did you not see him?"

The fortune-teller smacked her lips with satisfaction. "I've even shared a drink with him. His ship was anchored a short distance from Grenada. I was summoned out to see him, and we drank together. The best rum I've ever tasted. A little of it is still sitting in my hollow tooth. The rum was white like a baby tooth, distilled from the most exquisite syrup."

"Stolen, I presume?"

"There was nothing on Bull's ship that hadn't been stolen," said Zamora. "It's even said that his belt is made of human skin, and that his comb was carved from the bone of a German countess whose flesh was salted down and later eaten by the cannibals on board. When I saw him, he was naked but wrapped in his beloved flag, the black one on which the captain is toasting Death in the guise of a skeleton. Bull sold his soul to the Devil, you see."

"It's too bad they didn't eat you too," snickered Tom.

"Oh, I'm just a soup bone. Captain Bull's men are meat eaters."

Tom's gaze took on a dreamy look. "So he's just as fierce as his reputation?"

"He's your worst nightmare, and his crew includes the most bloodthirsty pirates ever to sail the seven seas. There are thirty-nine men in all. I know that because each and every one of them, from the first officer to the cook, has only nine fingers. The captain showed me his collection, which he keeps in a cupboard in his cabin. Inside, each blue-black finger hangs from its own hook."

Tom looked up at the ceiling with a dreamy smile.

"But listen to me now, Tom O'Connor," whispered Zamora. "Listen and learn, because you're going to be tempted."

"Tempted?"

"Yes, tempted—tempted by your greed, your eternal striving for gold, but don't listen to it. Instead think about the thirty-nine fingers. Think about the thirty-nine pirates, who for the rest of their lives will have to live with a black gap in their hands. These men will never be whole again, for it's a fact that in the middle joint of a sailor's ring finger resides his greed for gold."

With these words the old hag went behind the counter and helped herself to another tankard of wine. Afterward she opened the door to the deep night, and from its center emanated an emerald-green glow.

"Does the boy know where the darkness comes from?" she asked. "No, he doesn't, but once upon a time in the far-distant past there was no darkness, no night, and no sleep. Life was one long bright day, without interruption and without end, nothing by which to count the weeks, nothing by which to distinguish yesterday from today or tomorrow. Without knowing what it was, every living thing yearned for the dark carpet of night."

Zamora beckoned to Tom and said in a gentle, almost hypnotic voice, "Then the green pelican appeared and, as you may know, he is the wisest of birds. He had heard about twilight, dusk, and dawn, and he coaxed the night up from the river and into the world. Then came the toucan, the hummingbird, and the parrot. And after them followed the pangolin, the anteater, the tapir, and finally the spotted jaguar, the beast that hunts in the night. And just imagine, Tom, he devoured the green pelican. That's the reason why we have night and day, and why you never see a green pelican. Because whatever vanishes will never come back. So watch out for your ring finger, Tom O'Connor."

"Is that really the only advice you can give to a boy of fourteen?" grumbled Tom, spitting.

"Yes," muttered the fortune-teller, pulling up her hood. "That's what you get when you serve filthy water, and besides, you won't be fourteen until November. Lies cling to your tongue, but if you spit far enough, the truth is bound to come out. Maybe you have an excuse. When you were born there were seven crocodiles on the wharf by the bay. We threw them fish to placate them, but when they finally went back out to sea, there were only five left."

Zamora pulled her hood close and sniffed. "Farewell, young O'Connor," she said. "Never listen to a gecko, and beware of Orion's Belt, for that is the only constellation of the night that means you harm."

2 Feodora Dolores Vasgues

TOM SAT IN THE LOW-CEILINGED ROOM he shared with his mother and sister. This was where they kept their personal possessions, which for Tom consisted of a collection of unusual stones he had found on the beach and the ocean floor. Here he also kept his father's old leather belt and a sea chart, which, as far as Tom knew, covered most of the world. The map was homemade and no doubt the measurements were imprecise. On the other hand, all the good fishing spots were marked with an X. Europe had been given the shape of a sharp-snouted tapir, which, in the eyes of the artist, was a good likeness for most Spaniards. For the same reason, Spain was an insignificant wart on the continent, only half the size of Africa, which was depicted with long-legged giraffes and roaring lions. Between the Caribbean and Africa he had drawn five large ships, each more beautiful than the last. On the largest, a three-masted galleon, stood a bold captain with fiery-red hair and a gleaming dagger in his belt.

Tom knew that there were better and newer maps, and he dreamed of becoming the person who would one day put the world on paper. On the back of the page he had drawn a map of the constellations, and in his opinion this was much more accurate than the sea chart. He could name all the constellations and never had any trouble navigating by night.

His mother was lying on her back with her long blond hair spread out on the pillow and a faint smile playing on her lips. Her eyes were only half-closed, so it was hard to tell if she was asleep or merely stealing a nap before she had to get up again.

Tom kissed her cheek and took her hand. As always, she smelled of lime juice, which she put in the water she used for bathing. There was no scent

Tom liked better. He studied her hand, which was big and rough. A man's hand. But she also had to do a man's work.

Not if I have anything to say about it! he thought, getting up from the bed. In a matter of minutes he had gathered a tallow candle, the leather belt, and a tarred rope. With five light bounds he was down the stairs. In the dimly lit tavern he filled a flask with water and found the bucket with the freshly caught dolphin fish, floating belly up. Before he left he peeked in, as usual, on Señor López, who lay with his mouth open and his pants unbuttoned.

He did indeed have a corner of his nightshirt between his lips.

There was a peculiar wind that night—blowing first from the east, then from the west—but Tom paid it no mind. He was an experienced sailor if anyone was, and no fortune-teller was going to tell him anything about the wind or the weather. Tonight he had an odd but clear premonition of good luck. He could feel it in his body, which was sending him all the right signals. He had the strength, the energy, the tenacity, and the will.

Will was the most important. It was what gave him an advantage over the others. With his innate will, he would come out ahead. Nothing could break it. When Feo asked him why he believed that he would find the treasure before the hundreds of grown men did, his answer was always the same: because I have the will. Give me my skiff, a rock of suitable size, my father's old belt, and a flask of water. The rest will follow. Why? Because I have the will. He allowed himself a little smile as his feet paused in the brown sand.

His skiff was gone. He gnashed his teeth and tossed the rope aside, bending down to follow the tracks of the boat. They led from the shore out into the sea. "The Devil take you, Feodora Dolores Vasgues!" he shouted. "The Devil take all sisters."

He sat down on a rock and told himself it didn't pay to get upset. If he gave it some thought, he would quickly find a solution. He could try to borrow a skiff, but he knew they were all in use. There wasn't even a leaky one that hadn't put out to sea tonight. Señor López would be asleep for the next ten hours, so Tom had plenty of time—which made his sister's theft even worse. To think she had the nerve to steal his boat from right under his nose, when she knew full well that it was the only thing he thought about, the only thing he lived for.

He kicked at a rock, hurting his foot, and then stretched out on his back and looked up at the matte-black sky. He closed his eyes and relaxed, feeling weariness envelop his body. He lay there quite comfortably, listening to the gentle slap of the waves. The salty smell of the sea prompted dreamy images of scaled mermaids. It was said that they could sing. Tom's father was one of the few who had heard them. Mermaids sing lullabies, he had told Tom, wondrous, tender lullabies.

When he opened his eyes again, the sun was blazing on the horizon. The sea was pink and black. A pelican sat cackling on a fishing stake. Tom shielded his eyes with his hand and immediately caught sight of his sister.

She was sitting in his skiff not far from shore. The boat was rocking on the rippling waves with Feodora, erect as a reed, in profile. Her bright parasol made the sight even more intolerable. She knew that he was watching her and that at least for part of the night he had been cursing and fuming and carrying on.

He could easily swim out to her, but he wouldn't give her that satisfaction. He could wait. But could he really wait? Was there time for that? The other fortune hunters might have long since divided up the bounty, while that skinny girl sat there showing off. Tom put his knife between his teeth and was about to head out, when he saw that she was starting to turn the boat around.

She took her time about it and seemed to be enjoying the morning. She was dressed in her very best: the purple gown she had inherited from their mother. Her raven-black hair hung in a thick braid down her back, reaching to her waist. She had also been in the jewelry box.

"Properly decked herself out," he scoffed.

When she was close enough for them to hear each other, she lifted the oars out of the water and pretended to be surprised to see him. Even though she had been sitting out there for hours with only one objective in mind: to provoke him.

"Oh, is that you, Tom?" She shaded her eyes from the sun, although the sun was at her back.

Tom shifted his feet impatiently. "Who else would it be?" he shouted.

"From out there, I thought it was a dog. But now I can see that it's you."

"Is that so?"

"What are you doing down at the shore so early?"

"What do you think I'm doing? I'm looking for my skiff. The one you stole!"

"Mind your temper, Tom. You're getting all red in the face, just like the neighbor's pig. But that's how the Irish look."

Tom controlled himself and stepped into the water. "Bring my boat here."

"If you ask me nicely. Or else I might decide to go out rowing again."

Tom narrowed his eyes. The worst thing was that she was the kind who might actually do it. Feodora wasn't like other people. She went her own way, had odd thoughts, and said things that drove people crazy. Sometimes she came up with the most far-fetched tales. One of them was actually Tom's favorite story. It was about a magic powder that looked like crushed peppercorns and might in fact have been related to pepper. In any case, Feo spread the rumor that this powder possessed virile powers and was a source of eternal youth. The rumor had swiftly reached Señor López, who had summoned the girl to his presence.

"There was a certain fisherman," Feo had told the innkeeper, "and a more handsome man could not be found under the sun: tall, broad-shouldered, slim-waisted, lithe, and strong as a bull. The women flocked around this man, whom I assumed was about twenty years old. But just imagine, Señor López, when the truth came out, the man had actually reached his sixtieth year. You wouldn't believe your eyes. Some sort of sorcery had to be at work. It turned out that he had come into possession of this *aphrodisiacum*. Yes, that's what the powder is called in Latin. I myself keep a small supply of this fountain of youth under my pillow to be used when I grow old and gray."

Feo was told to produce the little pouch in which the powder was kept.

"Whether it should be ingested dry or with a small amount of pure water, I can't say for sure," she told the innkeeper when he got to his feet.

It turned out that Feo had acquired it during the course of her work serving the inn's guests, which is why Señor López claimed that the powder belonged to him, since the inn was, after all, his. Feo protested vigorously, but in the end had to watch the powder disappear into the Spaniard's mug and from there into his fat stomach. Afterward López went to bed, convinced that the next day he would awake to the spring of his youth.

They heard his bellows in the middle of the night. In fact, he sat in the privy for three days, where he shit his guts out, contracted a fever, and suffered hallucinations. Finally, sapped of all strength, he summoned Feo, who regretfully repeated that, as she had told him, she didn't know whether the powder should be ingested dry or with water. Several days later, after López had recovered, she was given a taste of Juan Carlos, which was the name of the leather strap that hung on the innkeeper's door. The blows reverberated through the inn for a full hour before Tom and his mother were allowed to drag her up to their room, where her mother could tend to her bloody back.

Not a single complaint crossed the girl's lips. Not one peep.

Most of the fights between Tom and Feo had to do with their fathers' different nationalities. The fact that Tom's father had succumbed to fever was, in Feo's eyes, a most undignified way to die. "But then again," as she said, "the Irish have no honor, no spine, and no pride. They die in their sheets."

That type of remark was delivered only when she was at a suitable distance from Tom or if their mother was present. And yet one day when she was feeling particularly cynical, such a remark had nearly cost Feo her life. After fighting for an hour, Tom sent her dashing up to the roof of the inn. From there she peered down at him with a scornful smile.

He was at that moment so overwrought that tears were rolling down his cheeks. "Come down, you half-breed," he raged.

"Spaniards die in battle," said Feo. "The Irish die with compresses on their brows."

"I'll make you eat your words."

The knife landed in the wood less than an inch from her forehead, plunging up to the hilt. Her face white, she stared at her brother, who was on his way up the olive tree that grew next to the gable of the building.

"Your father," he shouted, "died because he was a shrimp, a Spanish runt who was stupid enough to get involved in a duel but not man enough to win. People even said that his opponent was old and decrepit, weak and half-blind. But when it comes right down to it, a Spaniard is nothing more than a cross between a mule who shits and the fly who gorges on it."

Tom reached the roof as Feodora pulled the knife out of the gable and held it to his throat. With her other hand she grabbed hold of his red hair. "I dare you to say that again, Tom O'Connor."

Tom felt the knife blade against his skin; he knew quite well how sharp it was. No one on Nevis was more meticulous about his weapon than he was.

"Repeat what you said!"

"Do you mean the part about the mule or the part about the fly?" sneered Tom.

"Then die, half-breed," growled Feo, and gave Tom the first scar of his life. If he hadn't lost his footing and slid two feet down the roof, she would have slit his throat.

That evening they were both given a taste of Juan Carlos, which Señor López generously lent to the children's mother. After bandaging up her son, she turned all her strength to punishing her daughter who, true to form, remained dry-eyed.

"She could have killed me," yelled Tom.

"You started it. If you're going to throw knives, you need to learn to hit your mark."

"Next time there's going to be one less Spaniard on Nevis. That's a promise," he replied.

But there would be no next time, because that very evening their mother fell ill and took to her bed. Why she began to bleed no one ever explained, but the doctor told them that if the bleeding did not stop of its own accord, their mother would die in a matter of hours. All night long she lay there, pale as moonlight, but she didn't call for her children until the next day had dawned. Her bed was soaked with blood, though she had tried to stanch its flow.

Tom wept and Feodora washed and bandaged as she prayed to all the gods she could remember. None of it helped. Their mother's life ebbed out in a gentle stream. Until Feo, in desperation, cast herself over her mother, took her white face in her hands, and promised that she and Tom would never fight again. And that they would always look out for each other, no matter what happened.

"Take my hand, Tom," whispered Feo.

Tom clutched his sister's hand tightly.

"See, Mother," said Feo, "no matter what happens, you should know that we will never be parted, and we will always take care of each other."

"Always," vowed Tom. "Always."

Whether this was what stopped the bleeding or something else entirely, they never knew. In any case their mother regained her health, and from that day forward, her children may not have loved each other but at least they threw no more knives.

There was also another side to Feodora.

Tom held in his memory a series of images of a girl running along the shore beneath the tilted orange moon of the night sea, barefoot and with hair like coal, wild as the trade winds, happy as the world's first rainbow fish from whose eggs the stars had been born.

Sometimes she would pull him close and ask whether he could feel her heart. "Your life and mine, Tom," she would whisper, "are listening to each other." Then she would spin on her heel, laugh out loud, and disappear.

"Take me along, Feo," calls the little boy, attempting to keep up.

"Where, Tommy?"

"Wherever you like," replies the tot.

"You have to make a wish, little man."

"Then take me to the ends of the Earth."

She holds his face between her warm brown hands.

"You're already there, Tom O'Connor."

"Then take me to the beginnings of the Earth," shouts the insatiable boy.

"You'll have to learn to swim first."

Tom sat down on the beach and watched her pull the skiff ashore. He didn't say a word to his sister as she strolled up toward the inn, her parasol on her shoulder, humming a melody of her own devising. Half-breed, he thought, tossing his things on board. I wish you'd be sold as a slave and sent to Bahía with the first ship. An hour later he was out at sea, rowing with strong, steady strokes. His fury had given him new strength. His arms and shoulders ached, but he didn't care. The wind had died down and the heat was rising, but he had brought plenty of water and knew enough to use it sparingly. The day was not to be wasted; this time he would not return home empty-handed.

Four hours later the sun was high overhead. He could not see land but the ocean was so familiar to him that he knew he would soon reach the spot where the galleon had gone down.

The sea was his friend, his only true friend, and a friend should never be betrayed. He often talked to the waves, and occasionally he would take a handful of his prettiest stones and offer them as a sacrifice to appease the god who gave and took in such abundant measure that even the largest frigate could never feel safe. It was important to remain good friends with this elemental power. Never speak ill of it or use derogatory terms. And whenever Tom folded his hands and said his Our Father, it was not to God on high but to the One in the sea. The one who made the waves roll and the ships capsize. The God of the Sea lived in an ice-cold grave. His castle was built of the most beautiful corals and surrounded by the most precious treasures. There was no king who could match him in wealth, for the God of the Sea took whatever he pleased. And now it had pleased him to send his mighty hand up from the deep to claim a Spanish galleon that had disappeared with over four hundred souls on board. But the God of the Sea was not a greedy fellow who merely kept everything for himself. No, he was also a merciful lord who at times tossed tidbits, both large and small, up to those who waited patiently. And even though, for Tom's part, this had resulted only in a rusty dagger, a few planks, and a chest full of sea anemones, it might still pay to be patient.

After rowing for another hour, he stripped off his clothes and wrapped the rope around his waist, sitting for a moment to calm his breathing. There was nothing in sight but the sky and the sea and the chalk-white glowing spot where the world stopped, where the ocean rushed over a terrifying waterfall toward an ever-enticing rainbow, whose false glimmerings had sent many a good sailor to his grave.

He tossed the drag anchor over the side, tied a rock to the rope, and slipped down into the water. "Here I come, great Sea-God," he murmured. "Please welcome this poor boy from Nevis." One last breath and he was underwater. Quickly he spun around and felt the tug of the rock, which pulled him down with all its weight. There was a rushing in his ears and a roar in his nose. He used different muscles underwater, and he felt taut with vigor and energy.

He sank deeper and deeper until he could glimpse the seafloor and the huge reef that had lain on the bottom of the ocean ever since the days of the primal frog. It was a whole world unto itself, an enormous silent realm populated by the most beautiful creatures with unearthly colors. Some of the fish had names like emperor fish, damselfish, and marbled grouper, but others had to swim around with no more than a nickname, such as satchel fish, porcupine fish, and clown fish. Tom was convinced he knew them all, including those he ought to avoid.

Unfortunately, the fish and the corals were all that he could see. He spun around in the water and considered going back to the surface to row out a little farther. Surely Portuguese full-riggers rode so low that they would choose a more distant course. The sea was clear and he could see his skiff rocking on the watery mirror above like a little gray seashell. Swiftly he untied the rock and pushed off. A minute later he was hanging on to the side of the boat, winded and tired, but not so worn out that he didn't think he had air and energy for more attempts.

He drank a little water, listened to the wind, and let his thoughts drift. It was the same daydream he always had. About the square chest that stood amid the seaweed and reefs. Much too massive to lift. So the treasure had to be hauled up piecemeal. The dream of gold was so splendid that he decided to revise his course and row due east. The day had grown even hotter, and the sun's rays scorched his back and legs, but he didn't notice; nor did he notice when blisters formed on his hands.

He made two more dives before he began to think about heading home. The sun had passed its zenith, although he wasn't quite certain of this because it felt as if the light took on a different quality this far out.

Maybe I'm just tired, he thought. He had no more rocks, but he had tried diving without their help before, so that shouldn't stop him. A rest would do him good. A short nap, a drop of water, and then he would turn his nose homeward.

He lay down in the bottom of the skiff and closed his eyes.

When he woke, the wind was in the south. The waves slapped against the boat, which pitched up and down. The light was fading. He had slept for hours. He felt hungry and his body ached all over.

He took his bearings from the sun, put the oars in the water, and began to row. The palms of his hands stung, but there was nothing to be done about it. Back home a reprimand of the worst kind awaited him, maybe even a round with Juan Carlos. But if he could just manage to get a little food before the punishment, he wouldn't complain.

He rowed for three more hours without sighting land. The ocean was dark green, the sun was gone, and the wind had now subsided. The temperature had fallen, creating a fog that hovered like a veil over the surface of the water.

I suppose I'll have to wait for the stars to appear in the sky, he thought. But the last few nights had been starless. In that case, he would have to stay out in order not to row even farther away. He shouldn't waste his strength unnecessarily, or exhaust himself, and most important of all, he had to ration his water. "This is no way for a person to end his days," he said aloud. "I'm much too young for that. Do you hear me, Sea-God? I'm only fourteen years old—well, if the truth be told, I haven't even turned fourteen yet. And the two of us have been friends all our days. I've given you back my best stones." He lay down, muttering reassurances to himself.

Strange how still it was. It was said that when a large ship went down, it cast a deathlike stillness on the ocean that kept watch over the grave where so many souls had been lost. Maybe he was at precisely the spot where the Portuguese galleon had disappeared. Maybe that's why it was now so calm.

An hour later it was completely dark.

Tom tried to see his hands, which trembled in the night wind. Not from the cold, but from exhaustion and a sense of disquiet that he had never felt before. He looked out across the black waves, marveling at the fog, which was solidifying like porridge in a pot. He spoke to the sea in the hope of assuaging it. Finally he took off his father's belt, his dearest possession and the only thing left of the man whose name he bore.

Tom held the belt over the side. His hand shook and his voice quavered. "Receive this gift," he whispered, blinking back his tears. "Receive this belt that belonged to my father, Tom O'Connor. Take good care of it, great Sea-God."

The belt floated on the water momentarily and then the weight of the buckle pulled it down. He felt a lurch in the pit of his stomach when it disappeared, but he was certain that the ocean would now be more kindly disposed and that he would soon see the first constellations, by which he would be able to navigate. "It can't be any other way; anything else is unthinkable."

He knelt down, fighting back the sobs that had risen in his throat.

By midnight the sky was still black as pitch. The fog had closed in tighter around the skiff, in the bottom of which long white stripes had appeared. Tom's fingernails had made deep gouges in the boards, and he had carved his name on the thwart—as neatly as possible with a knife that was not meant for writing. His mother had taught him his letters so that as a five-year-old he could spell his own name. Feodora was better at reading than he was, of course, and her skill was one of the reasons that they were still living with Señor López, who had never learned the alphabet.

Now their names were on the thwart: Tom O'Connor, Elinore O'Connor, and Feodora Dolores Vasgues. Underneath he had printed the date and year.

He suddenly thought of the dolphin fish that had kept fresh in the bucket. Its flesh was still firm. He knew that he should remember to eat, and fish was his favorite food. Especially dolphin fish. That's what he told himself as he set his foot on the fish and sliced it open from gullet to tail. He removed the entrails, cleaned it, and threw the guts overboard.

"I love dolphin fish," he said aloud as he rinsed the meat in the water. "Damn, it tastes good," he groaned, allowing himself a little of the freshwater. He lay down on his back and stared up at all that blackness, thinking about the scent of lime and the filthy water he had offered Zamora. She hadn't said anything about his ending his days out here.

"You unpredictable old hag," he whispered just as something struck the hull.

He started up, terrified. Something was banging against the bottom of the skiff. He pressed his hand to his mouth to stop from screaming in fright. Stories about creatures that lived at the bottom of the sea were as numerous as they were ghastly. Above all else he feared the half-creatures, the lost souls that lived restless lives, half-man and half-fish, with shiny scales and wet fish eyes, fingers like jellyfish and snouts like a shark.

Tom clasped his hands and huddled against the gunwale as the monster struck again, this time with even greater force. Quickly Tom pulled out his knife. "Come and get me."

But nothing happened. For a moment it was utterly quiet, so quiet that he was convinced the abomination had vanished. He crawled forward in the boat and leaned over the side.

Nothing. He heaved a sigh of relief just as the monster once more rammed the skiff, which rose up from the blow. Paralyzed with terror, Tom stared down into the black water.

A face appeared below him. A rigid face with red cheeks, clear blue eyes, and wavy golden hair.

Furiously Tom lunged with his knife, which lodged in the face and nearly pulled him into the water. Only then did it dawn on him what had struck his boat. He felt his heart pounding with relief as he leaned over the side and grabbed hold of the post. Quickly he slipped into the water and wrestled the meticulously painted figurehead around to the side of the boat, where he lashed it tight. Then he flung himself back into the skiff, confused and despairing, happy and completely morose, certain that it was the figurehead of the proud galleon. He had found the right spot, but he would be unable to make any use of it.

He leaned over the gunwale and stared at the painted face, striking it again and again with his knife and cursing his misfortune. Finally he collapsed with his arm across his eyes, and lay there for another hour, half asleep with an old man's smile on his lips. Now I'm going to die, he thought. But when they eventually find my skiff, they'll also find the figurehead. People will say that Tom O'Connor was the only one to locate the wreckage. They'll tell stories about me. "To hell with your stories," he yelled and sat up.

He gave a start and smiled in disbelief. The fog had lifted, and overhead, sprinkled with a light but generous hand, sparkled not only the stars he knew but those that were unknown to him. Yes, it was as if everything that could shine was in the sky that night. They were all there: the long twisting golden diadems and the gossamer-soft brush strokes, which sat like frescoes on the firmament, heavenly pictures yellowed with age.

He was crying and laughing all at the same time. "Stars," he shouted, "the sea chart of the night. Tom O'Connor loves you and thanks you with all his heart."

Now it would be no trouble to find his way home. He had strength enough, no doubt about that. But he would have to let the figurehead go.

She would have to stay out here. No one would believe him when he told how he had found her, but that's the way it was with the best stories.

Quickly he untied the rope and shoved the figurehead loose. It set its own course at once and drifted away under the stars with its eternal smile, thankful to be free again.

Maybe, he thought, she'll find the rest of the wreckage and end her days among sunken cannons, barrels full of lard, and chests of ivory and precious stones. The last part he said aloud, quite softly and not without a certain bitterness. "Maybe that's how it goes. Figureheads from sunken ships must forever search for those who were shipwrecked. She'll drift from sloop to galleon to skiff in the hope of finding the lost crew in their watery grave. Live well," he murmured as he dipped the oars.

He rowed for almost an hour, then raised the oars and stared across the sea. Somewhere a voice had called out for help.

Ramón
the Pious

3

FOR A BRIEF MOMENT he thought it was the figurehead that had suddenly come to life. But the delusion left him when he caught sight of a murky figure floating some distance from the skiff. It came and went, rather like a dream image, but stayed long enough for him to recognize a body and a face.

There was no doubt that the poor soul had heard the strokes of the oars from the skiff. Maybe it was a victim from one of those merciless battles when two desperate men each take hold of one end of a long anticipated bounty. The sea was ruled by one law: only the strongest survive. And as Tom's mother so often had said, only the victor remains to tell the story.

He pulled his oars on board. Judging by the man's feeble call for help, he had been in the water a good long time. Tom hesitated to make himself known. If the man was drifting around alone, once on board the skiff, he might acquire a renewed faith in life. It was unlikely that Tom would be able to take on a grown man, no matter how exhausted the man might be. He had to be cautious—either that or simply row away.

At that moment he heard a loud groan and a suppressed plea. A hoarse voice said, "Help me, my friend, and you will be rewarded, I promise you that . . . promise you, or my name isn't . . ." The rest was lost in a hopeless rattling sound.

Tom set his knife on the thwart and paddled with his hands in the direction of the sound. He could now see the outline of the castaway: a man hanging on to a piece of wood that looked to be the base of a mast. Tom retreated a bit so that there was just enough fog between him and the man that they remained shadowy figures. Tom took time to mull things over. Then he gathered his courage and asked, "Who's there?"

"A friend, a friend," was the swift reply. "Oh God, I thank you with all my heart."

"Who are you?"

"My name is Ramón el Piadoso," said the man in Spanish. "I'm from Cádiz but I have served the Portuguese merchant fleet for fifteen years. Dear friend, please help me. I haven't had any water to drink in four days."

Tom cast a glance at his water flask and realized there wasn't enough for two if they were to make it back to Nevis in good condition. Especially not if the man was as parched as Ramón, also known as the Pious, claimed.

"Were you shipwrecked, Ramón?" asked Tom.

A moment passed in which the man uttered a series of plaintive sounds. Then he said, "The worst thing a sailor can imagine: mutiny! But tell me who it is I'm talking to. You sound young, dear friend."

Tom hesitated for a moment, then answered, "My name is Tom O'Connor and I'm fourteen years old. I'll soon be fifteen."

"May Heaven bless you, Tom O'Connor," moaned the man. "You will be rewarded for your good deed."

"Tell me about the shipwreck. We're talking about the Portuguese galleon, aren't we?"

"First a little water, Tom, first a few drops, my throat is twisted shut, and the sun has turned my lips into bloody crusts. But yes, yes, there was once a proud galleon by the name of *Santa Helena*, the pride of Porto. But she is no more. All that remains is a half-dead boatswain from Cádiz and a blessed scrap of lumber from the mast that bore our topsail."

And a figurehead with blue eyes, thought Tom, adding to himself that hopefully there was a good deal more that Ramón the Pious with the cracked lips knew nothing about.

At that instant the fog drifted away from between the skiff and the shipwrecked seaman. Tom gave a start. The man's condition was worse than Tom expected.

He lay with the upper part of his body and his bare arms wrapped around the piece of mast. His shirt, which in the dawn of time had been white, was tattered and filthy, while the color of the man's skin was the same as the shell of a crab. His matted hair looked like scabs on his gaunt cheeks. His hands and arms were blue, and the look in his eyes was imploring and desperate.

Only now did Tom realize that the man was not alone. At his side hung yet another figure, half his size. It was impossible to tell whether the figure was alive or rigid with death. The face lay partly in the water, partly on the post to which he was clinging.

This figure, somewhat hidden by Ramón's body, was quite clearly African and, Tom realized, about his own age. Without thinking, he paddled closer and saw gratitude cast a little life over the cadaverous face of the Spaniard.

"Thank you, Master, thank you, Master O'Connor," the man whispered and made a move as if to abandon the piece of wood that separated him from death by drowning.

Tom put one oar in the water, still uncertain how to handle the situation. He felt repulsed by the castaway, by his manner of speech and his appearance. At the same time there was something else, something unfamiliar, that drew Tom.

Just a few hours ago, when it was still night, he had clasped his hands and prayed for mercy himself, then scratched his epitaph in the wood of the skiff. Now he had been saved and held the fate of another man in his hands. The man had mentioned something about a reward. The word flitted around in Tom's head, but he saw no evidence of the Spaniard's promise and thought it best to keep an oar's length away.

"Who's the black?" Tom asked. He had seen many Africans when Spanish and Portuguese and British slave ships lay at anchor off Nevis, when the blacks came up on deck to be deloused or to get fresh air. Tom and Feodora had often gone on board to sell beer, rum, and wine as well as salted meat, fresh treacle, salt, and corn.

The slaves never spoke, though Tom had heard their high-pitched shrieks when the ships, in the night, rid themselves of their dead. It was said that sometimes half the slaves perished during the voyage from Africa to the Caribbean. Whenever Tom, as a little boy, awoke to the screams from a foreign frigate, he would crawl over to his mother, who would tuck him in and tell him that he should thank God for his green Irish eyes and his white skin.

"Who is he, you ask," groaned Ramón as he moved the black head that lay in the water and gave no sign of life. "This is a slave that I've dragged with me . . . I can hardly remember for how many days now. I know, you're thinking: Has Ramón the crazy boatswain actually rescued a slave boy? Has the sea devoured his mind and corroded his reason? No, Master Tom, this boy, no matter how black he is and how wretched he now appears, this boy is worth his weight in pure gold."

A demented smile spread across the Spaniard's bearded face. "I can understand if you're surprised, Tom. You will have the complete and truthful account as soon as I've tasted a little water. A little water, Tom, and you shall have the truth about this boy. You know, don't you, that slaves are called black gold?"

Tom leaned back. Of course he had never dealt in slaves, but he knew that the price for a grown man was not terribly high. Taking stock of the puny, half-dead boy hanging at Ramón's side, it was hard to see any trace of the black gold.

"Help me, Tom O'Connor," begged the Spaniard, "and you will be rewarded. Do you think I would be dragging around a black for my own pleasure and sharing with him the few drops of water that I had left? Do you think I've been keeping him alive, day and night, because it amuses me? Think about it, Tom. You look to be a healthy and sensible fellow."

Tom looked away but acknowledged that Ramón's words had made some impression. He lifted the water flask to assess its contents and heard the Spaniard's deep sigh and half-stifled whimper. "It's a long way to shore." Tom made his voice sound as authoritative as possible. "And I've been out here quite a long time, so there's not much to go around."

Ramón wet his lips, which were split by salt and sun. "A few drops, Tom, a few drops."

"What about him? Is he dead or alive?"

"Oh, he's alive, all right, Master Tom. The blacks can get by on less than the rest of us. I've seen slaves that could live on the dew that fell on their skin." Ramón poked his elbow at the black boy, whose small head hardly budged. The Spaniard tipped his face back so that the bloodshot eyes opened. "Say something to your rescuer," ordered Ramón. "Say something or the waves will take you. I've dragged you around long enough."

For a brief moment the boy looked at Tom. His cracked lips moved, as if he wanted to speak.

"There, you see, Master Tom," said the Spaniard. "Damned if there isn't life in the little devil. Now a little water, a few drops, Tom. Have mercy on me and I will turn your life golden on this day, which you will remember as the best of your young life."

"Do you really have gold coins?" asked Tom.

"Better than that."

"Precious gems?"

"A little water, Tom, and you shall have the whole story."

Tom maneuvered the skiff around so that only the mast was between him and the Spaniard. He held up the water flask and saw the man open his mouth and lay his head back.

The first drops struck his cheeks, but the next ones hit their mark. The Spaniard laughed and cried, drank greedily, and whined for more. "Just a few more drops, Tom, just a few more drops for Ramón."

Tom took measure of the contents and gave the Spaniard a little more and then put back the cork. He had given the seaman no more than half a glass, but his eyes had livened up considerably.

"Now your hand, Tom. Give me your hand and let's be friends."

"What about the reward?" Tom studied his knife.

"Would a man in such dire straits and so close to his Maker, would such a man lie to you, Tom?"

Tom looked out across the sea, where the fog was about to lift, pondering the question. Finally he said, "Yes."

His reply seemed to break the Spaniard, who dipped his head underwater for a moment. When he looked up again, he wore a lost expression. "Then leave me, Master Tom, row home to your family. I thank you for the water and I will not curse your name, only the unlucky fact that when you met fortune at sea, you did not understand how to gather it up. Closer to riches you will never come."

As the man spoke, Tom made room in the stern. He had already decided to take the Spaniard on board; there was no other choice. And the man's condition meant he was not exactly dangerous. "Grab hold of the skiff," said Tom, "grab hold and pull yourself up."

"You're a wise boy, Master Tom. You make your parents proud. Unfortunately my right arm was injured in the battle to save our ship, and the left one, which has been my lifeline these many days, could hardly hold even a pipe of tobacco." Ramón placed his bad arm along the gunwale, where it lay like a dead fish. With the left one he tried to hoist himself into the skiff but soon discovered that he didn't have the strength to manage it alone.

Tom reached out his hand, and with both their efforts the Spaniard made it into the skiff. He lay there for a moment with his eyes shut, shedding tears, and then clasped his weather-beaten hands. "Praise be with you, Tom O'Connor," he whispered. "Praise be with you." Ramón sat up, still quite dizzy, blew his nose, and laughed up at the sky, gnashing his teeth and shedding one last tear. "As close to death as I've been, a man learns to appreciate life," he whispered. "Back home in Cádiz I have a boy who's a few years older than you are. It was his picture I saw before me when things seemed the most hopeless. Thanks to you, Tom, I will see my beloved son again. Your father must be a very happy man."

"My father is dead."

Ramón narrowed his eyes. "Forgive me, Tom. But you still have your mother, don't you?"

Tom nodded and looked at the mast where the slave boy lay, as if wrapped around the wood.

Ramón smiled and blinked. "Let's get him on board, Tom."

They took hold of the boy's arms, which were ice-cold and limp. He weighed no more than a bird and was so thin that it was possible to count all his bones, which threatened to break through his skin at the shoulders and hips. The black shackles that still held his frail ankles were the heaviest part. Safely on board, he collapsed in a heap in the bottom of the boat. It seemed to Tom that it wouldn't be long before they would have to heave him over the side again.

"The blacks can stand more than you think," said Ramón, "and this one here is made of special stuff."

"Maybe we ought to give him a drop of water," murmured Tom.

"If you do, it would be an extraordinarily sensible investment, Master Tom."

"That's not how it seems to me."

"Look at his necklace," whispered Ramón, winking. "Look at what's hanging from it, for it will determine the rest of your life."

Tom leaned over the boy. The necklace was a black cord made of some unidentifiable material. It fit snugly, without any kind of fastening or hook.

Ramón stuck his hand under the slave's neck and turned the cord to bring into view a ring, which was its only adornment. It was not gold, at any rate. And why would a slave be wearing gold around his neck?

"Are you curious, Tom?" whispered Ramón. "Oh, I can see that you're curious."

"What is the ring made of?" muttered Tom.

"It is said," whispered Ramón, "that it's made from the bone of a beast that lives deep inside Africa, and that it gives whoever wears it extraordinary powers."

"I know all about stories like that," said Tom.

"So do I, Tom, so do I. The seven seas are filled with them, and now we have one more. You see, the reason that a full-rigger with twenty-one cannons and a crew that included eighty armed soldiers, a cargo hold free of rats, plague, and other pestilences—the reason that such a magnificent ship would go down on its maiden voyage is now lying in the bottom of your skiff." The moment Ramón uttered the last word, the slave opened his eyes and looked straight at Tom. His gaze lacked all joy and held no anger, gratitude, or sorrow.

The Spaniard smiled slyly. "He understands everything we say."

"Do they speak Spanish in Africa?"

"I have no idea what language they speak, but some of them, especially the children, learn quite a few Spanish words. When the voyage lasts for months, some of it is bound to stick. And for a slave, this fellow is no fool. You see, Tom, when two souls lie side by side on the same plank for several days, waiting to die, they quickly find things to talk about. Not that I would confide anything to a slave. But I'm not too proud to admit that, for lack of anyone better, it was a relief to have company when God had forsaken me. Now don't misunderstand me, Tom, the black and I do not have the same God. Whether he has one at all, I couldn't say. I myself am a God-fearing man and therefore was surprised that not a single prayer issued from the black's lips. I beg you to remember this, Tom, never turn your back to a slave, and especially not to this one."

"Is he supposed to be something special?"

In a flash Ramón grabbed hold of Tom's wrist. His lips were quivering and his voice broke. "This black boy is the son of a chieftain. In our latitudes we would call him a prince. His father and his tribe reside on a remote part of the Bissagos Islands, where no white man has ever set foot. Many have tried, oh yes, a great many—honorable men in galleons, crude buccaneers in homemade ships, pirates under black flags, and distinguished governors in four-masted barks—every one of them has been forced back. But that's not all, that's not all, Tom. This coal-black chieftain has been lucky enough to plunder good ships from Spain as well as Portugal so that today he is richer than any nobleman. In those parts he is regarded as something of a god. The blacks are not believers, but for them he is just as great as the Almighty. And when it was rumored that his only son was on board the *Santa Helena*, all hell broke loose. Rebellion, mutiny, plundering, murder, and finally fire and shipwreck—all because of this little round ring. Proof that this boy is the son of a chieftain. Do you realize the ramifications of what I'm telling you, Master O'Connor? Do you understand why it's your blessed good fortune that on this September day you met Ramón from Cádiz?"

Tom reacted with a shrug of his shoulders.

Ramón grabbed his arm, this time gently. "I myself am an invalid and of no use. My arms have given out but my soul is alive. Row me to land and I will reward you in a princely manner. The ring this black boy wears around his neck belongs to a king. No matter how black he is, he's worth a fortune back in his homeland. Save me, Tom O'Connor, and you will have a share in this king's ransom."

"A share?" whispered Tom.

The boatswain nodded and his eyes smoldered. "Half of him will be yours."

4 Father Innocent

HE IS STANDING OUTSIDE of the little garret that is right above Señor López's bedroom. It's the wee hours of the morning, and he has just come in from the sea. The garret is the smallest room on the second floor and usually used for storing sails and twine, casks of bacon and jars of treacle. All of that has now been removed and a straw pallet has been dragged in under the long shelf, where a thoughtful person has placed a vase with purple jacaranda flowers. That person might very well be the one who is lying on the pallet: the seaman from Cádiz.

After recuperating and nursing his wounds, Ramón had started doing carpentry and carving fishing stakes. His efforts pleased the innkeeper, especially after Ramón successfully repaired his favorite chair, and the Far Beyond could continue to grow big and strong and still have something on which to sit.

Ramón's ability to make himself useful worried Tom. Every morning he would ask the seaman when the slave was going back to the Bissagos Islands, and every morning he received the same answer: as soon as a ship appeared, Ramón would hire on and set off to recoup their shared reward.

"You're not going without me," replied Tom. "Don't forget our agreement."

"I wouldn't dream of going without you, Tom," said the Spaniard, "but the black isn't about to run off anywhere. I think it's probably the same with him as with pigs: the bigger he grows, the more we'll get for him."

Tom would often stand outside the seaman's door and study him in secret. He couldn't figure out this Ramón, who had shown himself to be grateful for all that was done for him. Besides being clever with his hands, he was also hardworking and amiable. And he turned a deaf ear whenever the innkeeper complained about the extra mouth to feed.

He may have had a deaf ear, but his tongue was sugar-coated. "Seldom has the world seen a more generous man than you, Señor López." Ramón closed his eyes with gratitude. "No, señor, I refuse to hear any objections. Here we are, four grown people, who daily enjoy your generosity and tolerance."

"A man does what he can," mumbled López, uncertain whether he was being ridiculed or whether he was indeed such a kindhearted person.

"Allow me to fill one of the big glasses with beer for the innkeeper. I will make do with a small one myself."

"So he is going to partake as well?" López squirmed in his chair.

"What kind of upbringing did you have, señor?" Ramón sipped at his beer and listened to Señor López, who gladly told him about his harsh upbringing, which in such a singular way had given him this kindhearted reputation.

After three weeks had passed, the man from Cádiz had Señor López right where he wanted him. He continued to be polite and helpful, especially to Tom's mother, although she rarely spoke to him. In her view the Spaniard's eyes concealed a completely different Rámon, who had not yet made an appearance. Tom couldn't see this, so he settled for marveling that a hardened seaman would see fit to decorate his room with fresh flowers.

The black boy had been stowed temporarily under the kitchen floor in a cubbyhole next to the provisions. Tom was the one who made sure that he had something to eat and that there was fresh water in his dish. The thought that the lad might perish from thirst was unbearable. He was still Tom's only prospect for ever acquiring any money.

There was never any light in the tiny space, but Ramón said that light was bad for a slave's eyes. "Besides," he added, "we don't want to attract any attention. Just imagine what would happen if it were rumored that we were holding a king's son in the cellar."

For that very reason Ramón and Tom decided to keep their fortune a secret. But Tom had told his mother and sister the truth—not that it had made much of an impression. "I now have my own slave," he told Feodora.

"You own *half* a slave," she corrected him. "And who cares about half a slave! By the way, is it the right half or the left that you own? Or have you divided him at the waist?"

"Jealous as usual," snorted Tom. "It radiates from you, half-breed."

Feodora smiled and ran her fingers through her thick black hair. "Why are the Irish more stupid than other people? Anybody can see that the scrawny fledgling isn't worth five pots of piss. You've been had, Tom O'Connor. Ramón has tricked you good and proper."

"You'll change your tune," replied Tom. "That slave boy is worth his weight in gold, and the day we deliver him to the Bissagos Islands, Tom O'Connor will be a wealthy man, able to buy half of Nevis if he likes."

At that remark, his sister doubled over with laughter and exclaimed that if this slave were to be sold by weight, the most he could possibly bring would be a decrepit hen.

That evening Tom decided to give food to the black twice a day instead of just once, in the hope that it would put a little more meat on his bones. The slave didn't say a word, merely ate what was set before him. But after a few weeks of double rations, when the boy hadn't grown any stronger or any healthier in appearance, Tom realized that his thinness was probably innate, and he decided to save the extra portion.

He knocked on the door.

Ramón sat up with a start and in a flash pulled his knife from under his pillow. But when he recognized Tom through the cracks in the wall, he smiled and opened the door. "So early, Master Tom."

Tom slipped into the garret and sat down on the only chair in the room. "I've been out to sea," he said. "By the way, we're going to have a visitor soon."

"A visitor? Who might that be?"

"A distinguished visitor. Why do you think the inn has been scoured and scrubbed from cellar to attic?"

Ramón tested the blade of his knife. "Tell me what you know."

It was all on account of a man who called himself Father Innocent, named for the eighth Pope. In reality his name was Felix Salazar and he was an inquisitor, dispatched by the church to hunt down heretics and witches. Father Innocent had won a certain reputation on the islands neighboring

Saint Kitts. If truth be told, fear of the pious father surpassed that of plague, pox, and fever. Many of the islanders even refused to leave their homes whenever he came to visit. The reports of the inquisitor's methods, when he sought to force a confession, had long since reached Nevis. In Spain many heretics had been burned at the stake.

It was two years since Innocent had last been to the island. He always arrived with a small retinue consisting of ten soldiers, a scribe, and an executioner. And his word was law. He had no friends but enjoyed great respect. During his sojourn he usually stayed with Señor López, who catered to the inquisitor's every whim. For the two days that his visit lasted, the innkeeper would be overcome by such strong religious fervor that it was difficult to understand what he was saying. And the inn, which was otherwise known for being both clean and God-fearing and could not be accused of housing heretics, witches, or folk of dubious reputation, was turned upside down from cellar to attic. The crucifixes that did not hang on the walls were immediately hung on hooks so that everyone could see that here lived a man of whom the Pope in Rome and all of devout Spain could be proud. For the same reason Señor López was also washed and deloused, and his best clothes were cleaned and mended.

Ramón stared off into space with a meditative expression.

"What are you thinking about?" asked Tom. "Are you afraid of the Inquisition?"

The Spaniard abruptly stood up and said that he was in all ways a God-fearing man who would help Father Innocent with everything he required.

"Do you know him?"

Ramón sighed. "I have heard of him, but who can claim to know Father Innocent?"

"But we don't have any witches here," said Tom.

Ramón gave him an uneasy look. "If there were no witch on Nevis," he whispered, "Innocent would not be coming here. He's known as the most zealous of all inquisitors. His methods of torture are so gruesome that the poor victims long for the gallows in order to escape more horrors."

Tom put a finger to his lips and then pushed aside the straw pallet that served as Ramón's bed. With a little smile he opened a trapdoor in the floor. Ramón knelt down and listened.

"Has His Excellency's room been prepared?" he heard López ask.

"Everything is ready," replied Tom's mother, as she sewed the last button on the Spaniard's vest, to which an insert had been added in the back so that the vest wouldn't split apart when he bowed before the pious father.

"I don't want to see a single rat dashing across this floor," snarled the innkeeper.

"Tom has set traps everywhere," said Tom's mother, "and Ramón has sealed up the cracks in the pantry and cellar."

"And that girl over there," said the innkeeper, pointing to Feodora, "she has to be deaf and dumb while our visitor is here."

Tom's mother swore holy oaths that her daughter's lips would be locked with seven seals.

"It's said that Father Innocent is coming to Nevis for a very specific purpose," gasped López. "Yes, you may stare, but there's good reason for it. Now we're going to put a stop to the heresy."

"Heresy?" Tom's mother glanced at her daughter.

"That's right, heresy! As if I haven't been saying the very same thing for years, but have any of you bothered to listen? Well, it's over now. The Inquisition is here, and now you shall see."

Tom closed the trapdoor. Ramón was standing at the window, in the process of exchanging his nightshirt for a tunic. He was naked from the waist up. It surprised Tom that Ramón always had fresh welts on his back. Maybe what Tom's mother had said was true, that the Spaniard had a peculiar temperament. No matter how happy he might seem, he could turn equally morose.

Occasionally Tom found him down at the shore, where the man would be clutching his cap in his hands and sobbing like a child, intractable and impossible to talk to. Sometimes he would borrow Juan Carlos from Señor López's room. At first Tom thought this was to punish their shared fortune, but he soon discovered that Ramón was exacting penance from himself. "Why, Ramón?" Tom had asked him.

"Because I deserve it," said the Spaniard. "Every single lash of the whip."

"Deserve it? In what way, Ramón?"

"You don't want to know, Tom O'Connor. I deserve all the torments of Hell, or my name isn't Ramón from Cádiz."

Tom had heard him moaning in his sleep. The strangest, eeriest sounds came from his room, with the Spaniard speaking in several different voices. But when dawn arrived, he was once again the friendliest, most carefree person in the world.

Tom felt the Spaniard's hand on his shoulder. "We should be glad," said Ramón, "that the Church looks after us. Keep in mind, Tom, that God the Almighty, who created all living things, had to do battle Himself with a serpent in the Garden of Eden. Evil is everywhere and must be fought with all possible means. That is why we have the Inquisition."

"Tell me what you know about it."

The Spaniard sighed. "The Inquisition is an interrogation that rids us of heretics."

"Am I a heretic, Ramón?"

Ramón smiled. "No," he said, "you're not a heretic, Tom. You're just ambitious, full of lies, and reckless as a shark. Heresy is much more serious."

"Tell me what a heretic is."

Ramón took time to think. "You know what a witch is, don't you?"

Tom nodded, uncertain whether he had ever met a witch.

Ramón put out the candle in the candlestick and got his pipe. "There are women who were born witches," he said, "who consort with toads and snakes and perform strange tricks, changing people's shapes and carrying on. They're in league with Beelzebub, the Devil himself. People also say that they can't sink."

Tom stared at him. "They can't sink?"

"It's true," said the Spaniard. "I've seen it myself in Cádiz, where they threw an old woman into the river again and again, but they could not make her sink."

"She must have been swimming."

"Tom, you don't understand. The woman was a witch. She was consorting with Satan. There are stories of witches who sneak into people's houses to suck the blood of infants."

Tom looked away, shaking his head.

"The Inquisition," said Rámon, putting tobacco in his pipe, "rids us of this sort of woman. We should be happy about that." The Spaniard turned his back to Tom and lowered his voice. "People say," he murmured, "that there's a witch on Nevis."

"Do you believe it?"

"We shall see."

"Who could it be?"

Ramón looked at his pipe and shook his head.

"I have no idea, but you can be certain that Father Innocent knows where to find her. Go in and get a little sleep now, Tom. And forget about all these evil thoughts. Think about that funny story I told you. The one about the pig that became the governor of Jamaica."

Soon afterward Tom lay on his worn bunk with his hands behind his head. But sleep refused to come. He looked at his sister, who lay on her cot with her hair spread out like a fan. Her skin was as white as ivory, and between her lips he glimpsed her pearly white teeth.

Tom stared up at the ceiling. Father Innocent had decided to stay with Señor López. Here, and nowhere else. He sighed heavily and studied his sister, feature by feature. She looks like one, he thought, she looks for all the world exactly like a witch. Now that he thought about it, there had always been problems with Feo whenever their mother asked her to say grace, to fold her hands and thank the Almighty for the meal. When they lit candles to the Holy Virgin, Feo could take it into her head to smile and squint her eyes, yes, even make faces, only to turn serious, quick as lightning—much too serious, in fact, as if she were showing off. Sometimes she would say, "Did you remember to fold your sweaty little hands, Tom, and thank God for the rooster you just ate?"

"Did *you* remember, Feodora?"

"I, who chopped off the bird's head and then plucked, boiled, and cut it up, have of course also remembered to thank God for this meal. And just think, Tom—afterward He said, 'You're welcome.'"

"You're a beast and a blasphemer, Feodora Dolores Vasgues, and if Señor López hears you talking that way, you'll get a taste of Juan Carlos this very night."

"Tom O'Connor, listen to me." His sister had lowered her voice to a confidential whisper. "Señor López can no longer swing the whip so it hurts—his blows do no more than tickle me. I think his arms have gotten too fat. So do me a favor and forget all about Juan Carlos and fold your filthy paws and pray that you don't get a rooster bone caught in your throat and end up choking in your sleep."

Tom closed his eyes. There had been plenty of conversations like this, with Feo talking in a heretical fashion. And now her punishment had come. Many people on the island would remember her impudent behavior, and just as many would curse her sharp tongue. And if it came to Father Innocent having to use Señor López as a witness, then Feo's days were numbered.

Against his will, Tom touched his sister's hair. How soft it was, so fine and so clean. She smelled of lime juice. She had put the juice in the water, just as her mother did. "Dear God," whispered Tom. "Dear God, Feodora."

Suddenly he recalled an episode from his childhood, when they had found a toad, a big brown one with a long slimy tongue.

"It will bring sickness and misfortune," Feo had told him. From her skirt she had pulled out a knife, which she used to cut the toad's throat. A swift, skillful slash. The toad hardly noticed it. But Tom threw up on the spot. "Dear God, Feo," he murmured, "are you really a witch?"

His sister opened her eyes. "Yes, I am," she said softly.

Tom fell to the floor in fright. "You don't know what you're saying."

"I don't?"

"No, you don't. Do you realize who's coming here day after tomorrow?"

"Is someone coming here?"

"Why do you think we've been cleaning all week?"

"Oh, that's right, the pious father is coming. I had forgotten all about it. Strange that I should forget when you consider how diligently I've been polishing our crucifixes. And that sanctimonious innkeeper is lying in his bed, stinking like a Cuban bordello."

"Father Innocent is coming because there's a witch on the island," whispered Tom.

Feo rolled her eyes. "That's not true, Tom."

Tom gripped her arm. "It's nothing to make fun of, damn it."

"Was that the only reason you woke me?"

"Tell me this, Feo. When you go swimming in the sea . . ."

"Yes, Tom? What about when I go swimming in the sea?"

Tom took a deep breath. "Can you sink?"

His sister gave him a penetrating look and then sat up and stroked her chin. "It's funny you should mention that, Tom." She snapped her fingers. "But no, I can't. I've tried many times, but I can't make myself sink."

Tom narrowed his eyes. "Are you serious?"

"Dead serious, Tom, dead serious. I can't sink."

Tom looked at her long, slender fingers, which seemed so untouched by the work that Señor López assigned her. Strangely untouched.

"Witches," he explained, "can't sink. Do you understand what I'm saying, Feo? Witches can't sink. I'm not making this up. Look at me. This is serious. Promise me that if Father Innocent tries to test you, promise me that you'll do everything you can to make yourself sink."

"I'll do my best, Tom. I promise."

Tom took his sister's hand. "You're a strange person, Feodora."

"Am I, Tom?"

"Yes, you are, but you're still my sister."

"Only your half sister, if we're going to be completely accurate."

"Only my half sister, but still. Still, I would hate to . . ."

"Hate to what, Tom?"

"Hate to lose you. I was thinking that maybe I could row you out to a skerry while Father Innocent is here."

"Oh, Tom, at heart you're a good person; and it's not your fault that you were born half-Irish. But don't you think it would attract attention if the girl who can't sink should suddenly disappear into thin air?"

Tom squeezed his sister's hand. "I'm just so afraid of what will happen."

Feodora nodded.

"Do you know," whispered Tom, "do you know what they do to witches?"

There was silence between them.

Feodora looked at Tom with a pensive expression. "They burn them," she said.

Two days later a storm began brewing, but by noon the wind had died down and turned brisk. The first fishing boats appeared on the horizon, heading for the coast.

Toward evening the waves rose up, and the old one-legged tar who hobbled around by the bay entertained the children with stories about worms coming out of his wooden leg whenever a hurricane was gathering force. When darkness fell in earnest, the rain swept in from the sea and drummed against rooftops and doors. The howling storm rushed between the buildings, and people huddled together around tallow candles, in the hope that ropes and hawsers would hold.

Tom, Feodora, and their mother did the same, having decided to spend the night in the tavern room of the inn. They were joined by Señor López, who had closed the inn because of the storm. He squeaked like a hungry mouse every time the wooden beams groaned, and he gazed with horror at the water trickling in through cracks and rafters.

In other words, it was a perfect night for good stories. Feodora, who was known as a splendid storyteller, had just started on an account of a sailing ship and the Southern Cross when they heard a knock on the door.

The innkeeper told Tom to explain to the intruder that the inn was closed. But since it was impossible to hear a thing in the roar of the storm, Tom had to open the door just a crack.

"Unfortunately," he said, "we are . . ." That was as far as he got because the door was slammed wide open. In strode a tall, slender man wearing a dark red cloak. Behind him came a thin little fellow in more ordinary garb. When the tall man flung off his cloak, a gasp issued from Señor López, who recognized Father Innocent.

Without a word, the inquisitor walked over to the fireplace, where he took up a position with his back to the flames. He flashed a fierce glance from López to Feodora and from Feodora to Tom, as if he wanted to hold them responsible for the storm that had soaked his garments.

Tom studied the man's features: the piercing eyes, the enormous hawk nose, and the high cheekbones. He looked even more magnificent than Tom remembered.

Señor López, who had fallen to his knees at the man's feet, was mumbling a slew of incomprehensible words that sounded like an apology, a prayer, and a welcome.

The inquisitor ignored him and went over to the table and sat down in Señor López's chair. With a snap of his fingers, he bade Tom pull off his wet boots. Cloths were then wrapped around his feet and he was served a glass of the best wine in the house. Señor López scurried around like a broody hen, lashing out at Tom and yelling at Feo whenever they didn't obey his orders quickly enough. "Father Innocent must excuse the bad weather we have to put up with," he said. "Rarely has it been so despicable."

"Despicable," said the pious father, stretching. "How can you call God's weather despicable?"

Señor López crossed himself and replied with a quavering voice that it certainly had not been his intention to say anything derogatory about God's weather.

Father Innocent told him to keep quiet and aimed his gaze at Tom. Sparks from the hearth lit up his dark eyes. "God's finger has struck Nevis to tell us that it is here we must seek. Here is where a blasphemer lives."

At these words Señor López threw himself to the floor. This seemed to amuse the pious father, who with a slight shake of his head pointed at Tom's mother. "Might there be a scrap of supper left?" His voice now sounded more gentle.

Tom's mother headed at once for the kitchen but was stopped by Señor López.

"You're to cook a fresh meal for His Excellency," he scolded her, apologizing for his staff's poor behavior.

"We will accept whatever we are given," said Innocent.

"His Excellency must have the best the house has to offer," whispered López.

It turned out to be a long night. Father Innocent and his scribe ate and drank, rested a bit, and then demanded more food. No one slept a wink.

Tom and his mother spent most of their time tending to the pots and pans. Feo ran back and forth, still without uttering a word. Tom was pleased that, in spite of everything, his sister had enough good manners to know when to keep silent.

Having finally eaten their fill, the men sat lolling around the table. Feodora started clearing away the dishes. The little scribe was in the midst of a story about a mule from Trinidad that was capable of adding up sums, when Father Innocent suddenly grabbed Feo's white hand, which he examined, finger by finger. "What's your name, young lady?" he asked.

"My name is Feodora Dolores Vasgues," replied Feo in a high, clear voice.

"And she has the sharpest tongue on the island," added Señor López.

The inquisitor looked up at Feo. "Is that true? Can so sharp a tongue actually reside in such a lovely mouth?"

"Judge for yourself," said Feo. She stuck out her tongue.

Tom shut his eyes.

With an effort Señor López lumbered to his feet, presumably to get Juan Carlos, but he was stopped by Father Innocent. "As far as I can tell," he said, "it looks like she has quite an ordinary tongue. But her hands are lily-white. Does she really have no work to tend to? It's not good for a girl of her age to be idle."

"Bone lazy," said López, "indolent and shameless. People don't get hands like that from tending to their work."

The inquisitor looked at Feo who, with a little smile, withdrew her hand as she turned to face the innkeeper. "Might the same hold true for our generous host?" she said. "His hands, as far as I can tell, are just as exquisite as mine."

Now Tom's mother stepped in, a frown on her face, but Father Innocent held her back. "Are you Spanish, Feodora?" he asked.

"Yes, I'm Spanish," she said, bobbing her head. "My mother is half-Spanish and half-British, but my father was Spanish from head to toe, and it's his blood that flows in my veins." Feodora smiled at her mother, who gazed at the floor.

A moment passed in which the silence lay heavy in the dimly lit tavern. Father Innocent sat lost in his own thoughts until suddenly, as if waking from a nap, he straightened up. "Your brother, Feodora," he said, "where did he disappear to?"

Tom emerged from the kitchen, drying his hands on his apron as he approached the great man, who regarded him through slightly narrowed eyes. "Your name, my son?"

"Tom O'Connor, Your Excellency, named after my father." Tom glanced at his sister, who was watching him with a little, mocking smile.

Father Innocent tilted his head back and closed his eyes. "Can you be trusted, Tom?"

Tom's eyes darted from his mother to Señor López, who seemed uncertain whether to laugh or cry.

"Tom's a good boy." Tom's mother put her arm around her son.

Father Innocent nodded to his scribe, who stood up and opened the door to the back room. Visible inside was the innkeeper's bed and the two huge candlesticks that always burned on his table. "This way." Innocent took Tom by the scruff of his neck—a tight grip that turned Tom to ice. They went over to the door, where Innocent paused when Tom's mother, this time more shrilly, repeated that Tom had always been a good boy.

"Isn't that what every mother says?" Innocent smiled to himself and hustled Tom into the back room. As the door fell shut, a change came over the man. The cold spiritual figure suddenly displayed a fiery temperament. His eyes flashed, and his narrow lips drew back to expose his gums.

Tom could fully understand the terror that surrounded this man and the turmoil that accompanied him.

"Now, Tom O'Connor," he whispered, "now we'll get to the truth about this island."

The inquisitor placed his hands on Tom's shoulders and fixed a burning gaze on him. The pious father had loathsome breath that testified to rotting gums. Quite ordinary-smelling breath, Tom realized, feeling a bit encouraged by the thought that there was actually something commonplace about this man.

"You know why I'm here, don't you?"

Tom nodded uncertainly.

"Tell me why the Inquisition is here."

"To look for heretics," whispered Tom.

The pious father responded by squeezing Tom's shoulders. "Are there any heretics?" he whispered.

"I don't think so," stammered Tom.

"Think, Tom, think."

Tom felt the man's grip tighten. "Maybe," he whispered, "but I don't know everybody on Nevis. Maybe if you asked my mother, who has lived here all her life."

"But I'm asking you, Tom. In your eyes I see an honest boy who wants nothing more than to make his mother proud. Although there is also a sliver of stubbornness. But slivers can always be extracted. Won't you tell me?"

Tom took several short little breaths and murmured that he had no intention except to help the Inquisition, but he knew nothing about any sliver in his eyes.

Abruptly the man released his grip and placed his hand on Tom's cheek. He pulled him close and patted him on the back. "Relax, young O'Connor," he whispered, "relax. No one means you any harm."

Tom felt the sobs rising in his throat and was annoyed by his own weakness.

"The boy may kiss my ring."

Tom bent down and kissed the man's red signet ring.

The inquisitor gazed at him and wiped away a tear from the corner of Tom's eye. "In this stone," whispered Innocent, "resides a terrible power and a heavy responsibility. But I gladly accept the loneliness that comes with it, for I am merely an instrument. Nothing more. My profession has taught me how to judge people. So I know that I can rely on you—isn't that so, Tom?"

Tom nodded, sniffling.

"You would never dream of hiding anything from me, would you?"

"Never ever."

The tall man stood up and took down from the wall López's golden crucifix, the one that Feo had polished especially for the occasion.

"Receive the Holy Cross. Hold it to your breast."

Tom did as he was told, watching the inquisitor gather up Juan Carlos, the thin leather strap, from its corner. With a lightning-fast movement and terrifying force, Father Innocent slammed the strap against the innkeeper's bed. Even though the bed had been thoroughly cleaned, a tremendous cloud of dust rose up in the room. Father Innocent was breathing hard and fast. "Press the Cross to your breast, Tom O'Connor." The bed suffered another blow.

Tom stared at the door to the tavern, where he could hear his mother crying and Señor López trying to hush her.

For the next five minutes the inquisitor pounded the poor mattress so hard that the straw burst through the ticking and the wooden frame threatened to break. Sweat poured down the man's face. His big nostrils flared like those of a horse and his eyes shot bolts of lightning.

Suddenly he pulled Tom close and pressed the crucifix to his chin. A drop of blood trickled out and struck the Christ figure. "You know there's a she-devil on this island," whispered Innocent. "You've eaten with her and served her wine. A witch of the worst kind. Think, Tom. Think, for your own sake. For your mother's sake, and especially for your sister's sake. In silence the Church has tolerated her impertinences, her misplaced contempt, but there are limits to what this ring can tolerate. I hope you understand, Tom. And now listen carefully, because Nevis is harboring a witch. You know it, Tom. Everyone knows it. Any child knows it." Innocent raised his voice. "Do not conceal it from the Inquisition, Tom O'Connor. Do not make yourself an instrument of the Evil One."

Tom wracked his brain, thinking like crazy, but could not come up with any name other than his sister's, which he refused to say aloud, even if the man beat him ten times worse than the mattress.

"Speak to me, Tom," whispered Innocent. "Speak to me so I can hear it."

"No matter how much I'd like to tell you, I know nothing of the evil you're talking about. I'm just a poor fisherman's boy, who . . ."

"In your silence, Tom, lives a lie."

The inquisitor put his lips to the crucifix and with the tip of his tongue he lifted the round little drop of blood from the cross, closed his eyes, and swallowed it. "And lies," he whispered with his eyes still closed, "lies are the language of Satan. Does the name Zamora mean anything to you?"

Tom gave a start, meeting the inquisitor's glance with a mixture of relief and uneasiness. The image of the old woman with the milky eye appeared before him as clearly as the pious father standing there. But she was harmless. A poor creature who had never hurt anyone. Was she supposed to be a witch?

"You know her." The inquisitor unbuttoned his collar.

Tom nodded.

"You've spoken to her often? No doubt that cannot be avoided, living as you do on such a small island."

"Not very often, just a few times."

Innocent took off his signet ring and put it on Tom's thumb. "Can you feel it burning your skin, Tom?"

Tom stared at the ring, but now his mouth was so dry that he couldn't utter a word.

The inquisitor opened his eyes wide, feigning astonishment. "Or is it cold the boy feels? It has come to my attention that this Zamora assists at births, is that correct?"

Tom looked away and nodded.

"Doesn't it frighten you that the Evil One has sent a witch to Nevis to attend the birth of children? Don't you realize what power Satan acquires over these newborn lives?"

"Yes," whispered Tom.

"Is it not true, Tom O'Connor," said the inquisitor, pulling the ring off Tom's finger and letting it slip back to its proper place, "that this woman also attended your birth? Look me in the eye, boy, and tell me the truth."

"I think she was there," whispered Tom.

For a moment the pious father stood twisting his head from side to side, as if his neck hurt. Then he opened the door to the tavern. Tom's mother was still standing in the middle of the room, her cheeks flushed with anger. At the table sat López, wearing a hopeful expression. The scribe seemed to have fallen asleep.

"Not a hair on the boy's head has been harmed," said Innocent, putting his arm around Tom.

Tom's mother sighed with relief.

The inquisitor gave Tom a somber look. "It will soon be daybreak," he said, "and a boy of your age needs his sleep. But tomorrow, Tom, tomorrow you'll be off as fast as your legs can carry you. No one knows the island better than you do. The Inquisition has appointed you as its holy instrument."

"Instrument?" murmured Tom.

"You could be given no greater task. Your mother can be proud of you. The whole island can be proud of you."

Father Innocent went over to the fireplace, stuck a piece of kindling in the flames, and then held it over Tom's head. "Tom O'Connor," he bellowed, "find the woman who in Satan's service brings children into the world. Find her and deliver her to the Inquisition."

5   Bibido

TOM HAD LAIN ON HIS BUNK for about an hour and now decided to get up. He splashed a little water on his face and was just going to open the door when his mother called his name. The sound of her voice gave him a start. For some reason he had thought he was alone.

His mother stretched out her hand and fixed her gaze on him. Tom looked away as though he were guilty of something. But why should he feel guilty? There was no reason for it.

And yet he felt a burning inside him. The flames licked at his thoughts, which turned black and charred. If this is what it's like to be grown-up, he thought, I want to keep on being a boy. Until then, he had always dreamed of the day he would be master of his own life, free as a bird.

Maybe life held a surprise. After all, his mother wasn't free; she was a house slave for Señor López. She owned only the clothes on her back and the clasp she put in her hair. By the end of each day she had earned only enough for the meal that she herself prepared. The shackles around her ankles were invisible, but they were there.

Was Señor López a free man? Yes, he was a free man. Master in his own house. He had achieved the ultimate that a human being could achieve: the innkeeper was free. And rich. Maybe not rich, but rich enough so that he could have people in his keep, people to do the work so he could sit all day long in his well-upholstered chair and have his hair deloused whenever it suited him. Tom stared off into space. López might be a rich man, but he was far from free. His girth and his laziness had wrapped a chain around the chair in which he sat.

Was Ramón a free man? Apparently, but the scars on his back told a different story.

My sister, thought Tom, my sister is a free person. Free as the wind in her hair. She does what she pleases. At the moment it pleased her to serve Señor López, to cook his food, to do the cleaning and wait on tables. But when the day came that this no longer pleased her, no one would be able to hold back Feodora Dolores Vasgues. Then she'd be gone. Damn half-breed. Tom murmured that he had to be off.

His mother looked at him and took his hand. "Before you go," she whispered, "you should know that no matter what happens, no matter what you do, I'll help you. I've always been proud of you, and I always will be."

Tom withdrew his hand. "Why are you telling me this now?"

She gave him a somber look. "Because you are my son and because I love you."

Tom went to the door and stood there a moment with his back to her. "Zamora is a heretic," he muttered. "A witch."

His mother made no reply.

He turned and looked at her. "You know she's a witch."

She sat up and started brushing her hair.

Tom went over to her bed. "There's plenty of proof."

"If the Inquisition says that Zamora is a witch, then she's a witch." His mother put the hair clasp between her teeth and gathered her hair into a knot. "And when the Inquisition asks my son to find her, then he has no choice. That's the way things are, Tom. You don't need to fret so much about it."

"I'm not," he snapped. "Besides, Ramón says that we should be grateful to the Inquisition for ridding us of heretics."

"You should just do the task you've been given to do."

Tom sighed in exasperation and sat down on the edge of the bed. "Who's going to help the women give birth now?"

"That's not your concern. And besides, it's not certain that Zamora is even on Nevis."

"What do you mean?"

His mother looked away. "Your sister has taken the skiff. She's rowing north."

"North? Why is she rowing north?"

"That's where she thinks Zamora may be hiding."

Tom stared at Feodora's empty bed. "Is she daring to defy Father Innocent?"

Once more his mother did not reply.

"She's defying the Inquisition. Feodora Dolores Vasgues is flouting Father Innocent and the Pope in Rome and the whole Catholic Church. Has she lost her mind? Yes, she must have lost her mind." Tom slapped his hand to his forehead. "What if Father Innocent hears about this?"

"He won't."

"Oh, you don't think so? But what about me? What about the task I'm supposed to carry out?"

"Dear God, Tom, just do what you've been told to do. Why make the whole thing so difficult?"

"No one asked my half sister about anything. I'm the one who's been given a task by the Inquisition, and now Feo's doing everything she can to prevent me from carrying it out. And you haven't tried to stop her."

"When Feo gets an idea in her head . . ."

Tom angrily flung open the door. "I'll find the old hag all right," he said. "I'll find her before Feo does, I promise you that. Because I'm loyal to the Inquisition. We don't want any heretics on this island."

His mother looked away and nodded. "You're absolutely right."

Tom searched for two days, going everywhere on the island, making inquiries, but no one would help him. In several places he even encountered men who spat at him and women who threw stones when he asked about the woman with the milky eye. They knew, of course, whom he was looking for, and some of them took the time to tell him that they often sought help from Zamora and had never done so in vain.

One day Tom found a cave in the dense rain forest from which the sea was visible only as a narrow strip of turquoise. Overhead was the cone of the volcano.

Except for the sound of monkeys screeching, the world was so beautiful, just as it had been when the ocean emerged for the first time from the mouth of the frog. Just like the first time Tom had opened his eyes and looked into his mother's face. He was so little then—not a word had crossed his lips, not a thought had formed in his mind. Just the sounds of his mother singing and of the waves pounding against the shore.

The shore and the sea, the stars and the palm trees—it was all still there, but now he was a different person. In his mind, words were writhing like twisted garlands, weighing him to the ground. Making him hide like a hunted animal in the deepest caves of the island, in the hope that he could return to his earliest childhood and see the world with the eyes of a newborn.

But he was neither a child nor an innocent, and the stars were not a mystery but something by which to navigate, and the great ocean could tell him nothing that he didn't already know.

"I'm grown-up," he said out loud. "I don't need to be afraid of anything. I don't need to have a guilty conscience because I'm just doing what I've been told to do. Like an ax or a knife or a fishhook, I'm just an instrument."

He looked around and raised his voice. "Just an instrument."

At that moment he caught sight of a little algae-colored gecko. It was clinging to the roof of the cave, looking right at him. If he didn't know better, he'd say the gecko was smiling as it licked its lips with its forked tongue. "There are only the two of us," whispered Tom, "only the two of us in the whole world."

The gecko came closer.

"You and me, little gecko, just you and me."

"And fear." The lizard seemed to smirk. "Don't forget that."

Tom narrowed his eyes. "Fear?"

"Oh, can't the boy feel it?" said the gecko. "Yes, of course he can. Why else would we be meeting in a nook of the forest, far away from everything?"

"Tell me about fear," whispered Tom.

"He wants to know about fear?"

"Yes, tell me about it."

"It's the same way with fear," said the lizard, "as it is with the eagle, the scorpion, the leopard, the cockatoo, and you and me. Without nourishment, we die. That's the way it is with fear too."

Tom sighed and gazed at the damp ceiling of the cave. "Go on. Tell me something I don't already know."

"What do I get in return?" asked the lizard, smiling. "Little as I am, I can't afford the luxury of not demanding something in return."

"You can't pluck hair from a bald man," muttered Tom, glancing around.

The gecko cast a superior little gaze around the deep cave. "I, who belong to a lower order of lizards, have few joys in this life. Compared to human beings, I live an impoverished existence. If I could only share in the joy of seeing a waterfall as more than rushing water, the stars as more than light, and the moon's beams as more than night, then my brief life would be so much richer."

"You certainly have a high opinion of me," sighed Tom. "How am I supposed to give you all that?"

"By granting me your heart."

"My heart? You want my heart?"

"Yes, give me your heart and I will tell you about fear, which is nourished by doubt. I will teach you to conquer it and tame it; the one who conquers fear is invincible."

"And what about the one who gives away his heart?" asked Tom. "To a gecko? A damn lizard? Go away, you hideous lizard, and never speak to me again."

The gecko raced across the ceiling of the cave. "We'll meet again, Tom," it whispered. "We'll meet again when life has given you a greater talent for commerce."

Tom left the cave in the rocks and made his way to the shore, where he lay down to sleep. That was where his mother found him. She didn't say anything, just took him along home. But when he asked about Father Innocent, she told him that Zamora had been found by the Inquisition's soldiers, and that the interrogation had begun.

The next few days Tom stayed out at sea, doing what he usually did: fishing. But one evening, as he steered the skiff homeward, he heard the sound of drums. Against his will, he rowed toward the sound. A short time later he caught sight of a long procession on its way toward the farthermost spit of land, whose crab's claw stuck out into the sea to the northeast. The sun was setting, and a throng of people, preceded by a banner and standard, moved like a column of black ants. Tom turned the skiff and rowed faster. From the sea he could keep an eye on the procession, which numbered at least a hundred islanders.

He pulled in closer and could now make out soldiers among the people. When the banner turned in the wind, he recognized the Inquisition's green cross on white cloth. He also recognized Father Innocent and his little scribe. They were walking behind a cloaked figure who was limping badly, hampered by heavy shackles.

Tom shifted his gaze and caught sight of a bonfire framework that had been built at the very tip of the spit of land. The sight made him curl up in the bottom of his skiff. He lay with his face pressed against the floorboards, with his knees tucked up to his chin, like a fetus, an unborn life whose palms had lines that revealed nothing. Nothing at all.

"I'll go to sea," he whispered, "to sea on the trade winds, far away, farther away than any man. Let them take me to the Old World, to Portugal and Spain, but most of all to Ireland, where the people speak my father's language and have green eyes and red hair. Where no one has ever heard of Father Innocent or the Inquisition. I'm a foreigner here. Yes, I'm an outsider. That's why my soul is split, so that one minute I'm jubilantly happy and the next I'm gloomy and sad." He sat up. Maybe I've been struck by Ramón's sickness, he thought. He clasped his hands and bent forward.

"Dear God," he whispered, "help a poor boy whose soul is split in two and who can't understand what's happening all around him. Help him to understand the world. My sister won't speak to me, and my mother tries to humor me, while my only friend, Ramón of Cádiz, tortures himself every night for no apparent reason. I thank Father Innocent for freeing us from another heretic, but I confess that it disgusts me to watch him eat. Not that it's important, because my own manners are far from perfect. I've gotten used to the innkeeper's manners, though in truth he eats like a swine. On the other hand, the pious father sits as erect as a pillar of salt and always uses a fork and knife, never touching the food with his hands, and still he washes them before every mouthful. He has even asked to have a basin of water next to his place. This is a sign of cleanliness, but I am revolted by the quantity he consumes—the inconceivable number of servings—and the grinding way in which he chews, slow and rhythmic and with his mouth open enough so that you can watch his tongue working at the meat. And as he chews he wipes his hands. He never looks at anything or seems aware of his surroundings, he simply chews. After the hour-long meal, he sits with his eyes half-closed and digests. Afterward he disappears into the privy, where he shits for hours. Father Innocent eats no vegetables, no herbs, and no bread—only meat. Endless amounts of meat. Ramón says that meat eaters get very thin and very tall, and that the time the pious father spends in the privy is a cleansing process, because it all has to come out so that he can be pure in his deeds. If only I could achieve the same thing: to be pure in my deeds." Tom wiped his eyes.

On the spit of land the drumming had stopped. He couldn't hear what was taking place, but after a while he saw the cloaked figure being led over to the stake in the woodpile. The hood of the cowl was thrown back, and Zamora's hands and feet were bound. She looked frail and small and offered no resistance. Now a brief drumroll sounded, followed by a high-pitched murmuring. Whereupon the wood was ignited and the flames flared up.

Tom would have preferred to row away as quickly as possible, but he sat riveted. His mouth agape and his eyes wide, he watched the fire make its way toward the stunted figure.

Tom fell backward, staring at the sunburned face with the milky iris. For a fraction of a second he felt that they had made eye contact. For a long, drawn-out, dizzying second he felt her gaze upon him and felt the strength of her hand. *It's called the breeze of the will. It comes from the great maw of Fate, and whoever knows how to listen will learn a great deal.* He remembered every word she had said, and he whispered a word of apology as he watched her gaunt body go up in flames and her face crumple, turning quickly into a coal-black skull with a smile of silver.

"Filthy water," muttered Tom, "filthy water."

He studied the lines in his hands, hands that were covered with tough skin and sores and hollows from blisters, both old and new. Hands that were used to working, that were made for rowing swiftly and steadily. It was good to think about that, just as it was good to put his oars in the water and toil with long, hard strokes. Because he was going away, far away.

But tendrils of smoke drifted out across the water and refused to release the skiff, which seemed to be pulling the gray smoke behind it.

He rowed with all his might but couldn't escape the thick, nauseating smell. It was still clinging to his clothes when he hauled the skiff onto land and dragged the basket of fish up to the inn.

No one mourned the loss of Zamora the fortune-teller. On the contrary, everyone agreed that it was a relief to be rid of the old crone with the milky eye. Everyone agreed that the Inquisition had acted properly. Even those who had spat at Tom and told him of Zamora's healing powers now said that Nevis had become a purer place to live.

· · ·

"There, you see, my dear half sister," Tom said to Feodora when he found her at the washtub beneath the olive tree, "you see that I was right, and that once again you made the wrong choice. The whole island is overjoyed about what happened."

"Are you talking to me or to yourself?" she replied calmly.

"I'm talking to the girl who is lucky enough to have a half brother who kept quiet when she decided to defy the Inquisition."

"So you think that Zamora is gone?"

Tom stared at his sister. "I was there, Feodora. Not that I enjoyed the sight, but I was there, and I saw that she went up in flames when her soul returned to the Devil."

Feo put the wet laundry on the washing bench and began pounding it with her stick. "So you saw that too, did you?" she said. "You certainly must have had sharp eyes."

Tom shook his head in annoyance and was about to leave, but his sister grabbed his arm. "Do you really believe more in your eyes than in your soul, Tom O'Connor? Don't you realize that Zamora is still here?"

Tom pulled away. "Don't be silly. She was turned to ashes."

Feodora smiled. "That's right: to ashes. And her ashes have flown out to sea on the trade winds. And were swallowed by the fish you catch and put on the table. And what happens to that fish, Tom? I'll tell you what happens: you eat it."

While the pious father consumed enormous quantities, Bibido ate very little. Bibido was the name of Tom's fortune. The one who was kept underground, where he lived in darkness and still had not uttered a single word, even though one of his owners claimed that he spoke Spanish. Tom had tried several times to engage the slave boy in conversation. At first with kind, enticing words and later with remarks of a cruder sort. He had even neglected to fill the water bowl, but nothing did any good. Not a word crossed the black's lips.

One night when the house was quiet, Tom tiptoed down to the cellar and found the boy awake. For reasons that Tom could not comprehend, the slave was always awake whenever Tom came downstairs. Maybe he never slept, maybe he had a supernatural sense of hearing that enabled him to sit up straight whenever anyone approached.

Tom had brought along a bottle of wine. A pint of the sweetest wine in the house. And a hunk of chicken that he proceeded to eat as he looked at the boy, who watched him in the dark.

"I might give you a piece if you say my name," said Tom. "You know very well what my name is. Every slave has to know the name of his master. Say my name and I'll give you a little meat, but you have to hurry or soon I'll have eaten the whole thing."

Not a word came from the darkness.

"I suppose I could go and get Juan Carlos," muttered Tom. "He could probably grease your tongue."

Tom ate the last piece of chicken and opened the door to the boy, who was sitting in the corner with his legs tucked under him. He was as skinny as ever. Tom poked at him with his foot. "Say something, slave. Say something or your master will get angry. I could beat you with one hand tied behind my back—you know that. Nothing can stop me, because I own you. You're mine, and I can do with you as I please. If I wanted to, I could break both of your arms and cast you into the sea, where you would sink like a stone. Like a stone, I said."

Tom sat down in front of the boy and for once managed to make eye contact with him. "Did you know, slave, that witches can't sink? No, you don't know that, because you don't know anything. Your black little head is as empty as a coconut. You're looking at me. Do you know what you're looking at? You're looking at the master swimmer of Nevis." A big smile lit up Tom's face. A splendid idea had suddenly occurred to him. He pulled the boy to his feet.

For a moment it looked as if the slave wouldn't be able to keep his balance, but then he recovered.

"I'm thinking of taking off your shackles," said Tom. "Do you understand what I'm saying?"

The slave showed no reaction.

Tom went upstairs and came back with some tools, a rope, and a thick leather strap. After half an hour he managed to break the hinge of the iron lock. The heavy shackles fell off the thin ankles, leaving a circle of pink scars.

He didn't look at Tom when the leather strap was placed around his neck. Nor did he react when Tom tied a rope to it. Soon afterward they were standing on the shore beneath a grinning orange moon that had edged the black-velvet sea with pale-pink scallops. Tom took hold of the skiff, which lay ten yards from the water's edge. With his other hand he held on to the rope that was around the boy's neck. "Wait a minute," he said, "this is slave work. Drag my boat out, slave."

Again there was no reaction.

"Can't you hear?" Tom gave the boy a shove and then showed him what he was supposed to do. But there was no strength left in the boy. Tom shook his head and pulled the boat out into the water. "Get in," he said gruffly. "Now we'll see what you're made of."

He rowed for half an hour, just long enough to stay within sight of land. Then he tossed the anchor over the side and put his shirt on the thwart. He was surprised by the boy's interest in the white fabric. His black fingers cautiously touched the three buttons, turning them around, as if he were studying how they had been sewn on. Tom smiled. "Go ahead and look," he muttered, "but you'll never have a shirt like that."

It was a mild night with no wind. All around them stretched the ocean, with no visible line dividing it from the starry sky. They sat as if in a dome. A hint of a smile appeared on Tom's face. He tied the rope that was fastened around the boy's neck to his own ankle. "Now we'll see," he said, moving over to the slave, "now we'll see how much of a fish you are."

The boy looked out across the water with the same despondent yet indomitable expression.

"You first," said Tom, grabbing hold of his arm. "Are you afraid? I think you're afraid. But you're attached to a rope. Your master won't let go of his fortune that easily, so you shouldn't worry about coming back up." Tom gave the slave a push and watched him edge over to the gunwale. He put one leg over the side and slid down into the water.

Tom jumped in, dived under, and then swam over to the boy, who gazed at him with an expression Tom couldn't figure out. At the same moment the slave turned onto his back, shoved off with his feet, and was gone. Tom watched the rope straighten out and barely managed to dive before he was yanked by the ankle.

Now he was really moving.

Tom had never seen anyone swim like that before. The black boy hardly used his limbs at all as he wove through the water like an eel. It took all Tom's strength to keep up. They were underwater for several minutes before the boy resurfaced, only to fill his lungs in a flash and dive again.

Tom didn't hesitate to show him that he was not yet in need of air. They continued like that for a few more minutes, until Tom hoisted himself back into the boat and from there watched the black boy swim back and forth. "He's enjoying himself," muttered Tom. "But we're not here so you can enjoy yourself." He yanked on the rope and got the slave back on board.

They sat there for a while, catching their breath. A new glow had appeared in the boy's eyes, which remained fixed on the black sea.

"Don't start thinking that we're going to do this every day," said Tom as he began rowing back. But when he pulled the skiff up on shore, still without the slightest help from the boy, he suddenly toppled the slave to the ground and sat astride him. Tom smiled. "What a little mealworm you are. If it weren't for the ring you have around your neck, we would have sold you at the nearest market. Like a dog." Tom had always wanted a dog. A dog that would come when he called. And that's how he happened to think up the idea.

"I'm going to call you Bibido," said Tom. "That's a good name for a gnome like you."

And that's how it was. Another three months passed, and still not a word from Bibido. Tom never took him out swimming again. There was no reason to pamper a slave who was unwilling to learn. But as the year came to an end and the year of Our Lord 1640 approached, the boatswain from Cádiz, known as Ramón the Pious, suddenly disappeared. He took three things with him: a silver candlestick, a silk shirt, and Bibido from Cape Verde.

Tom was left sitting on the cellar floor among the slave's dishes and the rusty leg irons that he had hammered off the boy's ankles. He heard footsteps on the stairs. The last thing he wanted was Feodora's company. Of course that's who it was. And it took only a second for her to guess what had happened.

"Cheated once again, Tom O'Connor," she said with a sigh and not the least trace of sympathy. "Cheated again."

"For the last time," answered Tom.

• • •

Six hours later he has tied two bags onto the back of López's old mule. Without saying a word to anyone, not even the innkeeper, who was the beast's owner.

The mule is standing at the end of the building, which is tinted pink by the morning sun. The mule is actually a worn-out old nag that López has threatened to put down because it attracts flies. But Tom has held a protective hand over the animal. Now it is weighed down with the two bags, a rolled-up rug, and a half-gallon cask of water.

This early, Señor López is still sleeping soundly. He won't be pleased when Tom's mother tells him that her son has set off on some unknown mission. And he will have a hysterical fit when he hears that Tom has stolen his mule, which will suddenly take on special value.

Tom looks at his mother standing the way she always does, her weight on one leg, gazing at him skeptically with her arms crossed. Her hair is unpinned, and the wind has caught hold of her skirts. In her hand she is holding a silver coin, the only one she owns. She wants to give it to him for his journey, but Tom refuses to take it.

He turns to the beast and raises his hand in farewell. For a long time he rides facing backward in the saddle in the hope that his mother will go into the house, but she remains outside until he disappears in the warm haze.

Part II

Nicolaus
6 Copernicus

HE PRESSED HIMSELF AGAINST THE WALL of the building, feeling his lungs heave inside his chest. His eyes were popping out of his head, and his ears were tingling. With trembling fingers he tore apart the pieces of meat and stuffed them in his mouth, but he hardly had enough breath to chew with. Sweat was dripping from his brow. He knew that if he didn't get the meat into his stomach, he'd be caught red-handed. So he had to devour it in huge chunks. He doubled over and coughed. It made him drop a piece. He gathered it up and swallowed it, then coughed again. He glanced from side to side. Though there was no moon that night, he was not invisible. In the dark all cats are gray. "Does the same hold true for rats?" he muttered. "In that case, I don't need to worry."

Stealing food was a serious crime, and in a city like Port Royal a person could be strung up for less. He had stolen the meat from a merchant's house. The smell of freshly salted fish and newly smoked bacon had attracted more than one thief creeping around in the dark along with the city's rats. If he had learned anything about life in a big city, it was this: people and rats live in the same buildings, and they eat the same food. It was a rat that had shown him the way to the house with the fresh meat. For lack of anything better to eat, he had been hunting a well-nourished rodent in the hope of sticking his knife into it. Rat meat tasted the same as chicken. Once it had been flayed and chopped up, you couldn't tell what kind of life it had lived. "Only a full stomach can be choosy," he said.

Port Royal was the name of Jamaica's largest port and a haunt for all sorts of people. The city was famed for being lively and lawless. It was a place where a person might easily disappear, whether because of drink or a duel, or merely because he happened to walk down the wrong alley.

There was always a stench of rotting food and overfilled privies. But people quickly grew accustomed to the smell and ignored the filth. Everywhere swarmed crowds of merchants, slave dealers, and gamblers. Scoundrels both big and small wandered among the farmworkers from the savannas, where banana and sugarcane plantations offered work to those who had had enough of the sea.

Tom had been away from home for five months now. He had lost count of how many slave auctions he had witnessed and how many ships he had boarded to make inquiries about a certain Señor Ramón from Cádiz. One week gave way to the next, and he had learned to ration his bread, to go to bed hungry, and to make do with food that was not meant for humans. After a month he had had to slaughter Señor López's mule so he could sell the hide and buy himself a machete. The weapon was invaluable in Port Royal, and he had stuck it in his belt at the marketplace where he had bought it.

He had learned to keep moving, to avoid sleeping in groups, to be evasive in his replies, and otherwise to pretend to be older than he was. For a while he had painted fake scars on his cheeks and strutted around with his legs apart and his arm muscles tensed, puffing out his chest and imitating all the others who made it through life this way.

From the fit of his clothes, he could tell that he had grown thinner and that his legs were longer. He had started to resemble a vagabond, a tramp, and a thief—in short, a native Jamaican. He missed Nevis and he missed his mother, and many times he was on the verge of turning homeward. But each time he would pack up his knapsack and sleep out under a skiff, cursing his hunger; then he would steal some food before cockcrow and pray for forgiveness after he had eaten his fill. He spent the nights repeating to himself that nobody was going to cheat Tom O'Connor. He was going to find Bibido, and his journey would end at the Bissagos Islands.

Life in the city was a harsh but excellent teacher. His former naïveté was worn as thin as a horse-dealer's boots.

At first the world seemed full of Ramóns. Tom thought he must have met them all. And paid dearly for his knowledge—both in coins and in experience. He saw them in his sleep. The treacherous eyes that lied without blinking and the open hands that closed around the coin, like a spider around a fly.

"In this day and age," said the Egyptian down at the harbor, "knowledge is the most precious of all treasures. Empty your wallet, young man, and I will tell you where you will find your true friends."

"Nothing is free these days," said the gypsy woman, with a sigh, "but give me what you have, and I will show you the way."

"Ramón from Cádiz," exclaimed the juggler at the marketplace, "I talked to him just the other day. And I even know where he was headed. You shall have the information cheap, young friend, because I'm in a kindly frame of mind."

After half a year Tom knew that nothing was easier than tricking a boy from the small island of Nevis.

But the world was not all lies and malice. It was also fabulous and grand, beautiful and, above all, insatiable. He had never dreamed that such a big city existed or such large buildings, such incomparable ships, such colorful buccaneers. They were all there: officers in sky-blue uniforms, noble-women in gowns, like freshly opened rosebuds. The women's arms were round and soft and so creamy-white that they seemed almost transparent. They were enveloped in a fragrance that tantalized the nose. They walked around on tiptoe, fearing they might tread in the city's filth and vigorously fluttering their fans to escape the stench of the alleyways. All around them swarmed servants and attendants, white serving maids wearing brightly colored clothes, and coal-black slaves in red uniforms with shiny buttons. The most distinguished parties were rowed ashore from frigates and galleons that had anchored in the bay to take on fresh water and provisions.

The whole world was gathered in Port Royal. People spoke French, English, Spanish, Portuguese, and five or six other languages that Tom didn't recognize. If only he could take a scrap of this world home with him so his mother might see its splendor. Instead he kept his eyes and ears open, pressing himself against the wall whenever the slave dealers trundled past and applauding the marketplace performers. All kinds of them came: goats that could dance, parrots that could talk, men who could swallow fire, women with beards. There was life and merriment, death and disease, rumors and stories, tall tales and great wisdom.

Tom learned to frequent the alehouses, where he drank beer and rum and wiped his mouth on the back of his sleeve as he scowled at whoever sat next to him. And here he listened. Because it was in the city's alehouses that stories about the wide world were told. And by people who had seen it with their own eyes. Although it was just as likely that the storyteller had never ventured farther than that very tavern where, for a fee, he would report on all sorts of splendors.

Fibs and lies were mixed together and served up in the same dish. And Tom was not a squeamish eater. Doubt made a good knife for carving out the truth in the evening, but the next day he would show up just as hungry as before. And there seemed to be no end to the stories about sultans with fourteen wives and queens whose hearts had frozen solid.

One night in this rogues' paradise, the conversation turned to that very topic: the world. There were eight men at the table, and at the head sat an old fellow in a gray coat, as bald as a coot and without a tooth in his head. Three times he was thrown out the door by the tavernkeeper for singing satirical songs about the Pope in Rome. But this didn't seem to bother the old man, who wriggled like a fish in water. And he certainly knew how to spin a yarn. It turned out that in his younger days he had traveled far and wide and even spent a night in the belly of a whale. There was a great deal of laughter that night.

Later it was Tom's turn to buy a round of beer and tell stories, and he did so gladly since he had enjoyed the hospitality of the others. Lively and in fine form, he told the story about the girl who gave her employer powder that he thought was an elixir of life, but that sent him to the privy for four-teen days and fourteen nights. The story was well received, and the men slapped Tom on the back. He stood them to another round of beer, al-though he could feel his courage sinking at the thought of his sharp-tongued half sister, whom he suddenly missed so badly that his stomach hurt. Maybe it's just that we'd gotten used to each other's company, he thought, because she was not a sweet girl, by the Devil, and she did have a mean mouth.

At that moment the old man spat on the floor and leaned across the table. "All right, now listen here and I'll tell you what they've been talking about in Europe," he lisped conspiratorially, looking around as if to ensure that only those closest to him would hear what he had to say. "In Europe, which I have seen with my own eyes, the buildings are twice as big as they are in this city, the people wear clothes that are much more splendid, their wigs are made from the finest silk, and the women, well, let me tell you!" The old man closed his eyes in blissful joy. "But the learned men, my honored audience, the learned men of Europe talk about only one thing: the astronomer and mathematician Nicolaus Copernicus." The old man sniggered and shook his head as if he had said something funny, but then he went on.

"You see, Copernicus studied the stars more thoroughly than any ship's officer on the seven seas, and he discovered the most astonishing thing you could ever imagine." The old man licked his lips and narrowed his eyes. "Move closer, lads, move closer, because this is in truth a shocking piece of news. For the sun, which you observe coming up from the sea and disappearing again toward evening, does not actually move at all!"

The seamen gave each other skeptical looks, and a couple of them seemed about to lose interest.

"In fact," said the old man with a grin, "it's this round Earth we're standing on that is constantly in motion."

"Well, I'll be damned if I can feel it," growled a sailor from Madrid, stamping his foot on the floorboards.

The idea that the Earth might be moving brought the old man to his feet. "Copernicus says that the Earth turns on its own axis."

"No more beer for Grandpa," someone shouted.

"And that's why," continued the old man, "we have spring, summer, fall, and winter. In Europe . . ."

"Shut your trap, you madman, or move on to somewhere else," growled the fellow from Madrid. "Now I'm going to tell you all about the world's tallest woman—she's seven feet tall and has three breasts."

The seamen banged their tankards on the table and laughed their encouragement to the Spaniard. But as the yarn about the woman with three breasts got started, Tom's own thoughts embarked on a voyage. An hour later, when he stretched out on the shore to sleep, he lay for a long time staring up at the full moon. There was in fact one thing that he had always wondered about. No matter how familiar he was with the sea and how much he knew about the wind and the weather, ocean currents, hurricanes, trade winds, and navigation, it had always puzzled him that the ocean didn't flow out at the world's end. Why didn't it get any smaller? And why was the sun so big when it came up and yet so small when it stood overhead and burned the hottest?

As he lay on the shore, he thought that this Copernicus might have wondered the same things.

The next day he went looking for the old man, who was begging near a warehouse at the harbor. The man had no memory of the conversation from the night before and just kept rambling on about his adventures in Europe until Tom grabbed his arm and bluntly asked, "How can it be that the world's ocean doesn't fall off if it's true what you say, that the Earth is round?"

The old man lay down on his side and smacked his toothless gums. "You have to view the universe, dear friend, like your own skull. By necessity the sun's place has to be in the middle of the universe, since all living things are in need of its fire. You see, the source of life must be found in the center of things. That should be as obvious as shit from a mule." The old man gave a shiver, which seemed to make him livelier. "Now tell me, young friend, where is a man's seed located?"

Tom stared at the old man, who wrapped his arms around his body and laughed so hard that his whole skeleton shook. "You do know what I mean by seed, don't you?" he snickered.

Tom replied cautiously that of course he knew.

"Where is a man's seed located?"

"In his genitals," murmured Tom, glancing around, not sure whether this conversation was suitable for anyone's ears but his own.

"The seed is located exactly halfway between a man's head and his feet," exclaimed the old man gleefully. "And aren't the seeds in an apple in the very core? And the pit in the middle of the peach? Yes, they all are. And now we have to demand from the Earth that it divide up the life-giving light of the sun so that there is enough for all kingdoms and countries. How can this be done?"

"Tell me," snapped Tom.

"By spinning around and around and around. Spinning on its own and also spinning around the sun."

The old man was now standing, and he had started twirling on his own axis.

Tom stared straight ahead, his thoughts confused, and yet he had an uneasy feeling that the madman with the child's mouth was speaking a measure of truth.

"Hence, in twenty-four hours," said the toothless man with a laugh, "we've moved around and around and around and yet haven't budged because we're right back where we started. Then it's morning once again and our lives can start all over, though we're one day older. For all living things must age, like the seed that becomes an olive tree, like the boy who becomes toothless and wise. Do you have any money, my son?" The old man scuttled closer to Tom.

"Not a bean," sighed Tom. "But keep talking, and I'll find you some food before nightfall."

The old man scratched his backside and seemed to ponder the offer. He beckoned Tom to come nearer. "At times," he whispered, "I have slurped from the inn's biggest tankard, and sleep has granted me a right wing, while the rum has given me a left. I became a bird, and under the golden light of the moon, I have flown across the globe like an albatross. And I have seen the Earth roll by beneath me, and I have gazed on so many different faces: white, black, yellow, and olive. Some with hats, others with turbans; cities with bell towers, some pointed, some round; churches with crosses and churches with crescents; palaces of porcelain with roof tiles of gold. And then I've returned, my feet still dry, ready to watch the sun rise once more, although it hadn't moved even the width of a finger. Life is an endless dancing in place, and yet we age, losing our teeth and our hair, our hearing and our eyesight. Only the heavenly bodies are eternal, and among them the sun is the greatest of all. For it is around the sun that everything revolves. You and I and the Pope are nothing but lard. Where will you find me some supper, dear friend?"

"I know a house where the bacon hangs outside," replied Tom.

The old man shrugged and said that, in his experience, stolen food had no savor.

"So the Earth that I'm walking on," murmured Tom, "is supposed to be as round as the lemon in Señor López's garden? And it's moving?"

"Exactly. You're no dimwit, my boy; perhaps we should join forces."

Tom looked down at his feet, tentatively raising and lowering them while thoughts flew through his mind. If the Earth he stood on was actually turning, shouldn't he be able to feel it? "But if the Earth is round," murmured Tom, "why doesn't the ocean fall off and land on the ceiling of the sky?"

"The ocean," chortled the old man, "is stuck to the surface of the Earth like a man's skin is stuck to his body."

Tom slapped a hand to his forehead. "What nonsense," he muttered, "what damned foolishness."

Tom's remark made the man open his toothless mouth and beam happily as he chanted:

> *The Pope in Rome*
> *Has an empty dome.*
> *On him the biggest lump*
> *Is his paunch and his rump.*

After that outburst, Tom realized that he'd been wasting his time on a lunatic. Yet he kept his promise and brought the old man supper from what he called the rat house, where newly smoked fish and salted bacon were hung up in abundance. And even though Tom didn't believe everything he had heard, he stayed for a while with the old man, who happily chattered on with his mouth full, attempting to teach a boy from Nevis about Copernicus from Poland.

Three days later, when he took leave of his instructor, Tom told himself that for all he didn't know about astronomy, he knew a great deal about the Pope in Rome. For on him the biggest lump was his paunch and his rump.

Tom is standing down at the harbor. The horizon has sliced the sun in half. The Earth is turning around. It's the Earth that's turning, he thinks, as he watches a fishing boat pull into the dock. On board, two men are visible. One of them is short and old, the other as big as a bear. Tom has been waiting for this moment. He realizes that he doesn't want to stay in Port Royal—unless he wants to end his life toothless and crazy, living under a skiff. He runs down to the boat and hails the fisherman.

The old man wipes his nose as he takes Tom's measure. "Work?" he says. "What sort of work?"

"Anything at all," replies Tom.

"What can the boy do?"

"I can do anything," says Tom, hitching up his pants.

The old man climbs out of the boat and pauses for a moment to study the sun, which is lying on the water like lava. "Thus ends another day in the short life of a man." He scratches his white beard. "But tomorrow the sun will come up again, and Bruno and I don't need any extra hands."

Tom smiles at the man. "The sun," he says, "doesn't move. It's the Earth you're standing on that's turning around."

The old man looks at him and suddenly breaks out in a big smile. "Who the devil are you?" he chuckles.

Tom moves closer. "I'm the world's best storyteller, and I know a thousand and one tall tales and just as many that are true."

The old man's name was Albert and his grandson was Bruno. He had an odd look in his dark little eyes and a childlike nature, but he was as good as the day is long and just as simpleminded as an ox. They plied the sea between Saint Croix and Saint John, fishing for their own enjoyment, and their greatest pleasure came from catching sharks. But otherwise they took life as it came.

Tom learned to handle the huge sea turtles that were flayed the minute they were brought on deck. The meat was flavorful and the shells could be made into jewelry and sold in the harbors for good money. A sea turtle's heart would continue beating for hours after the animal had been cut up. This amused the enormous Bruno, who would stare at the heart until it beat no more, and then, disappointed, he would fling it over the side.

In shark waters they would tie bait to the side of the boat and in this way lure the ravenous beasts. Catching a shark was a job that demanded patience, resourcefulness, cunning, and respect. If a person lost patience, he would catch nothing. But if he lost respect, he could also lose his life.

On a quiet evening in the glow of the stars, they were rocking on the waves five miles from Puerto Rico. The bait was fresh, and the smell of blood was mixed with salt water. Tom was sitting with Albert and Bruno, regaling them with the story about the princess whose heart had frozen to ice until the day when a sailor brought the sun from the warm countries and thawed out the girl. "This sailor," said Tom, "was given his very own castle by the girl's father, who was the Prince of Darkness. A richer sailor the world has never seen."

Tom paused, thinking about Bibido and the reward that he might never get. He glanced impatiently at the bait and cursed his unlucky fate, taking his anger out on Albert and Bruno, who obviously had no idea where to find the good fishing spots.

"Take it easy, Tom," said Albert, filling his pipe. "I promise you that we're at the very spot where the biggest fellows gather. Some of them are five yards long and just as clever as Copernicus from Poland." He winked at his grandson, who grinned and slapped Tom on the back.

"No beast is as clever as Copernicus," muttered Tom as he gazed out across the sea, "and especially not a shark."

The shark took a bite of the bait around midnight, and its attack on the bloody flesh of the fish was so powerful that the whole boat shuddered.

"Shark!" shouted Albert, swinging his legs out of his bunk.

In a matter of minutes all three of them were on deck. "He's under the boat," whispered Albert, rolling his eyes.

Bruno leaned over to see.

Silence.

"He's gone," said Tom.

"Patience," said Albert.

They waited a few more minutes in silence. Then Tom had his first glimpse of the shark, which swam with terrifying speed around the old vessel.

Bruno shrieked with enthusiasm and fright, but Tom ran along the gunwale, following the animal. Everything about it was beautiful: its back was blue and its belly gleamed like silver.

"He has eight rows of teeth," explained Albert, "and they're like a man's fingers curled up like claws. The cutting edges on both sides are as sharp as newly honed daggers. Nothing is as bold as a shark—he has no enemies and knows no fear."

"We'll see about that." Tom took out a harpoon.

Albert went over to him. "Remember what I taught you, Tom: respect!"

"For a shark? Not on your life."

Tom raised the harpoon and heard Bruno's hysterical laughter as the shark went for the bait again. They saw its ice-cold eyes and heard its teeth snap as it threw itself at the meat.

"Now," screamed Albert, "now, Tom!"

But all of a sudden the shark was gone.

That's the way it went all night. Abruptly the shark would disappear, and then just as suddenly they would catch sight of its dorsal fin, first close to the ship, then under the ship, and then with a crash the shark would throw itself at the bait.

"The shark is sneaky," the old fisherman told Tom, with a grin. "Sometimes a man gets cheated."

"I'm not about to be cheated by a fish," said Tom. "Before this night is over, we'll have ourselves a shark."

Albert laughed and shouted something to Bruno, but Tom didn't care. Now it was him and the beast. The beast that was gorging itself on the flesh of the fish.

The weariness Tom felt earlier has now been replaced by a knot in his stomach and a tension in his arms such as occur only when a person is close to death. It will be him or the shark. The shark that believes it lives in a world without enemies. That thinks it can blithely swim around below the surface of the water and fear nothing.

"I'll teach you to know fear," Tom murmurs as he raises the harpoon and stares at the beast banging its snout against the bait, devouring it with a greediness and indifference that make Tom cold and tense. When the shark surfaces for the third time, Tom strikes. He hurls the harpoon with all his might, putting his full weight behind it, and nearly falls over the side.

The harpoon skewers the shark's skull. But instead of keeping his eye on the line, Tom stares at the fish, which dives down into the sea, flapping its tail and snapping its jaws as the water foams. All of a sudden it reappears, as if it wants to say a last farewell to God's blue Heaven. Its eyes are dead and its body is still.

Tom looks at the line, which is tightly fastened to the capstan. When the shark sinks to the bottom, the line straightens out. The boat shudders.

Albert and Bruno are standing at Tom's side. "He's too heavy," says Albert. "We'll never pull him up. That devil has cheated us in the end. Now we're going to lose the harpoon and line."

Tom looks at him. He knows the harpoon is valuable. He stares down at the water. The line is taut, extended to its full three hundred feet, making the boat list to port.

Albert has already taken out his knife to cut it loose. "That's what some-times happens when you fish for shark," he says with a sigh. "You think you have him, but in the end, he cheats you."

Tom tells him to wait. "I'll go get your harpoon. I can easily dive down and cut the shark loose."

The old fisherman gazes across the water, where the light is starting to come up. "The problem," he mutters, "the problem is that he might not be alone anymore. Sharks hunt in groups, and it might not even be the same fellow that we've been fighting with all night long. If there's more than one, the others will show up at the smell of their dead comrade, and then Tom O'Connor will stay down there with the shark. And the two of you will meet the same end."

Bruno looks at Tom and breaks out in a big smile.

Tom assesses the situation. Of course it would be best to remain on board, and since Albert has accepted that the battle is lost and that the har-poon will stay with the shark, there's no reason to be so stubborn. But Tom can't stand being cheated, especially not by a dead fish. A harpoon in the skull of a shark is useless. He crawls up on the gunwale and puts his knife between his teeth.

"Do what you like, you Irish blighter," shouts Albert.

"Yes," Bruno joins in, "he does what he likes."

The boat lists in the wind. Tom looks at the line and the crimson hori-zon. For a moment he thinks about the scent of lime juice on his mother's skin and about the filthy water he poured into a mug and gave to a witch, who was later burned at the stake. He also thinks about his half sister and about his father's belt, the one he offered to the sea. And about Ramón and the share he owned in the slave boy with the ring.

"Are you going or aren't you?" asks the old man, with a grin.

Bruno bends double with suspense.

"I'm going to get that harpoon," says Tom.

He swam with strong strokes. Now that the blood from the bait had drifted away, he could see the shark, which lay twenty yards from the seafloor, the harpoon in its forehead.

All I have to do is pull it out, Tom thought, gathering his strength. Halfway down he realized that he should have enlisted the aid of a rock, the way he did when he had gone diving at Nevis. It was still a long way down, and just as long back up. He had enough air, no doubt about that, but would he also have enough to cut the harpoon free? How much of his strength would it take to work his knife around it, buried so deep in the shark's flesh?

He swam faster and soon reached the shark. He avoided looking at its dead eyes, which didn't seem much different from the gaze of the beast when it had been alive. He could feel the pressure in his lungs and glanced up. Had he ever been this far down? He couldn't remember feeling such enormous pressure.

With difficulty, he began the job of cutting. He had decided that it would be wisest to leave the harpoon fastened to the line so the tension on it would help him when he tried to pull it free. It was hard work; he shut his eyes and opened them again. Where the black spots were coming from, he had no idea, but there were more and more of them. He couldn't understand it. Something must be wrong. The hand with the knife kept hacking away, even though he had told himself that he should cut carefully and waste no energy.

A peculiar form of lassitude overcame him. A drowsiness that he couldn't explain. He could hardly hold on to the knife.

He had grabbed the line to begin his ascent when he noticed a blue shadow to his left. He blinked and turned, but no matter which way he twisted, the shadow stayed behind him.

Then he saw it: five yards above him, a twenty-foot-long shark was hovering over its dead relative, taking the measure of the boy with the knife. At that moment there was a tug on the line, which slipped out of the harpoon's eyelet. Tom stared at the line winding its way up through the water.

He stretched out his arm and grabbed it just as the shark attacked. It came rushing at him, its head at an angle, its clawlike teeth exposed. It was after the boy's leg.

He was now holding on to the line with both hands. He could feel the men working up on deck, hauling the line with all their might. He put his trust in the naive Bruno, whose enormous strength was made for tasks like this, turning the capstan faster and faster. Tom could practically hear the old fisherman yelling at his grandson while he leaned over the gunwale.

"Keep going, keep going, Bruno, don't stop, turn, turn, turn!"

The shark apparently couldn't make up its mind which meal it preferred. It circled its dead comrade while it took stock of the kicking legs.

Tom's hands were locked around the line, but his lungs were emptied of oxygen. He saw the last bubbles leave his lips and had to release his grip. The shark raced up from the depths at a horrific speed.

The last thing Tom thought he glimpsed before he lost consciousness was a spark of life in the otherwise dead eyes.

The old fisherman was leaning over him. The sail fluttered in the wind—a familiar sound. Am I dead? thought Tom. Of course he wasn't dead. Albert's toothless mouth came closer, smiling.

"Look at me, Tommy," he said. "Look at me, boy. Say something!"

"Say something," Tom repeated.

Bruno found this amusing, as did the old man—and it also amused Tom, who sat up. Then he started vomiting.

He had a great urge to lie down and go to sleep, but each time he closed his eyes, Albert would slap his cheek. Tom said to leave him alone, but the old man ignored him and hauled Tom to his feet, pouring a glass of rum down his throat, which did him good. He was given another and then heard himself say that he had lost the harpoon, but at least they had rescued the line. He looked down to see whether his legs and feet were still there. They were.

When night fell and they had eaten their customary meal of porridge and bacon, Tom told the story of the dead shark, which suddenly came alive and chased him with the harpoon sitting like a horn in its forehead. In a matter of ten days the story became just as good a tale as the one about Feodora Dolores Vasgues, who gave her employer a laxative powder that made him spend three weeks in the privy.

"Feo," whispers Tom, who is lying on his stomach in the bow as they pull into yet another unfamiliar port. Six months is a long time, and his half sister's face has started to blur. As hard as he tries, he can't remember whether her nose is curved or straight, whether her eyes are almond-shaped or round. He has to make an effort to recall her voice, and he tells himself that this is probably because he's seen practically the whole world and experienced more than his mother and the obese Señor López put together. "It's the same with the mind as with a barrel," he mutters. "It can hold only a certain amount. If you pour in too much, some of it will run out, and right now Feodora Dolores Vasgues is on her way out." The thought makes him gloomy.

The people on Nevis know nothing about the world, he decides, especially those who spend their time in the tavern at the harbor. Tom laughs bitterly and drinks another glass of sweet rum. As far as his half sister is concerned, she's probably still decking herself out, going for walks beneath her parasol, and acting so impertinent to the customers that she has to suffer the blows of Juan Carlos in the evening.

He rolls over and looks up at the furled sail. "I miss all of you," he whispers.

He had learned to handle a ship, to tie knots and splice rope, to take care of the hemp lines, and to grease the block and tackle. He had been given his own marlinespike, which he used whenever he had to work with the ropes. And he had become a master caulker, pounding hemp into the cracks between the ship's planks, filling in all the wounds. His diving skills were put to good use whenever he went down to knock mussels off the keel and rudder—a job that spared Albert from having to drag the ship on land to put it in dry dock. For his part, the old man had taught Tom how to use the cross-staff, a magnificent instrument that could measure the height of the sun to determine the ship's position. But best of all Albert had told Tom stories about the famous Captain C. W. Bull and his nine-fingered crew. About the ocean's mermaids, and about the gold in the sailors' graves.

They are sitting in the faint glow of the new moon while the boat drifts on the wind and the starry sky glitters like phosphorescence. They have set course for Port Royal, where they will take on fresh water before once again heading out at dawn.

Tom sees the city appear in the distance and ends the storytelling with the tale of how darkness came to the world, coaxed up from the river by the green pelican.

7 Lucifer's Boot

WHEN HE OPENED HIS EYES, he had no idea where he was. The smell of sour beer and two or three other things he didn't want to name gave him a clue. It was the familiar alehouse in Port Royal. With an effort he got to his feet, feeling a little confused, until he located the exit. Out in the alleyway he squinted, noting how the headache rolled from his forehead around to the back of his neck.

He had a vague memory of the night before. Saying farewell to Albert and Bruno, telling them that he was going into town to quell his thirst, he stepped ashore with the promise that he would be back shortly. The old man didn't care for Port Royal and had only tied up at the dock to take on fresh water.

In the town Tom ran into a couple of youths his own age who had gotten him drunk. Tom listened to himself saying that he never got drunk. No matter how much he drank, he would always remain sober, because he had once put his whole head inside the jaws of a shark. After an experience like that, alcohol had no effect on him.

They stole his machete, his knife, his boots, and his belt.

He was now barefoot, cleaned out, and with not a penny in his pocket. He looked down at himself and set off running. His head was hammering and his chest was pounding. His stomach was also turning upside down. His whole body was protesting, but he didn't care. He rounded a corner and tried to determine the height of the sun. Their agreement had been quite clear. Tom had even heard himself say that if he wasn't back before daybreak, they should sail without him. He had added that it was just a matter of visiting one of his old haunts. Now his only hope was that Albert had overslept.

When he reached the shore, he immediately caught sight of the fishing boat's black silhouette against the crimson dawn. He fell to his knees on the sand, murmuring their names: Albert and Bruno. On their way out to where the sharks live. He broke down, forgetting his headache. "By the Devil, how I hate you, Tom O'Connor!"

The sight of the old boat reminded him of something else that had just as certainly slipped out of his grasp. The hammering demons in his head announced in unison, Face it, Tom! You're never going back to Nevis as a wealthy man. You're going to appear on the doorstep just as destitute as when you left. Maybe even more so. Back then at least you had boots on your feet, a knife in your belt, and a mule to ride. If you stay another two weeks in Port Royal, the corruption will devour you skin and all, and you'll end your days toothless and friendless, blabbering some satirical song about the Pope's paunch, with the rest of the rhyme lost in a thousand glasses of rum. "This should teach me that it's possible after all to pluck hair from the head of a bald man," he muttered.

He rolled over onto his back and closed his eyes. Whenever he thought about his native island, he saw it as a paradise, with its clear waters, damp echoing rain forest, fresh springs, and vast skies.

His mother is standing near the corner of the house under the olive tree, washing laundry. She puts her hand up to shade her eyes from the sun and catches sight of a young man in fine clothes, riding a gleaming black stallion. "Can it be true?" she asks.

"Yes, it's true," replies the horseman. "It is I, Tom, your son. And I come back a wealthy man. I have been to the Bissagos Islands, where I was rewarded by the king himself; my bags are filled with pure gold. You shall no longer slave away for Señor López, for now the inn is ours."

It's late in the evening.

He's on his way out of the town, running like the coward he is. Without a knapsack or any other possession, barefoot and penniless. Driven off by the merchant in whose courtyard he and a couple of the local rats have been taking their daily meals.

Later Tom falls to the ground from exhaustion and hunger. In desperation he tears at a tuft of grass and devours it like an animal. He turns over and whispers to the night sky, "You shall no longer slave away for Señor López, for now the inn is ours."

He hears a cart come to a halt. A voice addresses him. Tom answers as if speaking through water. Maybe there's something wrong with his hearing. He gets to his feet and tries to brush the worst of the dirt from his pants, but his legs give way under him. He feels an arm around his waist and then the boards of a cart against his back.

The stars have been lit. The wheels clatter beneath him. He turns around to see who is driving the cart, but sleep strikes him like a hammer.

The smithy lies a day's journey from Port Royal. The master is a short broad-shouldered man with arms like a galley slave. He studies Tom's hands and feels his bones. "Because I have no use for a weakling."

"I'm used to hard work, señor."

The blacksmith spits in the fire. "The boy didn't look like much when I found him outside town."

"For a plate of food I can do the work of two, señor."

"Can the boy start at once?"

"I'm at your disposal, señor."

He started off by lending a hand, but he knew how to listen whenever the blacksmith had a mind to instruct him. His job consisted of keeping the forge going. It was tedious work, but he had two meals a day and a bunk to sleep in. During that first month he learned to appreciate the simple labor and the silence between the blows of the hammer. Before long he had so much to tend to that images of Nevis retreated into the background.

He quickly caught on to the task of preparing a glowing piece of iron and attaching it to a shaft; dealing with strange horses also came easily to him. He listened carefully, absorbing all the details whenever the smith decided to share the secrets of his craft. Not every animal cared to have its shoes changed, but the smith knew an incantation to whisper in the horse's ear as he stroked the beast's head. It was pure magic but not impossible to imitate.

They tended to the plantation windmills and the farmers' horse-driven mills. Tom learned to grease the machinery, change the gear wheels, and adjust the bearings. With a glance he could tell whether axles or rollers were properly placed. He inspected the woodwork for termites and dry rot. From his days at sea he knew how to deal with sails, so he found it easy to mend the large pieces of canvas before they were stretched on the vanes.

"Hell of a lad," said the blacksmith, and that was the closest he ever came to any kind of praise. He was in truth a man of few words. Sometimes several days would go by before he and Tom spoke to each other, but when the master finally did talk, it was about women. "There's a trace of mermaid in every one of them," he would say, spitting black juice. "No matter how warm-blooded they may seem from a distance, all of them are cold when you get close."

The subject never bored Tom, who often encountered girls his own age. They would come with various tools that needed repair or knives that needed sharpening. As far as Tom could tell, they weren't particularly cold. He had even spoken to a local girl who was a servant in a house on the edge of town, where the owner made his living selling salted meat to ships that crossed the Atlantic. Sometimes she would walk past carrying a water jug on her head. The big golden earrings that she wore looked good against her brown skin, and when she set her feet in the sand she did so in a most gentle and elegant manner. Her eyes were black like prunes and slightly slanted, like people from the Orient.

One day when they were alone she said, "It's rare to see someone with your skin color."

For some reason that left Tom speechless.

She came all the way into the smithy where he was standing with a red-hot horseshoe. "And those eyes aren't very common either," she continued. "What part of the world do you come from?"

"From Nevis," he mumbled, as he dipped the horseshoe in the water trough, where it sizzled and bubbled.

The girl had a way of moving one eyebrow, the left one, which she would suddenly arch high up. It gave her a lopsided and slightly mischievous expression. But her mouth was smiling. She had very red lips that complemented her black curly hair and the golden earrings.

"Does he have a name?" she asked.

"Who?"

"Why, the boy with the eyes the color of water."

"Tom," said Tom, staring at the horseshoe. "Tom O'Connor."

The girl gave him a sharp look. "You must have sailed a great deal, Tom O'Connor, to make your eyes turn so green."

"My father was from Ireland," replied Tom, "but otherwise it's true that I've sailed a great deal." He walked over to the farthest corner of the smithy, where it was dark enough that he dared to ask what a person had to do to acquire eyes the color of hers.

The girl picked up her water jug from the floor and set it on top of her head, then stood lost in thought for a moment before she said, "You have to yearn."

"Yearn?" said the voice from the dark corner.

"When you yearn, you get eyes like mine."

A moment later she was gone. But the drops from her water jug still lay on the floor, and the fire from the forge was reflected in them.

During the next few days, Tom kept on seeing her before him, even in his sleep. He was restless and distracted at his work, and he finally had to tell the smith that he had met a girl who was sweet and not impossible to talk to. He didn't understand it, but the fact that his fingers refused to obey him must have something to do with her.

"That's how every comedy starts," grumbled the master.

Tom didn't hear him. "I was thinking of picking flowers and paying her a visit. She's in service up at the merchant's house."

"Has it really come to this? Well, go on then, if you want to have the ears of an ass."

Three days later Tom was standing near the big house, though without flowers. He had been there several times but had never caught sight of the girl. Tonight he was in luck.

She was just putting an infant to bed in a hammock stretched between two posts. There was a marvelous scent from the lemon trees that grew along the slope. And a calm that made Tom feel weak inside.

When she finally noticed him, she said nothing but disappeared inside the house. A short while later she reappeared with a little shawl over her shoulders. This time her lips were not red, and there were no golden hoops in her ears.

Tom couldn't decide if this made her look older or younger, but he told himself that no matter what she did, she was the most beautiful creature he had ever seen. He explained that he just happened to be walking past.

They looked at a small green lizard clinging to a fig tree.

"It's a little lizard," said Tom, and he could have bitten his tongue in half.

In his confusion he thought of pulling out his new dagger to show her his prowess when it came to lizards, but he stopped himself. There was no way of telling whether the girl was particularly fond of lizards.

"I thought we might go for a walk."

"Do you want to go for a walk, Tom O'Connor?"

He shrugged his shoulders, regretting his foolish suggestion.

On his way back to the smithy he made a list of his talents: he was skilled at caulking and navigating, at reshoeing nervous horses and killing sharks, but when it came to girls he had much to learn. Yet nothing in life was impossible; it was just a matter of setting the right course and the rest would follow on its own.

The next night he lay awake memorizing sentences that he could use to navigate. He told himself that it wasn't enough to say the right words. They had to be said in the proper way. In a casual and natural manner, as if he had just thought them up—not as if they were lines he had spent all night rehearsing. The following day he was back, and the day after that, always at the same time, and each day the same thing happened. The words remained stuck in his throat. Until one evening, when he ventured onto the grounds.

The girl was standing at the cradle humming to the baby.

Tom had planned to say, "My great dream is to show you Nevis, the lovely island of my birth."

But when the girl caught sight of him, she smiled and said, "Aha, it looks like a thief is sneaking up."

Aside from the fact that he actually had been a thief in the past, it was suddenly impossible for him to say anything about the lovely island of his birth. Instead he said, "Is it a boy or a girl you're taking care of?"

"It's a girl. She's six months old. Her name is Annabelle." The girl bent over the cradle and smiled.

Tom cleared his throat and set one foot in front of the other. "My great dream . . ." he began.

The girl held a finger to her lips and hushed him. "She has such trouble falling asleep."

Tom apologized.

The girl came closer and asked him in a soft whisper what it was he wanted to say.

Tom clenched his teeth and felt a knot at the nape of his neck. He was annoyed to find that for some reason the rhyme about the Pope kept getting mixed up with the line about Nevis.

"Perhaps you didn't want to say anything?"

"Yes, I do," said Tom. "Yes, because my great dream is to show you . . . show you my lovely . . . island."

The girl frowned and stepped so close that they were almost touching. "Did you say island?" she asked.

"No," replied Tom swiftly, "no, I didn't."

"Yes, you said something about an island."

"It's possible I did say something about an island, but I've forgotten what it was."

"That's too bad," said the girl, with a smile.

Tom cleared his throat. "No, it's not. Because it doesn't matter. Do you know the Pope in Rome? No, of course you don't know the Pope in Rome. But over in Port Royal, where I often go to slake my thirst . . ."

Tom stopped. The girl gave him an encouraging nod.

"Over there," he went on, "we sing a funny song."

"Is that right? May I hear it?"

"Hear it? Well, yes, I suppose so. It goes like this: The Pope in Rome/ Has an empty paunch/On him the biggest lump/Is his skull and that's empty too. Is that the merchant's baby you're taking care of?"

"No," said the girl, catching hold of Tom's sleeve. "No, she doesn't belong to the merchant."

"So she's your baby sister, then?" muttered Tom as he tried to straighten out the rhyme about the Pope in Rome.

"No," said the girl, "Annabelle is mine."

The last three words were spoken as she stared at something beyond Tom. Maybe she wasn't looking at anything at all. She certainly wasn't looking at him.

• • •

The night is pitch-black and the moon is waning. He's lying on his bunk in the back of the smithy, listening to the cicadas. Tom has a bandage on his hand, a tightly wrapped compress made from shirt rags. He has cut his hand. He felt a pain and saw the blood come gushing out. A couple of drops are still on the earth under his bed, brown and dull-looking.

The wound has been closed up, and the smith, who helped him tend to it, told him a story about a customer who had his leg amputated at the knee. "We sealed the wound with tar, and that's something you can really feel."

"Yes," sighed Tom, "that's something that stings."

They sat in silence for a while. Then the blacksmith stood up and said what he usually said: "To each his own."

A good expression, thought Tom, nice to have at hand, especially when your hand has been cut up.

The next day when Tom bungled his work, the smith came over to him and said, "Forget about her. The world is full of girls. You'll see—there's bound to be one for you too."

Tom didn't reply because he had imagined that the girl with the earrings would be his girl. But she was the mother of a child named Annabelle, so that's not how things were going to turn out.

That night he looked deep into the rum bottle. The smith said nothing, since he was an understanding man. He himself had only one vice. Whenever there was money in the till, he would climb into his skiff and row out to an island that was known for its alehouse, its cheap liquor, its women, and its peculiar form of entertainment.

Tom thought he had seen it all when it came to sword swallowers, whistling birds, and fire-eaters. But the smith told him that the island's form of entertainment was unique: men who, for a fee, would put their lives at risk.

"Want to come along, Tom O'Connor?" bellows the blacksmith after receiving money from the plantation owners. "If you do, you'll get to see the seamy side of life. No, never you mind, it's not something for a greenhorn."

Tom says farewell to the smith, who rows out into the dark waves. Eight hours later he returns, looking like a candle that has been snuffed out. Yet something draws him back, and two weeks later he's off again.

"To each his own," mutters Tom, sketching a gray circle in the brown sand. A little ring-shaped fortune, stolen from him by the man who called himself pious. And yet Ramón owed Tom something much greater: his very life. Maybe the Spaniard had reached the Bissagos Islands, maybe he had been given his finder's reward and was living a life of luxury. "While I lie here in the straw behind a smithy, drawing rings in the sand. I end up falling for a girl who's the mother of a child, then cut my hand, and behave like a damn fool."

The smith is all dressed up. He's not a vain man and has never had a wife, and he normally washes only when a customer wants to have a tooth pulled. Now he's counting his money, and he gives Tom final instructions regarding the open hearth and the work he expects to be finished by the time he returns.

As usual, Tom follows him down to the shore, where he helps the blacksmith push the skiff into the water. And as usual when heading off to the island, the smith is in an odd mood, at once elated and dejected, full of both anticipation and fury. It's never good to say too much, so Tom keeps quiet until the smith tells him, "This is my last trip to the island. I can't take the excitement; I wake up bathed in sweat, seeing the flames of Hell licking at my body. Strange-looking people are gathered around my bunk, their faces fiery red. They're from Lucifer's Boot, and this is my last trip."

Tom gives the skiff a shove and is just about to go back to shore when he stops. He is looking at the smith haul himself into the boat, but it's an entirely different body and an entirely different face that appears. A rasping voice says: *In Jamaica there's a so-called public house named Lucifer's Boot. That's where you should go when all other possibilities are used up and your life has lost its meaning, for the Boot is the graveyard of lost souls.*

Like a sleepwalker Tom wades out into the water and takes hold of the skiff.

"Let go, lad," snarls the smith.

Tom says nothing but climbs into the boat.

The smith shakes his head as Tom grabs the oars. "It's no place for you, young O'Connor, and it's not free either."

"I assume you'd like to have someone to row you back when the carousing is over," says Tom.

There were only a few buildings on the island, but in the harbor, which was dotted with mooring posts, there were a great many skiffs, sailboats big and small, and a single sloop. From a distance Tom could hear that Lucifer's Boot was heavily patronized. People were going in and out, both men and women, the latter of the sort that could be bought for money.

Tom wasn't the least bit interested. He merely kept on rowing until they struck bottom, then looped a knot around the nearest post and helped the blacksmith ashore.

The smoke-filled alehouse was packed to the rafters. Men were drinking and playing cards, having a grand time telling stories, placing bets, and making deals. But in the back of the low-ceilinged room a platform had been set up on which four huge candlesticks burned. Behind the platform hung a large black curtain.

Tom was standing by himself when the smith came over to him with a mug of beer in his hand. "If anyone offers you a throwing knife, Tom, tell them no. Promise me that. It's much too expensive for you, both in cash and bad dreams."

Tom nodded to his master, who patted him on the cheek. The black-smith was drunk, but the liquor didn't seem to have improved his mood. Tom watched him disappear into the haze of smoke, not knowing it was the last he would ever see of him.

Now began the entertainment that Lucifer's Boot had made its specialty. An elderly gent in a black cloak had appeared on the stage and was hushing the applause. He introduced a man from Brazil who proceeded to stick pins into his arms.

Tom shrugged, feeling cold and indifferent.

At the tables the audience was divided into three groups: those who were already dead drunk; those who were paying attention to the women; and those who sat with their eyes alert, sipping at their beers and simply waiting. Their faces were like masks.

The elderly gent introduced yet another act, this time involving fire. Next came three women who flounced around in veils, which they shed, one after the other. The dance ended with the women doing handstands. The audience hardly saw fit to applaud, and then there was silence.

A tray was passed around. On the tray lay fifty small throwing knives that were for sale. Not everyone was allowed to buy, only those who had remained sober. Armed with the knives, they made their way to the front of the rows.

The elderly gent in the black cloak reappeared. He had painted long black stripes from his eyes to his chin and looked quite sinister. Tom shifted his feet uneasily, noting that the mood seemed hostile. He regretted coming along and stared anxiously at the curtain, which was soon pulled aside.

A round wooden disk shaped like a big wheel came into view. Fastened to the disk were four thick leather straps. The old gent bowed and made a sweeping gesture with his arm, whereupon a man in a black mask stepped forward. A gray coat of mail covered most of his body, although his arms and legs were bare and hideously scarred.

The sight of this man made some of the alehouse guests head for the door, while others moved closer to the stage.

"Ladies and gentlemen," said the elderly man, "allow me to present Jacques Emil Morte of Marseilles."

Applause followed. Some clapped wildly as drunks do, but others were more apathetic, as if they just wanted to get the formalities over with.

The man was strapped to the disk as a drum began to beat. Two assistants set the disk in motion. Faster and faster it spun, louder and louder sounded the drum. On stage stood the old gent with his arm raised. In his hand he held a banner, and when the disk was spinning so fast that it was impossible to distinguish one leg from the other, he let the banner fall.

At once a roar went up from the crowd, and those who had purchased knives sprang to their feet. They took turns throwing. Most of the knives struck the wooden disk, some missed entirely, but a few of them bored into the man's hands, knees, and arms.

By that time Tom had slipped outdoors, where the cool of the evening did him good. He felt disgusted and again regretted having come. He heard more drumming and decided to find his master. He went back into the alehouse, where the audience sat like waxen figures.

The man's mask had been removed. His long black hair was spread out like a corona. He wore a patch over one eye, and the expression in the other was that of a madman.

Tom took three steps closer and felt his knees buckle. The disk was set in motion. There was no longer any doubt what this was all about: a lunatic was putting his life at risk for the sake of entertainment. One knife after the other plunged into the wood.

And now the disk slowed down. The knife-throwers' odds increased. The only men left were those who had saved their last knives for just this opportunity. None of these men was interested in the man's limbs. It was his face they were after.

The knives whistled through the air and sliced into the man's hair. The disk was barely turning anymore. A knife thrower went down on his knees.

For a brief moment Tom felt he made eye contact with the poor wretch up on stage; then a knife raced through the air and plunged into the man's ear.

A cheer went up.

The end of the performance came as a relief to most people and, as the man was dragged backstage, many took their leave.

Tom watched the whole thing through the smoke and dim light, then slipped unnoticed backstage. When the man was alone, Tom stepped out of the shadows and went over to his cot.

"Ramón," he whispered, "I've found you at last."

At first it was impossible to get anything sensible out of the Spaniard. He rolled his eyes in delirium and muttered in some strange language. Tom shook him but could not rouse his attention. "Water, water," groaned Ramón, "the water is flowing over me, I see nothing but water, the endless ocean. I'm drifting, drifting."

"Look at me Ramón," said Tom, beginning to lose patience.

The Spaniard stared straight ahead. "I think I'm losing my sight," he babbled.

"It was your ear that was hit." Tom glanced at Ramón's left eye, which as far as he could tell had nothing wrong with it.

"The pictures come and go," muttered the Spaniard, who now spoke with a peculiar accent.

"Look at me, Ramón. Don't you recognize me?"

"My name is Jacques Emil Morte. I was born in Marseilles. I am an artist, and death is my speciality."

"Your name is Ramón," sighed Tom, "and I've been traveling all over the Caribbean looking for you. I've been away from home for almost a year, so stop this playacting."

"I hear that you speak Spanish."

"Yes, I speak Spanish. My mother is half-Spanish and you are from Cádiz. Now spare me the lies."

"I understand only a little Spanish," moaned Ramón. "What did you say your name was?"

Tom grimaced and shut his eyes. He sat for a moment, thinking. Suddenly he shoved the big man onto his side and pulled up his shirt. "These scars were made with a strap called Juan Carlos," he exclaimed. "Look at me, Ramón! I saved you from drowning, so show me the respect of admitting who you are."

Ramón looked at Tom with dismay, then buried his face in his hands and wept like a beaten man.

"I'm not worthy," he sobbed, "I'm not worthy."

Tom sighed and went to get a mug of water, which Ramón gulped down with a long-suffering expression.

"Forgive me, my dear boy," he said. "Forgive this eye, from which the light is slowly ebbing so that for the rest of my days I will have to walk around blind, carrying a beggar's bowl. Forgive this eye for not recognizing at once my rescuer and only friend. Let me look at you, Master Tom." Ramón held a candle up to Tom's face.

"You've grown tall, and filled out. Your hair is darker, but you're still the same Irish lad you were when you were a babe."

"You didn't know me when I was a babe, you miserable liar."

Ramón lay back on his cot with an arm over his forehead. "How many times have I prayed to God that I might see you again, Tom? In my sleep I laughed as if I were walking on feathers."

Tom slapped a hand to his brow. "As if you were walking on feathers? A person could go mad listening to this sort of drivel."

"Oh Tom, Tom, Tom, my dear boy. How many times have I regretted my actions? I, who believed that I could help you win the fortune you deserve. I, who believed that I was acting properly and wisely, but ended up in this rotten hell of a place, far from those I love." The Spaniard rolled his eyes and put his hand on Tom's arm. "Be kind enough to look at me."

Tom shook off the man's hand. "We don't need to prolong the torment, Ramón. Just tell me where he is."

"Who, Tom?"

"Who do you think?"

"Oh, the prince, our little black investment. Sit down here beside me, Tom. Let me tell you what happened. You see, when the boy and I arrived in Jamiaca . . ."

Tom raised his hand. "Start from the beginning, please. When you ran off from Nevis."

Ramón reacted by rolling over so that he lay with his back to Tom. "My conscience made me leave. I could no longer live off the charity of your mother and Señor López. A man has his pride, after all."

"Oh God," groaned Tom. "You could live off charity to the end of your days; I don't think you've ever lived by anything else. And as for your pride, I think it vanished with the umbilical cord when you emerged from your mother's womb."

Ramón put his hand to his lips, as if in horror. "How vulgar you've become, Tom. Is there nothing left of the gentle boy from Nevis?"

"He's gone," replied Tom. "Gone just like the boy I won a share of when I saved your life, you lying scoundrel. I ought to slice you up right now and throw you to the hogs."

"I'm not worthy," whispered Ramón. "But Tom, it's the will of Fate that I always wish to do the right thing but end up doing wrong."

"That at least is no lie."

The Spaniard looked at Tom, putting on his favorite long-suffering expression. "Aren't you at all glad to see your old friend again, Tom?"

Tom shook his head. In his heart he *was* glad to see Ramón. He was actually quite fond of the man, even though he was furious about what the Spaniard had done.

The seaman broke into a big smile. "Then take the hand of Ramón the Pious and let the bad blood go. Let's be friends again—we're united by Fate, after all."

"The only thing that binds us," said Tom, "is a sixty-pound African slave."

Ramón got to his feet with difficulty and proceeded to search for a liquor flask. When he found it, he started pacing back and forth as he moaned about his pains.

Tom made him sit down. "Tell me how a person could end up earning his keep by putting his life at risk. What's the matter with you, Ramón?"

"I don't want to live, Tom." The Spaniard groaned loudly. "Look at this!"

He ripped the patch from his eye, revealing a black hole, partially stitched together.

"As you can see, there have been nights when the audience took better shots, but it doesn't matter. One fine day, Tom, some conceited sailor will hit Ramón in the heart. And that man will be my friend, for he will have freed me from the greatest pain of all, which has tortured and tormented me so that in drunken desperation I have placed my fate in the hands of others."

"What have you done to deserve such a fate?"

"I have three hundred lives on my conscience, Tom. Mammon is a merciless lord. First he takes your pride, then your soul vanishes, and finally he demands your life."

The Spaniard fell silent for a moment, then lowered his voice to a sad whisper. "My name truly is Ramón Suárez Emilio Sánchez Rodrigues, known as el Piadoso, but I was not a seaman on the *Santa Helena*. I was the first mate, a highly esteemed officer with my own cabin and a lackey to polish my boots."

"Am I supposed to believe this?"

"Ask me anything about navigation. No one is better at it than Ramón. How do you think I found my way to Nevis? If I didn't know every single constellation and was able to set a course, even half-dead, I would not be sitting here today."

"Tell me everything, and start with the shipwreck!"

Ramón sighed, but a glimmer of liveliness appeared in his good eye.

"We could do fourteen knots under the best of conditions. She was a hundred twenty-four feet, that magnificent galleon. The anchor weighed a ton and a half. It took twelve men around our capstan to hoist it. That was her maiden voyage, Tom. No one could have known that we had the Devil on board. *Un pobre diablo*. A poor devil. He turned our heads, first the captain's, then mine, and finally the heads of the whole crew. And one night, when a storm was gathering force, a riot broke out in the hold. We had three hundred slaves crowded below deck. By that time we had been at sea for five weeks and had lost a hundred of the blacks. The mood wasn't good. No one could have known what there was about that boy that could make grown men behave like wild men. He looked like all the others."

Ramón folded his hands and bowed his head.

"When the captain finally realized that we had put a prince in chains, it was too late. Some of the blacks broke free—don't ask me how. Several of them jumped over the side and disappeared. Others launched an attack on the crew. The captain gave orders for the boy to be set free, but the slave rebellion was now so close to mutiny that I took matters into my own hands. I wanted to turn the vessel around and sail back to West Africa to pick up a new cargo of slaves. On the way we would stop at the Bissagos Islands and get the ransom money. The thought of how rich we were going to be became an obsession, and I convinced the crew to back me. But the blacks had something else in mind. They're not human, Tom; they're wild animals."

Ramón rolled his eye. "How many slaves we shot that night, I have no idea. At the same time, the storm got worse. The ship was taking on water, so I ordered some of the men below to start pumping. Others had begun to reef the sails. It was utter chaos. We withdrew to the officers' cabins to defend ourselves against the blacks. I saw my men filling their pockets with the ship's cash, but I knew what was coming, so I grabbed a water keg and began working my way toward the foredeck, when the ship started to heave onto its side. I was knocked down into the galley and passed out. When I came to, half the vessel was underwater. The sea was filled with dead bodies and screaming people, black and white. I saw the mainsail rip in half. The yard of the topgallant fell and split open the cook's skull. Terrified, I started for the bowsprit, which was still sticking up like a flagpole, and that's where I caught sight of him."

Ramón took Tom's hand. "He looked straight at me. As you know, the blacks all look alike, but this one was wearing that necklace with the ring, which the captain had showed me late one night when he was talking about the Bissagos Islands. I'll never forget the first time I heard about the chieftain they called their king and about the boy they called their prince. These many months later it's perfectly obvious that many things would have been different if the captain had never told that story.

"If I think about it, I can clearly remember the circumstances when we reached the islands. We had come from the west coast of Africa where we had taken four hundred blacks on board. That was fifty too many, but the captain was a greedy man and would be paid per head. By the time we arrived at the islands, we had already lost a few, who had either died or jumped overboard. The captain was eager to make up for these losses at the Bissagos Islands. As we approached the islands, we were greeted by a small group of boys who paddled their canoes up to the ship. They brought us gifts. I don't think they had ever seen such a big ship before."

Ramón wiped his eye. "Soon after, they were put in chains. I can still hear them screaming and their screams must have summoned the others in the tribe, because suddenly all hell broke loose. I can't even tell you how many canoes there were in the water, but there must have been hundreds, and the men were like wild animals. It was at that moment that I first heard about the chieftain. We lowered a couple of cannons, and the captain ordered the oars into the water. Soon after, we were out far enough to set sail and escape."

Ramón fell back onto his cot and went on with his tale of the shipwreck. "I can still see him before me. He was standing by the foremast, with the rain whipping at his face. And yet he stood there so calmly and just stared at me, as if I were the only other person in the whole world. I knew it would only be minutes before the galleon vanished completely, so I called out to him. We grabbed each other's hands when the bowsprit cracked in half like a twig. We were washed overboard. Everything was dark until I caught sight of part of the mainmast that was still floating on the water. The rest of that night we lay side by side and let the current and raging seas carry us. Nothing remained of the galleon, not so much as a barrel. I thought I would never see land again, but I tried to keep up my courage. I had a little water left, and the black had a couple of biscuits, which we shared. But when night fell for the second time, I could feel the life seeping out of me. Just as I was weeping the last tears of a dying man, I heard the sound of oars, and out of the mist came a splendid red-haired lad."

Ramón looked at Tom as if to plead his case. "And that's my story," he said, sighing. "No matter how awful it may be, it's the truth. Greed is a merciless master and cannot be beaten out of you. I know that now."

Tom put his hand on Ramón's shoulder. "Tell me what happened after you left Nevis. Did you sell him?"

Ramón looked away.

"Answer me, Ramón!"

The Spaniard sighed and nodded.

"Whom did you sell him to?"

"To a plantation owner. But you haven't heard the worst of it." Ramón held his hand to his forehead. "I didn't get a thing for him," he whispered. "You see, Tom, I didn't have any money for food, so I had no other choice. The plantation owners want big strong men, and that boy could barely even lift a hoe."

"How long ago did this happen?"

"Half a year, I would guess."

Tom stood up. "Splendid!" he said. "Give me your money, Ramón!"

"I don't have any money, Tommy."

"I said give me your money. You owe me."

"Dearest Tommy, I haven't got a penny."

"You can't tell me that night after night you risk your life for a glass of rum and a bowl of porridge. Do yourself a favor and give me what you have so I won't have to turn this whole place upside down and then for the rest of my days remember Ramón of Cádiz as a swine."

The money pouch wasn't big, but Tom could tell there was enough to buy a slave's freedom. At least a small slave.

"Where do I find this plantation?"

"Don't you ever give up, Tom O'Connor?"

Tom seized hold of the Spaniard and looked him right in his good eye. "No," he said, "I never give up. Never!"

The Spaniard shook his head and smiled to himself. "You're an odd creature, Tom, but it's your life and I'm not about to speculate as to your fate. The plantation is Aron Hill, the largest in all of Jamaica. You head west and continue until you come to the big sugarcane fields. I've heard there are more than two hundred blacks out there. The owner is apparently British, and he has a good reputation. His overseer often comes to our inn, and let me tell you he has given me many a scar on my body. His name is Joop van den Arle. He's easy to spot because he's pure white."

Tom went to the door and gave one last look at the Spaniard, who was leaning back on his cot with bloody wounds all over his body and a hole where his right eye used to be. If possible, he looked even worse now than when Tom had seen him for the first time, hanging on to a piece of timber.

"Live well, Ramón," said Tom.

"Live well, Tom O'Connor," whispered Ramón, shedding a tear. "Give my greetings to your mother and sister. And even though I won't ask you to mince words, tell them that Ramón from Cádiz, known as el Piadoso, wasn't all bad."

8   Joop van den Arle

THEY STOOD LIKE A DENSE FOREST OF TREES clacking faintly in the wind. Each plant was as tall as a man, each stalk the thickness of a finger. For as far as the eye could see there was nothing but sugarcane.

Tom had allowed himself a much-needed rest at the top of a hill. From there he could make out a large uncultivated area where an army of slaves was at work with their hoes. They seemed to work in groups, moving with a steady, monotonous rhythm. And when the wind shifted, Tom could hear a quiet hum.

He squinted at the sun and realized that he had been walking along the border of the plantation for nearly an hour. He had left the smithy at dawn. His few possessions were packed up in a bag with a strap attached so that he could sling the bundle over his shoulder. Inside the bag were Ramón's money, a comb made of tortoiseshell, and a little shell that his sister had given him for his last birthday. Rarely did Feo give anything away. When she was little she had always demanded the gift back. Maybe she had forgotten about this shell, painted with light floral colors that reminded him of the flowers on the lemon tree behind the inn on Nevis. He had discovered that the colors tended to change according to the mood he was in. He remembered Feo saying that whatever you gather from the sea will always remind you of your loved ones.

It was now midday and the sun was beating down on the earth like blows to an anvil. He drank the last drops from his water flask and wiped his forehead, thinking about what it must be like to work in a field with no shade. He had taken the liberty of breaking off a piece of sugarcane and enjoying the sweet juice. But the same was true of sugar as of salt: it merely increased his thirst.

Tom looked around. It was completely still; only the wind could be heard. The wind and the distant humming of the slaves. He thought about his friend Ramón, who was apparently born with a difficult temperament and an unlucky fate. And about the smith, who had finally sworn off a bad habit. He also thought about Bibido.

Maybe he was only a short distance away, working with the other blacks. The thought made Tom weak, yet tense. Was it true that when a person was about to reach a goal, he was always struck by a sense of fullness that wasn't half as satisfying as the hunger that had driven him? On the plantation the boy would have been given a new name, of course. If slaves *had* names, that is. But surely they had to call each other something. And the plantation owner could do as he pleased with the boy. Bibido was now his property, thanks to Ramón the Pious. "If I want him back," muttered Tom, "I'll have to buy his freedom. But that shouldn't be a problem. I have enough money, after all."

He grimaced bitterly. There was only one way to proceed. There ought to be plenty of work on such a big plantation. He decided to look for the main building and turned onto a gravel road that cut like a gray scar through the sugarcane. It was like moving through another world. The air was utterly motionless, making the heat unbearable. He found himself breathing heavily and had to stop. Even he, who was used to hard work and had good lungs and a young heart, started to feel faint. He thought it must be for lack of water. Maybe he was heading the wrong way. He couldn't hear the slaves anymore—in fact he couldn't hear anything at all. It didn't seem to matter whether he went right or left. In this wilderness it would be easy to disappear, never to be found, or at least not until harvest-time.

It was like walking on the bottom of the ocean, Tom thought. The lack of air pressed on his lungs. He licked his lips, crouched down, and shouted his name. The plantation swallowed up the sound; his voice vanished the instant it left his lips. He lay down on his back and breathed hard. He had started out with plenty of water, but unfortunately he had been greedy about drinking it. He closed his eyes, put one arm over his face, and didn't wake up until the ground thundered beneath him.

The sound was familiar—the sound of a horse. He placed the palms of his hands against the earth, which shuddered under the heavy hoofbeats.

The horseman must be very close. At that moment Tom caught sight of a fat rat looking right at him. It was sitting among the reeds, baring its yellow teeth. "You'll soon be a dead rat," Tom whispered.

Suddenly the horse was in front of him, rearing up on its hind legs. Tom stared in terror at the rider, who appeared like a pitch-black silhouette fused to the horse. The rider pulled the horse sideways and let it dance around Tom.

The man was wearing riding breeches and a bandanna, but nothing else. His skin was white as goat's milk, as was his hair, which hung down his back like a whip. The man's eyes were pink, with long pale lashes.

Tom was just about to say something when the rider jumped down from his saddle. His body was slim and supple. He stood in front of Tom with his legs spread. "What's this boy doing here?"

Tom cleared his throat but his mouth was so dry that he couldn't utter a sound.

"Do you speak English?"

Tom nodded vigorously. "Yes, sir. Yes, I do."

"Get up."

Tom stood up as quickly as he could.

The man walked around him. "Where does the boy come from?"

"From the smithy outside of Port Royal, sir."

"What was he doing there?"

"Helping out, sir. Tending the forge and . . ."

"What's he doing here?"

Tom was prepared for this question. The man was now standing behind him, so Tom had to turn around to look him in the eye. Tom said that he wanted work.

"Work? What kind of work?"

"Anything at all, sir."

"Are you British?"

"My mother is British, my father was Irish."

The man's face came close. The pink eyes stared at Tom with a mixture of indifference and loathing. The man said that he couldn't abide Irishmen. "They drink too much, fight too much, and they're full of lies. How old are you?"

"Fourteen, sir."

The man took Tom's measure. "I take it that you're also thirsty. The Irish are always thirsty."

Tom looked away and tried to moisten his lips, but he didn't have anything to moisten them with.

"Maybe you're too proud to say that you're thirsty?"

"No, sir. My water ran out several hours ago."

"Do you have a name?"

Tom said that his name was Tom O'Connor.

The man went over to his horse and opened the flat water bag. He placed the bag to his lips and took a long, greedy swallow. Then he put the cork back in, wiped his mouth, and mounted his horse. With his back still turned to Tom, he snapped his fingers and got the horse moving at a walk.

Tom followed as best as he could. They turned off from the gravel road and came to a network of smaller paths. The horseman picked up the pace. At first Tom had enough air and strength to keep up, but gradually he fell farther and farther behind. He stumbled, regained his footing, lost his bearings, and hurried on. The horseman kept changing direction, turning first to the right, then to the left, seeming to move in circles, and at last came back to the gravel road. Tom had only the sound to guide him. He was having trouble seeing clearly and keeping his balance.

He sat down on the ground and shaded his eyes, instantly catching sight of the shimmering silhouette of a man and a horse heading up toward Aron Hill.

The main building was whitewashed and enormous. Behind it stood the cabins of the house slaves. There were stables, manure heaps, two cattle pens, and four flat-roofed buildings used for the slave markets. Also on the grounds were a sugar mill, a cookhouse, and three mud-walled houses.

In the pen closest to the main building stood ten fat-bellied mules, looking as if they had been hewn from granite. Only their tails moved to shoo away the flies.

To the right of the main building rose up a small wooden church with a pale-blue tower. The bell swayed faintly in the breeze, creaking reluctantly. An odd silence reigned over the entire place.

As he came closer, Tom caught sight of several older slaves sweeping the pathways around the main building. The work seemed pointless, but Tom knew that it was important to keep slaves busy, and these men appeared to have passed the age for working in the fields.

He looked around for the horseman and stepped closer. The slaves paid him no mind. Even when he stood on the stairway to the main entrance, they did not react. He was surprised that they weren't in chains, though he had heard of blacks who had served on the same plantation for so long that they were allowed to go unshackled.

A rusty bellpull hung on the blue-painted front door. He dusted off his pants, smoothed down his hair, and tugged on the pull. A delicate little sound came from inside.

It was only a moment before the door was opened by a thin black woman, who looked at him with a suspicious expression.

"My name is O'Connor," said Tom with a bow. "I'm looking for work."

"What did you say?"

"Work. I'm looking for work."

She stared at him, dumbfounded. "Go on and get out of here. He'll have to speak to Master Joop or one of the other bombas. I've never seen the like."

"Who is it, Fanny?"

The voice coming from inside the house sounded as if it belonged to a child. Tom couldn't tell whether it was a girl or a boy.

"It's nothing," grumbled the house slave, but she was pushed aside by a girl Tom's age. He thought she was white in the way that only refined people are white. As if her skin, for lack of sunshine, had invented its own coloring, a peculiar cross between blue and white. Her arms were thin and sprinkled with freckles. In contrast to Tom's freckles, which were brown, the girl's freckles seemed greenish. She was wearing a flowered dress and black boots. Around her neck hung a gold cross, and on her head a straw hat was pressed down over long, blond braids. Her nose was small and slightly upturned, her eyes light blue and dull.

"Who is he?" the girl asked, staring inquisitively at Tom, as if she wanted to remember every detail.

"Someone looking for work. I told him he needs to talk to . . ."

"Does he speak English?" the girl interrupted. The house slave sighed loudly and crossed her arms.

Maybe he could at least get a cup of water. "Yes, I speak English," said Tom, adding that his parents were English.

"English parents!" The girl's voice rose to a shrill pitch, as if Tom had insulted her. "How amusing," she added, chewing on a fingertip. "How very, very, very amusing. Not amusing at all. Not in the least."

"Just look at his clothes," gasped the house slave, fanning her nose with one hand. "They haven't been washed in weeks. And besides, we have all the help we need. Miss Missy knows that quite well."

"I come from Nevis," said Tom.

"Nevis," repeated the girl with the high voice. "What on earth is Nevis?"

"Nevis is an island," replied Tom. "Far away from here. I was wondering . . ."

"What were you wondering?" asked the house slave.

"Whether I might have something to drink?"

They stared at him. "Is he crazy?" The slave slammed the door shut.

"No," muttered Tom as he walked down the stairs, "just thirsty." For a moment he merely stood there, staring. Then he went over to one of the blacks who was sweeping. "The bomba," said Tom, "where do I find him?"

The slave didn't answer but just kept on sweeping. After a while he straightened up and stretched his back, pointing beyond the mud-walled house. "But the bombas aren't home."

Tom threw up his hands in resignation and at that moment caught sight of the water trough that stood in the pen with the mules. The merciless blue sky was reflected in it. He cast a sidelong glance at the slave, who had returned to his sweeping and refused even to look at him. Tom went over to the pen, practically crawled over to the trough, and lowered his head.

The water wasn't cold, nor was it clean, since it was meant for the livestock; yet it must have been clean enough when they brought it up from the well. He cupped the water in his hands and let the worst muck sift through his fingers. Then he drank in big, greedy gulps. The dregs cask, he thought. This is truly the dregs cask. Here I am drinking water that ten dumb mules have had in their mouths, and I'm savoring it.

"A person can't be choosy," he whispered, catching the eye of the nearest beast, who looked back at him in astonishment.

Tom didn't care. He took another drink, enjoying how the water was giving him his strength back. He closed his eyes and sighed deeply, thanking the mules as he got to his feet.

She was standing at the corner of the house, looking right at him. The girl from before. Tom wiped his mouth, gave a wave, and was about to leave when she pointed out that he was drinking the animals' water. Now the thin house slave appeared. She had a stick in her hand. "Go on and get out of here!"

The girl approached with her hands behind her back. She set one foot in front of the other, like a tightrope walker, then spun around and made a coquettish little hop. "Leave him alone, Fanny. If he's to be punished, the bomba will have to do it. He's white, after all, and blacks don't hit whites. What's your name, boy?"

"My name is O'Connor," said Tom. "Tom O'Connor."

"Where are your parents, boy?"

Tom cleared his throat and looked away. If they had been alone, maybe in some alleyway in Port Royal . . . He didn't finish the thought.

"Perhaps he doesn't have any family?" The girl was studying one of her braids.

"My father is dead," said Tom. "My mother is back home on Nevis. We own an inn. I've served on a fishing boat and worked in a smithy. I can do all kinds of jobs and I'm not afraid to work hard. I can navigate and . . ."

She was standing right in front of him. "Navigate? Did he say navigate? On a sugar plantation?" She suddenly started laughing hysterically. She bent double and backed away, her laughter wild and shrill.

Tiny, sharp teeth, he thought, and some of them had already turned brown. Gets whatever she points at, if she's who I think she is, meaning the plantation owner's daughter, the only heir to five million sugarcane plants, two hundred blacks, fifteen horses, and ten bars of gold. She sleeps in a real bed under fancy quilts on sheets of smooth cotton. Slumbers beneath a fan tended by five blacks. She has never peeled a fruit with her own fingers but has someone else feed her. When the time is right, she will marry the eldest son on the neighboring estate. Together they will have a daughter who will be just as spoiled and dull-eyed as her mother. Every night she folds her flabby hands and prays to God to protect her from the fever and sores that come from the blacks. She also prays for a lovelier complexion and for fingernails that won't break. Tom looked away and smiled to himself.

The girl came over to him and tipped her head back, asking him what he found so amusing. Before Tom could answer she said, "JayJay is dead, but maybe you don't know who JayJay is. No, how would you know? Someone like you who comes from out on the water, where you can navigate and all sorts of other things. As if a person should believe everything she hears from a red-haired tramp."

Tom shook his head apologetically.

"JayJay was the smartest dog in the whole world. He was smarter than anybody, especially smarter than you. Do you want to see his grave?"

"Miss Missy," scolded the Negro woman.

The girl ignored her.

Tom had no idea what he should do, but he followed the girl, who marched around the corner of the house and into a garden with lemon and olive trees. A small swing was adorned with flowering vines.

The house slave followed Tom, still holding the stick in her hand.

Tom smiled at her. If she so much as touches me with that stick, I'll rip her ears off, he thought.

"He was seven years old." The girl pointed at a small mound with a wooden cross on which was inscribed: *James Jerome Briggs*.

Tom looked at her. "Is your name Briggs too?" he asked.

There was a pause and then the girl moved away with a new expression on her face. As if she were suddenly frightened. She stared at him with big eyes, partially hiding behind the house slave.

"He can read," whispered the girl.

"Of course he can't read." The slave waved the stick.

"Of course I can read." Tom kicked at a stone. He wanted to get away from that garden and find the bomba so that he could clarify his situation. He was about to leave when the girl grabbed the stick and marched right up to him, ready to strike. They were standing face to face. The stick trembled in her hands, and she was breathing hard. But then she dropped it and ran sobbing around the side of the house.

Tom stared after her and shrugged. He picked up the stick and handed it to the house slave, who snatched it away from him. "We don't like tramps," she said. "Just wait until Master Joop gets hold of you. Then we'll see how bold you are."

Tom looked up at the blue sky. "A person sure does lose his appetite when he sees an old witch like you," he said quietly.

The woman's face unfolded like a fan. "Just you wait," she fumed.

In a flash Tom tore the stick from her hand and broke it in half over his knee. "¡*Cállate, cerdo estúpido!*" *Shut up, you stupid pig!* he said in Spanish. He walked toward the corner of the house and stopped with his back to the woman, who stood with her hands pressed to her lips. "The bomba," said Tom, "where do I find him?"

"Here!" The man was standing behind Tom, about to light his clay pipe. Tom recognized him as the horseman who had found him by the fields.

"Master should certainly give him what he deserves," scolded the Negro woman. "He made Miss Missy cry, and he was downright rude and said nasty words in Spanish."

The man blew out a puff of smoke and watched the gray rings rise into the air. He showed no reaction to what the house slave had said but merely looked at Tom.

Tom noticed that the small pink eyes hadn't changed since he saw him the first time.

"Still thirsty?" the man asked.

"A little," replied Tom, pleased with the man's amiable tone.

"He drank out of the livestock trough," shouted the house slave.

The hint of a smile crossed the man's face. He spat and then stepped over to Tom, took him by the arm, and led him around the side of the house. They crossed the courtyard and went down to the mud-walled buildings, where the man tapped out his pipe and abruptly struck Tom hard with the back of his hand. The blow came so suddenly that Tom fell over backward. He stared at the pale man, who regarded him with a languid expression.

"You're not to go into the garden again. Is that understood, boy?"

"Yes, sir."

"Stand up."

Tom got to his feet and brushed himself off.

"You see, there is only one person in charge here, and that's Joop van den Arle. Are you listening, boy?"

"Yes, sir, I'm listening."

"And your Spanish curse words will be remembered. Spanish is the language of the Devil, and Spain is the name of the hell where he lives. One word in Spanish and you've seen Aron Hill for the last time. Two Spanish words and you've seen Heaven for the last time. Three little words in

Spanish and you'll see nothing more. And as for oaths and curses . . ." The man's pink eyes lit up, and he licked his lips and shook his head. "I'll leave the rest to your imagination."

The overseer showed his chalk-white teeth in what looked like a smile before he stuck out his hand and opened Tom's mouth to inspect his teeth. "As I told you, I can't abide Irishmen," he said. "They're just as unreliable as the blacks. But in contrast to the blacks, they have a hard time learning."

"I learn quickly, sir."

"Did I ask you a question, boy?"

"No, sir."

The pink eyes had taken on that lethargic look again. "Do you know about horses?"

"Yes, sir."

"And what do you mean by that?"

Tom took a deep breath and explained that he could ride, groom, muck out, and shoe even the most difficult animals. And that in general there was no kind of job that he hadn't done.

"Shoe horses?"

"Yes, sir."

"What was your name?"

"O'Connor, sir. Tom O'Connor."

The overseer took Tom's arm and led him into the stable. In addition to the black stallion Tom had seen out in the field there were four saddle horses and a pony.

"The black one is mine," said the overseer. "He's lame. I ride him anyway because I think it's probably just a splinter that has bored its way up from the hoof and into the bone. Right foreleg. Is that something you can handle?"

"Yes, sir," murmured Tom, looking the horse over.

"Then what are you waiting for? But I should warn you that he's been a little irritable lately. He has a hot temper and doesn't like anyone to touch his bad leg. But the splinter has to come out. You'll find a pair of tongs hanging on the wall under the harness," said the overseer, fussing with his pipe.

Tom kept his eyes on the stallion as he approached, whispering reassuring sounds that he had learned from the blacksmith. Cautiously he patted the horse on the neck and then gently stroked his chest. He was a magnificent animal, well-built with strong, slender legs. His head was small but his neck was powerful, with a glossy mane.

Tom stroked his muzzle and spoke sweetly and soothingly. The smith had taught him a little trick for dealing with nervous animals. If you ran a finger between their ears and over the forehead to the muzzle as you let the animal get used to your smell, it had a calming effect. When the stallion grew still enough for Tom to dare walk around him, he leaned down to have a look at the bad leg. There was nothing to see, so he had to lift up the hoof. He hesitated a moment, counted to three, and then grabbed the foreleg and held it tightly between his thighs. The horse reacted with a whinny but otherwise didn't move.

Tom caught sight of the splinter at once. Two fingers long, it sat in a lump of dried blood and had obviously been there awhile. The splinter had bored its way into the side of the shoe on the outer edge of the hoof, where it had entered the bone. To remove it, the shoe would have to come off.

He went to get the tongs and looked around for a hammer. He found one, put the horse's leg between his thighs, and started working. It had been a long time since the horse had been reshod, much too long.

Tom loosened the nails one by one and finally wriggled the shoe off. Then he put the leg down. The instant his hoof struck the ground the horse went berserk, rearing up on his hind legs and kicking wildly with his forelegs, neighing in pain and showing the whites of his eyes.

Tom held his hands over his face, aware of the enormous power so close to his head, expecting any minute to be kicked to death. But gradually the horse calmed down. The animal was still snorting, but he was no longer supporting his weight on his bad hoof.

Tom tried to speak slowly and soothingly, but it was difficult with his heart pounding in his chest. He wiped his face on his sleeve, but the sleeve was soaked with sweat. He closed his eyes and paused a moment to slow his pulse. There was nothing to do but start over, stroking the horse on the neck and muzzle, speaking kindly but firmly, demonstrating his composure to the animal. Finally he lifted the bad foot between his legs and waited a moment before daring to approach the splinter with the rusty tongs.

The problem was that he had no idea whether he would be able to pull it out with one yank or whether the splinter would break off and make the rest of the job impossible. He also didn't know how the horse would react. He was beginning to lose his nerve when the overseer said, "Drop it, lad, and let a grown man do a grown man's work." Tom heard him tapping out his pipe.

When the sparks struck the ground, Tom put the tongs around the splinter, shut his eyes, and pulled.

A second later he was lifted five feet in the air and tossed into another stall, where he landed between two geldings. The animals stared at him with wild eyes, seized by the panic in the neighboring stall.

The black stallion neighed and kicked his back legs, raising clouds of dust. Little streaks of light issued from the dark each time his hooves struck the wall.

The overseer peered down at Tom, who was lying in the straw with a stabbing pain in his back and what felt like paralysis in his left arm. "Has the Irish boy who dared call Miss Missy's black maid a pig, and in Spanish at that, has he finally had enough?"

Tom got to his feet and limped out of the stall. The small of his back hurt, his shoulder ached, and his left elbow was bleeding profusely, but he was grateful that he hadn't broken anything. Without a word he handed the rusty tongs to the overseer.

The man curled back his upper lip. "Little boys," he sighed, "should learn to take care or they might never grow up to be big men. When my men come in from the field, I'll show you how to handle a case like this. As I said before, I can't abide the Irish, and especially not Irish who try to show off."

Tom held out his hand. "I know," he gasped, peering at the horse, "but I think I'd wait a day or two to shoe him."

He handed the overseer a splinter of wood eight inches long, then walked out into the dry grass and collapsed.

9 Master Briggs

HE HAD BEEN GIVEN LODGINGS in a little building that was barely fourteen square yards. It seemed almost like a playhouse, although it had been made of the best materials, with a good roof and a solid floor.

Tom's new home turned out to be the former doghouse, which the deceased JayJay had left behind. The overseer found this entertaining, as did his companions, eight men in all, who were all called bombas. In Tom's eyes they resembled a band of murderers and pickpockets. Their manners were ghastly and their language a disgrace. Only when Joop appeared did they put a damper on their vulgarities. But they were masters at the art of making slaves work, and Aron Hill was said to be a model plantation, the pride of the island.

After living two weeks in the doghouse, Tom had still not been introduced to the owner of the plantation, Master Briggs. Tom had seen the man when he left for town in the morning and when he relaxed with his daughter in the garden in the evening. Just a glimpse, but enough for Tom to form an impression of a sympathetic man. Arthur Briggs was slight of stature, with short legs and short arms. Tom guessed he was about forty years old. He was always well-dressed and had a good reputation among his house slaves, who described him as jovial and amiable but incapable of making any decisions.

It was said that Joop van den Arle was the one in charge at Aron Hill, since Master Briggs had too many other things to attend to that had nothing to do with sugar. But among Joop's men, stories circulated that made Briggs a laughingstock. They claimed that he would start a sentence but seldom manage to finish it, simply because he couldn't remember how it had begun. They also called him a milksop who preferred to daydream and build models of English cathedrals.

Tom himself had noticed that there was something childlike about Briggs when the plantation owner played with his daughter in the evening. But Tom did not consider it demeaning for a father to amuse his daughter, especially if the daughter had trouble amusing herself.

The mistress of the house was almost never seen. She was practically bedridden. Exactly what ailed her, nobody knew, not even the doctor who attended her. He had confided to Joop that the mistress's illness was related to a melancholy spirit. If she left the house at all it was to go to church, and it was on these occasions that Tom had glimpsed her. She was small and thin but quite beautiful in a fragile sort of way. In Tom's eyes there was an air of persecution about the way she moved. Her hands were seldom at rest, and her eyes blinked nervously, like the eyes of a rodent. She and her daughter had the same skin color. According to the kitchen staff, she rarely joined her family at meals, leaving them to dine alone. She was considered a very religious woman. Tom knew that the mistress's father had been a pastor in London, and he guessed that Mrs. Briggs suffered not only from melancholy but also from homesickness.

One morning he stayed behind and watched the ranks of blacks heading for the fields. First the men, then the women. He had been told to wait, but he didn't know why. He had seen Miss Missy walking around with the little girl called Sunday, the daughter of the house slaves Ina and George. That morning Sunday was being pulled around on a leash, presumably as a substitute for the dog that had died.

Sunday was the favorite playmate of Miss Briggs. For that reason she led a different life from the other slave children, who were sent to work in the fields by the age of four—provided they weren't taken from their parents and sold.

When Sunday wasn't pretending to be a Negro doll or a dog, she helped out in the kitchen.

It was Fanny who on that morning had called Tom over to the kitchen door. She and Tom weren't getting on any better than when they had first met. She still regarded him as a poor replacement for the dog whose house he had taken over.

• • •

"He'd better wash up good," said Fanny, "hands and face and feet. Phew, how he smells."

"I don't smell at all."

"You stink of the hay that you sleep in." She ushered him into the kitchen. There he was given a thorough washing.

Fanny's assistant, the young Ina, found an orange-colored shirt that fitted Tom perfectly. Then she sewed on a few buttons and ran a comb through Tom's hair. Now he was ready to say hello to Master Briggs.

"Bow politely and speak only if the master asks you a question, and don't you dare use any of your Spanish words, because then it's out the door in a trice." Fanny's eyes flashed.

Tom looked at Ina, who was standing with her arms crossed. "Tom will be nice," she said, giving Tom a wink.

The three parlors of the house were connected, one next to the other. Tom had never seen anything like it. The floors were so shiny that you could see your reflection in them, and the carpets were so brightly colored that only the coral reefs could rival them. On the walls hung the most life-like paintings, many depicting scenes from the Bible. In a glass cupboard that reached from floor to ceiling, crystal glasses stood side by side with carafes and silverware, ivory boxes, and jewelry cases.

Master Briggs was standing at his desk when Tom made his entrance. He looked up. "Ah yes, young O'Connor, come closer, come closer. Let me have a look at you, my boy."

Tom cautiously skirted the carpets and went over to Briggs. The two of them were just about the same height.

"Well, well, well," murmured Briggs. "British, as I understand it."

"Half, sir. My father was . . ." Tom hesitated, lowered his voice, and said that his father was from Ireland.

For a brief moment it looked as if Master Briggs were experiencing severe indigestion. Then he gave a loud mirthless laugh and led Tom over to the terrace, which had a splendid view of almost the whole plantation. "I know nothing better than to stand here in the morning and watch them head out. If there's a more beautiful sight, I don't know what it would be. The black bodies glistening in the sun, and then their song—you know, many of them have excellent voices. Now where was I? Oh yes, Ina tells me that she'd heard the boy can read, is that right?"

Tom nodded eagerly.

"How did he learn to read, I wonder?" Briggs tugged at his ear.

"From my mother, Master Briggs."

"Oh, your mother could read too. I see. Well, that's excellent. Yes, we Europeans have to stick together, especially those of us from the British Isles. There are plenty of Spaniards out here. But we'll take care of them, you can be sure of that. The English fleet . . ."

Briggs lost his train of thought and proceeded to teeter back and forth on the balls of his feet, as if trying to rock his way back to the conversation. "The overseer tells me that it might be possible to train you to become a bomba one day."

"A bomba, sir?"

"It requires hard work—you won't get far without hard work." Briggs clenched his fists and began walking around the room. "I myself . . . and if you keep at it and know how to win respect, because it's no good without respect, then perhaps one day, who knows." Briggs came over to Tom. The man's small pale-blue eyes gazed guilelessly at Tom's chin. "This is a good plantation we have here, Tom, a good plantation. With nice Negroes. We treat them properly, that we do. Of course they have to obey, but otherwise they have an excellent life. I can tell you that we don't have nearly as many sick or dead as they have on other plantations. They're given decent food, and we have plans to teach the best of them to read. Naturally Joop has to show them that we expect obedience. We expect that, Tom. Obedience. We've seen how things can go when there's a lack of discipline. What was it I wanted to say? Oh yes, I think you should see what we just received by courier."

Briggs went over to his desk on which stood a bouquet of flowers, a black granite lion, and an English flag.

"Previously," he continued, "we had to make do with an iron brand that was heated up in the flames of a charcoal fire. The problem was that it left such unpleasant oozing sores. But this brand with the ivory handle is heated up in a spirit flame, and as the boy can see, it has my initials and the words *Aron Hill* spelled out in reverse. Yes, the brand is made of silver. We've been waiting a whole year for it to be delivered."

"It's very handsome," muttered Tom, having no idea what the brand was to be used for.

"Joop and his men should get started by next week, I think. . . ." Briggs lost his train of thought again. "It doesn't prevent them from running away, of course, but the brand on their skin does make it easier for us to find them. Does the boy know how it's done?"

Briggs looked at Tom with a big childlike smile.

Tom replied that he didn't know how it was done. He was beginning to suspect what Briggs was talking about.

"Well, you see, to make a clear imprint you put a little piece of oiled paper on the skin. No, the pain doesn't last long. But they do carry on, that they do. So my wife and I are taking a little trip to . . . I mean, until it's all over."

"So this is a branding iron?" Tom said, forgetting that he wasn't supposed to speak unless he was asked a question.

"It's the plantation's seal. We brand them on the chest or on the arms. First the men, then the women, and finally their offspring." Master Briggs looked at the branding iron. "Exquisitely made, don't you think? The handle and all."

"Oh, absolutely, sir, absolutely."

Briggs looked Tom up and down. "Are those the only clothes you have?"

"Yes, sir. Except for my other shirt."

"Tell Ina in the kitchen that you're to have . . . You see, each month Aron Hill arranges . . . No, I'd better say it straight out: we've been hearing about incidents of poisoning. Well, of course we don't think it would happen here, but one never knows."

"Poisoning, sir?"

Briggs gave Tom a confused look, lost his train of thought, and then found it again. "Whites that have been poisoned. By food or by wine. It happens in certain places. And my wife has grown uneasy because of these rumors, and since we're about to have guests . . . We're speaking of refined people, Tom. Extremely refined people. I mean, one should be able to trust the food one is served. Do you understand what I'm getting at, young man?"

"Yes, sir," replied Tom, without having any idea what Briggs was talking about.

"That was the one thing. The other is . . . on those plantations where they've had Negroes to taste the wine, precisely for the purposes of avoiding these problems, well, unfortunately a high degree of drunkenness has developed among these blacks. I won't elaborate on that any further. But my wife and I would like to have a white taster, and you're quite a presentable boy. Some of the bombas . . . but we won't go into that. And you look as if you're in good health. Are you in good health, Tom?"

"Yes, sir."

"The boy has never been sick?"

"No, sir."

"No pox, no contagion?"

"Absolutely not, neither pox nor contagion."

"Because there's certainly a lot of that, you know." Briggs sighed, rocking back and forth on his feet. "I myself have suffered from pain in my side. A little powder helps a bit. But all the better, I say, if the boy is hale and hearty. And an agreement is an agreement. Isn't that right, Cummings?"

"O'Connor, sir," said Tom. "My name is O'Connor."

"O'Connor? That's odd, I was quite certain he said Cummings." Master Briggs tugged at his beard pensively.

"But never mind that. What were we talking about? Oh yes, the wine. And the taster. Yes, because it's an honorable post he'll be taking on. I've always thought that trust builds on . . . Do we have an agreement, Cummings?"

"Most definitely, sir," said Tom, wondering what on earth a taster was.

He was ushered to the door. Briggs took his arm. "Do you know anything about wine, Tom?"

"My mother ran an inn, sir."

"Oh, she did, did she? Well, it's . . . what should I say, it's most fortunate that it should turn out this way. So you do know about wine, then?"

"I venture to say that I do, sir."

"And about rum and the like?"

"Rum as well, sir."

"But you're not . . . I mean, there are those who peer a bit too deeply into the glass."

"Oh no, sir, I've never been tipsy," replied Tom, who had once been so drunk that he couldn't even remember his own name.

Briggs gave his arm a squeeze and opened the door to the kitchen regions. "It's been a good discussion," he said warmly. "Now, unfortunately,

I must . . . I'm in the process of building." He lowered his voice. "I'm in the process of building Saint Paul's Cathedral. Just imagine"—Briggs raised his eyebrows—"the tower was destroyed by a lightning bolt in 1561. Nowadays they let mules, donkeys, and cattle roam through the church. I am shocked, Tom, shocked. Naturally, I haven't told Mrs. Briggs. It's just between the two of us."

"You can count on me," said Tom.

Briggs held him back. "England is on the verge of civil war," he whispered. "Cromwell and Parliament, utter riffraff. I won't say any more."

Tom nodded sympathetically.

"And it's no good without law and order," added Master Briggs.

With that, the audience was over.

Whether it was Joop or Master Briggs himself who had thought up the idea, the rules regarding law and order had been pinned up at the entrance to the slaves' quarters. They were printed in big easy-to-read letters, and although none of the slaves could read, even the smallest child knew what they said.

1

Runaway slaves shall be burned three times with red-hot tongs and thereafter hanged.

2

A slave who with malice raises his hand toward a white person, or threatens him, shall be burned three times with red-hot tongs and thereafter hanged, if the white person so demands. If not, the slave shall lose a hand.

3

A slave who meets a white person on the road shall step aside and stand motionless until the white person has passed. Neglecting to do so shall be punished by a flogging.

4

No Negro may be seen with a stick or knife, and it is forbidden for slaves to fight with each other. This is punishable by 50 lashes.

Witchcraft among the slaves shall be punished by a severe flogging. However, if the witchcraft is directed toward a white person, the slave shall lose a hand.

Joop van den Arle's personal servant, named Sugar George, is in the process of clearing away the overseer's dinner. George is married to Ina and the father of Sunday Morning. The slave children are named after the day of the week on which they're born. And it's become a bit of a joke on the plantation that whenever anyone asks Ina's little girl what her name is, she replies, "My first name is Sunday. My last name is Morning."

Sugar George is not like the other slaves. He's just as tall as Joop, but more powerfully built, and he seems unmarked by a life spent imprisoned. He is the overseer's personal slave, and he doesn't do work in the fields. George goes alone to the market and moves about freely, along with the parlor maids and Fanny.

Sugar George is the only male slave that Tom talks to, and he is just as friendly and kind as his wife. Sometimes Tom eats with George and Ina, who treat him like one of the family. They laugh at his tall tales and shake their heads when he insists that every word is true.

Joop is sitting in his old rocking chair, smoking his pipe, while George cleans up.

"The question is what to do with an Irish lad like this," says Joop. "Does he have any kind of future at Aron Hill? What do you think, George? You and Ina have been spoiling this Irish puppy. Do you think we should keep him?"

"Yes, I think we should, Master Joop," says George with a smile. "Especially if we're going to go hunting for sharks."

The overseer sighs and searches Tom's face. "You're being too lenient, George, but maybe you're right. With time, the lad might absorb enough that he could turn out to be one of my bombas. How about it, O'Connor? Want to have your own horse, your own stick, and your own whip? Maybe even a hut that doesn't stink of dog?"

The overseer smiles and winks at George. "With time, he might actually demand respect from other people and have blacks serve his food. I don't trust French overseers—not that I trust Irish overseers either—and old

Smith has been looking too deep into the bottle. I've even seen him delay using his whip when the blacks start acting up. You see, O'Connor, out in the field with a hundred slaves, all of them armed with hoes, an overseer has to keep an eye out in every direction. When they work the way you want them to, digging and harvesting, bundling and weeding, it's only because they're afraid of the cat-o'-nine-tails. The only thing they have any respect for is its claws on a slave's back. And if you neglect even once to keep their fear alive, then what happened twelve years ago on a neighboring plantation with three hundred slaves in the field could happen again. Six overseers hacked to death, the master and his wife found in the barn, each swinging from a rope. The main building was burned to the ground."

Tom looks from Joop to George, wondering why the overseer is speaking so openly in front of the slave.

Joop smiles and hands his glass to the slave, who fills it with wine from the carafe.

"George agrees with me," says the Dutchman. "Don't you, George?"

"Of course, Master Joop," says Sugar George, continuing to clear the table.

Joop sprawls in his chair. "You see, O'Connor, George is my property, just as this rocking chair is mine. If I feel like splitting it apart with an ax and then burning it, I can. This old rocking chair knows that, and so does George. Don't you, George?"

"Oh yes, sir, I do."

"Yes, you do," sighs Joop. "The thing is that the only person in the whole world who can give good old George his freedom is Joop van den Arle. And George also knows that if he's faithful to his master and minds his work, then one day George will have his own place and can settle down with Ina and Sunday, and maybe they'll even name their first dog after Joop of Holland."

The last remark makes Sugar George break out in a big smile. But Joop isn't laughing. As a rule he rarely laughs, and Tom is surprised to have been invited so frequently to visit the overseer, who seems to want to confide in him.

Tom mentioned this to George one evening as they were walking along the fields. Sunday was with them. She kept on running after Tom when he wasn't carrying her on his back, asking him when they were going to get married. She was never in a bad mood, not even after a scolding or thrashing from Miss Missy.

"I think," said Sugar George, "that Master Joop sees you as his successor in a few years. He's told me that the Irish O'Connor has what it takes. Stubbornness and a clever mind."

"Then will Tom get to have Master Joop's whip?" asked Sunday, giggling.

"That he will, and then you'll have to look out for him," replied George, smiling at Tom, who stuck his hands into his pockets, uncertain what to say about his prospects.

One morning, shortly before it was time to set out for the fields, Joop again confided in Tom, who by then had been at Aron Hill for five weeks. This time they were alone. And Joop was more somber. He closed the door behind him and told Tom to listen closely.

"I want you to be extra-vigilant," said the overseer. "We've got some troublemakers among the blacks. One of them is named Kanuno. A big fellow, never says anything, never whines, and he's never sick like the rest of them, who stay in bed for the slightest reason. But the look in his eyes, O'Connor, the way he glares with those big bloodshot eyes of his. Kanuno is an animal. Watch him using a hoe, and you'll see what I'm talking about. If he gets the chance, he'll slam that hoe into your back."

"So why do you keep him?" asked Tom.

"Because he's strong and good at his work, and because when the day comes, Master Joop wants to show all the young men who look up to him who's really in charge here. You see, Tom, we're not going to flog Kanuno; we're going to break him. And Joop van den Arle knows how."

The overseer opened the door and leaned against the door frame. "You can learn a lot about life on a sugar plantation, young O'Connor. Learn about the evil that certain people are born with and about the whip that keeps it in check. If you're clever, you'll learn to hold your own, and the only way to do that is by keeping the powder dry. By sleeping with a knife under your pillow. So use your eyes and keep your ears open. But above all, use your head. That's what separates you from the blacks. No matter how big or how muscular a slave is, he's still as dumb as an ox. It's by using our heads that we keep them under control. Don't forget, keep a close watch on Kanuno; listen to what he's not saying. Watch him when he's obeying, but never look him in the eye. Show him who's in charge, but never show him any weakness. If you can store all of that in your Irish head and at the same time keep away from the rum, then you'll make a great bomba and earn good wages—enough for you to put some aside so that you won't have to beg as an old man. And so you won't end your days in a doghouse. Get out of here now; there's work to be done. But mark my words."

The male slaves are lined up in a long row, two by two. They're all equipped with hoes, and no one is talking because it's not permitted in line. The bombas are riding around the group to make sure that no one is missing. Their commands are brief and easy to understand, and the slaves obey at once. Many of them bear the marks and scars of the whip and stick, and Master Joop has a reputation as the overseer who has beaten the most blacks to death.

Tom is sitting on his brown gelding, following the work of getting the blacks to stand exactly the way Master Joop prefers. Involuntarily he lets his eyes glide over the rows of young slaves, most of whom aren't much older than he is. Something about them looks the same, though they vary in height and breadth. None wears any type of jewelry, because that is forbidden. Of course Tom has kept an eye out for Bibido, but he's come to the conclusion that either the boy has never been at Aron Hill or else was sold. He has asked Joop, not outright, but indirectly. And Joop has told him that they only buy grown men.

Men and women were working side by side, some of the women with children on their backs. The work proceeded rhythmically and according to a set pattern. Each group consisted of fifty blacks. Many of them sang as they worked. Master Joop had nothing against their songs as long as they kept working. The slaves were out in the fields from sunup until sundown. Every three hours they were allowed a swallow of sugar water, sometimes with a tad of rum in it. That livened them up. Then they would banter with the bombas, who had nothing against being teased, though only up to a point, and no slave had any doubts about where that point was.

Tom had been inside the men's quarters. It stank of sweat and urine and partially rotten bacon. The first time, he went not only to look for Bibido, but also out of sheer curiosity. Silence fell as he walked down the aisle that divided the narrow cots. Some of the men were resting; others were tending to their aching joints or sores. The second time he went to the slave quarters it was to find an elderly man who had not shown up for the morning inspection.

"Get him out here, O'Connor," shouts the overseer named Brüggen, who is considered the most brutal of them all. The rest of the slaves are already in the courtyard, ready to go out to the fields.

Tom approaches the motionless figure. "You have to go out to the courtyard. Do you hear me?"

But the man doesn't hear because he's dead. He's lying on his back with his eyes wide open and with his hands clasped around a necklace made from little round beads of wood. Tom stands there for a moment, then goes to tell Brüggen the bad news. At that instant a big black man tears himself away from the group. He hasn't been given permission to move.

Brüggen stands up in his saddle and bellows the man's name. "Stay here, Kanuno!"

But the slave is already inside. Before the bombas manage to maneuver the horses around the rows of slaves, Kanuno is standing in the doorway with the dead man in his arms. He looks at Brüggen, who swings his whip.

Kanuno says nothing. Maybe it's the silence that summons Master Joop. Without looking at Kanuno, the dead man, or Frans Brüggen, he gives orders to have the body buried and then get on with the work.

The pattern for sowing the fields was a simple one. Holes were dug and then the tops of two sugarcanes were placed in each hole and covered with earth. When the plant sprouted, the earth was cleared of weeds. Once the plants had been thinned out four or five times, they were big enough to prevent new weeds from cropping up. In four months the plants grew to the height of a man and stood thicker than corn. When one field was done, the slaves were herded on to the next.

Tom learned that rain was all-important when it came to growing sugarcane. If there was no rain, the fields became parched and yellow. Then the slaves would be ordered out to start all over again. On the other hand, a few days of heavy rain could make the plants shoot up in the air so fast that you practically heard them growing. Six months after sowing, the plants would start to form reeds, and after a year they were ready for harvesting. Then another danger would arise. A single bite from a rat could spoil the juice, and that could ruin the entire batch during cooking. Yet the rat nuisance was nothing compared to the greatest danger of all: fire. The dry leaves would ignite in a matter of seconds, and once the fire caught hold, it could spread to the whole plantation in no time. For that reason, the most trustworthy slaves were sent out to watch for fire. They were equipped with conch shells to blow if they caught sight of smoke. Master Joop had forbidden any pipe smoking, because a single spark was enough.

But as the Dutchman said to Tom, "The truth about fires often has nothing to do with pipes. Plantation fires seldom occur on their own. They're set. A shard of glass used as a magnifying glass, and suddenly the whole place is in flames."

The Dutchman smiled slyly. "So be watchful, because that's what the blacks are always plotting. When night falls and Kanuno is lying there surrounded by his admirers, it's the only thing they talk about. How do I know? I can see it in him. So we'll just keep waiting. He and I. Does it scare you, Tom?"

"No, Master Joop," replied Tom. "It doesn't scare me."

The overseer was no longer smiling as he glanced around with a withdrawn expression. "It ought to," he murmured.

10 Sugar George

WHEN THEY STARTED HARVESTING, Tom was sent out to the fields along with overseer Brüggen and the women who had been chosen for the job. Each cutter had been given a so-called sugar knife, a tool that was seldom entrusted to male slaves. They also took with them the plantation's mules, who would haul home the sugarcane, and a handful of little children to ride the beasts.

Tom was perched high up on his horse next to the short, broad-shouldered Brüggen. The man's face was grimy with the type of stubble that never looked like anything more than soot. His nose was flat and boneless, and his little eyes were hidden behind a thick glaze that came from too much rum and too little sleep. In the bomba's ear glittered a gold ring. The earring had its own story, which the overseer enjoyed telling. The tale had to do with the time when Brüggen had found three black arsonists and had strung them all up at once. He then had claimed his reward, which he had molded into his very own trademark. Whenever there were rumblings of unrest among the slaves, Frans Brüggen would touch the earring to remind them of its story.

He spoke of Tom only as the dog. Whether this was because Tom slept in a doghouse or because the bomba equated Tom with a dog, it was impossible to say. But one evening after the rum had made its rounds among the eight overseers, Joop had called for Tom.

Tom had just finished grooming the horses and mucking out the stable, and reluctantly he went over to the bombas' cabins. Sugar George was also there.

"Brüggen wants to ask you something." Joop leaned back in his rocking chair, which had been dragged outside.

Frans Brüggen was sitting with his back to the barrel of drinking water.

He had a bottle of rum in his hands and was grinning about something known only to himself. The others looked at him expectantly.

"Well, it's just that a few of us were wondering whether it was your mother or your father who was an Irish mongrel. I thought the puppy dog might be able to help these ignorant men straighten out the pedigree." The amusement of the other overseers could be overlooked, but Frans Brüggen was laughing so hard that he had to wipe the saliva from his mouth.

Tom tried to gauge Joop's mood, but as usual it was locked behind a mask of indifference.

"The boy ought to answer when somebody asks him a question." Brüggen was on his feet. His body swayed a bit at the hips and then he grabbed Tom by the hair, yanked his head back, and attempted to pour rum into his mouth.

Tom coughed and spat, pulled away, and started punching the overseer. Maybe that's what Brüggen was waiting for, because suddenly his mood shifted. "Some dogs don't have any training. That's generally because they've never known a father—a situation that results when even the mother doesn't know the bastard's name."

"Speak decently about my parents," demanded Tom.

"Pardon me, what did he say?" Brüggen had hold of Tom's ear. "Repeat what you just said."

"I said that you're a swine, Frans Brüggen."

Brüggen glanced around, grinning in disbelief. Suddenly he knocked the lid off the water barrel and tossed Tom headfirst into the container, which was filled to the brim.

Underwater Tom got himself turned around and managed to hear Brüggen say something about the rat nuisance before the lid was slammed back on. It was pitch dark inside the barrel. The sounds from outside became a secretive muttering. But from his days on Nevis, Tom knew a thing or two about being underwater. And when he realized that a minute's time had passed, he closed his eyes and concentrated on the air he had left.

After two more minutes he began to notice that it was quite a while since he had been diving. He looked up and caught sight of the wooden block that held the boards of the lid together. It was actually possible to squeeze his fingers in between the block and the lid. He braced his body against the wall behind him and seized hold.

After three minutes something happened. Frans Brüggen grabbed the lid and tipped the barrel. Tom could hear him grumbling, and then it sounded as if he was getting help from the others. But Tom held on tight. Now the barrel was knocked over and rolled around. An ax shattered the barrel staves.

Water gushed out, and Tom let go of the lid. When Sugar George pulled him out, he lay limp and lifeless on the ground.

There was utter silence.

"I think he's drowned," whispered George.

Tom heard them gathering around. Brüggen said how the devil could he have known that the lid would stick. Master Joop came over and began shaking Tom. "O'Connor," he shouted, "O'Connor. Damn it all, boy." A couple of the other bombas swore quietly. "This will cost you, Brüggen," growled Joop. "You know the rules. We'll have to notify Mr. Briggs."

Frans Brüggen's voice sounded desperate. "By the Devil, it was an accident, you saw for yourselves. Do you hear me? He wanted to climb into the barrel. It happened exactly the way he wanted. We warned him, but he just had to show us. The damned fool."

"Poor Tom," whispered George.

"You keep your trap shut," snarled Brüggen. "We're all in this together. Go back to your quarters, George. And remember this: you didn't see anything, not a thing." Brüggen lowered his voice. "Damn it all, Joop," he groaned. "You can't very well hang me for this. Do you hear? The Devil take the lousy kid. I thought he could breathe through gills."

Tom opened his eyes. "I can."

Brüggen threw himself to the ground in terror.

Tom pulled off his shirt and wrung it out while he looked around at the circle of men. Even Joop was wide-eyed. Without another word, Tom went back to his little house and lay down on the straw, thinking that life at sea had taught him a good deal.

Sunday Morning came over and sat with him and stroked his hair. "Were you really about to drown, Tom?"

"Of course I wasn't going to drown. I can't drown, little Sunday. Because I can't sink. I'm a devil from Ireland. That's why my hair is the same color as the flames of Hell." He laughed when he saw her fold her hands in fright.

Sunday laughed too. This time through tears. "Shall we get married when we're grown up, Tom?"

"If you will have me."

She looked at him somberly. "Of course I will have you, Tom."

"Then we can go fishing for sharks together." His voice was soft.

She shook her head. "No, we won't go fishing. We'll stay here on the plantation together with Mother and Father. Then you can be a bomba and I can cook your meals."

"It's agreed, then," said Tom. "Now we're engaged, Sunday."

Later that night he told himself that aside from Father Innocent, Frans Brüggen was the person he cared for least in this world. Nevertheless, life had been kind to him. He had found friends, such as the shark fishermen Albert and Bruno, Sugar George and Ina, and Ramón from Cádiz. He added the last name with an audible groan. Yet Tom had to admit that in quiet moments he actually missed that lying scoundrel, who on top of everything had had the nerve to call himself pious. Perhaps that was the reason Tom liked him so much.

The harvesting work was hard. The cane had to be cut as close to the ground as possible, and it took strength to stand bent over in the unbearable heat. The bombas had to keep after the blacks constantly. Brüggen had divided up the cutters so that the old and the sick came last, gathering up the severed canes and bundling and tying them.

Tom followed the bomba's lead and urged on the cutters. He and Brüggen avoided each other as much as possible, and they spoke only when it was absolutely necessary. Tom told himself that he wasn't good at hating anyone for long. His anger usually dissipated quickly. But it was different with Frans Brüggen.

Joop had made it known that he wouldn't tolerate any ill feeling among the bombas, but Tom could sense a tiny, impatient chill inside himself that was waiting for the right moment. "When we're alone," he whispered into the bedstraw. "Let me get him when he's walking through the sugarcane, far away from the buildings, far away from everything. Just him and me and the knife I have in my belt."

In the fields he kept an eye on Brüggen's broad back, memorizing every word the man said as he issued commands to the women. Storing away every lash of the whip and every threat. And when the bomba tugged at his ear, Tom touched his belt and refused to look away when Brüggen scowled at him.

"What are you staring at?" The bomba's eyes roll. "He shouldn't just sit there staring like that. The dog could end up right back in the barrel if I felt like it."

Tom guides his horse over to the bomba and points at Brüggen's throat. "There," he whispers. "That's where I'm going to stick it."

The bomba's gaze wavers. "Joop will hear about this. He won't tolerate that sort of thing."

Tom is still pointing at the bomba's throat. "Now you know, Frans," he says. "It's a promise."

The harvesting had to be done swiftly because the sugarcane would be ruined if it was left lying in the fields for long. After the canes were cut, they had to be taken at once to the mill. The small mules, driven by the slave children, were shuttled quickly back and forth.

The mill had turned out to be in an unusually bad state. The evening before the harvest began, Joop and Sugar George had inspected both the windmill and the horse-driven mill, and finally had summoned Master Briggs.

"We can't possibly start tomorrow," said Joop. "We need to get the blacksmith out here."

Briggs wrung his hands.

Joop apologized for the delay, though he didn't sound particularly dispirited. "And the smith has so much to attend to right now," he added.

Tom was standing close by and moved toward Joop. "I worked for a blacksmith," he said.

Tom spent the rest of the night working with Sugar George, and when dawn came, they had finished with the mill's machinery. Master Joop said nothing, merely examined the mill, the vane, and the triangular sail. Afterward he gave Sugar George a cup of rum and went to bed.

There they stood, Tom and the big Negro, sharing the small mug of rum and giggling like little girls.

Tom enjoyed being with George, who was good with his hands and pleasant to talk to. He had an air of calm about him. Maybe that's why, on this occasion when the night was sultry and dark and everything was still, Tom decided to talk about himself. He told George about the inn back home and about his father, who had died of fever. Nor did he forget to mention his half sister, Feodora Dolores Vasgues, with the sharp tongue. George was amused and took an active interest in every part of Tom's story. Tom told him about his experience with Father Innocent and the Inquisition. And about the fortune-teller Zamora, who had ended her days burned at the stake. Then he raced forward to the time he had spent fishing for sharks, and finally he told the story about the powder that Feo had given to Señor López, which kept him sitting in the privy for three weeks.

Sugar George collapsed with mirth. "She must have gotten a thrashing for that, your wicked sister."

"She was given a taste of Juan Carlos," said Tom, winking. "But you see, George, the fat innkeeper didn't have enough strength to swing the whip, so he ended up hitting himself in the eye with it, and to this day he wears a patch."

Sugar George slapped his thigh, shook his head, and was about to ruffle Tom's red hair when he noticed the serious look on Tom's face.

"But George," Tom continued, "I didn't actually come to Aron Hill looking for work. I've been traveling for a whole year searching for one specific person. Someone who will make me a wealthy man. A black."

"A black, Tom? Is a black going to make Tom a wealthy man?"

Tom nodded. "A slave. Though not just an ordinary slave. But I found out long ago that he's not at Aron Hill. The question is whether he was ever here at all. Among all the liars in the world, Ramón the Pious is probably the worst of the lot." Then Tom told the story of Bibido—how he single-handedly had fished the boy out of the sea and saved him from drowning.

George had never heard of the Bissagos Islands. He said that in all likelihood Bibido was working on one of the other plantations that grew either bananas or coffee. "At any rate, I've never seen a boy with that sort of necklace. Besides, we're not allowed to wear jewelry of any kind."

"That doesn't mean I'm going to give up, George." Tom stretched. "You see, I never give up."

Sugar George's face brightened with a smile that quickly gave way to an anxious look. "Are you going to move on, Tom?"

"Maybe. I think about it every day. I miss my home and the island where I grew up. Especially the sea. I know that I don't belong on a plantation. Not that I feel I'm badly treated, but I'm a fisherman and I can't do without the surf and the sight of the vast horizon, or life on the shore and the long days spent in a skiff."

Tom was thinking about the inn on Nevis, about fat Señor López, and about Feodora Dolores Vasgues with the sharp tongue. He was also thinking about his mother, whom he could see before him, standing at the washing tub. His thoughts piled up and formed a lump in his stomach. Suddenly it occurred to him that George might have similar feelings about the place where he had grown up.

He looked at the big Negro, who smiled as if he had guessed what Tom was thinking.

"I live here, Tom," he said. "This is where I have my wife and my beloved little Sunday. They are my family, the best in all the world. Let me tell you, on the day Sunday was born, well, that was the most beautiful morning you could ever imagine, and she was one big smile from the very moment she left her mother's womb, and she's been like that ever since. Her name suits her. And one day we'll have our own place and a dog that we'll name after Joop."

Sugar George laughed, but Tom did not.

"What else, George?" he said quietly.

"Else, Tom?"

"You weren't born in Jamaica, were you?"

"Oh no, no. I come from the great land to the east." George cocked his head toward the house. "Africa," he said, "West Africa. From a small village. Today I remember our village as the sound of drums. Isn't that strange? Sometimes something from the past will suddenly appear. I think it must have to do with the earth. We all have a place that we come from, Tom."

"Tell me about it."

George stretched out on the grass with his head propped on his hand.

"My father was a farmer. He had two cows and seven children—I was the oldest. We lived in a village near the sea. I don't remember much. But one day a man came, one of my father's friends, someone we had known for years. He wanted me and two of my brothers to go out sailing with him. It turned out that he had gathered almost fifty half-grown boys down on the shore. That was the first time we saw a Spanish slave ship. It was anchored out in the bay. I don't know what I imagined, or why we didn't run away. Suddenly we were sitting in the skiffs. My father's friend came along and tried to calm us, but once we were on board, the friendly tone was over. Now you understand why I don't like Spaniards either, just like Master Briggs."

Sugar George smiled.

"Tell me more, George."

"More? Well, what more is there to tell! We were taken down into the cargo hold." The expression on George's face changed, and he looked away. "I think there were five hundred blacks down there. We were packed together with chains on our ankles, but it wasn't until we set sail and I saw the coast disappear, that I realized I would never see my mother or my father or my little brothers and sisters again. The adults cried and prayed. I don't think I cried. My older brother died during the voyage. They threw him overboard. We lost many, but my other brother, little Aruno, survived as I did. At last we arrived at Port Royal, where an auction was held. We were washed and given clean loincloths to wear and a little rum in our mouths, which was meant to liven us up. My brother had grown unbelievably thin. 'Aren't we going to sail anymore, Ntono?' he asked. 'No, Aruno,' I told him, 'that's over with now.' 'Are we going home to Mother and Father, then?' he asked. I didn't have time to answer before he was led away. That was the last time I saw him."

George sighed. "I was very lucky to come to Aron Hill. Just think, Tom, I now have a wife and child, and I can look forward to the day when I'll have my own place and I can watch Sunday grow up as a free girl. And get a dog that we'll name after Master Joop."

Sugar George got to his feet. He didn't look at Tom but headed back to the hut he had been allowed to share with his family. "Tomorrow is going to be a long day, Tom," he said. "Try to get some sleep."

That same night the overseer named Smith died. They found him in his bed and thought he died of drink. George and another slave buried him. Master Briggs came out wearing his dressing gown and said a few words, and afterward they sang a hymn. It was both too early and too late to summon the pastor.

· · ·

Tom is lying in his lovely doghouse, dreaming about life as the first mate on a huge galleon, when someone starts shaking him. It's Ina, waking him up. She tells him to come at once. Tom tumbles outside and is greeted by the first rays of the sun.

Master Joop is standing in front of the doghouse along with George, who is holding Smith's old horse by the reins. "You're going to the fields with the cutters," says Joop. "You're a bomba now and will ride Smith's horse, which is yours as long as you stay at Aron Hill. George, give him the horse."

In a daze Tom looks at the reins that George hands him, saying, "Here you are, Tom."

Joop, already on his way, turns around to give the slave a reproving look. "Bomba O'Connor—remember that, George."

"Yes, Master Joop. Bomba O'Connor. I'll remember."

Before the day was out, Tom had been given the name that he would bear the rest of the time he was at Aron Hill: Tombomba.

After the harvest there was a flurry of activity on the plantation. The mill turned day and night, and whenever the wind failed, they would switch to the horse-driven mill.

George was the plantation's sugar boiler, and an expert at it. It was said that just by biting into one of the canes, he could determine the density of the juice and set the boiling accordingly. That's how he had gotten the nickname Sugar George.

In the boiling-house Sugar George walked around with the sugar ladle and skimmer, because sugar production was a balancing act. He told Tom that the juice from low-lying fields had to have higher heat because it was more watery, and that red soil gave lighter sugar than black soil, because it contained more saltpeter and thus had to be treated with a dose of slaked lime.

George was the master of the boiling-house. He could tell when the warm sugar mash should be poured into cooling trays. Timing was everything. If he did it a few seconds too soon, the juice would crystallize; a few seconds too late, and the sugar would be burned.

Tom loved to watch George at work, admiring his concentration and the respect that, for a brief time, came his way.

As Ina told Tom while they were sitting outside near the gate with Sunday, "All that work in the fields, all that toil with digging and planting and weeding, now depends on George's instincts with the sugar. All of Master Briggs's fortune rests solely on him. Hard to imagine, isn't it?"

"You're proud of him, Ina," laughed Tom.

"Yes," she said quietly, "I'm proud of my George. He's carrying all of us on his broad back. Say good night to Tombomba, Sunday. It's time for a little missy to go home to bed."

If no one was watching, Sunday would give Tom a kiss on the cheek to say good night. Tom knew that a bomba wasn't supposed to be so friendly with the blacks, but it was hard not to like Sunday Morning.

That's what made it even harder when Master Briggs's new seal was to be inaugurated after the harvest. They started with the men's quarters, where the bombas set up a table. On it stood a spirit lamp, oiled paper, and the elegant silver branding iron with the ivory handle. For the occasion, the bombas had armed themselves with loaded shotguns.

The slaves came in, one by one, sat down on a chair, and had the red-hot seal burned onto their left arms. Between the seal and the skin Joop placed a piece of oiled paper. It served no purpose other than to hide the sight of the red-hot iron on bare skin.

Some of the men had to be forced to the table. Some fled in panic when they saw tears on the other men's faces. Some said not a word. Among them was Kanuno, who during the whole process looked directly at Joop without so much as blinking.

The last in line was Sugar George. He nodded to Tom and took off his shirt. Joop heated up the seal and placed the paper in between. George shut his eyes tightly as smoke rose up from the burned flesh.

"Okay, George," said Joop, "it's over now. Let's go get the women. Send the men out."

The trouble didn't start until it was time for the children, who had to be held by their parents. The seal looked enormous on the tiny thin arms, and it sounded as if the children's sobbing would never stop.

The last in line was Ina. Stifling her tears, she stood before Master Joop. "We can't find Sunday, Master Joop. George has looked everywhere."

Joop summoned Tom. "Get on your horse and find her, O'Connor."

Tom didn't need a horse. He knew where Sunday was. With heavy steps he went down to the doghouse. Huddled in the far corner, she looked at him with frightened eyes. "Don't tell them where I am, Tombomba," she whispered.

"Sunday, you have to come out of there."

"No, no, don't tell them where I am, sweet Tombomba, don't tell. I'll give you my pretty stones if you don't tell." She hid her face in her hands.

Tom crawled inside and took her hand. "Sunday," he said, "it's over in a second."

"No, no, please, Tombomba, please."

He grabbed hold of her. "Sunday, I promise you that it won't hurt. It's over quickly."

She looked at him. "Will you hold my hand, Tom?"

Tom looked away. "Your mother is over there, Sunday. Come on, now, do it for me."

She sits down on the chair. She is holding her mother's hand. George has vanished. Tom is standing behind Joop, who rolls up the sleeve of the girl's dress. Sunday's arm is not much wider than the ivory handle on the new seal. The smell of burned flesh is thick and nauseating.

Sunday looks at Tom and tries to smile. She clutches her mother's hand but she keeps her eyes on Tom, who has said that it won't hurt. The branding iron is heated in the spirit lamp until it's red-hot.

Tom glances at the ground, then goes over to Joop. "Is this necessary?" he whispers.

"Necessary? What do you mean?"

"She's so little. Can't it wait until she's older? Dear God, Sunday's not going to run off anywhere, Master Joop."

Joop looks back to where Brüggen and bomba Pierre are standing ready with their shotguns. "Take O'Connor out of here," he says.

But Tom leaves of his own accord. He squats down behind the barracks, holding his hands to his ears. With his eyes he follows a little yellow bird as it takes off from the fence and flies across the stubble fields that seem to burn with red and orange flames.

On the palm of his hand, from his time at the smithy, Tom has a scar the same color.

11　Sarah Briggs

TOM STOOD IN FRONT OF THE MIRROR in the big hall of the main house, wearing breeches, white stockings with yellow silk ribbons, and shoes with square toes. His jacket was red with shiny buttons, and his shirt was white. His hair had been washed, brushed, and gathered at the nape of his neck with a clasp he had borrowed from Ina. In fact, everything he wore was borrowed. And if truth be told, the clothes, the shoes, yes, the entire situation suited him very poorly. He felt constrained and idiotically dressed—he, who had stared wistfully at the fine people in their elegant clothes as they had strutted past him in Port Royal. Now he felt sorry for them. But there was no other way for a taster to look.

Ina had even suggested that the taster should borrow one of Master Briggs's old wigs—a suggestion that nearly paralyzed Tom. Fortunately it was only a joke. Otherwise it was the persevering Fanny who had outfitted him, and it was she who now stood beside him at the mirror.

"Let's hope that Tombomba can live up to his new clothes."

"Hmm, well, there's no telling what a person might accomplish." Tom sighed, looking at his shoes, which were too narrow in the width and too long in the toe.

Ina and Sunday came out of the kitchen. Tom didn't mind that they laughed at him.

"Isn't my betrothed a handsome servant?" Sunday asked her mother.

"I'm a taster," Tom corrected her. "That's something much finer than a servant. You see, I'm supposed to safeguard Master Briggs's health, yes, and the health of all the guests. It could even be said that, without me, the master and mistress might not survive the harvest festivities."

They went into the kitchen and Tom lifted Sunday up onto the table. "A taster, little Sunday, is like a bloodhound. He sniffs, sips, tastes, and drinks, and if he feels the slightest discomfort, the wine is taken away. If he actually falls ill, all of the carafes are dumped into the muck heap. And if it should happen that the taster drops to the floor with a rattling sound, dead as a herring, he will then have the honor of being sliced open by the local barber-surgeon. A more delightful life could not be imagined. I can hardly wait."

Sunday looked in horror at her mother, who took a swipe at Tom. In the meantime Fanny brought in a tiny bottle and sprayed him with it. "To keep the flies away," she said.

There was nothing left to do but wait for the guests to arrive. While they waited, Tom told stories about his days fishing for sharks. He held Sunday on his lap, and while Ina and Fanny prepared the dessert, Tom regaled them with his first encounter.

"Do you really expect anyone to believe that?" groaned Fanny.

"That's up to you," said Tom.

"I believe it," said Sunday.

"What exactly were you planning to do down there in the water?" asked her mother.

"I was going to retrieve the harpoon." Tom started all over again telling the story of the shark that was attracted by the smell of blood and circled the boat until Tom harpooned it.

"Thirty feet long," said Tom, "with forty-eight sharp teeth. The shark's eyes are black and cold. All it has to do is look at you and your blood turns to ice."

"Did you get the harpoon back?" Toto asked.

Tom grimaced. "The third time I was down there I salvaged it. By that time there were seven giant sharks in the process of devouring their dead comrade. But I didn't care; I had to get that harpoon even if it cost me my life. I killed six of them, but the biggest one of all was still left. A monster of a shark, the oldest and most hideous you could imagine. He was famous all over the Caribbean and was known as C. W. Bull. But just as I . . ."

That was as far as Tom got, because suddenly Sarah Briggs was standing in the kitchen, a stern look on her face. She asked if someone would pour her a glass of water. They all jumped up, Fanny apologizing as she shot Tom a warning glance. Ina took out a carafe and a glass of water. In the meantime the mistress disappeared into the parlor.

"That's what I get for listening to someone like you," scolded Fanny. "Get on in there now, you red-haired umba-umba-Tom. And remember to say yes, ma'am, and no, ma'am, and not a word about sharks."

Mrs. Briggs was standing in the middle of the good parlor with her hands clasped under her breasts. She was quite petite, and even though she was wearing her finest gown with pearls and gold jewelry, she looked pale and strangely lifeless.

Tom bowed, the way he had been taught.

"Oh, the bomba, yes." The mistress sat down on a chair and put the back of her hand up to her forehead.

Tom filled the glass with water, which he swiftly tasted before handing it to her.

She stared at him. "What is he doing?"

"I'm tasting it, ma'am," replied Tom. "I'm the taster."

"But what on earth could be wrong with the water from the well, aside from the fact that I wouldn't dream of drinking from a glass you've used?"

"Oh, I beg your pardon." Tom glanced around, and in his confusion he ended up pouring the water back into the carafe before he bowed clumsily and left the parlor, returning with a new glass and a new carafe. "The job of taster is something new for me, Mrs. Briggs," he said, pouring water into the clean glass.

The mistress took two small sips.

"What's your surname, bomba?" She tipped her head back slightly and peered at Tom through two small slits, her eyebrows raised and her lips parted, with the corners of her mouth turned down.

"O'Connor, ma'am. My name is O'Connor."

"Oh, that's right. My husband told me you were Irish." The mistress sighed and murmured something to herself, then gestured with her hand. "Is the boy happy here?"

"Oh, yes, ma'am, I'm quite content."

Mrs. Briggs got up and began walking around the room, straightening the plates and napkins, a task that she quickly abandoned.

"I've even heard that he can read, is that true?"

"It's true, Mrs. Briggs. I can read." Tom smiled and bowed.

"Does he read the Bible?"

"Yes, that too."

Mrs. Briggs brightened up a bit. "Then he must know the story of Jonah and the whale."

"Most certainly."

"Is that right? I'm so pleased. What else does he know?"

"He knows . . ." Tom tugged pensively at his ear. "Yes, he also knows the story of Jonah and the shark." Tom gave the mistress a hopeful smile.

Mrs. Briggs's eyes narrowed as she jutted out her lower lip. She gave him an appraising look and then said, "He may go."

But the next day the house taster was sent for again. Ina went to find him in the doghouse, where he was lying with a damp cloth on his forehead, still feeling dazed after a long evening of many different wines and a delicious French drink with a name he couldn't pronounce. She smiled and said that it looked as if they had gotten him home none too soon.

He got dressed, realizing that it was past time for going out to the fields. But since Joop hadn't come to wake him, it must be all right that he had slept so long.

It turned out that he was now supposed to take the mistress her tea. The tray stood ready in the kitchen.

Fanny scowled at him as he took a long drink of water. Unlike Ina, she had a good memory of Tom's debut as a taster and how, during the second serving of the main course, he had floated around the table, an outright disgrace to Aron Hill.

"A taster is a taster," muttered Tom, throwing water on his face.

"A taster tastes, he doesn't swill."

"I wasn't swilling."

Fanny poked her sharp forefinger at Tom's chest. "He was standing at the piano next to the British lieutenant, gulping port wine straight from the bottle and claiming that he had arrived from Jamaica on the back of a shark, which he only managed to tame by giving it a laxative powder."

"Did I say that?"

Fanny nodded sternly.

"Well then, I suppose it must be true," muttered Tom, rubbing his aching head.

A short time later the unfortunate taster was let into Sarah Briggs's bed-chamber, a dimly lit room with a high ceiling. Tom couldn't figure out what the room smelled of. It seemed like a mixture of chamomile, camphor, ladies' perfume, and dust.

Above the bed hung a painting of Christ on the Cross. The gaunt figure, with eyes turned heavenward, looked terribly tormented, Tom thought. He didn't like looking at him, yet he couldn't help it. Jesus had big oozing sores on his chest, and in Tom's eyes he seemed as battered as Ramón the Pious. From early childhood Tom had heard many stories about Jesus, and he had always imagined a large, powerful man, a real leader with a touch of warrior in him. So it was a surprise to see this weakling who had no more meat on his bones than Bibido. And it was hard to feel any sympathy. Tom thought that if Jesus hadn't died on the Cross, he surely would have died from dysentery. And if the taster had had such a painting over his bed, he never would have slept a wink. The idea of that painting in the doghouse made Tom smile, but he quickly turned serious when he noticed Mrs. Briggs staring at him. She was lying in the big canopy bed, wearing a night-gown and bonnet.

With a weary gesture, she summoned him over. The mistress said she would like him to make a little less noise when he moved about. And in addition, she wanted him to read her a passage from the Book of Psalms.

Tom looked at the Bible that lay on the nightstand.

"He can sit in that chair and hand me my pills and my glass." Mrs. Briggs put two pills in her hand and swallowed them with a gulp of water. "I take them for my health. I suffer from thin blood as well as a melancholy temperament. I bear this burden gladly, aware that God is testing me in order to see whether I am worthy of Him. All of us will be punished in this way, for as it is written: 'At the end of the world there will remain only a single island, and on this island shall live only one person, as witness to a time when humans occupied the Earth, which was lush and fruitful and teeming with life.'"

Tom muttered a few sympathetic words, opened the Bible, and began reading from the beginning of the Book of Psalms.

Mrs. Briggs interrupted him and said to start with Psalm 26.

Tom cleared his throat.

"'Judge me, O Lord,'" he murmured, "'for I have walked in mine integrity: I have trusted also in the Lord: *therefore* I shall not slide.'"

He noticed that it was unfortunately quite a while since he had last used his reading skills. He had to spell his way through the passage but received help from the mistress, who knew the verse by heart.

"'Examine me, O Lord, and prove me; try my reins and my heart.'"

"He can stop there. I myself suffer from kidney disease. I think it's because I'm not doing my utmost. Pain is the Lord's way of testing us, and I struggle with it every day. He can read from Psalm Seventeen."

Tom read a few more psalms, heaving a sigh of relief when he was permitted to leave. But the next day and the day after that he sat there again. The mood between them was now more relaxed, and on the fourth day he was given a cup of tea. After a week of reading, he was also given a biscuit.

He told Sugar George, "Before the month is over I'll be sitting at the dinner table, saying grace along with Mr. Briggs—not bad for a barefoot boy who sleeps in a doghouse."

George found it amusing, and his wife did too. Their sorrow after the cruel branding had been forgotten. As George said, "Mr. Briggs did it with good intentions. And little Sunday doesn't remember anymore how much it hurt."

Tom was not entirely convinced of this. Whenever he looked at Sunday, she still seemed the same happy girl, quick to laughter and quick to tears. But something was gone now, as when a butterfly lands on your finger and then flies off—a carefree feeling that had disappeared with the wind.

Tom was never invited to the dinner table, but the tea and cakes were something he looked forward to.

"'O Lord, rebuke me not in thy wrath: neither chasten me in thy hot displeasure. For thine arrows stick fast in me, and thy hand presseth me sore. There is no soundness in my flesh because of thine anger; neither is there any rest in my bones because of my sin. For mine iniquities are gone over mine head: as a heavy burden they are too heavy for me.'"

Tom sighed and shut the thick book.

The mistress was in bed with her eyes closed. Her hands were folded on top of the covers.

Tom glanced out at the courtyard, where Miss Missy was playing with Sunday, who was alternately pretending to be a doll and a maid. Miss Missy was sitting on a chair. The black girl was in the process of pinning up the young miss's fair locks, but had to keep stopping to fan her.

From above the mistress's bed, Christ gazed down on the taster. If Tom looked closely, the crucified Savior seemed to be staring straight at him. He had to lower his eyes. "If truth be told," he muttered, casting a glance at the painting, "I understand very little of what I'm reading."

Sarah Briggs opened her eyes. "I can hear that from the way you read, Tombomba. But you're not here for the sake of enjoyment. You're here for the sake of your education. My husband is exceedingly pleased with you. Mr. Briggs would like the standards among our bombas to be improved, and with time the job will be yours, so it's good to know that the boy is familiar with his Bible verses. But since you ask, I won't keep from you the wisdom contained in that text."

Mrs. Briggs smoothed out the covers. "You see, I'm lying here, forever ill and chained to my bed, because it is God's punishment. Sinners, both great and small, are not struck in this way by chance, but as a result of God's will."

Tom nodded sympathetically, studying Miss Missy, who had now begun to pull Sunday around like a dog. His thoughts drifted back to a night when he had been on his knees scrubbing the floor of Señor López's inn, as he had done so often. That evening he had received an uninvited guest, to whom he had served filthy water and a little wine from the dregs cask.

"Is he sitting there asleep?"

"No, no, not at all," said Tom. "I'm sitting here thinking." He remembered one statement in particular that had been uttered on that night.

"Is that so? What is he thinking about?"

Tom cleared his throat. "Does Mrs. Briggs know of Hippocrates?"

Sarah Briggs sat up with a peremptory expression on her face. "Is that one of the blacks?"

"I don't think so, ma'am. I believe he's a philosopher."

"Philosopher? Good gracious. Does Tombomba know a philosopher?"

Tom shrugged his shoulders. "Back home," he said casually, "we often said, 'Hail Hippocrates the Wise, for superstition is still the best friend of disease. God's will has nothing to do with fever, and the plague is something that people get from rats.'"

After that outburst, Mrs. Briggs turned over in bed and lay there for a long time with her back to Tom until, with a wave of her hand, she dismissed him from her room.

The following day he was not summoned to her bedchamber but was sent out to the fields to hunt rats with two other overseers. That evening as Tom sat on a stool in the kitchen eating leftovers, Fanny told him that there would be no more playing the cavalier. He had tasted his last biscuit.

"Did Tombomba misbehave?" asked Sunday.

Fanny sighed. "He probably just told the story about the laxative powder."

"In a sense, that's right," Tom agreed, and headed off to the doghouse.

But the next day he was summoned once again. To Tom's surprise, the mistress was sitting in the upholstered armchair, staring straight ahead, when he tiptoed in with the tea. She was fully dressed, and the drapes had been pulled open.

Tom let his glance slide over the crucified Savior, who also seemed to be feeling better. Even though it was impossible, he seemed to be glancing at the tray of biscuits.

"What is the boy looking at?" asked Mrs. Briggs.

"At Jesus, Mrs. Briggs."

The mistress raised her eyebrows and pursed her lips. "That painting is there as a reminder," she said. "Does it move you?"

Tom took a deep breath, uncertain how much paintings could actually move him, but convinced that he and Jesus could share an interest in biscuits. "Yes," he said, "it moves me a great deal."

"Why does it move you?" Mrs. Briggs gave Tom a stern look.

"I think it's because I once knew a man in the same condition."

The mistress's mouth fell open. "Oh, do spare me such nonsense," she groaned. "Who was this man?"

"His name was Ramón the Pious, Mrs. Briggs."

The mistress nibbled at a biscuit. "Quite a lovely name. But people who acquire such nicknames are usually just the opposite."

Tom nodded. "Mrs. Briggs is right about that. But he knew some amusing tricks."

"Is that so? What kind of tricks, if I might ask?"

"He could whistle with three biscuits in his mouth," replied Tom, glancing at the Christ figure. "I learned that trick myself," he added.

Mrs. Briggs rolled her eyes. "If the boy would like a biscuit, he should come right out and say so."

Tom apologized and took a biscuit.

"In England . . ." began Mrs. Briggs and stopped abruptly.

Tom looked at her, wondering whether she wanted him to finish her sentence.

The mistress leaned back with a forlorn expression. "In England, where I was born . . . I think about my native country every single day. It's my birthplace that I envision as I fall asleep, and it's the first thing I see when I open my eyes: England. That's where my ancestors come from, all the way back to the peasant rebellion, when we lost all our holdings. Just imagine, half the population of England perished during the plague. But today England is the greatest nation in the world. You must know that."

"I do, ma'am."

"A fabulous country." The mistress sighed.

"Quite fabulous," repeated the taster, eyeing the biscuits.

"London is an incomparable city, Tombomba, an utterly glorious city. Everything comes from London. As a young girl I often went to the theater. What drama, what costumes, and above all, what poetry." Sarah Briggs closed her eyes and, enraptured, whispered, " 'Now the dawn smiles at the gloomy night. / On morning clouds appear bands of light / and patchy darkness staggers aside / the sun chariot's torches swing wide.' "

She looked at Tom. "I want you to memorize these lines. Not for the meaning, but in order to feel the music of the words. Do you remember the first line?"

"Yes, ma'am. 'London is an incomparable city.' "

"Stop, you little fool. Try again. 'Now the dawn smiles at the gloomy night.' "

Tom repeated the line and the ones following, over and over again until he knew them by heart.

"Can you feel the words, Tom?"

"Yes, I can feel them, ma'am."

Mrs. Briggs looked away and began waving her hand, as if batting at a fly. "He doesn't feel a thing, absolutely nothing. Come closer."

Tom approached her chair. Sarah Briggs gave him a piercing look, as if she were searching for something. "When you walk along the streets of London," she whispered, "you're walking in the center of the world. Did you know that?"

"Yes, ma'am, I knew that."

The mistress drummed her fingertips on the table. "How can he know that if he's never been to London?"

"It must be the same with London as with the sun, Mrs. Briggs."

Mrs. Briggs frowned. "What on earth does he mean by that?"

Tom cleared his throat and tried to remember what the toothless old man had said when Tom sought him out in the harbor district of Port Royal. "Well, you see, ma'am, first off I have to ask you: where is a man's seed located?"

Silence fell in the stuffy room.

"What is he sitting there saying?" gasped the mistress.

"I'm going to tell you about Copernicus, ma'am. He was from Poland and very wise. He said of the sun that it sits in the middle of the universe. Just like the pit inside a peach or a seed inside an apple. Sometimes I dream that I have wings. Under the barren light of the moon, I have flown all around the globe like an albatross, and I've watched the Earth roll past beneath me and seen so many different faces, white, black, yellow, olive-colored. Some with hats, others with turbans. And I've seen cities with bell towers, some pointed, some round. And I've seen churches with crosses and churches with crescent moons, palaces made of porcelain with rooftops of gold, until I returned home, my feet dry, ready once again to watch the sun come up, even though it hadn't budged even the breadth of a finger. Life is an endless dancing in place, Sarah Briggs, and yet we grow old, lose our teeth and our hair, our hearing and our eyesight. Only the heavenly bodies are eternal, and among them the sun is the greatest of all."

Tom looked at Mrs. Briggs and Mrs. Briggs looked at Tom. At last she said, "Would he be kind enough to leave?"

Tom bowed and left the bedchamber, only to be called back ten minutes later. If the mistress previously had had a slight flush to her cheeks, she was now as crimson as a cockscomb. She was sitting up in bed. In the painting a spark of life had appeared in the crucified Savior's eyes, which gazed down at Tom with a touch of camaraderie.

"I've heard that sort of thing before," snorted Mrs. Briggs, "but I never thought I'd hear it in my own home."

"Copernicus . . ." began Tom.

"Is a heretic. And don't you dare utter his name again. Is that understood, Tombomba?"

"Yes, ma'am."

The mistress leaned forward and looked at Tom with a gentler expression. "I'm merely concerned about you. Where did you hear things like that?"

"I think it was at the harbor in Port Royal."

Mrs. Briggs crossed herself and pulled the covers closer. "I prefer that we change the subject."

"As do I, ma'am."

Mrs. Briggs gave her taster a sharp glance, then shifted her gaze in fright before she looked at him again, this time with a worried expression. "Does he believe in such things?"

"Absolutely not, ma'am."

"Then what does he believe in?"

"In God, ma'am."

Sarah Briggs snorted and pursed her lips. "Well, if that's what he says, I suppose one has to take him at his word. But let's see if he knows his catechism."

Tom smiled and nodded eagerly, having no clue what the word *catechism* might mean.

"I suppose at least we're in agreement about who created the Earth," stated Mrs. Briggs.

"In full agreement, ma'am. It was God."

"I assume that includes the sun, Tom O'Connor."

"Absolutely, ma'am. The sun and the Earth and the plants and the fish and the sea and the trade winds that howl south of the Tropic of Cancer."

Sarah Briggs raised her hand. "He can keep all that to himself." She narrowed her eyes. "But then who created Satan, Tom? Who created the great, vast darkness?"

"The green pelican, ma'am."

Mrs. Briggs frowned. "What did he say? The green pelican?"

"Yes, ma'am. The pelican coaxed the night up from the river, because once upon a time there was only daylight and no sleep. Then out of the darkness came the spotted jaguar, and the first thing the fierce beast did was to devour the green pelican. Have you ever seen a green pelican, Mrs. Briggs?"

"No, dear God, I never have." Sarah Briggs turned her face away.

"There you have it then—the story must be true."

"Enough of that! It wasn't primitive animals that we were going to talk about. But rather this . . . this Hippocrates, whom your family apparently worshiped like an idol."

Tom said that was not exactly how he would have described it.

"Then what kind of thing is that to say: Hail Hippocrates? Is everyone in your family a heretic?"

"No, no, not at all. In fact, my mother is quite biblical."

"But the moral to be drawn from the words of this Hippocrates seems to be that God's will has nothing to do with illness, and that the plague is something people get from rats?"

"Exactly. The plague comes from that disgusting animal."

"Enough of that! Do I have to sit here in my own bedchamber and hear about rats? If that's the only kind of stories he has to offer, I think it would be best for him to go outside to the sugarcane."

Tom bowed, grateful to be once again hunting rats, although he would miss the tea and Jesus and the warm cakes. But as he was slinking toward the door, the mistress stopped him. "I hear from Fanny that your mother is tyrannized by a Spaniard."

Tom nodded vigorously. "That is correct, Mrs. Briggs, one of the most Spanish of men you could imagine."

"Go on!"

"Well, he was terribly miserly and cruel and anything but God-fearing."

"A hypocrite, I would imagine."

"Of the worst kind," said Tom. "I've even seen him scratch his back with a crucifix and put the Holy Scriptures under a bedpost to level out a crooked bed. And when we mentioned these blasphemies, he beat us with a leather strap, just because we were of British heritage."

Sarah Briggs gave Tom a suspicious look. "He's not just trying to wheedle his way into my good graces, is he?"

"Wheedle? No, not in the least."

"He looks to me like a lad with much too wild an imagination."

Tom smiled and shook his head. "When it comes to money and wild imagination, Mrs. Briggs, I have equally small amounts of both."

Sarah Briggs narrowed her eyes, folded her arms under her breasts, and said, "I want to hear about the powder."

"The powder, ma'am?"

"Precisely, the powder. The one that your mother gave to the hypocritical Spaniard. The one that kept him in . . . you know . . . for six weeks."

"Oh, that." Tom cast an eye at the crucified Savior, who was smiling in anticipation.

"Well, it was an enormous scandal, of course. Oh, yes, yes, it certainly was. The story goes like this: Señor López was under the impression that the powder was an elixir that would give him back his youth. Yes, you may well smile, but nevertheless the innkeeper demanded that we put it in his food. Allow me to start from the beginning. You see, my sister, Feodora Dolores Vasgues . . ."

And thus the story about the unfortunate powder reached all the way to the bedchamber of Mrs. Briggs of Aron Hill. The following week when the mistress, quite contrary to custom, was out for a stroll around the plantation, she met Tom and raised her parasol in greeting.

"Good afternoon, Mrs. Briggs," said Tom, standing up in his stirrups.

"Hail Hippocrates," was the mistress's reply.

12 Sunday Morning

JOOP HAD COME HOME from town with three new slaves, all of them men. They waited in the courtyard in the scorching sun, the chains still around their necks. All three looked terrified. They wore only loincloths and their ankles bore the fresh marks of shackles. One of them was having such trouble with the sunlight that Tom realized they must have come straight from the harbor after spending months in a dark cargo hold.

Mr. Briggs uttered greetings right and left and clapped his hands, praising the glorious day. He didn't look directly at the slaves, but it sounded as if he were bidding them welcome. Afterward he conferred with Joop, presumably about the price.

Tom stood near the corner of the house along with Sugar George, following everything from a distance. Joop told the slaves to open their mouths. Mr. Briggs gave their teeth a brief inspection and settled for giving Joop a pat on the back, as if to say that he was satisfied with the deal.

The men were nothing but skin and bones and not much older than Tom. He cast a glance at George, who kept on saying that those three were lucky fellows because Aron Hill was known as one of the best plantations when it came to the treatment of its slaves.

Joop read aloud from the rule book. It was hard to say how much the new slaves understood, but they did react when Joop showed them his whip and pointed his finger to let them know who was in charge on the plantation.

By that time Mr. Briggs had disappeared inside the house.

There was always a certain amount of curiosity when new slaves arrived, not only from the other blacks, but also from the bombas and the house slaves, who all wanted to have a look at the newcomers. But this time the mood was marred by the fact that two male slaves had recently been lost.

Tom had no idea what had happened, but Sugar George told him that they had died of the disease called consumption. For some reason they had refused to eat, and one day out in the field they collapsed and died within a few hours of each other.

"How strange that it should happen at the same time," said Tom.

"They were brothers," replied George.

"Is that supposed to be an explanation?"

"Maybe not for you, Tombomba, but I knew those two men. They arrived three years ago, and they were inseparable. We knew they would kill themselves if we tried to keep them apart. And when the older one suddenly took sick with consumption, his brother refused to eat."

When slaves died, they were buried by the other slaves. A burial ground of sorts had been laid out behind the slave quarters, where the blacks had their garden plots. Here they could grow the vegetables and herbs that constituted their daily meals. Some of the house slaves and the oldest of the field slaves also kept a chicken or two in a special enclosure. Sugar George and Ina even had their own little pen with a few hens, a rooster, and a little black pig.

The rest of the slaves had to make do with the plots of ground they had been assigned. They would come home exhausted from their work in the fields and immediately set about weeding out the gardens that kept them alive.

After the three new men had left with the bombas, Tom followed George down to the quarters of the house slaves.

"Master Joop keeps a keen eye on the blacks every time we bury someone," George explained. "There have been cases of witchcraft and that sort of thing, and we don't want anything like that here at Aron Hill."

"Witchcraft?"

George nodded and told Tom that the feet of chickens had been found chopped off and other such things that he didn't like to talk about. It scared his wife, and there was something generally unpleasant about all that.

The next day, when Tom was with Joop in the alehouse, he learned more. The low-ceilinged room was crammed with seamen who were shouting and screaming and drinking until they were so far gone they had to be carried out.

"How pathetic," said the overseer, watching the crowd with his usual languid expression.

Tom had never seen Joop in a drunken state. The other bombas regularly drank too much, and several of them had had trouble staying in the saddle when they were out in the fields. Tom had seen the slaves exchange glances whenever a bomba started swaying back and forth. It was an ominous sight—twenty blacks standing there, each holding a long hoe, guarded only by a dead-drunk bomba. The temptation must have been tantalizing.

On one occasion, when bomba Pierre fell off his horse and big Kanuno helped him up, Tom saw the other slaves start muttering, only to be rebuked at once by Kanuno. He clearly had control of them, and he would also have control if someday there was a revolt. Bomba Pierre was so furious about having to be helped back onto his horse that he gave Kanuno a taste of his whip after they returned home. He claimed that the whole incident was Kanuno's fault—a story that Master Joop found no reason to doubt, even when Tom told him that the slave had done nothing more than put Pierre back in his saddle.

The comment had nearly cost Tom his job.

"You never speak against another bomba when the blacks are within earshot," snapped Joop. "You never speak against a white man. Is that understood?"

"It's understood, Master Joop. But the truth is . . ."

"The truth. I'll show you the truth. It's something you can touch and hold in your hand, and it's lying right there!" The Dutchman pointed to the whip on the table. "All the rest you can forget. There's so much brewing among the slaves that the smallest spark could ignite a bonfire. And I wouldn't want to be in your shoes if you're the one who lights the spark."

At the inn Joop was in the same frame of mind, although he was no longer angry with Tom. On the contrary. "We have to be alert," he said, sipping his beer. "Whenever one of them dies, it starts up again. There's a lot of witchcraft among them, and Kanuno takes the lead with all that. Sometimes they get so agitated they pass out; I've warned Mr. Briggs about it. A plantation may be struck by plague, fever, or dysentery, and that can be bad enough, but when the blacks get started with their witchcraft, a white man has to be on his guard."

"Witchcraft," said Tom. "Isn't that heresy?"

"Call it whatever you like. They have no god, at least not a god like ours. Don't misunderstand me, I'm not a churchgoing man myself, but I know the white God, and that's not who they worship. It's more like the Devil. I've heard stories about slaves who practiced so much witchcraft that it had an effect on their owners, who started suffering from aches, boils, and other illnesses. Whenever one of them dies, the others assume the strength from his soul, and our friend Kanuno is full of many souls. He's so stuffed with rage that he's about to burst. I can see it in him; he radiates hatred. He hasn't said a word since harvesttime. And the others obey his slightest wink."

"Why doesn't Mr. Briggs sell him, Master Joop?"

Joop van den Arle smiled and found a splinter he could use to clean his teeth. "I'll tell you why. If we sell Kanuno, it would be regarded as weakness. There's not a single slave at Aron Hill who doesn't know what I think of Kanuno. They also know what he's planning. There's even talk about him on the neighboring plantations, where he's worshiped like a god. Kanuno is like a chieftain to them. Their sole dream is that he will be the one to burn everything down, kill all the white bombas, and set the blacks free. You and me, Tombomba, you and me. Each of us dangling by his own rope from the nearest olive tree. The blacks call it white fruit."

Joop sighed and stretched contentedly. "That's the last thing Kanuno sees when he shuts his eyes, and the first thing he wakes up to at dawn. I don't think he can even look at us without seeing nooses around our necks. That's not the sort of man you sell; if you do, you'll make him a martyr. I don't want to see him on the neighbor's coffee plantation or sell him to the Portuguese in Port Royal. Kanuno's kind has only one dream, and that is to come back to Aron Hill and string up all the whites. He has to be broken, not sold. I know that Frans Brüggen thinks we ought to take out a good solid rope and be done with it. But his brain has been addled by too much rum. If I gave him permission to hang Kanuno, we'd have the whole pack at our throats. They'd come in the night with hoes and knives. Oh yes, they've got knives, little bomba. You may not see them, but they do have them. Keep them hidden in the ground, where they're ready for use. And then the gods only know what would become of Master Briggs's plantation. There are only eight of us bombas, and sometimes four out of the eight are so drunk that they can't even find their mouths with their tankards. So we're not going to string Kanuno up without good cause. Everyone has to see that it's justified."

Master Joop concentrated on cleaning his teeth, then suddenly grabbed Tom by the wrist and looked at him with a serious expression. "Are you trustworthy, O'Connor?"

"Yes, of course I'm trustworthy."

"An Irishman?" Joop shook his head. "Then the world must have come to an end." He leaned back and lit his white clay pipe. "But I hope you are, for your own sake as well."

"Master Joop can trust me."

The other man's pink eyes came closer. He was puffing hard on his pipe, and for a moment his white face disappeared in clouds of smoke. "Can you also be trusted when things get hot? You who have fire in your hair? I've seen how much you whisper together, you and Sugar George. I know that you eat all your meals with him and Ina."

"But George and Ina are different."

"There's no such thing as different." Joop leaned back. "They're blacks, aren't they?"

Tom looked away.

"The problem," muttered Joop, "the problem is that I can't trust George anymore. There was a time when he was just as faithful as JayJay, but these days George has changed. Instead of being dependable, he's merely polite, and there's a devil of a difference. When the time comes that we have to break Kanuno, we need to know how things stand with George. Many of the older slaves listen to George and look up to him. There isn't another man who knows as much about boiling sugar as he does. I've seen it before—it's a strange phenomenon. Certain house slaves start thinking that their skin can be as white as ours, but so far that's never happened, not as far as I know. Do you know of any blacks that have become white?"

Tom looked down at the table and shook his head.

Joop tipped Tom's face up and looked him straight in the eye. "You should know that I actually do trust you, O'Connor," he said. "Of all my bombas, you're the one I trust most. You and I are cut from the same cloth, you see. Oh yes, we are. We prefer things to run smoothly, but we won't stand for any trouble. And we don't hesitate when action is needed. Mr. and Mrs. Briggs also have certain expectations regarding Tombomba. Master has even talked to me about the plans he has for the likable boy with the many talents. The boy who rides better than anyone else, who can shoe horses, repair mills, and helps out at the fancy parties. He's even good at telling stories. And now the red-haired bomba has won entry to the mistress's bedchamber. Soon you'll be even whiter than I am, Tom."

Joop leaned back with a sly smile. "I wonder what it is that makes him so popular? What the devil is it about this Irish boy that makes people dance to his pipe? That charms Mr. Briggs into putting him on display in a red jacket at the fancy gatherings? I know what it is. You see, George heard from Ina, who heard from Fanny, who had it from the mistress's own lips. We like Tombomba, the mistress says, because he's untainted."

Master Joop emptied his glass and curled his lips back, patting his stomach. He made a move to get up, then all of a sudden leaned across the table. "Are you untainted, Tombomba? Are you really purer of heart than the rest of us?"

Tom did not reply. His thoughts went to his conversations with the green gecko.

Joop spat on the floor, yawned lazily, and shook his head. "You're not a whit better than me," he sighed. "Your eyes give you away, Tombomba. Nobody can hide anything from Joop, and I know you've been keeping your eye on Frans when you're out in the fields. You watch him, threaten him, and play with your knife. But you need to stop all that. Do you understand what I'm saying? You need to leave Brüggen alone. His time is past, anyway. Liquor has taken him over, and he won't last out the year. Why don't you say anything, Tom?"

"Because it's a matter between Brüggen and me," replied Tom.

Joop shaped his lips into a soundless laugh. "And he's supposed to be O'Connor the untainted? You make me laugh. And cry. Use your head, Tom. Leave Frans alone. He's not worth it. You have much bigger plans. Why waste them on a drunkard?"

Joop sighed and started to stand up, then changed his mind. "Do you know how I took care of a black who was on the verge of starting a revolt?

I'll tell you, you untainted Irishman. I sent him to town with one of my bombas. While he was gone, we discovered a thick plume of smoke at the far end of the fields. Anyone could see that the fire had been set. But before it destroyed everything, we managed to put it out. And when my bomba came back from town, he told us that the slave he had taken along had run off. And that the black had hidden among the sugarcane at the very spot where the fire had started."

Joop scraped out his pipe. "We found him that evening and strung him up, as regulations require. That's what you do, Tombomba. If you're smart."

During the next few days Tom stared out over the endless fields, looking for signs of smoke. He was just waiting for Frans Brüggen to order Kanuno to go to town with him, but nothing happened. Yet a peculiar sense of uneasiness remained, as happens out on the water when the wind suddenly dies down on orders from a hurricane.

What lay in wait was a hurricane so strong that it threatened to topple Aron Hill.

The dead had been buried and the new slaves put in place.

Each morning they all lined up according to the rules and each sundown they came back home. But the usual muttering in the ranks, not to mention the singing in the fields, had given way to an oppressive silence. After this situation had gone on for nearly a week, Master Joop took away the rum from his overseers, but that only made matters worse. Now they lashed out at the slightest infraction.

The ominous mood had even made its way into the kitchen, where the usually good-humored Ina walked around in silence. Fanny smoothed down her apron and clasped her hands, visibly nervous about what was brewing. "It's that Kanuno," she scolded. "He's turning all their heads."

But Ina said nothing.

Tom no longer talked to George, for fear the slave might say too much. Only Miss Missy and little Sunday kept on playing as usual.

Tom is standing in Mr. Briggs's office, a beautiful room with tall bookcases, polished furniture, and a sideboard with bottles on top. On the desk is a large model that Briggs is putting together. He has spent months carving wood for the veneer and cutting up colored paper to look like tiles. He has worked meticulously and patiently, and now he's very close to realizing his dream of building a faithful replica of Saint Paul's Cathedral in London. The model measures half the height of a man, and there's not much left to do before it's finished.

Mr. Briggs tells Tom that he has entered the most exciting phase of the building process, what's known as the buttressing. "You see, Tombomba, the whole thing has to be glued together, but I've been waiting until the last minute to join all the individual elements so I can be sure that everything fits before applying the glue. We have to proceed cautiously, so that Saint Paul's won't come to any harm." The little man rubs his fingers together and smiles at Tom, who nods, suitably impressed.

"I'm thinking," Master Briggs lowers his voice to a whisper as he kneels down, "I'm thinking that if our Lord God had a home, He would live at Saint Paul's. Where else would he live?"

Tom can see half of the man's face through the tall windows of the model.

"I've built the church to precise proportions. All the measurements have then been divided by . . ."

That's as far as Mr. Briggs gets. He is interrupted by a shrill scream. It turns into a loud howling that cuts right through the main building.

Tom glances at once toward the door, realizing that the sound is coming closer and closer.

A second later the door is flung open by the shrieking Miss Missy, who throws herself across her father's desk, causing the dome and the back part of Saint Paul's to collapse like a house of cards.

Half an hour later Miss Missy, Ina, Fanny, Master Briggs, and Sugar George were in the office, where Tom had taken up a position near the door. At first he focused most of his attention on the catastrophe with the model. His concern was shared by Master Briggs, who was close to tears.

In the meantime his daughter was screaming as if she had been jabbed with a red-hot iron. Fanny tried to calm her, but it was completely impossible, though there was nothing visible on the girl's clothing or body. But little by little, as Miss Missy regained enough of her voice, half-stifled by sobs and bitterness, to tell her father what had happened, only one name was mentioned. She pointed to the garden and whispered, "Sunday hit me with the reins."

It turned out that a welt was actually appearing on the girl's cheek, a long reddish stripe from her temple to her chin. By the time it had fully emerged, Ina and George had left the office, and Fanny had managed to carry the sobbing Miss Missy to her room. Only Tom and Master Briggs remained. The latter sank onto a chair with a dull expression in his eyes.

Tom slowly went over to him. "Master Briggs," he said cautiously, "if there's anything I can do . . ."

The plantation owner looked up at him with tears in his eyes. "Would you please go get Joop," he whispered.

In the next twenty-four hours a great deal happened, most of it without Tom's knowledge. He had been ordered out to the fields to relieve bomba Brüggen, and by the time he rode back to the main building in the evening, calm had been restored. At least temporarily. Miss Missy had been examined by a doctor, who concluded that the welt was not serious and would disappear over the course of a few days. The problem was Saint Paul's Cathedral, as well as the matter of a black child striking a white.

The story was familiar enough. The girls had been playing dog-on-a-leash, and Sunday had been the dog, but maybe she had grown bored with the game. At any rate, she had taken the strap off her neck. And when Miss Missy had ordered her to put it back on, Sunday had swung the leather rein and struck Miss Missy in the face. Now Sunday was no longer living in the hut with her parents, but in one of the barracks belonging to the bombas.

Joop had been in to see Mr. Briggs, and when the overseer came out of the main building, he summoned Tom.

They're sitting in Joop's house, late at night. Joop has put on his finest clothes. His boots are shiny, and his shirt is a dazzling white. He fastens his belt and checks his pistols.

"Now it's a matter of keeping the powder dry, Tom O'Connor."

"Is Master Joop going to town?"

"Yes, I'm going to town at dawn. I think you should come along with me. Put on some other clothes. It's only three hours until daybreak. We're going to the slave market."

"Are we going to buy more slaves, Master Joop?"

The Dutchman fills his pipe. "Buy? No, we're going to sell. When someone tears down half of Saint Paul's Cathedral, they have to pay for it."

Tom smiles uncertainly. "I don't think I understand."

"Understand?" grumbles Joop. "There's nothing to understand. She's going to be sold tomorrow. It's as simple as that."

"Who's going to be sold?" whispers Tom, feeling the hair standing up on his arms.

Joop opens the door. "Sunday is."

In his dream everything is colored green—green like the ocean, when you sail out far enough. The light is at once clearer and yet more hazy, and the sounds seem disquieting if you're not used to them.

Overhead the sky is crab-green, and the seafloor is swarming with people who are all talking at once. There are whites and blacks, bombas, slave dealers, first officers, boatswains, sailors, plantation owners, and soldiers in blue uniforms. It's swarming with animals: sheep, cows, horses, parrots, cockatoos, hooded birds of prey, and chickens in a cage. But before the dream takes him to the harbor district of Port Royal, it starts in the courtyard at daybreak. Tom is glad he's at the bottom of the ocean so he can't hear Ina's scream as they saddle up. He's glad the water is so murky that he can't make out Sugar George's face. The big Negro is on his knees, but fortunately Tom can't see his expression. All of the other bombas are outside, even though it's still so early. They have their flintlocks ready with the fuses lit. The rest of the slaves have been locked indoors. Bomba Brüggen is holding on to Sunday Morning, whose hands are tied behind her back. She is sitting on the small gelding, looking in terror from her mother to Tom and back again. But since this is happening underwater, her sobs cannot be heard. Soon her tears will be swallowed up by the all-consuming ocean.

In Port Royal the sun has come up and the auction has started.

Tom is sitting on his horse, following the sale. People are shouting and screaming, gesticulating and settling accounts. Some are trading, others selling, and even more are buying. Tom looks at a fat man and his even fatter bomba, who is feeling Sunday's arms and legs. Her teeth are also inspected, but as far as Tom knows, Sunday has healthy teeth.

Joop van den Arle is standing with his back turned, as if he has no part in all of it. But he accepts a money pouch and then walks over to his horse, which is next to Tom's.

The water is now beginning to heave violently, and the image of Sunday Morning vanishes into the ocean. The marketplace is cleared and everything is whirled away—the people and the animals, slaves and merchants, horse-drawn carts, pigs, cattle, and sheep.

Only God's night-blue sky remains above the green surface of the water, where the full moon shines a blue shaft down to the ocean—an oblique column uniting heaven and sea.

Inside the shaft a boy is swimming with long stubborn strokes. He is searching for the finest of all the wreckage, meaning the sun, which each day disappears into the sea.

13 Ina

THE RAT SAT AMONG THE YELLOW CANES, grooming itself. It was a large specimen, almost the size of a cat, old without being decrepit, and so fat that it must have lived a good life. Of all the animals, Tom hated rats the most, and the pleasure of killing them was something he had acquired at his mother's breast. He knew that only clever rats grow old, and that old rats are dangerous. Cats had nine lives, rats only one, but theirs lasted ten times as long.

Tom knew not to be fooled by a rat's appearance. Nothing in the world could look as wretched as a rat. If a rat could talk, it would be the world's best storyteller, capable of recounting the most gruesome narratives. Whether death by fire, shipwreck, or mutiny, afterward there was always a little furry witness with a long naked tail.

That's the way it is with rats, thought Tom, sneaking closer. Everyone knows that rats can't talk, but their history can be read in their eyes. And it's just as lengthy as the history of humankind. We've wandered together, men and rats, each with the thought of annihilating the other. So far the outcome hasn't been determined. When humans conquered the oceans and traveled to new worlds, it was always done with a blind passenger sitting in the hold among the timbers.

Their teeth are yellow, for in their bite resides the plague.

He has drawn his dagger but hesitates to move, aware that the slightest motion might give him away. He has been watching the rat for half an hour, both repelled and fascinated, and now he's sitting with the tip of his knife between the thumb and forefinger of his left hand, ready, tensed. He holds his breath, weighing how far he dares cock his arm back without revealing his presence.

The moon is bright over Aron Hill. The last few nights he has been out hunting, and even though luck hasn't been with him every time, he has knocked off five rodents. Sleep is impossible. The doghouse feels stuffy and the heat is oppressive.

In the daytime he rides around among the sugarcane, issuing commands to the blacks, who do as they always do, working in their own rhythm, ignoring him and turning their backs when they drink their sugar water.

All of the bombas are out in the fields, even Joop van den Arle, who keeps on changing the work teams.

"Stick with me, O'Connor," says the Dutchman, "and see about getting some sleep. You look terrible."

But Tom can't sleep.

He no longer goes to the kitchen, and he avoids George, who does his work and tends to his wife, now bedridden. Tom doesn't know what's wrong with Ina, but he supposes it's not serious, since no one has sent for the doctor. When Ina does leave her bed, it's to help Fanny. They don't speak to each other. And when the work is done, Ina goes back to her cabin and lies down with her face to the wall.

"Ina will get better," says Fanny, but Tom has seen Ina walking around at night. Like a blue ghost she wanders back and forth along the rutted road until George brings her inside.

In the afternoon Tom sits with Mrs. Briggs, who regales him with accounts of her perpetual illness, her righteous God, her fiercely missed parents, and her happy childhood. By this time Tom can reel off quite a few poems. He likes to recite them to the dead rats when he trudges home from the fields.

> *She sparkles brighter than all torchlight,*
> *Like a gem on the cheek of the night,*
> *A jewel in an African's ear,*
> *Far too lovely, too noble, too dear.*
> *She outshines others, even her foes,*
> *Like a white dove in a flock of crows.*

Miss Missy has started seeking Tom's company whenever she's released from the drudgery of her lessons and allowed outside. She hands out almond cakes, which Tom devours. One day she says that she wants to wash his hair. Tom has no wish to have his hair washed, but when Miss Missy wants something there's no denying her.

He is sitting on a chair outside the kitchen. At the washstand is Miss Missy, wearing an apron and with her sleeves rolled up. His hair has to be washed many times. Over and over, because it must be clean. "But at least he doesn't have lice," says the girl.

In the meantime Tom watches Sugar George, who is walking past the corner of the house. Maybe it's his wife's illness, or maybe George has hurt his back hauling things, but at any rate he is walking differently. And when he catches sight of Tom, who is sitting with Miss Missy's comb in his hair, he smiles in an unfamiliar way and nods to himself. Sugar George has a different smile now. It exposes his gums and makes his nostrils flare. He looks strange, but if anyone asks him what he's laughing at, he gives no answer. Fanny says that Tom should leave George alone, and Tom thinks that as matters now stand, she is right.

Two weeks have passed. Two weeks since George and Ina watched Sunday disappear down the rutted road. Two weeks, ten almond cakes, and five dead rats.

Miss Missy could fuss with Tom's hair for hours, but at some point Fanny says, "That's enough." A clasp is put in Tom's wet hair and he stands up and leaves.

"He doesn't have to say thank you," yells Miss Missy.

"And he most certainly won't."

She comes after him at once, catching up with him in the garden with the decorative swing. "What was that he said?"

"He said thank you for the hair wash, Miss Missy."

"Oh, so that's what I heard."

They measure each other with their glances. Suddenly she puts her hand on his cheek. Lets her fingers slide around his ear. Tom narrows his eyes and watches her. Her expression is obstinate and reproving. As if she wants to say, I can do whatever I like. Her hand is on its way around his chin, but when it reaches the other cheek she seizes hold of it and pinches him. At first gently, then harder, and when he doesn't react, she squeezes even more.

Miss Missy smiles. "He's not complaining. He's making himself hard. But he has a mark now. I'm sorry about that. Let me hear some poetry."

"This is normally just for rats." Tom spits. "Though it's always possible to make an exception. But I'm only going to recite one line."

"Go ahead then," growls the girl.

Tom looks at her. "He who laughs at scars can no wounds recall."

Miss Missy gives him a disappointed look. "Is that supposed to be poetry? Is that supposed to be beautiful? Say it again!"

Tom shrugs his shoulders and repeats the line.

"Tell me more, Tombomba."

"I can't remember any more."

"You're lying. I won't let you go until you tell me more. And this time something without disgusting scars."

"Then I guess I'll just have to stand here, because I don't know any other lines. Unless Miss Missy wants to hear something from the Book of Psalms."

Miss Missy's face moves in close, especially her tiny mouth. She looks at Tom's cheek; he can feel the tip of her nose brushing his skin, and he takes a step back.

She smiles, but the smile doesn't reach her eyes, which flicker uncertainly. "Did he think I wanted to kiss him? Oh God, he thought I wanted to kiss him."

Tom watches her run off, snickering, bent over, hysterical, halfway between tears and laughter.

The next day as he's reading from the Bible in Mrs. Briggs's room, the mistress says that she doesn't want Tom to be taking liberties with her daughter.

"Liberties, ma'am?"

"He knows what I mean. I've seen you together. But he needs to understand that there is a difference. He must learn to control himself."

Tom knew that rats could spend hours grooming themselves. They didn't look as if they would be vain creatures, but this particular rat might have made the trip all the way from Europe. The very idea was hard to comprehend, though it was not unlikely. Maybe it was a Spanish rat, father to several hundred young ones. Tom reached his arm back as far as he could without making any noise and then hurled the knife.

At night he walks through the big slave barracks on the heels of three other bombas, led by the pockmarked Pierre, nicknamed Lupo, who carries a spirit lamp in his hand. The blacks are asleep. Or maybe they're not sleeping at all, maybe they're wide awake and just pretending. It's impossible to tell. The bombas take a head count every two hours. The slaves need to know that they're under observation.

When they come to Kanuno's bunk, Pierre stops and lets the yellow light slide across the Negro's face. Kanuno is neither asleep nor pretending to be. He's lying on his side, staring at the wall.

"He never sleeps," whispers Pierre. "He's waiting. Right now he's pretending that we're not here, as if he were somewhere else altogether." Pierre squats down in front of the big Negro and lets the light slide back and forth across the black face.

Kanuno looks at him, but his expression reveals nothing.

Tom goes to visit Ina, who is still bedridden. When he enters the cabin, she turns over so she is lying with her back to him. Tom has brought her a bowl of soup, but she doesn't want any.

They're standing in the kitchen, he and Fanny. The pot of water has been set on the stove. Tom is busy chopping up a mixture of herbs consisting of basil, coriander, and dried horsetail. From his mother, he knows that soup made from this mixture is beneficial for consumption and a gloomy spirit.

Through most of it, Fanny merely watches him. But when he picks up the bowl of piping hot soup, she stands in front of the door, blocking his way. She looks tired and resigned, but there's plenty of force in her voice as she says, "Get out of here, you Irish boy. Go back to where you came from. You don't belong here. You're a bird of ill omen."

"What's that supposed to mean?"

"You and your manners. Turning everyone's head. Go back to where you came from. Take your wretched soup and get out. Nobody wants you here."

Tom pushes her aside, but she grabs hold of him. "I hate you, Tom O'Connor," she whispers. "Do you hear what I'm saying? I hate you! Every night I pray that you'll die in your sleep."

Tom puts down the soup and stands for a moment with his back to the house slave. Suddenly he spins around and presses his knife to her throat.

"A black doesn't talk like that to a white," he snarls. "If I wanted to I could cut her throat so the blood would flow, and nothing would happen to me. Nothing at all. They would just drag her body down behind the slave quarters and throw some dirt over her until there was nothing left to see. And the next day there would be a different Fanny out in the kitchen."

He presses the edge of the blade harder against her flesh. "Don't ever say another word to me. Don't ever speak my name. Whatever you do in your sleep or when you're alone doesn't interest me; I don't care a fig about your black god. But in Mr. Briggs's kitchen, you keep your mouth shut. In Mr. Briggs's kitchen, she is a black slave and I am a white bomba. Is that understood?"

"Yes, it's understood, bomba."

The knife missed its mark, plunging into the dry earth only inches from the rat, which gave a start and then scurried off through the sugarcane and disappeared with a dry little crackle.

Swift as lightning he pulled his knife out of the ground and raced after it. The rodent was hindered by its love of food. The tiny legs did their job well enough, but the big brown body quickly grew too heavy. Tom had the rat in sight in no time; he could practically step on its tail. But he refrained because he wanted to make the rat run until it was worn out. Tom's legs were still fresh. He was positive that the rat had a nest nearby, which it would instinctively head for. And he was right, it suddenly vanished into a hole, an insignificant hollow that was mercilessly exposed to the moon's yellow light. Maybe the rat thought it was invisible among all the leaves it had gathered and matted together. Maybe it was so exhausted from the chase that it was no longer thinking clearly.

Tom waited until his breathing had slowed, then knelt down close enough that he could hear the unmistakable squeaking of the rat's babies. He could hardly believe his luck. With the tip of his knife he removed the top layer of leaves and looked down at six pink baby rats lying close together, still blind and defenseless. The mother stared up at Tom, baring her long yellow teeth. He slowly rose to his feet. She followed him with her eyes but didn't see it coming. He planted his boot on her neck. When she finally sensed the danger, it was too late. There was nothing wrong with Tom's talent for throwing a knife.

The babies were so small that he could easily get rid of them with his heel.

He is sitting in his saddle, feeling sleep overtake him like a weight, starting in his shoulders. He tries to fight it off, but the heaviness is too great. He closes his eyes for a moment, and the monotonous thudding of the hoes lulls him to sleep. He leans his head back and sees a rat with Fanny's face.

Suddenly he feels a steady pain against his spine. He opens his eyes. Joop is next to him, prodding him with his stick.

"He's asleep!"

"I just closed my eyes."

"He's asleep. He ought to be whipped for sleeping during his watch. Get on home and go to bed. Go on."

When he reached the buildings, he slipped slowly off his horse. Normally he would have curried the animal after a ride to the fields, but today he didn't have the energy. It was only an hour before sundown. He left the stables and was heading for his little house when he caught sight of her. She was scurrying along the rutted road, down toward the big gate with the portal and the sign that said *Aron Hill*. She carried a bundle slung over each shoulder, but it was the way she was running that made him uneasy. When someone ran like that, someone was chasing her. But as far as Tom could tell, no one was chasing Ina. He had believed she was sick, but the way she was running didn't suggest illness. On the contrary.

As he threw himself onto the straw and shut his eyes, he thought that she had chosen a good moment. "All the bombas are out in the fields," he murmured. "The mistress is taking her afternoon nap. Miss Missy is doing her lessons. Mr. Briggs is in town and won't be home until nightfall."

"Ina is running away." He sighed, settling under the soft blanket of sleep. "She's running as if someone is after her with a knife. Maybe I should do something. Maybe I didn't see her at all, and most likely it doesn't mean a thing."

Ina's disappearance was not discovered until the following day. Mr. and Mrs. Briggs had known that their maid was ill and thus didn't miss her. And Fanny had apparently been struck dumb, as was Sugar George, who should have been the first to realize that his wife had disappeared.

"I've spoken to Mr. Briggs," Joop told Tom. "He thinks we ought to wait. Runaway slaves usually come back. Most of them end up changing their minds, and the same will happen to Sugar George's skinny wife."

"What does George say?" asked Tom.

The Dutchman went over to the door and peered out into the twilight. "George isn't saying anything. But we're going to leave old George alone. He'll be his old self again soon. There's nowhere for his wife to go. And after she's been raped three times in Port Royal, she'll be begging to come back here. Trust me, I've seen it happen hundreds of times. In the good old days we even used to say that a runaway slave who returned home on his own became a better slave. The blacks' accounts of what they experienced in so-called freedom kept the others from doing something equally stupid. I've seen them roaming around Port Royal at night, miserable and exhausted, with wild eyes and teeth like animals.

"But you need to sleep at night, O'Connor, and don't go out hunting rats unless we tell you to. Actually there's only one rat you need to keep an eye on. The time is near. The hourglass belonging to Kanuno and me doesn't have much sand left in it."

Tom is adjusting Mrs. Briggs's pillow so that it sits the way she likes it—not too high up because then it bothers her neck and gives her a headache, and not too far down because then it disturbs her posture.

Tom moves the pillow according to her instructions as he looks out the window and thinks about Ina, whose transparent image seems to glide by. With the laundry on her head. Tall and slender, always with a scent of something nice and clean about her. It was hard to imagine Ina in Port Royal's alleyways. Hard to picture her like a wild animal.

"And what she's looking for," Joop van den Arle had said with a sigh, "she's never going to find."

Tom can also see before him the daughter, little Sunday Morning with the thin arms and wayward lock of hair falling over her forehead.

"Today," says Mrs. Briggs, closing her eyes, "I feel a little bit better than yesterday. It all depends on how much sleep I get. I truly suffer in this climate. In England it was cool, with blessed rain. As you can see, my complexion is not meant for all this sunshine. My husband has promised me that we'll go home in the spring, but I dread the voyage. Mr. Briggs has already chosen a ship we can travel on. A ship with all British sailors. We will be escorted by a man-of-war with thirty-seven cannons and a crew of two hundred fifty. That's a comfort. Please open the window, Tom. No, close it again. There's a terrible draft. I sang in the choir as a child. Would he be so kind as to take the fan from the sideboard? I have these heat spells. Move the fan faster, bomba, faster. Like that, yes, but not so fast that a person can't breathe. Sometimes I feel such a vile nausea. Could he bring me some lemon water?"

Tom lies down on the straw, shuts his eyes, and thinks about the dog in whose house he now lives. "The family must have loved the poor beast," he mutters, "since they had this hut built for it, with so much space and such a good roof." Afterward he whispers his mother's name and tries without much luck to remember the sound of his half sister's voice. Were they still delousing Señor López and washing his feet? Serving beer to travelers and scrubbing the floor and wiping the counter? And was Feodora remembering to look after his skiff? Of course she was.

Tom murmurs a verse that came either from the Book of Psalms or from the poetry that Sarah Briggs brought with her from the London theaters. " 'Come, mild, gentle night with brows so dark.' "

He is far away on the back of a green pelican.

14 Kanuno

THE SMOKE APPEARED in the southwest corner, a narrow column drifting crookedly to the right, then vanishing quickly, as if it had died out. But soon it appeared again, now thicker and blacker.

Fanny was the first to notice it. Her screams woke Tom and then the rest of the plantation. It was shortly before dawn. She had been out to gather eggs. Instead of waking Master Joop, she simply began to scream.

Tom pulls on his pants as he runs. The first thing he sees, aside from the shrieking Fanny, is Joop van den Arle standing in front of the barracks with two pistols in his belt. Pouring out of their cabins come the other bombas, partially dressed but armed to the teeth. Joop blows the special conch shell that signifies fire. Then he calls for Tom and tells him to go find George.

On his way down to the slave quarters, Tom sees Mr. Briggs dashing around the courtyard with Miss Missy. The girl is pointing toward the smoke at the bottom of the fields. From where she stands, it looks like a black curl, a wayward lock of hair in the western sky where a faint light is beginning to spread.

Tom was racing toward George's house. The sugarcane was dry as tinder; it wouldn't take much for it to ignite on its own, he thought. At the same time a different voice said that a fire starting on its own at night was contrary to nature, unless human beings were considered part of nature. If someone set fires, then night was the best time for it.

He flung open the door to Sugar George's cabin and called his name. He could already hear hoofbeats thundering along the road toward the fields, and the church bell that someone had set in motion. He had often been to

Ina and George's cabin, which consisted of one large room with three chairs, all made by George's skillful hands. One small chair and two big ones. The chairs stood next to the table, where fresh flowers lay. On the whole it was remarkably neat, but the most noticeable thing about the place was that it was empty.

Tom ran back to the courtyard and immediately caught sight of Kanuno, who had been placed in chains. At the main entrance stood the entire Briggs family, but Joop ushered them back inside.

A team of slaves was already on its way down to the wide plantation road with rakes and shovels. The children were whimpering and the women shouting, but they were told to keep quiet.

In the southwest corner the smoke had now taken on a different form and was drifting like a carpet over the dry sugarcane. The fire was starting to spread. It was only a matter of time before the western part of the plantation would go up in flames.

"O'Connor," yelled Joop. "Where the devil were you? Where's George?"

"George wasn't there, Master Joop."

Joop came over and grabbed Tom by the arm. "Then he must be somewhere else, right? Find him!"

Tom looked everywhere, though he already knew that he would not find Sugar George. Finally he went into the stables, saddled his horse, and brought it out to the courtyard.

Joop was telling Mr. Briggs that everything was under control, but that it probably would be a very good idea for the Briggs family to pay a visit to the neighboring plantation while Joop and his men took the necessary precautions. Soon afterward the horses were harnessed and the carriage clattered off down the rutted road.

Joop ordered Tom back to the stables while he inspected the shackles around Kanuno's ankles. "We've locked his friends up in the barracks," he told Tom, following him. Lupo and the others will stay here while I go and see how bad it is." He leaned against a post and didn't seem particularly upset, surprised, or angry. "You understand how things are, don't you?" He winked at Tom.

"Well, yes. And no."

"The riding horses belonging to the Briggs family are all still here," said

Joop, "so he must be on foot. And as far as I can tell from the smoke and the spot where the fire was set, he must still be somewhere in the sugar-cane, because he wouldn't get far walking. I'm thinking he wants to watch the results of his work in the hopes that not only the crops, but all of Aron Hill will burn to the ground."

Joop hitched up his pants and narrowed his eyes. "But I think we'll have to disappoint him. Frans is already out there. And if there's anyone who can track down an arsonist, it's Frans Brüggen. He took the bloodhounds from the coffee plantation with him. There are twelve of them, and they love the blacks. If you happen to run into one of them, promise me you'll stay on your horse. As for Kanuno's friends, they've been locked inside the barracks. I've given orders to shoot the first one who sticks his head outdoors. That's sure to keep them from taking advantage of the situation."

"Shouldn't we get everybody out in the fields, Master Joop?"

"Have you lost your mind, O'Connor?" Joop's pink eyes took on a furious glow. "Can't you see what this is all about?"

"Tell me, Master Joop."

The Dutchman's mouth opened in a soundless laugh. "Why, bomba, this is . . ." Joop stuck out his tongue and rolled his eyes expectantly. "It's a plot."

Tom looked away and shook his head.

"Bring out my horse," said the overseer, walking out into the daylight.

Tom did as he was told. "Master Joop, I think this is something between George and us. I don't think Kanuno has anything to do with it. Aside from the fact that I can't understand how Sugar George could . . ."

"Good Lord. Good Lord, O'Connor." Joop swung himself up onto his horse. "You've certainly got a long way to go, young man. But that will have to wait. Our friend, Frans Brüggen, has gone out there with Mr. Briggs's blessing. He's been given a free hand. We'll find the culprit, I promise you that. And we're taking a rope along. I can already picture him dangling in his own smoke. Before the day is over, a big black fruit will be hanging from the plantation's tallest tree. And once George is gone, then it'll be his turn, the one standing in the courtyard over there. We have to clean things up, Tom. Do you understand what I'm saying? Clean things up."

Joop turned his horse. "You go out to the other bombas. Make those blacks work like they've never worked before. The whole lot of them, both women and children. Some of them will be terrified when they get near the fire, but to hell with that."

"Yes, Master Joop."

"Off with you then. And Tom, make yourself useful this time. Today could be your big day, the day when you pass the test as a bomba. I don't want to have my reputation ruined by a sugar Negro."

His horse flew through the ingenious labyrinth of pathways, wide and narrow. First to the right, then to the left. He wasn't following any specific route, merely relying on intuition. He had left the road through the wide field, and now the smoke was at his back, though its nauseating stench shrouded the plantation. The sun was high overhead. The sound of the stallion's hooves thundered against the ground, blending with the baying of the bloodhounds.

He looked over his shoulder to survey the damage. Tom had never had any experience with fire and didn't share the terror that filled the blacks, who had to be threatened with whips before they would go near the flames. "But there's no way around it," he muttered, coughing. The smell of smoke and the speed with which the fire was spreading seemed to seep into his blood. He began to understand what kind of force was approaching. He reined in his horse, trying to intercept some sound. But the only thing he heard was the dogs baying, a sound that came and went, swallowed up in the tremendous roar of the fire.

Tom looked up. It sounded like a gigantic billowing sail. He stood up in his stirrups and caught sight of an enormous cloud of smoke, which in a few seconds blacked out most of the plantation. For the first time he could glimpse the chalk-white sea of flames that seemed to be devouring the dry plants at lightning speed. It was unbearable to think that there were people in there. His horse reared up and whinnied, but Tom paid it no mind. He slapped the reins, dug his heels into the animal's flanks, and raced off to the east. Then he brought the horse to a halt, changed direction, and turned around to assess the situation. Should he ride back to the buildings or try to find the men out in the fields? Maybe they were already at work evacuating the houses. Tom couldn't figure out what to do. Finally he decided to ride toward the baying hounds to find Master Joop.

Suddenly his horse reared again, nearly throwing him off. On the ground lay a figure, curled up almost into a ball. It took a moment before Tom recognized Sugar George.

The slave stared up at him with a wild and terrified expression. He didn't move but just lay there, as if he had accepted his fate. He looked as if he'd been that way a long time, frightened and exhausted and on the verge of surrender. He knew what his fate would be if the hounds tracked him down.

Tom got off his horse. George started to crawl backward. He was filthy and soot-covered; scratches covered his arms and legs and his whole body was trembling.

"George," whispered Tom.

The black man shook his head.

"Damn it, George. What have you done?"

"Leave me alone."

"Leave you alone?" Tom clenched his fists. "You can choose to perish in the flames or to be strung up by Frans Brüggen."

"Leave me alone. Leave me alone, Tom."

George's fear gave way to a wrenching sob. He hid his face in his hands and called out his wife's name, weeping as if he were being whipped.

Tom stood over him, his horse's reins in one hand. "Get up, George."

Sugar George stared at Tom. "Ina will never find her. She's never going to find her," he cried.

Tom cast a swift glance at the leather pouch that hung from his saddle. It held bread and biscuits and enough water for many days.

"Why, George?" asked Tom.

"You ask me why? He's asking me why? Do I really have to tell you?"

Tom looked away. "What about your wife?" he whispered. "What about Ina?"

"Ina is far away."

"Do you know where she is?"

"I know that she's waiting for me, but Ina doesn't know anything about this." George studied his hands.

The noise from the fire was deafening. Smoke hung like a black ceiling over the whole plantation. Tom went over to him. "Get on out of here," said Tom. "Ride northeast and you'll come to the main road." He handed the reins to George.

The black man wiped his face on his sleeve. "You don't know what you're doing, Tombomba."

"Get going. Now!" Tom hustled George up into the saddle.

"But what will you tell Master Joop?"

"I won't tell him anything." Tom lowered his voice, feeling his courage sink and his speech growing thick. "Give my greetings to Ina when you find her."

George nodded, leaned down, and put his hand on the back of Tom's neck. "If you were black," he said with a little smile, "you'd be an awfully handsome boy."

Tom shrugged his shoulders.

"But you've got red hair."

"Yes, I do. And now off you go, George."

Tom slapped the horse on the hindquarters and watched George ride away.

Tom was back at the main house. The buildings were deserted. The sound of the bell in the church tower, creaking on its rusty hinges, blended with the heartrending braying of the mules in their pen.

Everyone was gone, even the slaves who had been locked up. Tom cast a glance at the fields. The smoke was starting to take on a different shape. Long black fingers shot out from the enormous cloud, which was gradually being dispersed by the wind. He ran down to the house that had been built for the dog JayJay, who had been nice enough to die so that there would be room for a boy called Tombomba.

But Tombomba was now deceased, just like JayJay.

"Tom O'Connor is my name." He said it out loud as he gathered up his things. Then he dug up the money he had hidden under the floorboards— his entire savings after half a year in Mr. Briggs's service.

"I arrived on foot, and I'll leave on foot. Of course a person might be bold enough to take one of the master's fine riding horses. But I just don't have it in me."

He looked at his hands, which had abruptly started shaking all on their own. His heart responded by pounding in his chest. His breath came in little gasps, and he suddenly had to put his hand to his lips to keep from screaming. Fear had taken hold of him, and it was spreading like the flames in the sugarcane. Everything had happened so fast. He had acted without thinking things through. But now came the doubts, the speculations, an uneasy, quivering sense of regret. It settled in his throat and tried to come out as a scream. But this was not the proper time. He said as much aloud, "Not the proper time, Tom O'Connor."

He sank to the floor and felt his strength ebbing away. "You reckless Irishman," he muttered. "Why can't you ever learn to think first? What the devil have you done? What's going to become of you? They'll find you, you know. Frans Brüggen and his bloodhounds, they'll find you, Tom. After the whole place has burned down and only stubble remains, they'll set out to search for the red-haired bomba who gave his horse to an arsonist. The bomba who betrayed his master, the hand that fed him. What will Mrs. Briggs say? Not to mention Jesus on the Cross. Will He also forsake me, or is there help to be found there?"

Tom looked around as his thoughts leaped like sparks. "Joop will braid a rope for your neck and string you up in the nearest tree. What the devil have you done, Tom? Is it your heart that's sick? They'll find Sugar George too; they'll find them all. Out here they spend a whole year looking for a slave, only to set another one free. What am I thinking?"

He glanced around. "I'm thinking of taking off," he muttered. He threw his knapsack over his shoulder and left the doghouse. He was just about to cross the courtyard when he caught sight of big Kanuno, standing with a stake driven through the chains around his ankles, his hands bound behind his back.

Tom didn't want to look, but something made him. There was no doubt about Kanuno's fate. When Joop failed to find George, he would string up Kanuno. It was a question of hours, maybe less. He could read it in the man's eyes. Kanuno was looking straight at Tom with a blend of surprise and acceptance.

"You found him," said Kanuno.

Tom gave a start; he had never heard Kanuno speak. He was surprised by his calm tone and the unexpected but very familiar accent that came from mixing Spanish and English.

Tom nodded.

A little smile spread over Kanuno's lips. "So George is far away."

Tom glanced at the mules in their pen and remembered the first time he had stood in the courtyard. He went into the stables, saddled up Master Briggs's and Miss Missy's horses, and brought them outside. He found two water flasks, filled them at the well, and got a hammer and chisel. He took up a position near Kanuno's feet and split the chain with one blow.

Kanuno gave him an astonished look.

"I once worked for a blacksmith." Tom untied the slave's hands.

"I can tell."

Tom nodded and tossed the tools aside. Yes, he thought, I've worked for a blacksmith and I've fished for sharks and I've scrubbed tables and drunk myself silly and hunted for rats and threatened people's lives. I've seen the underside of life and slept out under the open sky and been so hungry that I've eaten stolen food, and now I'm finishing things off so that I'll live the rest of my life as an outlaw. It's that damned Irish blood flowing in my veins. It has its own will, just like the lines in the palms of my hands. And it can't be changed because a person carves his own epitaph in the thwart of the boat he has launched himself. May the Devil take it all!

"Are there any other chains that need to be broken?" he shouted as he fell onto his back. He lay there for a moment, then jumped up and looked around. "Do you hear me, Joop?" Tom was laughing and crying at the same time. He wiped his nose, picked up the hammer, and flung it far off. He looked up at the sky, which was gray and threatening. Then he shifted his gaze and nodded at Kanuno.

The slave didn't move, just stared at Tom.

"If you want to say something, Kanuno," gasped Tom, "then say it now, while I'm still in a good mood."

Kanuno hesitated, then went over to Tom and looked at him with a solemn expression. "When I saw you walk through the barracks," he said, "I knew that this would happen." Kanuno touched his brand mark. "Because you have one of these yourself," he whispered. "In your eyes."

"Is it that obvious?"

Kanuno nodded and backed toward the slaves' quarters. For a moment he was gone, vanished behind the door to the huts that had been his home for eight years. Then he reappeared with a bundle and tied it to the saddle. He had put on a shirt and stuck a knife in his belt. "Is it time, bomba?" he asked.

"Yes, it's time," replied Tom. "But my name is O'Connor, Tom O'Connor."

Kanuno said he would try to remember that.

Together they rode toward the great portal that said *Aron Hill*. Tom reined in his horse.

Kanuno looked at him. "Where are you headed, Tom O'Connor?" he asked.

Tom shrugged. "Don't know . . . don't know, but out to sea, in any case."

The other man muttered something about that being a good idea.

"What about you?" Tom asked.

"I'll manage."

Tom nodded. He didn't have any doubt about that. "Good luck," he said and turned his horse.

Kanuno stopped him, stuck his hand under his shirt, and pulled out an amulet that hung from a leather strap. Without asking permission, he placed the strap around Tom's neck. "It will bring you luck," he said. "It belonged to my grandfather and it was the only thing I brought with me when I was sold eight years ago. But now I'm a free man, thanks to you, Tombomba."

"O'Connor," said Tom, looking at the amulet. "My name is Tom O'Connor."

Kanuno smiled and turned his horse. "Live well, Tom O'Connor."

Part III

El Casto Josephine

15

HE'S STANDING IN A GARRET ROOM of the little inn, beneath a roof that leaks whenever the trade winds bring rain from the sea. The heat is unbearable, and toward evening the air stands still. Heavy raindrops fall from the walls and ceiling and collect on the floor in quivering dishes.

The damp eaves have acquired the familiar sour smell of mold, and wherever the heat and the moisture meet in earnest, the sickly sweet stink of rotting vermin rises. The cockroaches are as fat as mice and as bold as rats. But what lives between the cracks in the plaster has never been given a name. It comes out at twilight and feeds off the mites that nobody else can see.

An old friend is paying Tom a visit. The gecko stares at him from the beam overhead where it has planted its little yellow feet.

Tom thinks he recognizes the quiet fellow, who again gives him a superior smile with a hint of menace. Only on special occasions is he honored with a visit.

"This is a good place," says the gecko as it feels its way forward with its tongue. "Although the smell could be better."

"It's probably coming from you," Tom says with a sigh.

"Oh no, it's coming from the fear, not to mention the dread, that is pouring down these walls. The dread of death smells like this, and it doesn't rise from the woodwork but from the lodger."

"I could cut you in half, you loathsome creature."

"That you could," agrees the gecko, "and as easy as pie. The question is what you would do with half a gecko. And I'm tempted to add, you who've had such bad experiences with things that are half."

"Shut up, you slimy lizard."

"I beg your pardon, I thought my company might cheer you up. But what does a lizard know about human sorrows?"

Tom gets to his feet and goes over to stand close to the gecko. He examines his hands. "I feel as if I'm about to turn green," he whispers. "That I'm the one who coaxed the darkness up from the river."

The gecko scrabbles down the wall. "Unfortunately, I don't see colors," it says. "But it seems to me that he has taken on a new sheen, as if his life has begun to seep away."

Tom looks out the window. "I gave the town this black night, and out of the darkness comes the spotted jaguar," he says to himself. "I am the pelican, and Joop is the predator. He's already here. The darkness has given me away, and it's only a matter of time before the predator finds his prey." He turns to face his guest. "Give me some advice, you old gecko. Tell me what I should do if I want to see my mother and my sister again."

"That kind of advice will require a much bigger spirit than the one inside a lizard." The gecko's tongue quivers with false modesty. "But if it should turn out that I might counsel so precious a creature as a human being who assuredly has one foot in the grave, then I would be a most peculiar creature if I did not demand some small token in return."

Tom presses the back of his head against the wall and shuts his eyes. "Can you pluck hair from the head of a bald man?" he murmurs.

"Modesty is a virtue, it certainly is, but avarice is a vice."

"I have nothing to offer you in trade," moans Tom.

"Oh, but he does. You see, a little lizard such as myself is no different from any other animal whose only desire is to be like you humans. And surely we can't be blamed, when we watch you laughing, crying, singing, and loving. A lizard's blood is always cool, and it feels neither sorrow nor joy."

"Is that what you want, gecko?"

"From the one who sees the sand in his hourglass running out, I ask for what is invisible: namely, his soul. If he gives me that, I will whisper in his ear how he can escape this situation that threatens to put an end to his young life. The whole town is swarming with bombas who have only one name on their lips. You can hear it everywhere. O'Connor, whisper the alleyways. Tom, echo the streets. Deadly arson, thunder the waves. That's what it says on the noose that is looped around his neck."

"You want my soul. But what would I do without a soul? What would I become?"

"A person without a soul feels no dread." The gecko pauses to savor its own words. "No pangs of conscience and no homesickness. A person without a soul has no nightmares and never mourns what is lost."

"My life," whispers Tom, "would be one long night."

"So take a lesson from the creatures of the night."

"I've known people who have made such a deal, and I say no thanks. Better to see the sun again, even if it's for the last time. Your price is too high, gecko, and your greed will cost you your life."

Tom pulls out his knife, but when he looks around the room, he discovers that he's alone.

It's been three days since he fled from Aron Hill. He has gone from sloop to fishing boat to galleon, offering himself and his talents, but there seems to be a curse hovering over him, a glow from the fire that burned down half a plantation. Maybe they can read it in his eyes. That he was a horse thief and an arsonist's accomplice. And to top it all off he had freed the most dangerous of all slaves, the black Kanuno, who had only one thought in his head—to take revenge on all whites.

If those sorts of crimes don't leave a mark on a man's brow, then a mule has five legs.

In the mirror he stares at the change, which has left its trace not in one particular spot but all over. He can't remember when he last looked at himself in a mirror, but he supposes it must have been in Señor López's room. He thinks about his brief career as a taster, dressed in black velvet pants, silk ribbons, and shoes with square toes. In the elegant mirror in the great hall of the plantation, he had smiled at a carefree lad with wild hair and bright eyes, a boy given to laughter and impudent remarks, sharp-witted, confident of himself.

The gleaming mirror of the plantation has been replaced by a spotted rectangle in a shabby frame. Instead of fine clothes, he now sees filthy riding breeches, a torn shirt, and a pair of boots that are a size too big. Yet the real change has occurred on the inside. It would take a long, hard search to find Tom O'Connor from Nevis—if he exists at all anymore. He has grown thinner, and his lips don't seem as willing to smile as before. And even though this may be only temporary, it pains him to see it. Yet the eyes that meet his gaze have probably undergone the most lasting transformation.

He looks at his reflection, which belongs to a stranger regarding him with doubt, mistrust, and sorrow. The red hair is now darker and plastered to his head like a hood of congealed blood. "They're after me," say the thin lips. "Hunting me like an animal. Seven bloodthirsty bombas with Joop van den Arle in the lead. And they won't quit until they find me. Won't sleep until they string me up. My name is already carved on the post from which my body will dangle. There aren't many red-haired youths in this town. Even though I've sold the horse and changed my clothes, my locks and green eyes will give me away. If I don't get hired on before sunrise tomorrow, then my final day has come. The town is swarming with sailors, boatswains, and whores who, for a glass of rum, would show the bombas up to the garret room where the runaway lad sits, armed with a rose-colored amulet and a seashell from Nevis. A shell that a girl by the name of Feodora Dolores Vasgues gave him at the dawn of time. She was known for her sharp tongue and her bad habit of demanding back whatever she gave away. Yet she made an exception for this seashell, maybe because there were five hundred million other shells exactly like it, maybe because this particular one was special. With Feodora you never could tell.

"It's at times like this," he says to himself, "that a lonely boy from Nevis must try to combat his superstitions, his melancholy, and his homesickness."

So he sits on the floor for another day and night, staring straight ahead and cursing his fate, his bad luck, and his temperament. If the truth be told, everything could have turned out very differently. Instead of sharing a room with rats, beetles, and cockroaches, he could have been lying in the warm straw at Aron Hill, with a tray of biscuits and a glass of beer into the bargain. He could have won praise from Joop van den Arle and Master Briggs.

Full of gratitude, he summons the Irish lad, who stands with his hands clasped behind his back, in front of the desk supporting the ruins of Saint Paul's Cathedral. "On behalf of my wife and myself, yes, on behalf of the entire plantation, I would like to offer you our thanks, Tom O'Connor, thanks for your great efforts. Without your help everything would have been lost in the fire. Without your efforts Sugar George and Kanuno would still be alive today." Tom bows and receives a coin. Afterward the hero is admitted to the room of Sarah Briggs, who smiles gratefully and asks him to sit down next to her bed. Today she is the one who reads aloud for him. Tom closes his eyes, feeling as if he knows the Book of Psalms by heart.

But that's not how things turned out. His stubborn nature had to spoil everything. And now here he sits on the floor, with his head halfway in a noose. And the rest of his life can be counted out in days. His money is gone, spent on lodgings and clothes, a bottle of rum to put him to sleep, and a worn pair of boots.

He looks at the door and the latch holding it shut. A grown man could easily kick it in. Tom puts his ear to the wall. It's evening, and folks have begun streaming into the Pink Boar, where entertainment, singing, and the clanging of tankards goes on until late into the night. The inn is a favorite spot for sailors waiting to be hired on.

High above the town, Tom scans the wide horizon where the sun has just vanished. Any hope of catching sight of the ship that will carry him off to sea again has slowly begun to ebb away. He drinks the last drop of rum and gathers up his things, realizing that he can no longer stay in Port Royal.

A few minutes later he goes downstairs to find the innkeeper and settle accounts. The innkeeper, who is a kind man, throws in a free mug of beer. Not a bad thing for someone to have in his belly before heading out into the night.

A short time later he's sitting in the dim light on a bench in the back of the tavern, watching the entertainment, which doesn't amuse him much. A man in a veil, wig, and women's clothing—El Casto Josephine—is waltzing around the stage. The man is tall and vulgar and singing in a shrill affected voice. It's hard to see any resemblance to a woman. The hairy legs, large body, and black patch over one eye don't help the illusion. Maybe that's what amuses the crowd, or maybe it's the song the man is singing. He urges the audience to join in, and they gladly do.

Tom has another swig of beer and moves closer to the stage, convinced that if he ever finds money for beer again or a reason to laugh, it won't be for a good long time, so why not make the most of things now and sing along.

The tall man in women's clothing dances a few awkward steps, winks his one good eye, and warbles another verse:

> *Adieu, my Negro master,*
> *Oh master, farewell to thee.*
> *The whites are all no good*
> *So now I'll take my leave.*
> *Farewell, my sister Tilda*
> *My husband and brother dear.*
> *I'm off into the wide world*
> *And nevermore will fear.*

"Everybody join in the chorus":

> *Sleep well, sweet dreams, oh master*
> *When I sneak off in the rain.*
> *Oh do not wake the evil whip*
> *With the rattle of my chain.*

People are standing on the benches, but the drinking is harmless, and Tom happily roars with the others. He can now see that El Casto Josephine has a talent for comedy. He follows the example of those sitting around him and tosses salted nuts and grain at the stage, where Josephine ducks and bellows abuse. It's all part of the entertainment. Everyone is in top form, and Tom clinks glasses with three sailors he doesn't know, all woes forgotten. They shout in unison:

> *Sleep well, sweet dreams, oh master*
> *When I sneak off in the rain.*
> *Oh do not wake the evil whip*
> *With the rattle of my chain.*

He has no more money, yet he orders one beer after another, for he's in a jolly mood and it has been a long time since he tasted beer. And there's nothing wrong with the entertainment.

Up onstage El Casto Josephine has started waltzing around with a cloth doll that's supposed to be her suitor, but that does nothing to dampen the lively mood. On the contrary.

Tom laughs his heart out, leans across the table, and freezes. Joop van den Arle is standing in the doorway, looking straight at him.

At that instant the whole crowd starts bellowing the popular refrain, led by the virtuous Josephine:

> *Sleep well, sweet dreams, oh master*
> *When I sneak off in the rain.*
> *Oh do not wake the evil whip*
> *With the rattle of my chain.*

Joop is not alone. He has Frans Brüggen with him, and they're in a hurry. The Dutchman's pink eyes brighten with triumph and the thirst for revenge. He shoves at people, toppling one man. But he wants only Tom, who is on his way toward the back of the tavern, where he trips over a chair, then moves around to the other side of a table. Bomba Brüggen takes a shortcut, catches hold of Tom's shirt, and pulls out a knife.

Tom spins around and stretches out his hand—the tankard of beer is filled to the brim and very heavy. Tom just manages to see its owner staring at him before he swings the tankard, which strikes its target. Brüggen sails backward, blood streaming from a split eyebrow.

Now it's Joop's turn. But unlike Tom, he is sober. Yet Tom is familiar with the tavern and the inn's winding corridors. He dashes up the back stairs, hearing the Dutchman close on his heels. He rounds a corner, Joop right behind him, and reaches out to grab him. Tom rolls like a cat and sees the Dutchman standing over him.

At that moment a door opens, striking Joop, who is momentarily forced to step aside for a stout-looking woman. Her screams slice through the building. Several guests appear, summoned by the alarm. In the confusion, Tom slips inside a room where a naked man is about to put on his wig. Tom sees Joop in the doorway and grabs a machete that is hanging from the bedpost.

"O'Connor, you're a dead man." Joop slams the door in the face of the screaming woman.

"You can either choose to endure a beating first or you can give yourself up voluntarily and get it over with. It's up to you. There are twenty of us bombas in town, all on your account. Mr. Briggs is also offering a reward." Joop tips his head back and smiles.

"Mrs. Briggs, who had such great expectations for you, has suffered a relapse. And before the night is over, Sugar George and your Kanuno will each dangle from his own rope. Seldom has the world seen so much misfortune at one time, brought about by so little. It will therefore be a true pleasure for me to skin your hide and at the same time earn a pretty shilling, although I admit that I need no payment for a job I will so enjoy." Joop steps over the bed where the naked man with the curly wig is staring in shock from one man to the other.

"I'm glad to hear that you haven't found George," whispers Tom.

Joop shakes his head. "My impression of Irishmen was always too forgiving," he growls. "But I hadn't yet encountered Tom O'Connor, the red-haired devil. To think this snake could have reached all the way inside the mistress's bedchamber, that with his forked tongue he read aloud from the Holy Scriptures while he conspired with the blacks to set the place on fire and then flee. Under that pale skin there must be hidden a different color, for worst of all are those who betray their own kind and pit black against white. He's going to end up paying for that, so it will serve to terrify and warn anyone of like mind. You will serve as an example of the gruesome death that awaits the likes of you."

Tom backs into a corner. He feels the wall behind him and looks at the cat-o'-nine-tails being shaken in front of his face. Then the door opens. Frans Brüggen, the blood gushing from his eyebrow, is staring with fury at Tom. "Let me have him," he says.

Joop van den Arle smiles at Tom. "Shall I leave you to Frans?" The Dutchman laughs his joyless laugh and makes room for Brüggen by yanking the stranger out of the bedstraw and kicking him out the door, which shuts with a bang.

As Frans approaches, Tom glances at the window. He knows there's a porch roof right underneath. He scurries to the right as the bomba pulls out his dagger.

Joop is standing behind the bed, near the door. Brüggen, with one leg on the floor and the other on the bed, is slightly off balance, while Tom can push off from the wall.

But Tom miscalculates. Frans Brüggen lunges sooner than Tom expects. A knife whistles past Tom's ear. When he sees Brüggen's pistol on its way out of his belt, Tom swings his machete, which opens up the bomba's throat like a lump of dough. Brüggen's expression changes, and he puts his hand to the gaping wound under his chin where the blood is pouring out.

Behind him Joop sizes up the situation. And before Brüggen hits the floor, the Dutchman is over by the window. But Tom has anticipated this. He leaps over the half-dead Brüggen, tears open the door, and dashes out into the hall.

He has a thirty-foot lead, but the corridor is crowded with people, all screaming at once. Above the din he can hear Joop's roar. Tom careens down the steep stairway, rounds the landing, then enters a room. He finds himself face to face with El Casto Josephine. The man is still wearing the veil and wig, but his big hand is quickly pressed to Tom's mouth.

Tom squirms but can't budge. Outside they hear the sound of stomping boots and Joop's voice, commanding his men. For a moment everything is quiet, then there's a loud pounding on the door. Tom looks into the eyes of the fake woman, who shoves him behind a curtain. El Casto Josephine straightens the draperies and opens the door with a swift yank. "Can't a body ever have any peace from you men?" El Casto Josephine chirps.

"We're looking for a red-haired boy." It is Joop's voice.

"Oh, but of course," laughs Josephine. "I know very well what you're looking for."

"Shut up and move aside so we can search the room."

"Certainly, be my guest."

Tom hears the men stomp into the room and sees their shadows on the thin fabric of the curtain. He turns around and sees the big cloth doll that Josephine waltzed with onstage. It's lying on top of a chest of drawers with its perpetually happy smile and staring eyes painted on the rough sacking. In a flash Tom pulls out his machete and cuts off the doll's head, tears out the straw stuffing, and just as quickly pulls the sacking over his own head. Wearing the doll's cape he sits down in the corner.

The next second the curtain is flung aside. Tom recognizes the smell of Joop's tobacco and hears the Dutchman opening the chest of drawers.

Tom is concentrating on his breathing, grateful that he has good lungs, but he fears his pulse will give him away. Now Joop's face appears, very close, and Tom can hear the Dutchman's heavy breathing. Joop stares right at the blue-painted eyes on the sacking. A dagger emerges.

At that moment a shout is heard. "He's here! Joop, he's down in the tavern!"

The next moment the man is gone and the door shuts.

Tom lets out his breath and pulls off the sacking. He wipes his brow and rushes over to the little window to look down at the back courtyard. He estimates the distance, praying that his legs will survive the leap.

Behind him the fake Josephine says, "No, wait. Wait a minute, Tom."

For a brief moment dizziness overtakes Tom. Then he spins around and recognizes the man who is removing his wig.

"Ramón," whispers Tom, and faints.

When he came to, he was lying on Ramón's bunk. The inn was quiet. Outside it was night. Ramón was dressed in his regular clothes, sitting and staring at Tom with a broad smile. He seemed in every way to be his old self once again, whatever that might mean.

"I have to say," groaned Tom but couldn't go on. He shook his head and dropped back onto the bunk. For a moment he lay there with one arm over his eyes, mumbling to himself.

Ramón came over to him. "Let me have a look at you, Tom O'Connor," he said kindly.

"Tom O'Connor, the horse thief." Tom sighed.

The tall Spaniard gave a chuckle. "Yes, well, you surely must have done something. And in these parts men are strung up for less than that."

Ramón grew serious and gave Tom a penetrating look. "You've changed—you have indeed. The boy is gone. The hands are bigger and the arms stronger, but the eyes are still as green as the sea at Nevis. That pleases old Ramón. In the depths of your soul, you're still the same."

Tom sat up. "I'm afraid the same is true of you, yet you did save my life."

"Then we're even, Tom. Fate demanded that our paths should cross again. What incomparable luck."

Tom grimaced. "I don't know how lucky it is. They're looking for me all over town."

Ramón laughed. "What could a red-haired lad like you have done?"

"Do you really want to know? I stole two horses. The best ones on the whole plantation. Mr. Briggs's riding horses."

Ramón shrugged as if this were a mere trifle. "Good Lord, I'm sure they'll get their horses back."

"And I freed two slaves."

"They'll be found too. Take it easy, Tom."

"One of them set fire to the sugarcane, and half of Aron Hill is gone."

"It'll grow back, Tom."

Tom rolled his eyes and slapped his forehead. "You don't know what you're talking about. At Aron Hill you can be beaten just for stepping inside the master's garden."

"Just so you haven't killed anyone," said Ramón, pouring beer into two mugs.

Tom went over to him. "An hour ago," he said, "I cut the throat of a bomba. With this very machete. Like this!" Tom showed Ramón with one swift movement what he had done.

Ramón tugged at his ear. "Let me see if I've understood it all. You steal two of the master's horses and then free two slaves who have set fire to the plantation. After this little episode you run away and then top it all off by cutting the throat of a white bomba. Did I get everything?"

Tom nodded. "Now do you believe they're going to hang me?"

Ramón pursed his lips. "If you're lucky. But there are other methods that aren't nearly as pleasant."

"You're taking it all very calmly."

Ramón flashed an entrancing smile and said he wasn't the one who was going to be hanged.

Tom went over to the little window. "I wonder if they're still here."

"The whole town is restless," said the Spaniard. "The whites have very little tolerance for anything these days. Port Royal is a hotbed. The world is changing, and we Spaniards have to watch out because now is when the English are going to bite. They want Jamaica for themselves. They've built forts and brought in a governor from England so they can really bully us Spanish dogs. God only knows what they think of Irish horse thieves, fourteen-year-old murderers, and red-haired arsonists."

Tom lowered his eyes.

"Killing a white bomba," sighed Ramón, "is probably the worst thing you could do. Especially if the whole plantation is in flames and the blacks are running around without shackles or supervision. Where will it all end? To think that Mama O'Connor's little boy has cut the throat of a white bomba."

"You don't know Frans Brüggen," groaned Tom. "If you only knew how he treated the blacks."

"The blacks, Tom? You haven't gone soft, have you?"

"Of course not. But he enjoyed punishing them. To beat someone up just because . . . sometimes, in my dreams, I see her before me, little Sunday Morning. We sold her, Ramón. Here in town, at the marketplace. Her mother . . ." Tom hid his face in his hands. "We broke her heart."

"Are we still talking about a slave, Tom?"

"We're talking about the bombas."

"I understand that. But it seems to me that you mentioned someone else. You were talking about a slave, weren't you?"

Tom waved his hand and changed the subject. "You and I still have an account to settle. You sent me to Aron Hill on a wild-goose chase. God knows, I think all your lies have changed into fluid and taken the place of your blood."

Ramón pressed his hands to his chest. "Good heavens," he moaned. "In a minute you're going to say that it was Ramón's fault that you cut the white bomba's throat, burned down the plantation, and freed two blacks. Sweet Jesus and Holy Mother, what will we hear next from the mouth of a child? I'll gladly accept part of the blame if you'll just listen to what I have to say, because why should I save a boy's life if the lad is just going to be hanged?"

"Bibido," snarled Tom. "My half of the fortune. Let's talk about him."

Ramón moved closer to Tom and placed his hand on his shoulder. "Of all my sins," he whispered, "the sale of that little black boy is the least of them. Even compared to you—and I have to say that you've certainly made a career for yourself—but even compared to your rotten deeds, I'm a much greater sinner. There isn't a crime that poor Ramón has not committed. Why do you think I perform in women's clothing and behave like an idiot? But Tom, you're cut from a different cloth. Even though your hands are bloody and you can still feel the stolen horse between your legs, your soul remains untainted. I can see it in you, boy. Those green eyes can't lie."

"Try them—they can lie faster than a horse can run."

Ramón smiled. "A liar would never describe himself that way. Oh, Tom O'Connor, you are and will always be Ramón's bright little star in the inconsolable heavens. The first time I saw you, I thought to myself, this boy will . . ."

"I don't give a damn what you thought," said Tom. "I'm sitting in the shadows of the gallows because of two people I never should have snatched from the jaws of death. I curse the day I met you, Ramón. Even at the hour of death you were full of lies."

"You do me an injustice, Tom."

"Where is Bibido? Tell me!"

Ramón sighed. "The boy you call Bibido is probably in Brazil by now, if he hasn't died on some coffee plantation someplace in the Caribbean. Negroes of his size don't last long—you ought to know that. Let's be realistic, Tom. That boy is never going to see his home again, and neither are we."

"Damn it all, Ramón! Damn it! I could have been rich. I could have bought the inn and kicked Señor López out on his Far Beyond. If your story was true, that is, but I've started to have my doubts. Lies come so easily to you that you probably can't even tell the difference. Look at me. Was it true that the slave boy was the son of a rich man, or was that just something you dreamed up? At this hour of the night, you might as well tell me the truth. What have you got to lose?"

"Oh, the story was true enough, all right. Bibido is the son of a king out there, but dearest Tom, let's face facts. How well do you know the ocean?"

"Like my own back pocket."

"It must be awfully big then, because the Bissagos Islands are infinitely far away. The new sea charts available in Port Royal are extremely reliable. And unless you can also steal full-riggers with two hundred cannons and three hundred soldiers, you won't reach them in less than three months. Listen to me, Tom, it was a splendid dream. I let myself be captivated by it too, I admit that. But in the hour of truth—and if this isn't the hour of truth, then my name isn't Ramón the Pious—at this hour we have to let the dream go. No matter how much it hurts."

"You stole him, Ramón. You stole him from me, even though I saved your life."

"And now we're even."

"I still haven't received the share you promised me."

"By the Devil, you're a determined boy. The whole town is looking for you. All of the bombas are out. Before dawn they'll bring in their abominable curs, and then I wouldn't want to be in the boots of an Irishman. Yet he can sit here, by God, and babble on about a Negro who disappeared two years ago. This surprises Josephine. It truly does, Tom. It surprises and offends her."

"Good God, Ramón, you're so rotten to the core that it makes me dizzy. There's more goddamned honor in your dancing partner than there is in you."

Ramón took Tom's hand. "Permit an old sinner to do one last good deed in this life. I don't have much time left and will soon have to face my Maker." He shed a tear and began sniffling.

"That should be some scene."

"Go ahead and make fun of a dying man."

"Don't worry, Ramón. Unfortunately there's something immortal about you. It's highly likely that for the next thousand years you will wander through the world, ridiculing truth. You've pawned your soul for a glass of rum, and no doubt you've sold your walleyed mother for even less. If there should actually be one good deed left in you, then I'll believe in mules who shit bars of silver."

Ramón replied by opening a chest and pulling out a handful of gaudy clothes that turned out to be the entire wardrobe of the virtuous Josephine. "The remark about my mother was rude," he said, "but I'll let it go. Wearing these clothes, you'll be able to pass safely through the streets of Port Royal."

Tom stared in disbelief at the tall Spaniard. "Do you really think I'm going to dress up like a girl?"

Ramón nodded confidently.

Tom slapped his hand to his forehead. "Over my dead body."

"Most likely."

"Splendid. Give me a glass of rum."

"I'll be damned if I'll let you drink rum, a half-pint like you," said Ramón. "What do you think your mother would say?"

"She's not here, and I need a glass."

Ramón pulled Tom over to the window. "What you need more than anything else is to stay sober. And now listen to what Ramón is going to tell you. At dawn a Spanish galleon is going to pass these coasts. She's called *The Flying Fortress*, but her real name is *Caballito del Diablo—The Dragonfly*. A magnificent ship. She's on her way from the Aztecs, carrying pure gold intended for Spain, that dear country. Here at the inn are two Italian sailors who are supposed to sign on when the galleon stops to take on fresh water. In the harbor there's a skiff that Ramón has been keeping ready just in case a situation like this should arise. You know, Tom, that we rats always have an escape route. *The Dragonfly* will be your salvation. If you do as I say, before sundown you'll be far from these shores and the rope that they've twisted in your honor."

"But I don't want to go to Spain," Tom said bitterly. "I want to go home."

"First and foremost, you have to get out of here. What you do at sea is none of my concern—that's up to your own audacity and your relationship to your god. But for now, put on these clothes. And if you've got any whiskers on your chin, scrape them off. In the meantime I'll find you a yellow wig and a touch of powder. Then you'll bid adieu to the virtuous Josephine and leave these infested lodgings behind."

16 Viva España

THEY WERE WALKING beneath a crescent moon under the cover of darkness. Tom tried to keep up with the virtuous Josephine, who was swinging her hips, taking quick, mincing steps, as if she were still onstage. At night Port Royal was even more sinister than by day, if that was possible. In addition to thieves there were the usual drunkards who cruised from inn to tavern, so broke that no one even bothered to assault them.

Tom and Ramón had decided on a route that cut through the worst sections of town. If the choice was between thieves and white bombas, they preferred the thieves. So far things had been fine, so fine, in fact, that Ramón suddenly had an impulse to start singing.

He stood in the shadows of a doorway, where his voice would have greater resonance. The alley was long and narrow, the doors were all closed, and the windows shuttered.

> *Sleep well, sweet dreams, oh master*
> *When I sneak off in the rain.*
> *Oh do not wake the evil whip*
> *With the rattle of my chain.*

Ramón blew his nose, moved by his own talent.

"Do you have to tempt fate like this?" complained Tom.

"That's how my life is, dear Tom," the Spaniard said quietly. "The closer I come to death, the more exuberantly I live. The fever won't get me, nor the plague. No, if Ramón is going to be stopped for good, it will take a bullet, and the same holds true for the virtuous Josephine. We're made from the same treacle." Ramón looked at Tom with a pensive expression. "I miss the whip," he whispered. "The whip on my back."

Tom glanced at him out the corner of his eye. "Why is that so important for you?"

"Pain," replied Ramón, "is the only thing that can soothe the eternal suffering that goes by the ridiculous label of bad conscience. As if it were a matter of a bad finger, a bad joke, or a bad wine." Ramón looked at Tom, his face dissolving in tears. The smeared powder didn't help matters.

"All the people I've disappointed," he whispered. "All the hopes that were pinned to Ramón, Victor, Filip, Juan, Hugo, and Albert, not to mention the virtuous Josephine and Jacques Emil Morte. I was born under thousands of stars and therefore had thousands of names. My mother I've forgotten, and my father could be anyone at all. Ramón from Cádiz couldn't help but turn out to be forgetful and a nobody. My talents were few and my opportunities limited, but I discovered that lying was my profession. I stole, betrayed, denied, and bewailed. I tortured myself at night for what I did during the day. I went to sea because the Earth was burning. And I called myself the Pious out of humility." Ramón smiled and placed his hand on Tom's cheek. "Life is like the wheel. Once it's worn crooked, the cart will follow suit."

It was quiet in the dark alleyway. Ramón took off his wig. "I would have liked to be a father to you, Tom. On Nevis that was my most fervent wish. But how does a man evade his own shadow? That's only possible in the dark. Make sure, Tom, that your life doesn't turn out crooked, as mine has, that you don't end up a one-eyed wretch with scars on body and soul. Damn it all, just look how I've botched my life."

"But surely it's never too late to change," murmured Tom.

"You see, that's exactly my point." Ramón put the wig back on. "Because one day it *will* be too late. And this crock has been mended for the last time. If I had never met you, Tom O'Connor, I would never have realized how corrupt I am. That's something that can be seen only in the purest of mirrors."

Ramón straightened his dress. "But it was my fate," he sighed, "to be saved from drowning so that life could continue to punish me."

Tom looked past Ramón. A man had appeared in the alleyway. He had stepped out of the shadows, as if he were waiting for them. Now he was standing in front of Ramón, who in Josephine's voice asked him to move aside.

In reply, Ramón was hoisted two feet up in the air. "Whether you're a man or a woman," growled the man, "you have to pay the bridge toll before you can go."

"I don't see any bridge," chirped Ramón.

"That's your problem."

"If you put me down, I'll take a look and see what I have."

The man tossed Josephine to the ground and spat in Tom's direction.

"I keep my fortune in this sock, you see," said Ramón.

"Just hand it over, if you value your life."

Ramón gave him an acid smile. "The unfortunate thing is that I don't."

In the sock was a stone, and it struck its mark with precision. It all happened so fast that the robber stood for a moment as if in doubt about some theoretical question before he hit the ground nose first.

"What we poor defenseless women have to put up with," said Ramón, shaking his head.

Tom was studying the sky. The eastern horizon was starting to brighten. The plan was for him to hide under Ramón's skiff. He would gladly stay there a whole week if it would save him from the bombas.

Ramón cast a glance inside a tavern where the last customers of the night were pressing their hands against the tables in an effort to get to their feet. "Maybe we could tip just one last glass before we part."

"There's no time for that," said Tom.

"Just one glass in farewell. For Josephine's sake."

"If we're going to part for good," replied Tom, "it's not going to be with me wearing women's clothing." He tore off his dress and wig.

They stepped inside. The mood in the tavern was just as listless as in all the other alehouses. Ramón waved over the innkeeper. "May we please have two glasses of rum and a mug of beer for our thirsty throats?"

When they had their drinks, Tom asked about the skiff.

"It's easy to find." Ramón downed the rum. "On the side it says *Alfredo*, which is the name of the previous owner. God be with him, and cheers, Tom, for never has there been a more beautiful friendship."

At that moment a commotion erupted outside in the alleyway.

"Wherever decent folks are, that's where decent folks gather," intoned a drunkard.

The door was shoved open. Tom instantly ducked down. Ramón turned away from the man who had come in. "Do you know him?"

Tom nodded. "He's called Lupo, but his real name is Pierre. He's one of the bombas from Aron Hill."

A few minutes later Lupo departed.

"I think we should go now," Tom said.

"And I think we should leave by the back door," replied Ramón as he stood up.

Tom turned around and caught sight of Joop van den Arle standing in the doorway with three other bombas. "The patient fisherman always gets a bite," said the Dutchman with a triumphant smile.

Tom dashed after the virtuous Josephine, who was making her way up a narrow staircase. On the landing Ramón shed his dress and tore the banister from the wall, hurling it down the stairwell. "The roof, Tom," he shouted. "Go on up there."

"What about you?"

"I'll stay here and have a little chat with your friends."

"Damn it, they'll murder you."

"Get going, Tom O'Connor." Ramón threw out his arm. "And I hope you'll live to be a hundred and have twelve healthy children."

Joop appeared on the stairs. He lunged for Ramón, who jumped aside and pulled out his dagger. Tom heard a shot, changed direction, and raced up three more flights until he was standing under the hatchway that led to the roof of the building. In a flash he hauled himself up and out, catching a glimpse of Joop, who had appeared below.

"You'll never make it, Irishman," he bellowed. "We'll get you sooner or later. I have the smell of your rat's blood in my nose."

The next second Tom was leaping and stumbling from rooftop to rooftop. He jumped across a passageway and slid down a neighboring roof, landing in a courtyard where a donkey and a small wagon stood. Above, on the roof of the tavern, he saw a silhouette of Joop and two of his men. It was almost light now. The sky had turned shades of pink, and the opportunity for passing through the town under the cover of darkness was gone.

"The gallows are waiting for you, Tombomba," yelled Joop.

Catch me first, thought Tom, as he rushed out the gate, rounded a corner, and set off at a run. He knew that the harbor was only a few hundred yards away. He looked back but couldn't see the bombas. He passed the first warehouses and paused to catch his breath. The town was slowly waking up. A cart rolled past. The driver swung his whip over a gaunt nag.

"The whip is the Devil's invention," gasped Tom and rounded another corner.

Joop was standing right in front of him. His eyebrows rose, and he laughed with all his might.

Tom's back slammed against the building. He began edging sideways.

Joop followed with long calm strides. "Run, bomba, run," he shouted. "We'll get you in the end."

Tom spun around and barged right into Lupo, who reached out to grab him, but Tom ducked and pulled free. His legs were churning like windmills. Behind him he heard Joop laughing. Ahead of him were the shore and the sea. Nowhere to hide. Nowhere to run.

"Run, bomba, run," shouted Joop.

Tom heard furious curses, horses stomping their hooves, more laughter, and more shouting. "Count to ten, Tombomba," muttered Tom, "and they'll nab you by the time you reach seven."

His feet sank into the sand. He stood as if paralyzed. Out in the bay, bathed by the first rays of the sun, was the most splendid vessel he had ever seen. A Spanish galleon, incomparable in size and beauty. Three-masted with spritsail, outer jib and inner jib, its hull and rigging spanking new. Judging by the size of the yards, she was a ship that could do fourteen knots. She lay at anchor as if the sun, the horizon, and the light breeze had been made for her alone. The big sails were reefed, but frantic activity reigned on every yardarm. They were making ready for departure. Eight rowboats were on their way out to the galleon, the oars manned by crews of six. Next to the large barrel in the middle of each boat sat two officers, issuing orders to the sailors.

The whole thing was so perfect, so infinitely removed from the stinking alleys of Port Royal, that it had to be a dream. "But she's not a vision in a dream," Tom murmured.

Soon she would be gone, relegated forever to the world of dreams. The crew had gotten what they came for: fresh water. And when the boats reached the ship, they would weigh anchor and set sail.

Tom glanced over his shoulder. Joop and his men were approaching in fan formation. There were twenty men in all, and they were heavily armed.

"This is where the journey ends, bomba," shouted the Dutchman.

Tom stuck his machete between his teeth and tore off his shirt and boots. A second later he cast himself into the waves and dived down, feeling the cold against his skin. He swam underwater for several minutes. When he surfaced, he saw the bombas coming after him in a small fast-moving skiff. Calm as always, Joop sat in the bow, commanding his men, who were rowing like crazy.

Tom was now midway between the galleon's rowboats and the pursuing skiff. The chance of reaching his destination before being overtaken was just about as poor as the chance of making it to the rowboats before they reached the galleon. Even though he was a strong swimmer, it was obvious that Joop was catching up.

Tom dived down and changed direction, but the water was so clear that Joop could easily follow his movements. Tom surfaced again, gasping for air, and felt something strike him on the back of his neck. For a brief moment he blacked out and went under, but then he regained control and came up, only to see the next oar lunge toward him.

Joop's skiff was now within reach. The furious bombas were shouting like dogs. Joop's joyless smile had been replaced by a blazing hatred. "Make sure he doesn't drown," he yelled as he lit his clay pipe.

"To hell with you, Joop," gasped Tom. "To hell with you and your bombas."

The Dutchman nodded to his men. "As you can see, I wasn't exaggerating. We're dealing with an animal here. Haul him in!"

Tom swam as fast as he could, but his strength was just about gone. The skiff came alongside him, the bombas hanging over the gunwale, ready with the boat hook.

Tom gasped and looked up at the bright blue sky. Using all the strength he had left, he gripped the machete, pushed off, and rose two feet out of the water. He had eyes only for Joop, who was standing in the boat, confident of his catch.

Tom threw himself with all his force, but missed. His machete flew past the Dutchman's nose and knocked the pipe out of his mouth. In a rage Joop grabbed the boat hook. "You Irish swine," he screamed, raising it.

Just then a shot rang out, Joop muttered something, and there was another shot. The Dutchman clutched his chest, where a red stain began to spread across his shirt.

A second later Joop van den Arle toppled over into the waves and sank like a rock.

Tom swam like crazy, hearing one shot after another. He could make out the shape of a rowboat ahead, and when he glanced back he saw the bombas maneuvering the skiff as they tried to duck the bullets. He had cramps in both legs, and the strength in his arms had long since given out. The fact that he still could get his head above water was due to force of will and will alone. Through the surface of the water he could see the shimmering outline of a uniform and a brown wig leaning down to him. The man was holding something that looked like a pistol in his hand. When Tom bobbed up out of the water briefly, it was pointed straight at him.

He gasped and swallowed a mouthful, sank down again, and then with the greatest exertion he grabbed the rowboat and held on with his fingernails. The water was roaring in his ears, yet he heard the officer shouting something that sounded like, "Spanish or British?"

Tom coughed and spat, swallowed more water, and gasped, "Spanish . . . señor."

Someone struck his fingers hard and he had to let go. He drifted ten feet or so, letting himself be pulled by the current. Then something grabbed him by the belt and hauled him up. He lay with his head down. Everything went black.

"Spanish or British?"

"Spanish . . . Spanish, señor. Spanish!"

"Name!"

"José Alonzo Emanuel Rodrigues Vasgues, señor."

Tom's head was plunged once again underwater but then pulled back up just as quickly. With a gasp he continued. "Born in Cádiz. Fourteen years old. I've served . . ."

"Why are the British after you, José?"

"To hell with all of them," Tom hiccuped. "Viva . . . viva España."

Laughter came from the boat.

But the sound vanished. Everything vanished. His head underwater. Shimmering. Light-colored pearls on the surface of the sea. The ocean's grave is green and silent.

He is sinking, filling up with water, becoming twice his size. He feels the bubbles in his head and the sea in his chest. Shoals of fish disappear inside his ear.

Then night arrives. Coaxed up from the river.

17   Caballito del Diablo

THE GALLEON PLOWED THROUGH THE WAVES, listing slightly to starboard, with all sails set. The wind from the east blew with a force that was steady and firm. As if the trade winds wanted to say: this is how a sailing ship should look in order for us to open our mouths wide.

Tom had to pinch his arm, blink, and cling to the railing. He looked up at the enormous sailcloth twisting in the rigging. The waves pounded against the hull, which gave off an intoxicating smell of fresh tar, salt, and resin. He leaned out, feeling the foam in his nose and the heaving in his chest. He had to clench his teeth to keep from sobbing with joy.

"I'm a spinning top, a wild and crazy spinning top." He laughed with all his might and danced barefoot on the deck, then bent forward and clasped his hands. "Oh, heavenly Father, holy God of the Sea, lucky star, I thank you with all my heart. With all my sinful heart, which I will never give to that damned gecko."

He turned around and let his glance slide up to the top of the mizzen-mast. "What a ship," he sighed, "and what good fortune. In spite of everything, God must be fond of those with red hair. I give my thanks to you, great galleon, and to you, the ocean. I hope you are still taking pleasure from my father's belt."

A hundred and thirty feet she measured in length, with thirty-eight oars that could be manned by seventy-six crew members in becalmed seas. There was a swarm of people—officers, boatswains, sailors, carpenters, and soldiers—but no one took any notice of a half-naked lad running from the bow to the aft cargo hold and back again.

"Can I be of assistance?" He repeated the question over and over again, to the boatswain, the officer, the sailor, and the carpenter. But they were all too busy to reply. Everyone knew exactly what to do. A shouted command was rarely heard. He took this to mean that the captain was firmly in command. There were no bottles of rum in sight, nor any drunken sailors. There were very few slaves, and they either stayed in the hold or helped out in the galley, ruled by the cook.

It was the cook to whom Tom was entrusted when an officer finally had time to pay attention to this newest arrival. Tom had to repeat his full name and come up with an equally fictitious tale regarding his relationship to the Englishmen, though he quickly realized that what his explanation lacked in credibility could be made up for by a fundamental hatred of everything British.

He followed the officer down a stairway at the base of the bowsprit. They emerged into the pantry, where all the food was stored. There were baskets of newly smoked fish; pyramids of coconuts; barrels of root vegetables and tropical fruits; sacks of flour, grain, and biscuits. At the very back of the room stood casks of water. Sulfur had been added to some to make them keep longer.

The cooked turned out to be a hotheaded little man who walked around humming as he issued orders to his staff.

"Felix," said the officer, "here he is then, that red-haired lad we fished out of the harbor in Port Royal. He's got a hell of a tongue on him, but since you've been complaining about being short on help, we're giving you an extra mouth to feed and two hands that for once aren't black."

The cook wiped his hands on his apron and looked Tom up and down. They were the same height and almost the same in breadth. "Is he used to doing any work?" The cook lifted Tom's hands and turned them over with a shrug of his shoulders that might be interpreted as approval.

"Yes, señor," said Tom, straightening his back. "I've never been a stranger to hard work."

This amused the officer, who with a roar of laughter left Tom to his new employer.

The cook walked around Tom. "What's your name, redhead?"

"My name is José Alonzo Emanuel Rodrigues Vasgues. I'm from Cádiz."

"What was he doing in Port Royal?"

"Those damned Englishmen, created by the Devil and spread all over

God's innocent Earth, captured and tortured me, just because I happened to shout *¡Viva España!* in the marketplace."

"But what was he doing in Port Royal? Does he have any skills? Or is he just another fool that's been inflicted on me?"

"I worked for a blacksmith, a Spaniard of course, who took me under his wing after my parents died of dysentery. I was only five years old, and as for my nine brothers and sisters . . ."

"Fine, fine, you can tell your life story to the coconuts. So your name is José. Well, listen here, José! In my galley there are certain rules. The first has to do with cleanliness. If I find you haven't washed your hands after a trip to the privy, you're finished in the galley and you can report to the hold, where they'll point you to the oar at the very back of the ship or make you hunt rats among the timbers. Is that understood, José?"

"Yes, Señor Felix."

"Felix will do. Keep the fancy titles for the captain. He'll be pleased to have his soup dished up by a white boy. It's taken me months to train the four blacks who were so kindly tossed down here to me. We call them Enero, Febrero, Marzo, and Abril, after the months of the year. That should be easy enough to remember, even for a black. Enero and Febrero are slothful, Marzo is delicate, and Abril has tried to jump ship. He's tied to a floorboard in the barrel room of the hold. And if he doesn't come to his senses very soon, he'll be sold at the first port or tossed overboard with a cannonball attached to his leg. If anything needs to be done, the cook has to do it himself. The crew has its own galley, thank God, but it's a long way home, and the sooner you figure out how things work around here, the better I'll feel. And when the cook is happy, everyone is happy. The second rule has to do with thievery! If I catch you stealing food or fresh water, that'll be your last day in the galley, and you can look forward to a keelhauling."

The cook paused for a moment, cheered up by the thought.

"Rule number three! Report to the ship's surgeon as soon as you develop a sore, a rash, or any other sort of discomfort. Better to go too often than not often enough. It's too late to make amends once the whole officers' mess is infected. Be ready to work from sunup until sundown, because we have a lot of mouths to feed. Besides the captain, there's the first officer, the boatswain, the chief gunner, the surgeon, the scribe, four lieutenants, the priest, the quartermaster, two sailmaker mates, three second mates, two artillery mates, ten cadets, two corporals, twenty constables, and a drummer. Even though this is a modern ship with a modern crew that understands about cleanliness, no ship is free from rats, and we have our share of them too. Most of your time will be spent making soup and cutting up meat, cracking nuts and cleaning up, as well as hunting rats. Right now the three blacks are all down in the hold. Their rations are measured out according to how much work they do, you see, and they're lazy by nature. We can only hope that the same doesn't hold true for José with the red hair. Am I making myself clear?"

"Yes, Señor Felix, perfectly clear, and if I may, I'd like to add that all my days I've been a quick learner, and I've caught many rats in my life. I've worked for a blacksmith and been a bomba on a sugar plantation. I know how to use a cross-staff and navigate by the stars, and my mother has taught me how to prepare all kinds of dishes."

"That'll do. Wash yourself all over and scrub your fingernails. Then put on that white jacket that's hanging above the utensils. Your pants we'll burn and toss the ashes overboard. I don't even want to think about how many times you must have taken a shit in them. I figure a pair of my pants ought to fit you. And then let's see if you can serve a tankard of beer to our captain without spilling foam all over the deck."

The cook came close to Tom and gave him a searching look. "It's seldom we see folk from Cádiz with your eye color, José."

"That's because I was given too much salt in my food as an infant," said Tom, staring steadily back at the cook, who shook his head, scratched his neck, and remarked that it had been a very long time since he'd met such a liar.

Half an hour later Tom was standing outside the captain's cabin, dressed in a white jacket and holding a big tankard of frothy beer. He was late. He had gotten distracted while standing next to the helmsman, a big hefty man wearing a striped sweater who looked like he wouldn't mind having his monotonous job interrupted. He had let Tom study the amazing compass floating in whale oil. On a slate, the first officer had recorded the ship's position and the time.

This ship, Tom had said to himself, is a dream. I have to pinch my arm to grasp my good fortune.

"You must be the lad they pulled out of the harbor," the helmsman had said with a sniff.

"That's me," Tom had replied. "My name is José."

"They say the English were after you, is that right?"

"Those damned idiots would have killed me if I hadn't been rescued by my countrymen." Tom had shaken his head and tried to look vengeful.

"What about your parents? Or maybe you don't have any?"

"Both are dead, señor. Hanged for a trifle by those selfsame men. You might say that my hatred is well-founded. Jamaica will soon be British through and through, with the governor and the fort and all the rest of it. Good thing I'll soon be back home in Cádiz."

The helmsman's face had lit up. "Are you from Cádiz? I am too. What did you say your last name was?"

"Er . . . Vasgues, señor."

"Are you from the family that makes clay pots?"

"That's my cousin's family," Tom had babbled, heading for the stairs.

The helmsman's face had taken on a somber look. "Sad about old Alonzo," he'd said, "but as long as he can still hear, I suppose he'll do fine."

"With a little help, but it's not easy."

"Can you tell me how it happened that he lost his eyesight?"

Tom tugged at his ear. "Well, I'm no doctor, but I heard it was due to a lack of vegetables."

"So it wasn't the heat from the kiln, after all, that ruined his eyes?"

Tom had looked around in confusion and, muttering something about the captain's beer, had hurried down the stairs and knocked on the door.

The captain was a corpulent man with a large bald head. His curly brown wig hung from a peg, which also held his uniform. He was sitting at an enormous desk covered with charts and drawings and a large piece of parchment with circles in red and black, representing the various phases of the moon. On the desk also lay the ship's log, a goose quill, a lovely ink holder made of brass, along with two telescopes and a ceramic item that turned out to be a water pipe from Arabia.

"Regiomontanus," said the captain.

Tom bowed politely and said, "José Vasgues," in the belief that the captain was introducing himself.

That was not the case. But he did pick up the beer tankard and empty it in one gulp, then patted his stomach and gave Tom a look of astonishment. "Now where were we?" he grumbled. "Oh, yes, Regiomontanus. An excellent man. From Nürnberg. I share an interest with Regiomontanus, namely lunar eclipses. As you can see, young Vasgues, these drawings are copies of Regiomontanus's original sketches." The captain gave Tom a disoriented look. "Er . . . doesn't a slave usually bring my beer?"

Tom bowed. "I'm new, Señor Capitán. My name is José Vasgues."

"Is that so? Is he from Jamaica?"

"Um, yes. Unfortunately my parents are no longer alive. The plague took them."

"How sad, sad, very sad."

"They were infected by a damned Englishman."

Tom was rocking vigorously back and forth, and he now had the captain's full attention.

"Did he say Vasgues was his name? Good! Now listen here, young man! I won't tolerate any cursing on my ship, is that understood? Not any kind whatsoever. The crew was chosen for its mastery of the Spanish language, and I crack down hard on any cursing. It's a contagion that comes from the Evil One himself. Has the boy been brought up in the true faith?"

"Yes, I have, Señor Capitán, especially when it comes to the Book of Psalms, which I know by heart."

"Is that right? That's certainly to the boy's credit. May we hear a sampling, Vasgues?"

"Certainly, Señor Capitán."

Tom cleared his throat and put one foot in front of the other as he translated poetry from English to Spanish for the very first time.

> She sparkles brighter than all torchlight,
> Like a gem on the cheek of the night,
> A jewel in an African's ear,
> Far too lovely, too noble, too dear.
> She outshines others, even her foes,
> Like a white dove in a flock of crows.

The captain stared into space, then stood up and went over to the window, which offered a magnificent view of the emerald-green ocean. "The Book of Psalms," he said. "How strange."

Tom lowered his eyes, aware that he might have mixed up the Bible with one of Sarah Briggs's theater pieces.

The captain came over to him. "What a remarkable color his eyes are."

"Inherited from my mother," said Tom, "due to a certain goat."

"Is that right? How so?"

"Well, you see, Señor Capitán . . ." Tom crossed his arms. "Back home we had twelve goats, all named for the months of the year, and the goat called Noviembre was an unusually generous specimen. We could milk her twice a day and get a whole quart each time. We had the most wonderful cheese on bread and the finest milk. My seven brothers and I received such an abundance of her milk that it gave us—if the captain will permit me to say so—these extraordinary green eyes."

"What a peculiar story, Vasgues. Most odd."

"Unfortunately, Noviembre was stolen from us. By the man we had rented our lodgings from. He was British." Tom rocked vigorously on the balls of his feet and gave a telling wink.

"Is that a fact?"

"And from London, to top it all off. He stole Noviembre and sold her at the marketplace. On the other hand, my sister gave him a so-called *aphrodisiacum. . . .*"

"You don't say."

Tom nodded, tugged at his ear, and told the story about the laxative powder that kept the goat thief in the privy for six weeks.

"Entirely deserved, and after my own spirit." The captain slapped Tom on the shoulder. "But now I must continue my studies. The boy may go."

Tom bowed, picked up the tankard, and shut the door behind him, feeling quite satisfied with himself. On his way back to the galley he thought that a misunderstanding might arise if the officers happened to compare accounts relating to the premature demise of his parents. In less than an hour he had presented three different explanations, from dysentery to execution to the black death. He told himself he must learn to curb his imagination and remember that a liar's rule of thumb was to say as little as possible.

By the end of the first week Tom had become accustomed to the galley routines, and the cook seemed to be pleased. But whenever his work was done, Tom would rush out to the railing and let the mild trade winds envelop him.

"What the devil is he doing here?" the cook shouts through the storm.

"I'm inhaling the wind, Señor Felix."

"He must be out of his mind."

"No, just happy," says Tom with a smile.

At night he can be found straddling the bowsprit, where he is rocked by the waves, exulting at life and the star under which he was born.

After two weeks Tom thought he knew the ship well, from hull to mast. He had learned to operate a cannon, to read a compass, and to measure the ship's speed with a string, a piece of wood, and an hourglass. He had been up to the topmost rigging, so high that the galleon looked no bigger than a banana peel on the endless ocean. From there he could feel in earnest the violent rolling, and he gained a sense of the forces at play. There weren't many seamen who cared to stand on the yard above the main royal sail, but whenever the opportunity arose, he would clamber up the rigging, swift as a gecko and strong as a monkey.

"Does he absolutely have to put his life at risk, that red-haired beggar?" bellows the cook.

Tom slides down the mast and looks at him with sparkling eyes. "When you're that close to death, Señor Felix, you feel truly alive."

On one occasion he nearly robbed the poor man of his senses. He leaped from the yard over the topgallant sail, a fall of a hundred fifty feet. He hovered in the air like a tern, spun around like an acrobat, and vanished into the waves without making so much as a ripple on the green surface of the sea.

"Now that's what I call a seaman," exclaimed the first officer, as the cadets fished the cheerful José out of the water.

"And I call it madness," scolded the cook. "Here I've finally gotten a little help, and the lunatic has to go behaving like that."

But Tom enjoyed every second. He couldn't get enough of the speed or the air or the excitement. He allowed himself only a few hours' sleep and gladly lent a hand on the quarterdeck, on deck, in the hold, and in the galley. He was happiest whenever they were plowing through the waves with all sails set.

But after three weeks of good wind and calm sailing, they reefed the sails and dropped anchor. They were to wait for two warships that would escort the gold-bearing galleon across the Atlantic.

Tom had met the three slaves Enero, Febrero, and Marzo, who seemed just as lazy as the cook had said. They spoke very little Spanish and had particular difficulty understanding orders. Whenever they helped out in the officers' mess, the men thought it was downright disgraceful the way they poured the wine and carved the meat, so these tasks were left to Tom.

"What did I tell you?" snarled the cook. "Those blacks are good-for-nothings."

"Maybe if we gave them a little more to eat," suggested Tom.

"Down there they get paid by how many rats they kill," said the cook, "but they're no good at that either."

Tom chose to hold his tongue. He knew that the slaves caught just as many rats as he did, but they ate most of them for lack of any better food. Yet they were nothing but skin and bones.

Things were quite different for Tom. After three weeks his cheeks had grown rounder, fattened up by the generous Felix, who dipped deep into the lentil pot each time Tom turned up with another rat on his spike. "It certainly was lucky for you that we gathered you up in Jamaica," said Felix with a grin. "Otherwise you would never have reached Europe. When were you last home in Cádiz?"

"Oh, a long time ago," replied Tom.

He had been thinking about his situation, aware that the galleon would soon set course for the north. Day by day for three weeks more and more distance had been put between him and Nevis. And now, as the sound of the mighty anchor chain had replaced the quiet roaring of the wind in the sails, they found themselves off the coast of Hispaniola, and Tom didn't care to sail much farther away than that. He had no intention of ending up in Spain.

At night he walked around the deck, which was manned by cadets at all the cannons. On the uppermost yards sat the sailors, keeping watch for pirates. If he was going to escape this ship, it would have to be done with stealth. Putting a skiff into the water without being discovered was unthinkable. And since no one in his right mind would dream of swimming from Hispaniola to Nevis, he had resigned himself to traveling along until a proper opportunity arose. Yet deep inside he knew that he might have to stay on board until the ship reached Europe. What was before a great warm feeling of happiness was now transformed into a knot in his stomach. Homesickness had changed to shame. Shame and sorrow. Maybe also regret.

He had been gone almost two years. He could still see his mother waving good-bye as he rode away astride Señor López's old mule. Leaving had been easy; he hadn't even said good-bye to his sister. Everyone had expected him to be back in two weeks. Now there were more and more indications that he might never see his mother and sister again, and the thought cut him to the heart. Maybe they had given up on him; maybe they thought he was dead. Maybe they dreamed that he had won riches and honor and forgotten all about the inn on Nevis.

But he was not a melancholy sort of person. Instead he turned his attention to the new navigational skills he could acquire. If he was lucky, he might be allowed to study the captain's maps and learn even more about astronomy and mathematics. His daily visits carrying beer had brought him closer to the captain, who besides being a God-fearing man had turned out to be a stern taskmaster when it came to punishments but generous when it came to imparting knowledge. So he was wildly enthusiastic when Tom told him about Copernicus and readily countered with a report of an Italian named Galileo, who, in the captain's opinion, was the greatest astronomer.

"Superstition was created by the Evil One," he told Tom, who replied at once, "Yes, and by the English."

On that occasion he was allowed to taste the officers' beer, and this unexpected kindness made the thought of Europe easier to bear.

18 Nyo Boto

FOR SOME SEAMEN, the time spent waiting for wind can seem very long. Just now, as the Spanish galleon rocked on its anchor, it was difficult for the crew members to keep themselves occupied. Felix, the cook, was among those who suffered the most beneath reefed sails. The officers had arranged for various types of entertainment so the crew would not succumb to drinking or brawling. They played cards and games of ninepins, and they practiced shooting at targets. But for Felix the waiting time was a nervous strain that made him retreat to the pantry, where he sat with glazed eyes, snorting like a bull. That was where Tom found him after midnight, when the ship's clock had struck five bells.

"The silence is seeping into my blood," whispered the cook, clenching his fists. "I can feel it hardening in my veins. It makes a man sick to see the naked masts sticking up like a shark's skeleton. A ship was born to sail, not to sit still. It gives me fevers and shivers. I feel sick to my stomach and short of breath. I poured the last of the soup into the sea to appease the sea gods. There wasn't much left, but a little goes a long way, as the mouse said when he pissed into the river. The worst part is the nights, when we sway back and forth. I roll around in my hammock, moaning in my own sweat and listening for the ship's bell, just waiting for something terrible to happen. You see, José, it's at times like this that calamities occur."

"Calamities, cook?" said Tom, who was in the process of devouring a brown banana and who experienced no problem with waiting. He had been given access to the captain's library, which, in addition to the newest sea charts, contained all manner of books. A vast amount of knowledge was just waiting to be plucked from the shelves. And since the cook couldn't read, he had also benefited from his red-haired assistant, who in idle hours would read aloud from the book of fables. Every evening half a dozen grown men would sit around listening. The large audience had an invigorating effect on Tom—he had nothing against putting the book aside and telling the story about the green pelican who had coaxed the darkness up from the river. And late one night he started in on what he called The Story of Ramón the Pious.

The sailors moved in closer.

"Together they drifted in the sea for eight days before they were gathered up by Alberto, the fishwife's boy, who then won a share of the slave." Tom had discovered that he had a talent for embroidering the story, and he was especially fond of describing Alberto's fight with the English bombas on the sugar plantation. The story of little Sunday Morning, who was sold into eternal slavery but released when Alberto bought her freedom, made a particularly strong impression.

"How does the story end?" asked the sailors.

"Happily," replied Tom and went off to his hammock, uncertain whether that was really true.

Most of the seamen had lively imaginations when it came to calamities. Many of them firmly believed in the sirens, who flew during the night and lured seafarers to shipwreck and death.

"It's when the sea is becalmed," whispered Felix, "that fire and mutiny break out. The crew goes crazy waiting, but worst of all is the fear of pirates." The cook poured himself a tankard of beer. "Of course, you know, José, that we find ourselves in pirate waters, don't you? At any moment they could be upon us. It always happens when you least expect it. Out of the fog appears the black flag, and then they come racing like demons from hell. Before you know it, they've taken over the ship. Don't forget what we have in the hold. That much gold is enticing to those scoundrels."

"Has the cook ever heard of the pirate named C. W. Bull?" asked Tom.

The cook glanced around and put a finger to his lips. "Don't say another word about him. They say that even mentioning his name is dangerous. There's a curse on that blackguard."

"Have you ever met him?"

The cook crossed himself and tapped three times on a water keg. "If I had, I wouldn't be sitting here now. But the boatswain tells a story about Bull, who six years ago sailed up to a Portuguese galleon heading for the colonies in Brazil. The galleon surrendered without a fight. But then it turned out that there wasn't much to steal, so Bull seized the ship's captain, bled him, and ate him right before the eyes of the terrified passengers. Later he burned the ship and left the Portuguese on an island. They may still be sitting there today. No, I've never seen Captain Bull, but I came close. Once, when we were anchored near Curaçao, I made an exception and went to an alehouse to quench my thirst. There I saw a man sitting all alone in the dim tavern. No one dared approach him, let alone speak to him, for that man, José, had only nine fingers. A sure sign that he was one of Bull's men."

Tom nodded. "Does the cook know why Bull's men have only nine fingers?"

"It's because Bull ate the tenth one," answered the cook.

Tom shook his head. "That's not so. You see, I *have* met Bull."

"That's a lie," snarled the cook.

"No, it's not a lie. I've even had a drink with him. Exactly one year ago. His ship lay at anchor a short distance from Grenada. I was sent to have a look at two of his cannons. As the cook knows, I've worked for a blacksmith. And since my master didn't dare pay a visit to Bull, I had to go in his place. Yes, those were the days." Tom sighed.

The cook narrowed his eyes. "Tell me more, you miserable liar."

Tom shrugged his shoulders. "What is there to tell? We drank together, the best rum I've ever tasted. A little of it is still sitting in my hollow tooth. It was white like a baby tooth and distilled from the most exquisite syrup."

"Satan himself must have shaped your tongue." The cook laughed, lunging for Tom, who ducked and chuckled, only to turn serious as he recalled the source of the story. That didn't make it any more believable, just tinged with sorrow.

"To be a good liar," he murmured, "you have to have a good memory." He suddenly remembered a different story, told by his mother many years ago. And he thought that it was at times like this, on the open sea beneath reefed sails, that a sailor remembered such things.

He is lying in his mother's arms, not yet too old for that sort of thing. She is singing to him before he goes to sleep. But Tom would rather hear about how he was born, and he is lucky enough to have a mother who isn't afraid to talk plainly about procreation. She reaches the part in the story about the night when Tom O'Connor came into the world.

"I was past due," his mother tells him, "three weeks, to be precise, but on that night she came without being called, old Zamora. She told me that there were seven plump crocodiles on the wharf, all of them with open jaws, and this was a sign that a boy would be born. I remember that I waddled out of the inn to stare at the big creatures. Zamora tossed some fish out to them. 'If they tear it apart, then it will be a tranquil child,' she said. 'But if they leave it alone, you will have a sickly son.' Zamora claimed that she had seen most everything, but never a battle like the one that ensued. It was so fierce that one piling of the wharf was torn loose. The tumult continued in the water, where the huge animals whipped the bay into a froth. At the end, only five were left. And before dawn you were born, little Tom, with no pain at all. 'But the pain,' said the old fortune-teller, 'the pain will come later.'"

Why Tom should think of this story right now, he didn't know, but at that instant, beneath the glittering stars of the night sky, he felt his heart grow heavy as a stone. He looked at the cook, who had gone back to his ruminations about pirates.

"The great pirate captains," he said, "can literally smell what a hold contains—they have a nose for gold. They know that we're coming from the Aztecs, so they know what we have on board. May the Lord be merciful toward the shabby soul of a poor cook. But we all have to die sometime, and the grave makes the crooked straight, as the saying goes."

The cook crossed himself and poured another glass of beer.

"That reminds me of something, José," he said. "I forgot all about the black who's tied to the floorboards down by the pumps. He's the one named Abril. See if you can find him a drop of water. Take what we used to scrub out the pots and pour it into a bottle. Don't forget the small lantern—it's pitch-dark down there. And don't let me ever hear you mention the name Bull again."

Soon after, Tom was on his way from the galley through the midship, where the cadets kept watch, two by two. Every half hour, "All's well" was shouted from the maintop between the mainsail and the topgallant sail, where the lookout was perched. Otherwise it was a quiet night with no wind and no moon.

He continued down to the uppermost cannon deck, where he greeted the night guards who were sitting in a huddle, illuminated by a single lantern. A short time later he opened the door to the ship's lowest deck, where the pumps and barrels of water were housed. This was where he and the slaves hunted for rats, but it was also a place that was said to be haunted.

The darkness in the vast space was as thick as cobbler's wax, and the smell of rancid timber filled his nostrils. The water pounding against the keel and hull made a hollow, ominous sound. Tom held up the lantern in front of him and cautiously moved forward, uncertain where the slave might be. One of the other blacks usually brought him food and drink. Exactly how long he had been imprisoned here, Tom wasn't sure, but judging by the smell, it must have been days.

Before long he could discern the outline of a body in the dark. He seemed about the same height as Tom, but leaner in build. He was wearing only a loincloth around his waist and his head had been shaved to prevent lice.

"It's me, José," growled Tom. "I've brought you water. You understand Spanish, don't you?"

There was no answer.

Tom held the bottle to the boy's lips and watched him drink greedily. The cracks in his lips and the way he stared wide-eyed at Tom suggested he had been locked up in the hold for a long time. He emptied the bottle to the last drop and fell against the mast, groaning loudly.

"You should have saved some of it," said Tom. "It's not certain that you'll get more water tomorrow."

He was walking back toward the door with the lantern held high above his head when he heard a hoarse whisper behind him.

Tom stopped. If he didn't know better, he could have sworn the slave had said his name. Not José, but Tom.

The lantern shook so hard that its candle flickered. With hesitant steps Tom went back toward the black boy and held the light close to his face, only to lurch backward, as if he'd been burned. The shaved head, the dull eyes, and the hollow cheeks had fooled him at first. Not to mention that almost two years had passed. He had seen the change in his own face, but in the black's face it was even more apparent. He still had the features of a boy, but it was a man's gaze that met his own.

"Bibido," Tom whispered, "is it . . . is it you?"

The boy's eyes rolled a bit, then his lips parted, as if he wanted to smile, but when this failed, he said, "You took me out swimming once, a long, long time ago."

Tom looked away in an attempt to regain control of his racing heart. There was of course a lot he needed to think about, but right now all thoughts had deserted him. "Wait here," he said. "Wait here, Bibido."

In a matter of minutes he was back on deck and running down to the galley, where the cook had surrounded himself with like-minded mates who were in the midst of recounting tall tales about mermaids, hellhounds, sirens, and bloodthirsty pirates who seized good Spanish galleons whenever they were waiting for wind.

Tom knew that it was on nights like this that you had to be careful. It had happened before that otherwise-hardened seamen ended up in a panic and threw themselves overboard for fear of something worse than death by drowning. But right now he had other things to worry about. Quick as lightning he filled a cask with water and stuffed his pockets with biscuits.

"Where are you off to in such a hurry, José?" asked the lieutenant who had the watch on the cannon deck.

Tom threw out his arms and said that he'd seen three rats in the hold. "They're as good as dead, Lieutenant, sir. I'm an expert at catching them."

"How do you go about it?"

"I know a trick that lures them right to me." Tom backed toward the stairway.

The lieutenant, who had the first traces of peach fuzz on his chin, followed Tom. "That I'd like to see."

"It would be my pleasure," said Tom, "but the lieutenant will have to watch out because the brown beasts will bite at anything, and you never know what they might be carrying. One bite of their yellow teeth can be enough to bring the plague on board. This way, Lieutenant, sir."

"You go ahead. I'm on watch." The officer turned on his heel.

Tom allowed himself a little smile. Fear of the plague was so great that they no longer made do with throwing the dead overboard. Now they stuffed each body into a sack and rowed far from the ship before dumping it into the sea.

• • •

A minute later he opened the door to the pump room and made straight for Bibido, to pour more water down him. Afterward Bibido took the biscuits and began stuffing them into his mouth so fast that he immediately threw up.

"That's not what I intended," muttered Tom, examining the rope tied around Bibido's wrists. The bracelet of dried blood said a little about the thoroughness that had been brought to bear when he was tied up. Tom sat still, lost in his own thoughts, then asked, "How . . . how are you?"

Bibido blinked.

"You're not about to, I mean, you're not going to die, are you?"

"I'm all right, but I can't feel my legs," whispered Bibido.

Tom scratched his head. "Just imagine finding my half of a fortune in the hold of a Spanish galleon. What's the matter with your legs? How long have you been sitting here?"

"I think . . . since the full moon."

Tom calculated that Bibido had been in the hold for twelve days. The slave's legs were ice-cold.

He took out his knife and cut the rope. When it split apart, Bibido fell over and lay still for a moment, as if the blow had killed him. Tom managed to pour a little more water into him. Then he rubbed Bibido's thin legs until the boy whimpered with pain. His gaunt body began shaking as he curled up and, with an effort, stretched out on his back.

"It's coming back to me," he whispered.

"What's coming back?"

"The feeling in my legs. I had a dream," he said. "I dreamed that my legs were going to be crushed by the waves."

Tom got him to sit up. "The ship is anchored. We're waiting for two warships that will escort us to Spain. Are you listening to me, Bibido?"

The boy looked up with a trace of his old will in his eyes. "My name is not Bibido." He tried to make his voice sound authoritative and proud but managed only a whisper. "My name is Abebe, but I've always been called Nyo Boto."

Tom stared at him. "Well, what do you know," he grumbled. "Is that right? But for me you're still Bibido, so you might as well forget about that other name. Half of you still belongs to Tom O'Connor. I thought you knew that."

"What about the other half? Is it mine? Or does it belong to the ship?"

Tom cleared his throat. "You remember Ramón, don't you?"

Bibido did not respond.

"The man who saved your life after the shipwreck off Saint Kitts? I rescued both of you. Have you forgotten all that?"

The boy looked at Tom with a reproachful frown. "How could I forget?"

Tom said something about Ramón possibly being dead, and then felt surprised that his heart could bleed at the memory of a soul that was so rotten. "In a sense," he said, "you're all mine now. That was the agreement with Ramón. And I've traveled half the world looking for you. So don't go on about any Nyo Boto here; your name is Bibido and that's final." Without realizing it, Tom had downed the last of the water in the cask. "But I can't stay here," he muttered. "I'm going to have to tie you up again. If we're discovered, I'll be keelhauled four times over. Damn it all."

"You're not allowed to curse on this ship," said Bibido.

Tom gave him a hard poke in the chest. "That's not for you to decide. You can't decide anything at all, do you understand? And by the way, my name is Master O'Connor. Aside from the fact that my name isn't O'Connor at all, but José. You'd better remember that."

"Should I call you Master José?"

"Yes, or rather, no. Don't call me anything at all."

Tom went over to the door and stood there a moment. "The question is," he said, "the question is whether you're actually worth all this trouble. Nyo Boto, you say. What does that mean? Are you really the son of a chieftain or a king's son or a prince or something like that? And where's the ring? Did they steal it from you or have you lost it? Not that I think it was worth anything, but Ramón said it was proof you were a prince. Is that true, or was that just another one of Ramón's lies? You can at least tell me that, can't you?"

"Yes, I am a prince," replied Bibido, "and my father will make you a very rich man if you take me back to the Bissagos Islands."

Tom smiled and nodded. "Oh sure, that's a good one. I don't know how you thought that would happen. Did you picture yourself sitting on my back while I swam like a damned dolphin? Was that what you imagined, Prince Boto? This boy who's been shitting all over himself, and who throws up when somebody gives him a biscuit. Good Lord, good Lord. But let me tell you something else. It would take us three months to sail to the Bissagos Islands, and you still haven't told me what's become of the ring. The Devil knows I'm tired of this whole business. Here I thought that I was going to . . . that there was a chance I could earn . . . but no . . . damn it, how unlucky can I be?"

Tom stopped when he saw Bibido open his mouth and tilt back his head. "What's that supposed to mean?" he asked.

Bibido picked up the lantern and held it to his open mouth.

Tom moved closer.

The little gray ring sat in his throat, all the way in the back, sewn on with a thin piece of string.

"It's placed there," he explained, "so I can hide it with my tongue."

"Hide it?" muttered Tom.

"When they inspect our teeth," said Bibido, "at the auctions."

Tom shook his head. "I don't even want to ask, but I can't help myself. Who did that?"

"I did," replied Bibido. "I don't know the name of the town, but after Ramón sold me to a shopkeeper, I was put on board a ship that took me and ten others to Jamaica, where we were to be sold at the marketplace. In a compartment of the hold, I got my hands on one of the needles that the fisherman used to repair his nets. I've had to change the string several times, but I still have the needle."

Bibido turned up the edge of his loincloth and showed Tom the curved needle stuck into the underside of the fabric.

Tom sighed and threw out his arm. "Dear God," he sighed. "The things a person hears. But now let me tell you something. I've actually made up my mind to go to Spain. Why? Because I'm happy and because I've found so many new friends. That's why! So you might as well forget all about your home—sitting here in the hold with a ring in your throat."

Tom leaned his head back against the timbers. "The cook is actually quite nice," he went on, "and the captain is an educated man. We talk about all kinds of things, the captain and I. About Galileo and Copernicus and about lunar eclipses, which happen to interest me. But what do you know about things like that? You, sitting down here gaping. You probably still believe that the sun is a moving ball, don't you? Well, it's not. It doesn't budge from its spot. The Devil knows I'm wasting my time here. But getting back to what I was saying, the idea is to stay on board until we put in at a Spanish port. That's what I've been planning."

"You have?"

"Yes, I have, that's what I've been sitting here telling you, isn't it? In a few days, maybe even tomorrow, the two warships will arrive and then we can set sail. Before long we'll be north of the Tropic of Cancer and won't make landfall until we reach Madeira. I've looked at the captain's sea charts and have the whole route at my fingertips. First the Azores, then Madeira."

"But where are we now, José?"

"Right now we're south of Hispaniola, and by the way, you don't have to call me José when we're alone."

"Should I call you Tom, then?"

"Don't call me anything at all, but if necessity demands it, you may call me Master O'Connor."

"Is it far to Nevis, Master O'Connor?"

"It's a hell of a long way to Nevis."

"Even by boat?"

Tom slapped his hand to his forehead. "Where are you going to get a boat, you skinny runt?"

"There are plenty of skiffs on this ship."

"Oh, good God, my dear sweet Lord and Creator. You don't know anything, do you? This vessel is sailing with so much gold on board that we could buy half of Spain and Madeira too. The cannons are manned around the clock, and the riggings and yards are swarming with sailors. You can't even swill a glass of water without someone asking you if the cook gave his permission. Do you really think we could put an eight-man rowboat into the water without being caught?"

Bibido pointed to the door leading to the stairwell.

"Behind that door," he said, "is the gunpowder room. The kegs are stacked up on the floorboards; I think one would be enough."

Tom's eyes opened wide. "Oh, you think one would be enough, do you? Is that what you're suggesting?"

Bibido looked at Tom with his half-closed eyes. He nodded.

Tom sighed deeply.

"Now let me tell you something, little Prince Pillarick. You don't know anything at all. If you blow up one of those fellows, half the ship will go with it. It'll make a hole the size of the aft deck. The water will come pouring in. And if the cook's two assistants, the red-haired José, and the slave they call Abril, don't get their behinds shot off when they set fire to the keg, then they're sure to be strung up from the mast."

"I would never blow up a whole keg," explained Bibido.

"Oh, is that right?"

"No, I'd take a handful of powder and put it where they store the coils of rope. They would catch fire in no time. I'm thinking that the smoke would rise up to the deck and . . ."

Tom put his hand in the air. He'd just noticed a rat scurrying across the floor and down through a hole in the boards. "Of course," he said, "of course." He stared straight ahead, speaking in a calm monotone. "Sometimes you get help from an unexpected source. And a long life has taught me that the rat is the cleverest animal of all. That's why the Devil has adopted its tail. You see, Bibido, we're not going to set fire to anything."

"We're not?"

"No, just the opposite. We're going to do what's expected of us. And if things go as I hope, we'll be out of here before daybreak. And with the officers' blessing, to boot. But we have to be quick. We won't get a chance like this again." Tom stopped and looked at Bibido. "You must have been born under a lucky star after all," he said, "but your luck may run out before the next grain of sand strikes the bottom of the hourglass. It all depends on your ability to pay attention when your lord and master speaks. Can you do that, Bibido?"

"Yes," replied Bibido.

"Pardon me, but I didn't hear what you said."

"I said, yes, Master O'Connor."

Tom stroked his chin pensively. "And will you leave everything to your master and do exactly what he says?"

"Yes, Master O'Connor."

"Be as loyal as a dog that knows no other master?"

"As loyal as a dog that knows no other master."

"And what I'm seeing on his face isn't a dumb little smile, is it?"

"No, Master O'Connor."

"And what is your name?"

"My name is Bibido, Master O'Connor."

"You learn faster than I thought."

"Thank you, master."

"You're welcome."

"Tell me what I'm supposed to do, master."

"You're going to prepare to die," replied Tom as he left the hold.

He's standing in front of the duty officer. Behind him is the cook, wringing his hands. The unpleasant business of assigning blame and responsibility has begun. The cook says that it wasn't his responsibility, and therefore he doesn't deserve to be reproached for anything. He adds that according to regulations, the slaves come under the authority of the first officer and that their health and well-being are a matter for the surgeon.

The cook's voice is unnaturally shrill. This is not because he fears being reprimanded or punished—his agitation is too great for that. It's the prospect of a cruel and premature death that is making the cook quake.

When the full extent of the situation dawns on the duty officer, he takes two steps back and then bites his knuckles and stomps on the deck. "Damn it all," he groans. He has just relieved the young lieutenant and is cursing his luck. But when he realizes that the problem is much more serious than an unfortunate watch, he hunches his shoulders and begins pacing back and forth. The horror of the situation makes him so dizzy that he has to lean on the cook. "Damn it, how I detest the savages," he snaps. "Almost as much as the plague. In our family we went to sea to avoid it. We thought ourselves lucky because that opportunity was open to us. Yet in death we are all equal."

"Yes," sighs Tom, "the rich man has only two nostrils, just like the poor."

The officer turns to face him, suddenly furious. "Is the boy mad? Spare me such witticisms."

Tom apologizes and receives a swat on the back of the neck from the cook.

"Certainly not very pleasant news to be bringing me right now," groans the duty officer.

"Maybe we should wake the captain," suggests the cook.

The officer gives this some thought.

While he's thinking, Tom says, "With the duty officer's permission, I don't think it's necessary to disturb the captain on this account."

"No? Doesn't the boy realize what we're talking about here?" The officer catches himself raising his voice and continues in a hoarse whisper. "Doesn't he understand what might happen if this gets out? The men are already irritable after all this waiting. It would be like setting fire to a keg of powder. Damn it. And it would have to be on my watch. To hell with the blacks. Is he absolutely positive about this?"

"Quite positive, señor," replies Tom.

"Damn. Well, I suppose I'd better have a look. Captains have a habit of making themselves scarce when things like this happen. *Cattus amat pisces, sed non vult crura madere*—the cat loves fish but doesn't want to get its paw wet . . . and I quote. Lead the way, José."

"Gladly, señor."

The officer makes a move to follow Tom but stops and stares in astonishment at the cook, who is already on his way down to his warm bunk. "Where does the cook think he's going?"

"I'm going down to catch up on my sleep."

"Absolutely not. You're coming with us, you miserable evader."

"Why should I come along?"

"Because you're the one who threw that black devil down there—that's why! Get going!"

Tom walks ahead of the officer, who is pushing the cook in front of him. They make their way to the passageway leading down to the supply room and light a couple of lanterns.

"I think it must have happened yesterday or the day before," says Tom. "Judging by how much the rats have eaten, they must have been at it for several days."

The officer stops abruptly. "How disgusting," he whispers. "A corpse like that isn't a pretty sight, is it?"

Tom wrings his hands. "It's not that bad, señor. Most of the face is still there, and after you get used to the smell . . ."

"Hold your tongue, boy." The officer puts his hand on his stomach and gives himself a shake. "This is no job for an officer. I can see that now. We need to get hold of the surgeon."

"I'll run and get him, señor."

"Excellent. Off with you, José. We'll wait here. But remember, not a word to anyone."

Tom bows, slaps a hand over his mouth, and makes it down to the surgeon's cabin in two minutes flat. He leans against the door, muttering to himself.

> *She sparkles brighter than all torchlight,*
> *Like a gem on the cheek of the night,*
> *A jewel in an African's ear,*
> *Far too lovely, too noble, too dear.*
> *She outshines others, even her foes,*
> *Like a white dove in a flock of crows.*

He repeats the verse and then rushes back to the officer and the cook, who are still standing on the stairs.

"What now, José?" asks the cook.

"I have both good and bad news, señor." Tom takes a deep breath. "According to the surgeon, the body is probably infected with the plague."

"Damn those blacks," groans the officer, slapping his hands together. "And damn the rats." He puts his fist to his forehead and rolls his eyes. "Then what was the good news, José?"

"That actually was the good news," says Tom, sighing. "The bad news, with your permission, is that the dead body could infect the whole crew in less than twenty-four hours if something isn't done. The sooner we get rid of the corpse, the better. Says the surgeon."

"We must get hold of the captain," decides the officer.

Tom allows himself to pluck at his sleeve. "There's a proverb, señor. It goes something like this: 'He who acts swiftly is he who wins the honor.' If you see what I mean."

The officer straightens up and gazes out across the motionless ocean as he tries to repeat it. Then he scowls at Tom with a skeptical expression. "But who can we get to . . ." He lowers his voice. "Who the hell can I get to do this filthy job? No white would touch a black that's been struck by the plague. And if word gets out that we have plague in the hold, there won't be a sailor left for miles around. We're risking riots and mutiny. And it's understandable. The Devil knows it's understandable. We can threaten them with a keelhauling and the whip. But faced with the plague, those threats will mean nothing to them."

The cook clasps his hands and smiles with satisfaction. "I've got it, señor," he says eagerly. "I've got it—it's perfectly elementary. We'll make Enero and Febrero do it."

"Who the hell are Enero and Febrero?" growls the officer.

"Two of the slaves."

The duty officer snaps his fingers. "Good idea, cook. Roust them out of bed at once."

The cook has already started on his way when Tom calls him back. "I don't want to meddle in the decisions of my superiors," he says, "but if we force the blacks to haul their dead comrade out of the hold, then won't we be left with a double problem? How can we be sure that they aren't infected too? And besides, we shouldn't forget that the blacks are at least as super-stitious as the whites. I've worked on a plantation where the slaves adorned themselves with feathers and parrot beaks and sang songs backward over their newborn children as they dripped fresh blood from eleven chicken feet onto the children's faces. All just to avoid the plague."

"Damn it, José is right," mutters the officer. "We can't use two blacks. Unless we shoot them afterward."

"So go ahead and shoot them," says the cook.

"But wouldn't it attract attention if we suddenly executed two blacks?" grumbles Tom.

"Not really," says the cook.

"And there are no other alternatives," exclaims the officer.

"Señor!" Tom straightens his back and salutes. "José Alonzo Emanuel Rodrigues Vasgues reporting for duty."

The officer clears his throat and squints through one eye. "For duty? What does the boy mean?"

"I volunteer, señor."

"Is he crazy? The slave has the plague."

"I know that, señor. But I believe that working on a plantation has given me strength against the plague."

The officer looks to the right and the left. "Has he been through this sort of thing before?"

"Three times," whispers Tom. "If only I can get someone to lower the boat into the sea, then the officer won't hear another word from me. And as for the black with his face gnawed off, I promise that he will be many miles away by daybreak."

The officer is lost in thought for a moment, then he puts one hand on his waist and strokes his beard with the other. "José," he says, "you're a boy after my own heart. Cook, find a sack for this brave lad, who's putting his life at risk in order to save the crew. I will personally see to it that the boat is put into the water. I'm certain that the captain will be thanking you when he hears about your actions tomorrow. Now Felix, keep your mouth shut and go find the sack."

Tom bows humbly and watches the cook trundle off. While the officer summons two cadets, Tom goes down to the galley, where he finds the cook in the process of emptying a sack of millet.

"I've just come to say good-bye," says Tom.

"Good-bye?" mutters the cook.

Tom nods. "I'm not coming back, Señor Felix. I didn't want to say so in front of the young officer, and I ask the cook to keep this to himself, but in the hour of need I had to lie to my superiors."

"You lied, José?"

Tom nods. "The truth is just the opposite of what I said. I'm afraid that I may already be carrying the infection."

The cook takes a step back.

"Don't worry, señor," says Tom. "I realize that I can't allow myself to stay on board if there's any suspicion of the plague in my blood. That's why I thought," Tom lowers his voice to a whisper, "I thought maybe I could have a few provisions, a little water and a handful of biscuits?"

"Damn it all, José," moans the cook. "I don't know what to say. It pains me to hear this news. I was actually starting to like you. But of course, you can have whatever you need. You'll be missed by many, José. Not to mention your stories."

Tom modestly shrugs.

The cook empties another sack and fills it with provisions. Then he pours water into two casks.

"Give me plenty," says Tom. "Even though the plague is hideous, the illness can take its time."

The cook gives him a commiserating glance and makes the sign of the Cross. "Tell me, José," he says, "before you leave us, how does the story about the fisherman's son Alberto end? Did he ever find the slave boy who was born a prince? I can't sleep in peace unless I know how it ends."

Tom looks up. "Oh, him. Well, yes, he did find him, and on a ship where the boy was working in the galley."

"He did?" The cook's eyes gleam.

"Unfortunately," Tom continues as he puts a coconut into the sack of provisions, "unfortunately, the slave was infected with the plague after being bitten by a rat."

The cook's mouth falls open. His fingers are laced together in front of his chest. Then he breaks out in a sly smile. "You're the world's biggest liar."

Tom throws out his arms and winks at the cook. "Actually my name is O'Connor and I'm from Ireland."

That too amuses the cook, but he quickly turns serious. "Good-bye, José," he whispers.

"Good-bye, Señor Felix," says Tom. "Live well. You're the best cook I've ever worked for."

The cook blows his nose on his apron. "Your good deed will be remembered."

"I will live in hope."

Tom picks up the sacks and goes back on deck, where he is met by two young cadets who tell him that the boat is on the starboard side, as requested. Then Tom goes down to the hold to find Bibido. Without a word the boy crawls inside the sack, which Tom just as soundlessly ties tightly. Then he quickly slings the slave over his shoulder.

The whole thing takes less than five minutes, and then Tom is back on deck. He catches sight of the duty officer standing with the cadets and the cook. They are staring hard at the brave boy dragging his heavy burden down the ladder to the rowboat, where he drops the sacks of provisions before placing the body in the bottom of the boat. He dips the oars in the water and rows two hundred feet away, then stands up and salutes.

From the deck of the galleon it sounds suspiciously as if the cook is sobbing, but the officer salutes Tom in return. His gesture is immediately copied by the two cadets, who with shining eyes stare at José from Cádiz, who got his odd eye color from eating too much goat cheese, and whose parents suffered the remarkable fate of dying from dysentery only later to be hanged before they expired from the plague.

Seldom have the two cadets seen a man row faster than this lad who, in the service of a greater cause, has gone to sea with the plague.

And when dawn came and the warships at last appeared, the captain held a short memorial service for José Alonzo Emanuel Rodrigues Vasgues, who, close to death, was hauled on board off the coast of Jamaica, and who, once again marked by death, left the proud galleon south of Hispaniola. The priest said a few well-chosen words about the spirit of self-sacrifice, whereupon they honored the red-haired ship's boy with two minutes of silence.

19 Island

HE'S LYING IN THE ROWBOAT with his hands behind his head, studying the stars. All the heavenly bodies have gathered above him. On this night the firmament has merged with the ocean, and there is no dividing line. The shark, the whale, and the algae-colored mermaid are swimming around between the sky and the sea, transformed into amber-yellow constellations in a phosphorescent veil.

Tom is dozing, in a state between sleep and wakefulness, pointing out Cetus, Aquarius, and Virgo. "They're watching us," he murmurs, "whispering and wondering, because stars are like mothers worrying about their children. Did you know that, Bibido? No, you didn't know that. You don't know a damn thing. And don't go talking to me, either. What blissful peace. Did you hear what I said, little man? I said, what blissful peace." Tom lowers his voice and mutters to himself. "What's the matter with him? Why doesn't he ever say anything?"

Tom sits up and looks at Bibido. Suddenly he feels a pang in his chest at the thought that Bibido also had a mother who, like the stars, worried about her children. Especially about the one who disappeared. Maybe a trace of her still remained inside of Bibido, and maybe it was this trace that made him so quiet.

For six days he has sat with the oars in his hands. It would be an exaggeration to say that he is good at rowing, but what he lacks in strength is balanced by his endurance. He rows without stopping, night and day.

Tom would like to ask about his mother, but he doesn't know how to formulate his question. Not to mention the fact that Bibido might have forgotten everything about his parents. He has been gone for a long time, after all. Almost two years. But was two years long enough? Could a person forget about his parents in only two years? His home, his language, his brothers and sisters? "As if it makes any difference to me. As if I didn't have anything better to think about."

He is annoyed by the voice that keeps asking these irksome questions regarding that skinny slave. Besides, thinks Tom, there's a difference between him and me. I would never dream of sewing a ring into my throat. That wasn't exactly proof, but it did say something about how great the difference was. Was a tapir capable of feeling sorrow when its young were eaten by the jaguar? Of course not. That's the way nature was set up; otherwise it would be unbearable to be a tapir. Without comparing Bibido to a tapir, it was probably the same with him and his mother, meaning that the blacks didn't have the same feelings as the whites. Otherwise it would be unbearable to be black. Tom permits himself a little smile. "If I were black," he says, "if I were you, Bibido, I would be downright happy right now."

The other boy looks at him as if he doesn't understand.

"Better than being tied to a water barrel, isn't it?"

Bibido frowns.

Tom moves closer to him. "You would probably say that you're glad to get out of those ropes. But maybe you don't know what it means to feel something? Don't answer." Tom sighs and rolls his eyes. "What's going on in that little black head of yours? We've been at sea for six days, so you must have been thinking about something."

"I'm thinking," replies Bibido, "that soon we won't have any water left. Do you know where we are, Tom?"

Tom cups his hand behind his ear. "Did you say Tom? Whatever happened to Master O'Connor? Or maybe you think you're free now and can call me Tom? But you're not, Bibido. You're mine. You belong to your master. On the sugar plantation, the blacks showed me real respect. There I was called Tombomba."

"That's a grand name," says Bibido.

"I hate that name," snarls Tom, "so for now on you'll call me Master O'Connor."

Bibido nods. "I just asked if Master O'Connor knows where we are?"

Tom replies in a carefree voice. "We're somewhere south of Puerto Rico, maybe a whole mile from Nevis, depending on how far south the wind has carried us. We should have had Saint Croix in sight, but it never showed up." He turns around. "Shall we talk about our fate? Are you prepared for it, Bibido? You know what it is as well as I do. So why keep rowing? I suggest that we write our names on the thwart so the people who find us will know who we are. Give me the water cask."

Tom sits up and watches Bibido pick up the cask, which he hugs close. "Oh, so he wants to fight over it, does he?"

Bibido shakes his head.

Tom narrows his eyes and studies him. He does look terrible. His soft lips have dried up into crusts, and his eyes have a dull look to them.

"It's good that you're watching out for the water." Tom gives a sigh. "By all means let's drag out the misery. But when I feel like having some water, I'll have some. Just so you know."

Two hours later daylight arrived. Bibido was still sitting in the bow, rowing with the same rhythm, the same monotonous lassitude.

Tom had started carving in the timber. Small splinters of wood lay in the bottom of the boat, as proof of his hatred. He held the rowboat responsible for his misfortune. He knew that unlucky boats existed, and this surely was one of them. He also knew that it hurt the rowboat to be cut. So he resumed his scratching at the boards and laughed loudly every time a splinter struck the bottom of the boat.

He had dreamed, no, he hadn't dreamed, he had actually seen it. One night, a couple of days earlier, when the sky was black and even the stars had deserted them, Bibido had danced. For hours and hours, as he intoned something that Tom couldn't understand. He claimed that it was a dance to placate the stars. This had amused Tom, especially since the stars hadn't come out.

Tom moved over to his slave and grabbed his ankle. "I could eat you, you know," he said.

Bibido did not react.

"I could start with your leg. Cut it off at the knee and let the water salt it before I devoured it, piece by piece. But what slim pickings. There's not even enough meat for one meal. Do you hear what I'm saying, Bibido? No, you're not listening, because you're stone-deaf. You're a jinx, God damn it. I could be sitting in the captain's cabin, studying the newest sea chart and drinking sweet wine from Madeira while eating one helping of pork after another, stuffing myself to the bursting point. And then I could trot down to see the cook, who would never refuse his galley boy a tankard of water. Fresh water that slides down the throat like thousands of tiny fish and tastes of the south wind when it blows into the bay off the island of Nevis. I can hear the monkeys in the forest. They too love the south wind. They're gorging themselves on fruit and sticking their blue tongues under the waterfall, drinking as much as they like. I've often drunk from that very same water. It tastes of iron, earth, and oranges. It comes from the big volcano with the white rim. I wonder whether the Almighty has forsaken us."

"Who?"

"Almighty God, you ignorant slave. I wonder whether He has forgotten about us. Maybe He's ignoring us because you're along."

"Doesn't the Almighty like me?"

Tom laughed. "Of course He doesn't like you, Bibido. Think about it. There must be some reason why you were born black and I was born white."

"My parents are black," answered Bibido.

"Yes, so they are, Bibido. And the Almighty doesn't like them either."

"There are lots of blacks," said Bibido. "Lots and lots of them."

Tom nodded and said that he was aware of that too.

"Do you know why the Almighty doesn't like the blacks?" asked Bibido.

"Because He's white. That's why," Tom answered.

Bibido looked at his hands. "Just think if there was another Almighty that was black," he murmured.

"But there isn't. The white God would never allow it."

Bibido said that it was unfortunate the Almighty didn't like all people.

Tom lay down and closed his eyes, listening to the waterfall on Nevis and to the monkeys screaming. For some reason it made him laugh. He laughed himself to sleep and didn't wake up until midday when Bibido started shaking him. Actually, Bibido wasn't shaking Tom at all. He was leaning over him, holding the water cask.

What had awakened Tom was the swell of the waves, which had grown enormous. The rowboat was rocking so violently that it was taking on water. They had to cling to the thwarts just to stay in the boat.

Tom sat up. His head felt terribly heavy. He couldn't understand it. What had happened to make his body suddenly feel too heavy to move? He felt dizzy and muddled, tired and weak.

Bibido held the water cask to Tom's lips. Tom opened his mouth and felt the drops strike his tongue. He laughed loudly. A dribble of water ran out of his mouth, but Bibido lifted it back to his lips on the curve of his forefinger. "Keep pouring," said Tom, "just keep on pouring, Bibido."

"There isn't any more." He tossed the cask aside.

Tom wiped his mouth. It was barely moist. He stared out at the ocean, which had been so flat but was now transformed into towering waves. They were rolling and pounding and smashing together in great cascades. He looked up at the sun, hidden behind a grayish-yellow mist. "The heading is good enough," he muttered. "If only we can manage to stay on board. Will we stay in the rowboat or will this cursed ocean finally swallow us up in one big gulp?"

"We're not going to die here," said the slave.

"Oh, is that so? Well, that's good news. We're not going to die here. Did you hear that, Almighty God? Forget all about devouring two tiny men and a Spanish rowboat. Bibido, the great chieftain's son, says that we're not going to die here."

At that moment a huge wave rolled under the boat and lifted it fifty feet in the air, only to vanish just as rapidly. For a brief second they hung in midair. Then the rowboat heeled over and fell sideways into the foaming sea, where it righted itself, now half-filled with water.

They bailed like crazy and were once again lifted up and thrown down. It went on like this for an hour. By that time, they had been tossed into the waves twice, and Tom had made a lifeline out of pants and shirts. Toward noon the waves seemed to subside a bit. On the other hand, a strong current had taken a firm hold on the rowboat.

Tom couldn't read their course, but he thought they were moving in a southwesterly direction. It was the worst thing that could happen.

When night fell, they were lying huddled together in the bottom of the boat. Tom calculated their heading by studying the stars. "We've been pulled eastward," he muttered, "due east, as far as I can tell. That's actually not so bad. With a little luck we should reach the Saint Martin islands by morning. Maybe even tonight. So maybe it did some good after all that you danced for the stars." Tom coughed and touched his cracked lips. "Maybe you should dance for the favorable current that has served us better than any sail." He turned around and looked at the slave, who was lying flat on his back with his eyes wide open. His lips were slightly parted. He looked like a baboon to Tom. His cheeks were so hollow that his teeth were visible under his skin.

Tom gave him a shake but got no response. "Bibido, are you listening to me? Bibido? Master O'Connor is talking to you." Tom raised his voice in anger and bent down over the lifeless form. "Damn it all, man, what are you looking at? Or maybe you're not looking at anything?" He moved his hand back and forth, but Bibido's eyes did not waver.

Tom grabbed the water cask before he remembered that he had drunk the last drop himself. Then he pressed his ear to Bibido's lips and shook him so hard that his head fell backward. In a rage Tom filled the cup of his hand with seawater and threw it over the lifeless face, over and over again, until he was screaming hysterically. He pulled the limp body close to his own. "Don't die now," he whispered. "Don't die now."

Tom clenched his teeth but couldn't stop the tears from trickling down his face. He rocked the lifeless form back and forth as he wept and cursed, begged and pleaded. "Stay with me," he whispered. "Stay with me, Nyo Boto. Do you hear me? Stay with me. If you want to be free, don't do it like this. I'm begging you, don't do it like this. Whisper in my ear, whisper my name, just once, and that very second you will be free. No more chains, no more ropes around your neck. Tom promises, he promises."

He laid the limp body down in the boat and opened Boto's mouth. He took out his knife and cut the string that held the gray-black ring. He rolled it between his fingers and then placed it on Boto's thumb.

"All right," he whispered. "Now the ring is back where it belongs. Can you feel it, Nyo Boto? Can you feel the ring on your finger?" Tom lifted up the boy and rocked him back and forth. "Say my name. You only have to whisper it."

A blue moonbeam had appeared on the sea. Tom squinted his eyes and moved forward to the bow. There was no doubt about it. Due east a reef was visible. No, not a reef but a misty coast, a hazy image that minute by minute was growing clearer and clearer.

Tom felt the hysteria roll out of his stomach and into the night. He laughed and he cried; he picked up Boto's head and turned it toward the re-demptive coast. "We're not going to die here," said Tom. "We're not going to die here, Nyo Boto. Do you hear me, boy! Damn it, then answer me. Look at the coast—we're saved. We'll be there in less than an hour. The current will carry us. It won't desert us. But is there a price? What is the price? What do I have to give? Oh, now I remember. But it's not going to depend on that. Nobody's going to say that Tom O'Connor is a stingy boy. No one can say that. Go ahead and take my heart, you slimy gecko. Take my heart, you green lizard, if only . . . if only he'll wake up. But his spirit has left him."

Tom's voice sank to a whisper. "His whole body is cold. Like the fish washed up onshore whose scales have lost their gleam, whose eyes see nothing. Maybe I should try to blow the life back into his lungs. Maybe I could blow some of my own air into him. Do you hear what I'm saying, Nyo Boto? Tom is going to open your mouth and you must accept the air that I give you."

Tom pressed his mouth to Nyo Boto's dry lips and blew as hard as he could. "Take it inside you," he said harshly, placing Boto's head on his knee and blowing again, but with no response. "Maybe," Tom muttered, "maybe it would be better to try his nose. What do you say Boto? Shall we try it?" Tom's voice broke and he began sobbing quietly. "Shall Tombomba try your nose?" He placed his mouth over Boto's nose and blew as best he could. Over and over again.

Then he collapsed, feeling faint and dizzy. "I have nothing more to give you, Nyo Boto."

He leaned over the gunwale and did the forbidden—he took a gulp of salt water. For a brief moment he enjoyed the refreshing sensation, only to feel the salt in his throat.

"The Devil take you, Almighty God. You've deserted both the blacks and the whites." He fell onto his side. "Is this your idea of a joke? In that case, I'm not amused. I'm not in the least amused."

Tom wept, then stood up in the boat. He clenched his fists and shook them at the sky. "First you give, and then you take away. Just like my stubborn sister, who always tied a string to her gifts." He stared down at the water. "But I won't let you have him. I'll take him with me onshore, and I'll bury him there. He's not going to end up in the sea. Do you hear me, Sea-God? You've gotten plenty, damn it all. But you won't get him, because he's mine."

"Fu-fu."

"Yes, fu-fu," muttered Tom and spat. Then he sat up with a start and looked down at Boto, who was still flat on his back. "Fu-fu," whispered Tom. "You said fu-fu."

The other boy's eyes flickered in three tiny movements. "It's a kind of mash," he said in a weak voice. "Made from yams that are crushed in a mortar."

Tom shut his eyes, his whole body shaking with sobs that went on and on. Finally he roared like a lion and laughed through his tears as he tenderly gathered Nyo Boto into his arms and held him close. "Fu-fu? What the hell is fu-fu? You miserable runt, I thought you were dead. But you're not, you're alive, you tough little slave. You impossible fu-fu man."

Tom laughed, pressing his nose against Boto's, and saw the glimmer of a smile in the boy's eyes. "Look, look toward the east. Land, an island. We're saved."

Nyo Boto nodded and lay back down. "You can also mix the yams with cooked bananas."

Before Tom even set foot on the rocky shore, he knew that he had made a mistake. He was familiar with most of the islands in the area. None of them looked like this one. It was not Saint Martin, at any rate.

From the sea, the island had looked as if it were covered with jungle. When they came closer, they caught sight of a number of wooden posts of the sort used for rolling large vessels into the water. What puzzled Tom the most were the crowds of monkeys occupying the shore. They lolled about, grooming one another, or concentrated on peeling some type of fruit from the forest. If any humans lived here, the monkeys would have kept to the trees.

When the rowboat reached calm waters, Tom slipped into the shallows and pulled the boat behind him until it touched bottom. He told Nyo Boto to stay where he was and received an inquisitive but veiled glance in return.

In no time Tom entered the suffocating heat of the forest, where droplets of moisture sat on the foliage. Overhead the parrots screamed, reinforcing his initial impression that the place was deserted. He found a couple of green coconuts, which he cracked open with his knife. The trick was to give them a hard rap, but not too hard. It wasn't really a problem, since he barely had enough strength left even to lift one. But as soon as a

hole appeared and the juice slid down his throat, he fell to his knees in gratitude.

After quenching his thirst, he gathered up three more coconuts and hurried back to the rowboat, where Nyo Boto lay with his face turned toward
the naked heavens. Tom poured the juice into a shell, and Nyo Boto drank
in small measured gulps.

"Did that help?" asked Tom.

Boto nodded and lay back down. Closing his eyes, he fell asleep.

For the next few hours Tom wandered along the shore. Even as a child he
knew that it was important to show the monkeys who was superior. So he
had enlisted the aid of a solid stick, which he waved in a threatening manner when a silver-gray monkey tried to test him.

After a while he came upon the remains of a campfire. In the ashes he
found charred branches, fish bones, and a larger bone. He figured he was
on the north side of the island and had gained some sense of its size. It was
much smaller than Nevis and not a place where you'd normally expect to
find humans. Tom knew of islands sufficiently remote that pirates used
them as places to abandon undesirable individuals. There the poor souls
could either rot away or attempt to make some sort of life, in the hope that
one day a ship might happen past.

He continued on into the forest, where he stumbled upon a cleared area
with a well and a kitchen midden. Greatly uneasy, he stared at the marks
where four houses had once stood. Ashes were all that remained. Quickly
he gathered up some fruit and lugged it back to Nyo Boto, who reluctantly
allowed Tom to feed him.

Tom had to make his voice sound stern. "I'm the one in charge here, and
you have to eat."

"This isn't Nevis," said Nyo Boto.

Tom told him about finding the burned-out village.

"Maybe there was a tribal war," said Nyo Boto.

"Maybe," said Tom.

He didn't wake up until the sun was high overhead. He would have liked to
sleep longer, but he was awakened by a terrible pain in his stomach. For the
next few hours he had diarrhea. Toward evening, feeling feeble and weak,

he lay on the beach where Nyo Boto had lit a fire. He had also found a stand and a pot, a rusty knife, and a shirt that smelled so powerfully of mold that the stench was noticeable from ten feet away.

"Burn it," moaned Tom, holding his nose.

"It's a fine shirt," said Boto. "It was once red."

"It stinks. Burn it."

But Boto refused to burn his shirt. He boiled a handful of herbs, filtered the salt from the water, and poured it down Tom's throat. Next he tended to the shirt, which had started to come apart. Boto still had his needle. With threads pulled from the canvas sacks, he tacked the shirt together. As he told Tom, "This is my very first shirt, and I never dreamed that one day I would have a red one."

By the third day, Tom had regained his strength. Together with Boto, he went back to the village, where they searched for anything else that had been left behind. Suddenly Tom pulled Boto away. "My God, how could I be so stupid?" he said. "What was I thinking? The island was struck by the plague. That's why the whole place was burned down. We can't use the well."

"Can houses get the plague?" Boto was standing a short distance away, picking through a heap of ashes.

Tom smiled and went over to him. "Didn't you know?" he said. "Of course houses can get the plague. No, they can't, you miserable runt, but people burn them down anyway, just to be sure."

Boto kept on sifting. "It's still here," he said.

"What's still here?" Tom was about to head for the beach. He wanted to make his way around the entire island.

"The soul of the house."

Tom watched him bring over the sack containing fruit, which he stacked up in the old ash heap. "What are you doing?"

"We need to give the soul back," explained Nyo Boto.

"It took us six hours to collect all that fruit. I don't see any soul."

"But it can see you, Tom."

"Oh, so the invisible soul has eyes."

"Can't the leopard see in the night?" Boto made a steady little flame from dried leaves.

Tom had never seen anyone make a fire as quickly as Nyo Boto. His ability to keep it going was amazing. Soon the flames were licking at the fruit, which shriveled up and turned black.

"And just what were you thinking of eating?" asked Tom.

"Tonight we will sit by the fire and honor the soul of the house by not eating."

Tom smiled in disbelief. "Boto, you are . . . I don't know what you are."

The boy looked at him. "I'm a free man in a red shirt."

They sat next to the fire until midnight. Tom amused himself by talking about the wild animals that were patiently waiting in the dark, ready to dig their claws into them as soon as they left the fire.

Boto said nothing. He merely sat hunched over, with his eyes closed. On his forehead he had drawn a black stripe, and when the moon rose and sent its blue light over the clearing, he stood up and announced that now it was all right to leave.

"How do you know?" asked Tom.

"The soul told me."

Tom smiled. "Did it say anything else?"

"Yes," said Boto as he put out the fire. "It said that we should walk around to the east side of the island, where there's an abandoned sloop and sails and oars and sound timbers. If we're lucky."

Tom opened his mouth but decided not to say anything. After an hour they reached the east coast of the island. It looked like all the other rocky beaches, except there were no monkeys. A flock of cranes stood in the shallow water, preening themselves.

Tom went over to Boto, who was digging in the sand with a stick. "Something tells me that we're not going to be so lucky," said Tom.

Boto didn't answer, but fished a few worms out of the sand, which he rinsed off and ate. "Good for the stomach. Stomach pains should be taken seriously."

Tom shook his head and dropped onto the still-cool beach. He didn't wake up until Nyo Boto roused him. "Leave me alone," groaned Tom. "I'm tired."

"You have to get up, Tom."

"No, I don't have to get up. I have to keep lying here; my soul says that I should stay here. I've been thinking about it. Do you realize that we're going to stay here for the rest of our days?"

"No," said Boto, "we're not going to stay here for the rest of our days. We're going to Nevis, Tom. Get up."

"Let go of me."

"We're in luck, Tom."

Tom shaded his eyes from the sun. "Luck?"

"Come with me."

It was around the point, rocking faintly on the rippling waves. The sail, which hung like a limp rag, had two big rips in it, and the anchor chain turned out to be rusty and crumbling. But otherwise she was in fine shape. The mast and tiller, the keel and rigging—everything was as it should be. They found nothing on board except for an ale tankard and an old scoop.

An hour later they had repaired the sail enough that it could be hoisted. Together they hauled up the anchor, and when the first breeze struck the east coast, the sailcloth billowed out.

Tom sat at the tiller and stared at Nyo Boto, who stood in the bow wearing his red shirt, absolutely convinced that they would find their way to Nevis. After they had sailed far enough from land and the wind was steady, Tom secured the tiller, went up to Boto, and held out his hand. They hugged each other, and Tom screamed for joy, tugging on the rigging and behaving like a wild man.

Boto raised his eyebrows and stared at him. The gentle twinkle that sometimes appeared in his brown eyes was for a brief moment joined by a warm smile.

For two days Tom navigated by the stars, the sun, and his own instincts. On the third day they hailed a passing fishing boat. The man was old and not especially communicative. He said these were his fishing waters, but when Tom pressed him about where they were, the fisherman suddenly pulled out his flint pistol and said that he had never heard of Nevis.

That evening the wind blew to the south. Nyo Boto sat in the crimson twilight, waiting for the stars to appear when the fog lifted. He called Tom, who was taking a nap since he knew that he would be up most of the night. "I think we may be in luck," Boto said.

"Another sloop?" mumbled Tom, getting to his feet.

"No, I think I see land." Boto pointed.

The island was a big, grayish-black mass. At first they feared that the darkness would hide their landmark and that the distance might be fooling them. Certain islands had a tendency to disappear at daybreak. But at the first light of dawn, this one stayed where it was, and Tom felt the hairs stand up on his arms and back. The sight of the tall volcano with the white rim made his chin start to quiver. He could feel the tears behind his eyelids, and for a moment he stood with his head bowed.

"It's Nevis," he whispered. "Where my mother and sister live. And good old Señor López with the big behind. It's Nevis, Boto, do you hear me?"

"Yes, I hear you. We've been very lucky."

They sat down with their backs against the starboard gunwale. "I'm going to see my mother again," whispered Tom. "The very thought makes me nervous. It's been almost two years, after all. And my half sister, Feodora Dolores Vasgues. Do you remember her, Boto?"

The other boy shook his head.

"She has a very sharp tongue," said Tom with a smile.

Boto nodded gravely. "Some people do."

Tom gazed at the starry sky giving way to dawn. "I'm the happiest person on Earth," he said. "I should be singing and dancing."

"You also should have eaten the worms," said Boto.

20 Gráinne Ni Mháille

BEFORE COCKCROW TOM WAS POLING the boat toward the familiar coast. Even from the water he could see that nothing had changed. The inn stood as it always had, looking sleepy, not particularly well-kept, and decidedly not well-to-do, but a place where decent beer was served for a reasonable price. Much could be said about Señor López, but when it came to prices, he was a fair man.

Tom smiled at Boto, who was sitting in the bow with his eyes fixed on some distant point. They had agreed that it would be best for him to stay in the boat. Tom wanted to have time for a proper reunion with his family.

But now that he was wading toward the flat shore, his heart was beating so hard that it made him uneasy. He didn't know where this uneasiness came from but ascribed it to some sort of guilty conscience. He could have sent them some word. Maybe they thought he was dead. On the other hand, his mother and sister were both strong women who had been through a lot, so his uneasiness must come from something else.

He looked at his old skiff, which lay just as he had left it, with the oars in the oarlocks. A sure sign that it was being used. He let his fingers slide over the block letters that were carved into the thwart, spelling out his name. Written long ago, when he thought his last hour had come. "Back when I was just a little child," he murmured.

He could feel that he needed to sit on the beach, in order to collect his thoughts and formulate the proper thing to say when he stood in front of his mother. He was not averse to showing her that he had grown up, that he had come home to take care of her. The fact that he had not returned to Nevis a rich man was something that she would understand and forgive—seeing him alive would be enough. He hadn't thought much about how he was going to support her, but Señor López was hardly a young man. With all the flesh he was carrying, it wouldn't be long before he had trouble walking and would have to entrust the inn to a more agile man familiar with the work. Someone he could rely on. Tom would do all he could to improve his relations with Señor López. His ability to carry out this decision would be a testament to his maturity. And on the day Señor López left this world, Tom O'Connor would be ready to take over. All of this he would tell his mother.

Having made that decision, he walked up to the main entrance, which was locked, of course. He knew that by pressing a stick between the door and the frame, he could wriggle the latch free. A moment later he was standing inside the dimly lit tavern. The familiar smell of a scoured floor, stale beer, and freshly smoked bacon spread from his nose to form a lump in his throat. Fortunately he could take all the time he needed, so his mother wouldn't see him blubbering. And fortunately a rasping, snoring sound was coming from Señor López's room. The Spaniard's door was ajar. Tom could see that the stout innkeeper still slept with a corner of his nightshirt in his mouth.

He poured himself a tankard of beer, contemplating the idea of taking some out to Boto, who no doubt would welcome a little nourishing drink. Instead he found a mirror, which he set on a shelf so he could smooth down his hair and remove the grime and dirt from his cheeks and forehead.

The last time he had looked at himself in a mirror was at the inn in Port Royal. Even though the face he now saw supported his notion of manhood, it also filled him with the kind of sorrow that accompanies the inevitable. "My mouth," he whispered as he stared at his lips, which had lost their fullness. "My nose, that Feo called a potato snout. It has disappeared. Or maybe it just shrank so that only the bone is left."

The kitchen was just the same, although the jars of herbs and spices were gone. There used to be a long row of jars labeled with his mother's meticulous script, proclaiming that this one contained horsetails for dying fabric, this one held fennel for colic, and this one balm for insect bites. But there were still limes in a basin of water, and the pots and pans were scoured clean and hanging as usual from a pole suspended from the ceiling.

He examined his fingernails, which were pitch-black—but that's how they had always looked. A moment later he climbed the stairs and went down the corridor to their room. In front of the door, he took a deep breath, then opened it.

She was lying on the wide bunk with a blanket pulled over her. Her hair was spread out on the pillow, and even in the dark it gleamed like raven feathers. Tom's bed had been taken down, but that had to be expected. For some reason Feodora was alone in the room. She hadn't changed.

He sat down near the bed, feeling his pulse racing, as if it wanted to tell him something. For a terrible moment he was overwhelmed by doubt. There was still time to escape. To shut the door behind him and set sail. To disappear for good. Would his homecoming make a bad situation worse? He was thinking about looking for his mother when he discovered that his sister was awake. She was staring right at him. Her expression was intense but empty of any emotion.

"Feo," he whispered, "it's me, Tom."

She didn't reply, merely looked at him.

"I've come home," he said, realizing that this was a meaningless thing to say. But he went on to tell her that he had a sloop out in the bay, and that he had found Bibido, whose name wasn't Bibido at all, but Boto. That he had been to thousands of different places and seen most of the world.

She sat up and pulled a shawl around her shoulders, as if he weren't there.

He wanted to touch her, mostly for the sake of recognition. But also to feel a familiar tenderness, a closeness that he hadn't felt for almost two years.

Cautiously he took her hand, lifting it up as if it were a bird that had fallen out of its nest. He turned her face toward him and saw that her eyes had grown shiny. She pulled him close and held him tightly. He couldn't remember that they had ever sat like this before, and he couldn't tell if her embrace was loving or harsh. His sister's body felt small and fragile, thin and resistant.

She took a deep breath and smiled. "Welcome home," she whispered. She took his hands. "Welcome home, Tom O'Connor."

"Did you think I wasn't coming home again?" he murmured.

"Maybe," she said. "Maybe I didn't think about you at all."

Tom wanted to pull his hands away, but she held on tightly. The look in her eyes was now clear. It wasn't sorrowful, warm, or cold, but black with loneliness. "I've missed both of you," he said.

"You have?"

He nodded. "Are you angry, Feodora? I understand if you are. I've been gone a long time, much too long, but . . ."

"You've changed." Her whispering voice had gathered strength; he was almost frightened by its deep pitch. She sounded like a grown woman. Even though she looked the same, she spoke like a grown woman.

"I've seen tons of things," he muttered.

"Has it made you wiser?"

Tom wasn't sure. He nodded and then shrugged.

"Stronger?"

"Yes," he said firmly. "I've certainly gotten stronger, that much I can say."

"That's good. You'll need it."

"You look like you're still mad at me."

She let go of his hands and smiled to herself, and then quickly turned serious. "No, I'm not mad at you. I've been jealous of you. But I'm not anymore."

"Jealous?"

"I've always envied you. Not because you could swim, row, fish, or navigate. I've envied the fact that you're a boy. That one fine day, whenever it pleased you, you could saddle up a mule and ride off without another thought, to seek your fortune."

"I found it, Feo. Well, maybe not my fortune, but Bibido. I found him. I've got at least a thousand things to tell you."

"I do too. But I don't know whether this is the right time." She put her hand to his cheek. Cautiously, tenderly. And stroked his forehead.

"I can remember," he whispered, "that sometimes, when we were little, you would ask me if I could feel your heart. I can feel it now."

"Your life and mine, Tom," she whispered, "are listening to each other."

"Yes, that's what you told me, that's it exactly."

"And you would shout, 'Take me with you, Feo, to the ends of the Earth.'"

Tom pulled away and looked at her eagerly. "I've been there," he said, "to the ends of the Earth."

"No, Tom, you're there now."

They both fell silent.

"Mother is dead," she told him.

He is standing behind her at the corner of the house. Under the olive tree a little mound has been formed, with a cross. Flowers, of the kind that might be weeds, are growing on the patch of ground. Tom is standing with his arms hanging limply, listening to his sister, who tells him that their mother started to bleed. That in less than a week the life seeped out of her like a red river, and afterward there was only darkness. Feodora of course summoned the doctor. He examined her and said that for this type of sickness there was no cure.

Feo pulls her shawl tighter, bends down, and starts ripping out the weeds. "As you can see, it's not much of a grave site. But since I didn't have any help, it was the best I could do." She straightens up and disappears around the side of the house.

Tom glances up at the sky, which for some reason looks the same as always. Then he falls to his knees, wondering why he isn't crying. He rakes the earth with his fingers, seeing glimpses of his mother. At the stove, in the tavern, washing laundry behind the house, putting flowers in a vase, combing Señor López's hair. He can't remember her voice, but he will never forget the scent of lime on her skin.

He buries his fingernails in the earth and falls onto his side, curled up, waiting for the tears to come. Later he staggers down to the shore and out into the water, then hauls himself into the boat. He goes over to Nyo Boto, who is sitting with the curved needle in his hand, mending his shirt.

Tom sits down across from him and carefully studies his features.

"Who's dead?" asks Boto.

"My mother is dead." And now the tears come. He doesn't try to hold them back, just sits there, his back erect, and weeps.

Boto doesn't say a word as he continues to sew.

Tom wipes his eyes and blows his nose. "She's gone," he whispers. "It seems unbelievable."

"I could see it in the building," says Boto with a toss of his head.

Tom gives him a sidelong glance.

"I was thinking about it when you dropped anchor. Now Tom will go in and hear some bad news—that's what I thought."

"Is that all you have to say, Nyo Boto?"

Boto replies by setting down his needle and putting on his shirt. He takes a minute to examine whether he has done a proper job. Then he jumps into the shallow water.

Tom trudges after him and together they walk around the corner of the house to the place beneath the olive tree, where Boto squats down and runs his hand through the dry earth.

Tom sits down beside him.

"But her soul is still here, isn't it, Boto?"

"No, it's gone," he says.

"It can't be gone, you fool."

"Oh yes, it's far away. I think it's searching for you. But it will come back, Tom. If you're lucky."

That night he slept in his old bed. Boto had been granted his wish to remain in the boat. As for the innkeeper, he had no trouble controlling any joy he felt at the reunion and only reluctantly allowed Tom to stay. He couldn't resist telling Tom that his mother had died of sorrow, and that until his dying day he, Señor López, would regard all the Irish as spineless.

Tom didn't utter a word but merely resumed his old duties, watching his sister do the work of two. Exactly as she had for the past six months. Moreover, the day had been filled with numerous travelers, demanding and impatient, recalcitrant and complaining loudly when it came time to pay the bill.

None of it bothered Tom. When he lay in bed, he felt strangely cleansed, his mind completely clear. He had not said anything to López about Nyo Boto. Feo knew only what he had already told her. There was plenty of time.

But one night after closing, as he sat next to the grave where he had placed some flowers, she appeared at his side.

"Before she died," said Feo, "she told me an odd story. About you, Tom O'Connor." Feo gave a toss of her head.

He followed her down to the beach where the waves were striking the shore in a quiet, steady tempo. Above them shone the moon, partially hidden by a blue mist. Fedora's mood had now changed, although she still seemed preoccupied. The teasing and sharp tone had apparently left her.

"Regarding your paternal grandmother." The trace of a mischievous expression appeared in her eyes, making him move closer. "Now I don't know whether it's true," she said, "but Mother was not the type to gossip." Feo looked him up and down and smiled. "Actually we both agreed that there was a good deal in the story that seemed to fit."

"What about my paternal grandmother?"

"Well, she was Irish through and through, and that doesn't bode well for future generations, but Irish she was. And of noble descent. It may not be visible to the naked eye, but according to Mother you have blue blood in your veins, Tom. Apparently. She was a noblewoman, but behaved quite otherwise."

Feo winked one eye and smiled. "You might even say, exactly the opposite. On the Irish Sea, far away from here, your blessed grandmother made her living as a simple pirate. She robbed and plundered and was a terror to all seafarers. It amused our mother, and it amused me too. I've written her name on an old shirt that Mother . . ." Feodora lowered her voice and looked away ". . . that she slept in during the time you were gone. Don't misunderstand me, Tom. I don't reproach you for anything, nor did Mother. We wished you all the luck and happiness in the world. Your paternal grandmother was named Gráinne Ni Mháille, and if I were you, I would be proud of her. According to your father she was pardoned by the English queen, but all of that has long since turned to dust and ashes. What interested our mother, and no doubt will interest you, is that old Gráinne expired in the year of our Lord 1591, on the thirteenth of November, to be precise. As far as I remember, the thirteenth of November happens to be your birthday, Tom." Feodora leaned back. "That makes a person think."

Tom looked away, in an attempt to digest this news, but strangely enough he felt as though he had heard it before. A hoarse rasping voice that had asked, "What do you get if you mix a drink from the noblest wine, the strongest rum, and the purest springwater?" Something totally undrinkable, he had replied. Whereupon Zamora had said, "You've just described yourself, Tom O'Connor."

They were sitting with their backs to the point, looking out across the still waters bathed in the gentle moonlight.

"I'll take care of you," he said quietly. "No matter what I'm made of, I'll take care of you. That's a promise, Feodora Dolores Vasgues. One day I'll take over the inn, and everything will be different. Completely different. Then it will be just you and me. Then you will have deloused a man's hair for the last time."

Feo sighed. "All your days you've had such high regard for yourself, Tom O'Connor. I think that the Irish, to counterbalance their barbarian souls, have to puff themselves up. And as for the delousing, you're mistaken about that."

Tom smiled broadly. "Half-breed," he whispered.

"But your help isn't necessary. You're not the only one in this family who's going to see the world."

"What does that mean?"

"And the one I'm thinking of has no intention of riding away on a stolen mule, in the hope of finding half a fortune disguised in a puny slave boy's body."

Feodora held out her right hand. On her forefinger was a silver ring.

Tom shrank back, as if in scorn at the ring. "Where did you get that?"

"It was given to me by my betrothed." Feo studied the ring. "It doesn't quite fit, but a person can't have everything."

Tom leaped up. "What the hell are you sitting there talking about?"

"Your language bears witness to the company you keep, Tom O'Connor."

"I don't give a damn about my language. Are you engaged?"

Feodora looked at him with a subdued expression. "Yes," she replied, "I'm engaged and I'm going to be married before the month is out. Aren't you going to congratulate me?"

Tom walked along the beach and picked up a stone, which he flung into the waves, only to return at once to his sister, who had taken off the ring. "It seems to me there's suddenly a lot of news," he said. "But no one is going to say that Tom O'Connor can't offer his congratulations. So congratulations on everything, Feodora Dolores Vasgues." He took a deep breath.

"I'm old enough, you know," said Feo in a casual voice.

"Yes, by God," said Tom, "it all fits. I give you that much. You certainly haven't wasted any time. And now she's going to see the world, I understand. Have fun, there's plenty to see."

Feodora sighed and cast a dreamy glance up at the dark night sky. "Spain," she said. "The mere sound of the name fills me with longing."

"She'll soon grow tired of it."

"Why is that?"

"Because it's packed with Spaniards."

"I would assume so."

Tom sat down with a different, more concerned, and above all more honest expression on his face. "Are you seriously considering traveling to Spain?"

Her eyes widened and she nodded.

"But what will you do there?"

"Live. Together with my husband. At least for a while. Later, when the time is right, we're going to Africa."

"Africa? Are you crazy? There are wild animals in Africa. It's swarming with cannibals whose only thought is to eat you alive. You're talking to someone who has been traveling for two years and met people who know these things. If you knew what I know about lunar eclipses, about the Earth and the world . . . Well, Feodora, you've never been anywhere but here on this island. How can you wish to go someplace that you know nothing about?"

"That's why."

"And what did you think the two of you would do in Africa? Trade in slaves?"

"Good God, no. We'll be missionaries. You see, Tom, we're not going to live out in the wilderness. We'll have servants and our own means of conveyance, and by the time we arrive, the mission will already be built. We'll be traveling with a letter from the Pope in Rome."

"If you're making fun of me, I'll . . ."

"No, no, I'm not. I've never been more serious."

Tom sighed and sat down. "What did you say my grandmother was named?"

"Gráinne Ni Mháille," replied Feo, as she put the ring on her finger.

They walked back to the deserted tavern and closed the door to Señor López's room. He had long since fallen into bed. Tom poured himself a glass from the dregs cask and then saw Feo opening a new bottle, which she confidently set on the table between them. "It's from Madeira," she said.

"And the best the house has to offer," gasped Tom.

Feo nodded and poured two glasses. "Don't you think we have something to celebrate, Tom O'Connor? You, who have just learned that you're of noble descent—well, there may be a few stains on your reputation, but still . . . And I, who will be traveling on a Spanish frigate, and as a married woman, no less. I'll stand in the bow as we cross the Atlantic Ocean, enjoying every second."

"It takes three months, my little señorita."

"Enjoying every second of the three months, taking in the strange breezes, filling my soul, my heart, and my mind. Maybe we can write to each other."

"Rats," Tom said with a hoarse laugh. "Plague-ridden rats; scurvy; dysentery; bad water; hurricanes; seasickness; diarrhea; lentils morning, noon, and night. And that's the nice version. Damn it all, Feo, you have no idea what you're talking about. The only thing awaiting you at sea is death by drowning, mutiny, pirates, corsairs, buccaneers, and rapists. I was hired on a Spanish ship, where we tossed a body overboard every single week, just to prevent contagion."

"Once we arrive in Europe, I'm going to find the biggest library that exists and sit there for months. Just imagine all that knowledge. All that poetry."

"Splendid, I'm talking to deaf ears. If you want to see the world, go ahead. But do you have to get married to do that?"

Feodora sipped her wine. "How can a girl see the world otherwise, Tom? Tell me that! There's only one way. And I jumped at the offer."

"You certainly have. You most certainly have. Well, be my guest! Missionaries, you say? Since when have you become so pious that you could actually teach such things?"

"Whatever life hasn't taught me, I can make up. It may sound rash, but my betrothed wasn't scared off when I told him my true feelings."

"What damned cynicism," snarled Tom. "What kind of marriage is that?"

"Quite an ordinary one, I should think. Built on the only emotion that lasts: common sense."

"My mother," said Tom, narrowing his eyes, "said that love is the only basis for marriage."

Feodora clapped her hands together, feigning astonishment. "Listen to the wise man speak. My half brother wants to teach me about love. Does he have anything more to say?"

"Not if you're going to act like that." Tom felt a pang in his heart as he suddenly remembered a certain girl on Jamaica. Oddly enough, he had forgotten her name, but her daughter was called Annabelle. Sometimes he thought about the young mother and hoped that she would also remember him.

"Falling in love," continued Feodora, "lasts no longer than a simple fever, and I have no intention of letting a cold stand in the way of my happiness."

"Are things really so distorted for you that you don't even love your betrothed?"

Feodora did not reply, but merely stared at Tom with a hard and self-satisfied expression.

Tom looked away. "I shouldn't presume to judge."

"No, you shouldn't, but you can pour me another glass. The night is young, and I have more to tell you that will make the hair on the back of your neck stand on end and your mouth fall open."

Tom grabbed the bottle and poured until the wine overflowed. Then he emptied his glass and pounded on the table.

"You'll wake Señor López," said Feo, not sounding especially distressed.

"I don't give a damn about the fat beast," said Tom. "Let him sail his own sea. After you're gone, Tom O'Connor will leave too. I have a goal and the means to get there."

"Oh, you must be thinking about your little skiff out there in the bay. The one with the black runt on board. What a puny boy he is."

Tom slammed his palm against the table. "You'd better speak well of him," he ordered.

"My dear half brother. The evening is getting more and more entertaining."

"Not another word. He may not be very big in size, but he's . . ."

"Yes, Tom? What is he?"

Tom leaned back on the bench. "His real name is Nyo Boto, and he has more will to live in his little finger than I have in my whole body. Do you feel like listening? If not, I'll stop."

"We have the whole night ahead of us," said Feo, with a smile. "And as the shrew said as she beat her husband, the best is yet to come."

Tom gave his sister a sidelong glance and cleared his throat. "When I first met him, he was wearing a ring on one finger. You remember Ramón from Cádiz, don't you? He told me about this boy and his ring. I know you don't believe me, but he really is the son of a king, Feo. I had proof of this after we left the good ship *Caballito del Diablo* and rowed off in an eight-man longboat. Alone at sea with nothing but a sack of food and two casks of water. Why did I do it? I did it because I had to. And besides, he showed me what he had sewn into his throat with his own hand. Nyo Boto is my best and only friend. And he's no longer a slave, anymore than you or I."

"And I suppose Tom has given him his freedom?"

"Yes, I have. Do you have any objections?"

Feodora pursed her lips and shook her head coquettishly. "I'm just listening." She ran her forefinger around the rim of her glass. "Sometimes it's hard to dislike you, Tom O'Connor. But tell me this, what did the beast have sewn into his gullet?"

"The ring, Feo, the ring. To hide it for later use. That lad is so brave that I don't even have words to describe him."

Feodora tilted her head back and laughed. "Dear God, pour your half sister another glass. So you've given up hope of the vast fortune?"

Tom shrugged his shoulders. "Maybe," he said. "Did you know that a man's greed can be found in his ring finger?"

"Is that what you heard out in the big world?"

"No, I learned that here on Nevis. Late one night two years ago. Damn, that wine has gone right to my head. I think I'm going to have to lie down."

"Not yet, dear brother. You can wait a bit. Isn't there something you still need to know about my marriage?"

Tom threw out his arms.

Feo smiled. "Aren't you going to ask me his name?"

"Do you mean your betrothed is someone I know?"

Feo nodded. "That he is. You're going to be proud of your sister, Tom."

"So tell me what the man's name is before I'm so drunk that I can't see straight."

Feodora leaned across the table and looked Tom deep in the eyes. "His name," she whispered, "is Salazar, Felix Salazar."

Tom shrugged his shoulders. "Should that mean something to me?"

"Oh yes. Although it's possible that you know him better by another name. I think that's probably true; I've just gotten used to calling him Señor Salazar."

Tom rolled his eyes. "What's his other name?" he groaned.

Feodora filled her glass to the brim, but then abruptly threw it in Tom's face, laughing hoarsely as she said, "Father Innocent was his former name. If that means anything to you, Tom O'Connor."

Nyo Boto is sitting under the crescent moon, telling the myth about the old man who with his stick punctured holes in the sky and created what humans call the stars.

He's telling the story as he calmly sews new buttons on to his red shirt. The buttons came from Feodora. They're not all the same, but he accepted them as if they were gold. And in a strange way, the story that he's telling suits what he's doing.

"And that's how the starry heavens were created," he concludes as he bites off the thread.

"It certainly must have taken a lot of work," mutters Tom from the bottom of the boat, where he is lying on his back.

"Yes," says Boto, "and a long stick."

Tom rolls onto his stomach. "Look at me, you little African man."

"I am looking at you, you big red-haired Irishman."

"Are you making fun of me?"

"No, I'm making buttonholes."

"What do you see when you look at me, Nyo Boto?"

"I see the only friend I have."

"You're looking at a man, only half-grown, who in less than a week has lost both his mother and his sister. The longing for my mother burns inside me like a fire, but the loss of my sister makes me as cold as ashes." Tom tells Boto about Father Innocent and the Inquisition. "I received the news three days ago and have felt sick ever since."

Either Boto isn't listening or he doesn't care.

"I've seen them together," Tom continues. "She waits on him. He's a glutton without equal, but he too has changed. He left his job as inquisitor, and now he wants to go home to Spain. The pious father speaks to me kindly but patronizingly, stroking my hair so I can smell how he reeks. Of dead flesh. And his betrothed, my half sister, floats around, obeying his slightest request. Seldom has a voyage been paid for so dearly. 'Come to me, young O'Connor,' says Salazar. 'Sit down beside me and let me hear about your days out in the wide world.' I refuse to tell him anything because I detest everything about him. There's so much blood, so much suffering in his cloying touch, that it makes my very soul freeze. Do you know what I've been dreaming, Boto?"

"What have you been dreaming, Tom?"

"Every night I dream about killing him. Cutting his skinny throat and listening to him rattle as the life gushes out of him. What do you think about that idea, Boto?"

"I think it sounds like a good idea, Tom."

Tom looks away and smiles. "But I don't dare," he sighs. "My sister would never forgive me. She talks of nothing else but the frigate that will soon drop anchor in the bay. Her trunk is packed, and that sanctimonious Salazar has even given fat Señor López a small fortune as a kind of dowry. That's why His Excellency is staying at the inn. The frigate could appear on the horizon at any moment. If I'm going to kill that swine, it has to be now, but Feo would never forgive me."

"Maybe she would never forgive you if you don't do it."

Tom goes over to Boto, who is now polishing his precious buttons. "Why can't I ever get a decent answer out of you? Why do you always say something that is neither fish nor fowl?"

"Would you prefer fish? Or fowl?"

"Is that a riddle?"

"Your dagger is neither fowl nor fish, Tom. But your hatred will stay with you and make you mean and bitter."

"There's a second possibility," says Tom. "I've been thinking about it."

"Have you, Tom?"

"Yes, that's what I'm sitting here telling you. Listen here. The two of us, Boto, the two of us could kidnap Feo, tie her up hand and foot, and carry her off to a foreign shore. What do you say to that?"

"That would be the same as turning your hatred on her," replies Boto.

"Who says so?"

"Someone who has experienced it himself."

Tom turns away. "Go back to your shirt. And by the way, it still stinks of mold." He goes over to the mast and pounds his forehead against the timber.

Boto comes over to him. "I think it's the same with my shirt as it is with Salazar. There's mold clinging to both of them. I also think my shirt may smell, but that kind of odor you can get rid of with time and when the wind is right. And the day will come when the trade winds will kiss my red shirt and make it as soft as honey and as fresh as springwater."

"You want to go back out to sea to get your shirt cleaned? Is that what you're saying?"

"Along with him."

"Along with who?"

"Along with His Excellency. They can go together, the man and the shirt. Who knows, Tom," Boto has a dreamy look in his big brown eyes, "maybe his ship will take us to the Bissagos Islands."

Tom smiles. "Do you think so?"

"Yes," replies Nyo Boto, "if we're lucky."

The three-masted frigate is rocking on the waves in the bay off of Nevis. A rowboat is on its way in from the ship. Ten men are at the oars because it's a long way to the coast, and the sea is rough.

On the beach, in the stiff wind, stands Feodora Dolores Vasgues, holding on to her new hat. She is clutching a satchel in one hand. Her dress is dark red, like the color of the Spanish flag. The fabric is too thin for the weather, but the dress has lain too long in her trunk, waiting for just this moment. Over it she is wearing a woolen sweater; she didn't have much to choose from. The sweater once belonged to her brother but is now too small for him. Under her arm is her parasol and two little books, one of them tied with a big bow. It contains her personal writings. On the cover it says, "Feodora Dolores Vasgues's Almanac." Besides being a diary, it is also a book of recipes from her mother. The names of herbs are listed alphabetically, and under the letter *A* there is a recipe for a so-called *aphrodisiacum* that is supposed to restore vitality to older men. As it says under the Latin names that make up this secret elixir, "Whether it should be ingested dry or with a small amount of water, I can't say for sure." This almanac and the catechism that Feo received from her betrothed make up her entire library.

Her room has been emptied down to the last conch shell, the last moonstone, and the last crab shell. The floor has been washed and the bedding placed on the shelf. Feo can leave the inn with a clear conscience.

On her mother's grave lie dried flowers and a seashell from Jamaica with the inscription: "To Mother from Tom."

Feodora has nothing left to do on the island. She has promised herself never to return.

Out of the inn steps a tall slender man wearing a dark-red coat and a flat hat. At his side walks a small insignificant man who in a former life served as a scribe for Father Innocent. Today he is carrying Señor Salazar's valises. The two men stack their possessions on top of Feodora's trunk and watch in silence as the sailors fight the waves. They nod encouragement to each other, convinced that everything will be fine since the rowboat is steadily making progress toward them.

Feodora smiles and feels the hand of her betrothed on her back. He says something to her that is carried off by the storm.

At the inn, which is still open for customers, Señor López is sitting with his feet in soapy water. He yells impatiently because his two new helpers aren't used to the work and fumble with the file, the comb, and the brush. López has taken the clasp out of his hair, which needs to be combed and inspected for lice. He mutters something to himself and tries to push open the door with his cane, but the chair is too far away and he has to shout.

The rowboat is so close that the sailors pole the rest of the way in. Soon afterward, they start loading the valises and bags on board.

Señor Salazar offers assistance to his betrothed, who needs no help but steps into the boat with a brisk, supple movement. She sits down next to the tiller so that she has her back to the coast. That's why she doesn't notice the boatswain conferring with two barefoot lads standing on the beach. One of them has a file and a comb in his hand. The other stands slightly behind the first boy, wearing a red shirt.

"Used to what kind of work?" the Spanish boatswain shouts over the wind.

"Any kind at all, señor," replies the lad with the file. "Galley, deck, cabin, anything."

"We have enough hands on board," grumbles the boatswain.

Tom moves closer to him. "Take us with you, señor, please take us with you. You won't regret it. We'll do the work of four—no job is too difficult."

"We have rats in the hold. How about that?" The boatswain grins as if he has said something funny.

"You won't find any rat hunters better than us. We'll sleep on deck and ask only for the food that the crew refuses to eat."

The boatswain blows his nose, spits black juice, and casts a glance behind him at the passengers. "Where are your things?"

"We're ready to go as we are." Tom takes Nyo Boto's hand.

The boatswain stares at him. "With a file and a comb?"

"At your service." Tom straightens his back and salutes with the comb.

A moment later they climb into the boat. The boatswain issues orders to his men. Feodora Dolores Vasgues casts a sidelong glance at her brother, who is sitting next to Boto. Then the oars are put in the water, and the only sound is the boatswain stomping on the floorboards, signaling the rowers.

The sea fog moves in over the crew and passengers, but no one pays it any mind. With brisk strokes they glide away from Nevis. For the first time, Feodora is leaving her birthplace. Briefly, doubt seems to fill her black eyes. There is a tug at the corner of her mouth, and she takes a last look at the familiar shore. Then she lifts her head high and stares steadfastly at the silhouette of the three-masted frigate that awaits her.

With the wind blowing as it is today, the ship will reach open waters in no time, and Nevis will be no bigger than a peppercorn in the ocean.

Tom O'Connor, on the other hand, does look back. For the second time in his brief life, he is leaving his native shores. He smiles slyly and winks at Nyo Boto, thinking that he can almost hear Señor López calling for the comb and the file.

Part IV

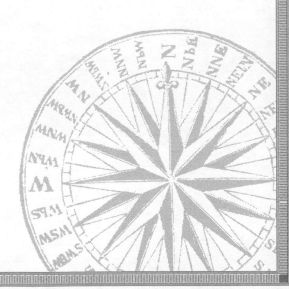

21   The Devil's Pate

THE FRIGATE *OCEANIA* was a much older, less comfortable, and above all less seaworthy ship than the one Tom and Boto had recently left. She had been built in Barcelona, had yards on every mast, but had only one cannon deck, situated on the port side. In the cannonball chamber, located next to the water barrels in the bottom of the ship, were six tons of ballast. The weight was of course meant to hold the ship on an even keel, but it made the frigate difficult to maneuver. In addition, the sails were frayed and the rigging worn and only minimally repaired.

After only a week, Tom could tell Boto that even the navigation was done using outdated methods. The sea charts, if not exactly incorrect, were ancient and, in Tom's opinion, misleading. The first officer, who set the course, did so using an old cross-staff whenever his drunken state prevented him from figuring out the sextant. Judging by the way the ship rolled, it also seemed very likely that her keel hadn't been repaired in years.

Nor had the boatswain exaggerated when it came to the rats. If there were any living things that thrived on the ship, it was the rats. Tom constantly found new nests, many of them alarmingly close to the storerooms and pantries. The cook didn't seem to care. And the captain, Eduardo Muñeco, was mainly preoccupied with his two daily promenades on deck, where in fair weather most of the ship's passengers spent their time.

The *Oceania* was a floating inn, sailing westward with families who dreamed of finding their fortune in the New World on Hispaniola, and sailing eastward with those who had seen enough. Hence the ship was loaded with homesickness, sorrow, expectations, hopes, and impatience, and the daily humdrum was broken only by Captain Muñeco's promenades. He was a short, rotund man who wore a big black, white, or orange wig. His preferred attire consisted of silk trousers and jacket, patterned stockings, and shiny shoes with square toes and high heels. He liked only pastel shades and took part in the work only when circumstances forced him to do so. His preferred occupation was conversing with the small but select group of passengers who possessed money or titles. These exclusive few had been given their own little corner on the middle deck where, due to the lack of cabins, their quarters were separated by blankets. By far the majority of passengers were crammed together on the lower deck.

Aside from the obligatory seasickness, there were the usual squabbles over missing possessions, irritation at the sheep and pigs in the hold, and complaints about the slowness of the crew.

After hunting rats for a while, Tom had been promoted to cabin boy and thus had access to places where Feo also spent her time.

Unlike the other passengers, she was never unhappy with the *Oceania*'s conditions. As a rule she would stand on the windward side and let her long hair blow as she waved to the dolphins and shivered whenever the sailors crawled up in the rigging, then cheered when they came back down. She ate whatever was served and never felt seasick, nor did she succumb to any of the usual stomach ailments.

Tom saw very little of her betrothed, Señor Salazar, who had become good friends with Muñeco. The two men secluded themselves in the captain's cabin and appeared only when the captain promenaded or when the boatswain arranged a conference in order to pass the time.

Boto had become a sail maker of sorts. Equipped with a sail needle and a special kind of glove, he mended the holes in the old sails. It was hard work because the canvas was thick, but the leather glove was furnished with a lead plate, which made it possible to force the needle through the fabric. Day and night he could be seen sitting in the rigging or on one of the middle yardarms, sewing. Whenever Tom couldn't find Boto, he simply had to look up to see a little red spot against the azure sky.

Tom was on friendly terms with the second officer, who was quite young and who quelled his homesickness by listening to Tom's stories. He was the one who had warned Tom that the first officer was no champion at navigating. On the ninth day, with the wind coming from the south, Tom's suspicions were confirmed. It was obvious that they were off course, which could mean a delay of several weeks if not corrected.

That night he sat with Boto and studied the stars and his homemade map of the Atlantic Ocean. "If we don't head northeast, we'll never hit the Azores," said Tom. "We're sailing near the Tropic of Cancer, almost due east, and that's all wrong."

The next day he sought out the second officer, who let the cabin boy in to see the captain. He was in the midst of his weekly manicure.

"Speak up, young man." Muñeco was wearing a bright red robe and a skullcap, with a long tassel, that hid his bald head. From a rack hung his three wigs.

Felix Salazar was also present. He was sitting comfortably behind the captain's desk, which was covered with calipers, rulers, telescopes, and various sea charts. There was also a sextant of newer vintage. Tom thought to himself that it ought to be up on the quarterdeck and not down here. Salazar himself was holding a little black catechism that he pretended to read while Tom stated his business, which was that he thought they were off course.

Hearing that, Muñeco uttered a shrill squeal and, twittering like a woman, withdrew his hand and slapped the brown wig on his head. He studied himself in the mirror for a while, then said, "Who does this young ruffian think he is?" The captain spun around and looked at Salazar. "Is this one of your acquaintances, señor?"

"Tom O'Connor," said Salazar, closing the holy text. "He's famous for his temper, but he has a good head on his shoulders, captain, sir. Not that I would approve of all his actions, but according to his sister, he has spent a great deal of time at sea, so if he says that we're off course, I would advise you to evaluate the situation."

Tom smiled at Salazar, pleased at his unexpected support. Even so, it was common knowledge that the first officer was lazy, given to drink, and rarely on the quarterdeck.

The captain went over to Tom and looked him up and down. He was at least half a head shorter than the youth, though he compensated for this by standing on his toes. "Let's see if he can use a sextant."

Tom bowed, walked to the desk, and unrolled a sea chart. Quickly he grabbed another one, studied it, and laid it aside, only to examine two others before he sighed and said that all of the charts were old—not necessarily incorrect, but probably misleading.

This prompted a genuinely furious outburst from the captain, who calmed down only upon hearing Salazar's soothing voice. "I think perhaps we should listen to what the young man has on his mind," he said.

"Am I supposed to take instruction from a red-haired newcomer?" The captain puffed himself up and changed his wig.

"Why don't we just say that we're testing him." Salazar gave Tom a nod of encouragement.

"If we actually reach the Azores within the next ten weeks," Tom began, "we may have enough water and provisions. But if we continue on this course, it will extend the voyage by at least two more weeks. That's why we need to start rationing our water more sparingly."

"Is that so? How amusing," said Muñeco. "Does the boy know how many years I've spent at sea? No, he doesn't. But including the time I devoted to my job as second-in-command on the English Channel, we're talking about thirty years. And he thinks he can come in here and give me instructions? It's enough to give me apoplexy. Be so kind as to calculate our latitude."

Tom picked up the sextant, talking to himself out loud. "This degree scale is of an older vintage, and it shows us one-sixth of a circle. According to the hourglass, in a very short time the sun will be at its zenith. With the sextant, no matter how ancient it is, I can determine the angle between the sun and the horizon and calculate the latitude. Will the captain permit me to go out on deck?"

Tom was back in no time.

By now Muñeco was fully dressed, sitting with a magisterial expression behind his desk. "What does he have to say, this Irish scamp?"

Tom cleared his throat. "He says that we're sailing two to three degrees north of the Tropic of Cancer, señor. That means latitude twenty-five degrees north. And that's the wrong course, if the captain will permit me to speak my mind."

The captain looked at his second officer, who was staring at the floor. Reluctantly, the young man declared himself in agreement with Tom.

After this little exchange, the ship's course was duly changed. The first officer received a reprimand, and Tom was demoted to the task of hunting rats.

One week gave way to the next, and the daily routine assumed its own quiet rhythm. People had grown accustomed to the limitations of the galley and the rolling motion of the ship, not to mention the idleness.

One night Tom met his sister on deck. True to form, she was taking a walk alone. Most of the passengers were asleep. The crew members who were on watch had gathered in small groups around lanterns to play cards or they had joined the cook, who was singing lewd ditties.

They had been at sea for four weeks, and Feo, who had always managed to keep her complexion pale and unblemished, now looked tan and sunburned. Tom teased her about her new colors and let her chase him around the masts. He tried to keep his balance, carrying the two rattraps that he and Boto had constructed.

"Go ahead and stick to your rats," said Feodora, out of breath. "That's where you belong."

"When I say the ship should be turned, the captain turns it," replied Tom, striking a cocksure pose.

Beneath them rolled the great waves of the Atlantic Ocean, rocking the frigate from side to side. They could hear sheep bleating and pigs squealing down in the hold.

"This is the life." Feo looked at Tom with glowing eyes. The wind seemed to intensify, and it began to rain.

He nodded. "The wilder, the better, is that how it is?"

Feodora went over to the railing, threw out her arms, and shouted into the night, "I wish for storms and hurricanes, rough seas, and thunderbolts. Have you ever been in a real hurricane, Tom?"

He thought for a moment. Unfortunately he had to disappoint her. "But there's a good substitute." He smiled slyly. "The question is whether you have what it takes."

"Just tell me."

"You might have to change your clothes." Tom cast an eye at his sister's dress. "Where we're going it would be best to wear something more practical."

"And where are we going?" Feo shut one eye.

Tom gave her a penetrating look and pointed upward. "It's called the Devil's pate," he said, "the yards above the main royal sail."

Feo tilted her head back.

The mainmast measured one hundred and thirty feet. From this distance the uppermost yard looked like a giant needle. The enormous sails billowed in the wind, and the rigging hammered and pounded whenever the ship heeled over and the wind took hold. On a night like this, the forces of nature had free rein. A storm was holding a rendezvous with the sea. With the sky as the only witness, the lovers raged and their ardor split open the cloud cover and sent splinters of morning light straight through the night and across the firmament. It was not so strange that the moon was looking away and had taken on a chilly color. Nothing is new for that pale orb, whose smile turns inward and whose gaze can frighten small children.

All of this was reflected in Feo's eyes. She stared in disbelief at her brother. "You're out of your wits."

Tom cocked his head to the side. "What do you mean?"

Feo pointed, her thick tresses rising like a pitch-black halo. "No sensible person would crawl up there."

"But my dear sister," replied Tom, "how do you think we change the line that holds the main royal sail if we don't climb up to the uppermost yard?"

Feodora swallowed and moved closer. "So you've been up there?"

"Plenty of times. It's up on the Devil's pate that you truly experience what it means to sail. That's where you feel the ship rolling, sense the power of the wind, and realize how big the world is. And how small you are."

She shouted into his ear, "Is that why I should go up there, Tom? To realize how small I am?"

"I thought I would give you this experience as a wedding present. When you're sitting at the dinner table in Andalusia, sweltering in the heat together with your meat-eating husband, you can think back on the wind at the top of the mainsail, the tremendous forces of nature, the sinking in your stomach, the dread in your heart, and the jubilation that follows when you live life to the fullest."

She gave him a furious look. "How dare you speak to me that way," she shrieked.

Tom did not reply.

"Find me some pants and a jacket," she said firmly.

"Feo, it was meant to be a joke."

"I said, find me some pants and a jacket. You've thrown down the gauntlet for the last time, half brother. And I'm accepting the challenge. In three days my name will no longer be Vasgues, like my father's, but Salazar, like my husband's. Captain Muñeco is going to marry us so that we can share a cabin and enjoy a more comfortable voyage. So the view from the Devil's pate will suit me fine. Now go get me some pants and a jacket."

When Tom went to get his old spare pants and the jacket he wore when he hunted rats, he happened to wake Boto. They had found a provisions room in front of the main rudder where they could be left in peace by drunken sailors and malcontent passengers.

"One day I'm going to make you a pair of red pants," said Boto sleepily.

"Go back to sleep," murmured Tom.

"They'll have pockets in the front and back, because you're the sort of person who needs pockets. And they'll be just as red as my shirt."

"Good night, Nyo Boto."

"Where are you going?"

Tom sighed. "I'm going out with my sister."

"Out dancing?"

Tom smiled, but quickly turned serious. "I might have done something that I'll later regret. She's going to be married this week. Feo, who has never seen anything, is going to marry Father Innocent."

"That would be like wandering through an endless night," said Boto, turning over onto his side.

Tom sat down next to him. "I'm taking her up to the Devil's pate."

"Are you really?"

"Yes, that's what I just said, didn't I? If she should fall from the uppermost yard, it would be preferable to the marriage that awaits her. Doesn't that sound reasonable, Boto?"

"No, I don't think so, Tom." Boto was still lying with his back turned.

Tom gathered the clothes into a bundle. "Why doesn't it sound reasonable, if I might take the liberty of asking you, who are apparently so wise that even in your sleep you can speak one truth after another."

"You ought to invite Señor Salazar up there."

Tom suppressed a little smile and tucked the blanket closer around Boto's back.

She is standing in front of him wearing his woolen pants and old jacket. Her hair is tied in a knot on top of her head. She looks like a boy. An unusually attractive boy.

"We'll start with the maintop," shouts Tom. "That's the platform that sits above the mainsail. You might decide that's high enough, because the view from the maintop is really quite splendid."

"You go first, Tom O'Connor."

"You can still change your mind."

Feodora looks past Tom and whispers something to herself, then she stares into his eyes. "It's too late to change my mind."

Tom hesitates, then puts his feet in the rigging and pulls himself up, foot by foot. He doesn't look back, just steadily and calmly works his way up. After a few minutes he is standing on the square platform between the mainsail and the main gallant sail, where the noise is indescribable. The wind has picked up, and the swells are slamming onto the deck, washing in great surges from side to side, then rolling from stem to stern, only to begin all over again.

He looks down at his sister, whose jaw is set. She's no weakling, but she's not accustomed to this kind of work. Using far too much energy, she manages to make it to the maintop and refuses his outstretched hand as she crawls up onto the platform. But when she gets to her feet, she hugs the mast with an openly terrified expression.

"Glorious, isn't it?" shouts Tom.

"Wonderful." She gives him a stony look.

"The thundering and roaring up here is magnificent." Tom leaps out and grabs hold of the outermost rigging, swinging like a monkey and laughing into the wind.

Feo watches him but doesn't utter a sound. She clings to the mast and presses her lips together.

"Boto suggested that we should bring your betrothed up here with us." Tom gives her a wink.

Feo raises one eyebrow and speaks through tightly pressed lips. "I thought we were going all the way up. Maybe you don't want to go any higher, half-breed?"

Tom moves closer to her and puts his arm around her waist. "Like the shrew said as she beat her husband, the best is yet to come. Let's go, Feodora!"

Tom leaps into the rigging above the maintop, now working his way up like a madman. Higher and higher, faster and faster, he pays no mind to the wind or the sail but crawls with his hands and feet close together, his body arched, all his muscles tensed, and his senses wide open. Soon he has the yard of the gallant sail overhead and can feel in earnest how much the ship is rolling.

It's not every day that a person finds himself so high up. Even though Tom thinks he's tried a little of everything, he can feel his heart pounding and his legs trembling. He looks down and smiles. She's working her way up like a lunatic, battling not just the rigging and fatigue but herself. Her eyes are flashing lightning and the knot of her hair has partially come undone, making her look like a wild creature, a fearsome foe. It occurs to him that if he ever has to fight for his life, it would be good to have Feodora Dolores Vasgues nearby.

"Three more feet and you're there, Feo," he shouts, placing his elbow against the yard of the gallant sail.

"Move over, Irishman." She uses her last strength to haul herself up.

Tom makes room and watches her throw herself at the yard like a shipwrecked soul, breathing hard, her eyes wild.

It seems a terrifying distance down to the deck.

"The sea is violent, isn't it?" says Tom with a smile. "You feel so close to the universe, part of God's own sea chart. Boto knows a story about how the starry sky was created. Do you want to hear it, Feodora?"

She turns to face him and presses her lips to his ear. "This, Tom, is the ends of the Earth."

"Maybe we should go back down."

She shakes her head and smiles harshly. Tom recognizes that expression and isn't sure that he likes it. "I shouldn't have brought you up here, Feo."

"Of course you should have. I'll never forget it. And I'll always remember how much I loved life."

He touches her cheek. "Let's go back down now, Feo."

She shakes her head. "Not yet, Tom, not yet."

"I don't like the look in your eye."

Feo doesn't answer.

"If you love life," shouts Tom, "how can you marry Father Innocent?"

"I broke off our engagement yesterday."

Tom grabs her arm. "Splendid, Feo, that's splendid."

"It wasn't my intention to cheat anyone," she says, "not even Salazar. But for the first time, after four weeks at sea beneath this vast black, gray, but above all, infinitely blue sky, I've gained a sense of what freedom is. And what a person can lose." She looks up. "Can you explain what freedom is, Tom?"

"The uppermost yard." Tom laughs.

Feo stares straight ahead. "Freedom is the opposite of Señor Salazar."

Tom pulls her close. "You have no idea how relieved I am. You're right, freedom is the opposite of Salazar. That's just as it should be, Feo, precisely as it should be."

"No," she says, pulling away. "That's not as it should be. Because my betrothed refuses to allow me to break off the engagement. He has gone to the ship's highest authority, Captain Muñeco, who has ruled that we should be married as planned. It has been decided that we will be joined in holy matrimony when the sun rises the day after tomorrow, on Salazar's birthday. At the exact moment when the first light breaks through the darkness, I will become his wife."

Tom stares at her. "Can't you refuse?"

Feo doesn't answer, so he takes her arm and gives her a shake. "There must be some way out," he yells.

She looks at him. "There is. Because you're right, you know. This is freedom, and I will never give it up."

Tom clasps her face between his hands and presses his forehead to hers. "Feo look at me. Listen to me. I don't know what you're thinking, but . . . but I just want to say that there is always a way out. I've been in much worse trouble, much worse. They've chased me with knives, daggers, and clubs. But Feo, you owe it to life to . . . you owe it to life . . ."

"What does a person owe to life?"

"To hold on to it, Feo, to hold on."

"Do you think death is the worst thing that exists, Tom?" Feo smiles wanly. "If that's the case, then you're mistaken. Loneliness is worse. You'll never understand that, Tom. Not because you're Irish but because you're a man."

"Let's go back down now, Feo."

But instead of grabbing hold of the rigging, Feo lets go and presses her lips hard against Tom's in a kiss. "I've always loved you, Tom O'Connor, always. I've also hated you like the plague. But deep inside I loved you. Look up, little man. Take a brief look at the Devil's pate."

"I would rather look at you."

She gives him a smile and stretches out her arms. The wind catches hold of her hair. Her eyes are blazing. For the first time Tom sees tears in her eyes.

Then she takes off. She hovers for a second in midair with her head tilted back, with all of her senses wide open. For one giddy second, time stands still.

Then she vanishes beneath him. Strikes the rigging, somersaults, stops. Keeps on falling.

Hand. Fingers. Grip.

Mind, reason, thought. Gone.

Only a body in the wind.

He slides down and lunges outward, his feet locked in the rigging, his body extended, his head down.

Hand, fingers, grip. Around her wrist.

The sudden roar when sound returns to him. The roar from the sea and the thundering of the sail. She's dangling beneath him. Her eyes are wide open and as black as coal. "Let . . . me . . . go, Tom!"

"Never!"

She tosses her head and flails her body. He can feel her weight threatening to tear his arm off. But he clenches his teeth and holds on tightly.

"Damn it, you Irish half-breed," she screams. "Let go!"

"Never, Feo, never. If you want to be free, don't do it like this."

At that instant her wrist threatens to slide out of his grip. He hears her scream and feels his strength ebbing away. "You'll take me with you," he bellows. "If you don't catch hold of the rigging, Feo, you'll take me with you."

"Let go of me, Tom."

He looks up. "Here we come, heavenly Father," he shouts. "Here we come. My name is O'Connor, and I'm bringing my sister with me."

She's hanging in the rigging at his side. They're gasping loudly.

For a long time neither of them has the strength to utter anything but a few fierce curses. Tom is still holding on to Feo's wrist. He refuses to let go until they're standing on deck.

The ship's clock struck three bells. The sound of the clock merely reinforced the silence that had descended over the *Oceania*. Tom went to the galley to get a mug of water that they could share. She still had not said a word. They wiped their faces and hands, which were sticky from the salty sea fog.

Tom emptied the mug. He could feel her looking at him.

"I was left alone with López," she said. "Mother was gone. You were gone. López and I were the only ones left. I started hating the inn and hating my work; in the end I hated all of Nevis. I dreamed only of getting away. Even if it had to be in your old skiff. Every evening I would talk to the guests in the hope that one of them would take me along. But the ones who offered either had as few prospects as I did or had quite different desires in mind. Another year passed. I started to give up hope. Then one evening he came, Señor Salazar. No longer an inquisitor but a free man. I think he could see how full of longing I was. He thought this meant that I was eager for marriage. I didn't care. I packed my bags that very evening, even though it would be two months before we could leave."

Tom sat lost in his own thoughts for a moment, then he took Feo's hand. "I'll go with you, Feo."

"With me? Where?"

Tom smiled. "To the ends of the Earth."

Feo shook her head. "You impossible Irishman, what would we do there?"

"Get rid of him."

"Oh, so you want to kill Señor Salazar?"

Tom nodded.

Feo closed her eyes and sighed. "You are truly the grandson of Gráinne. Good heavens! First you save my life and then you want to get rid of another—is that how it is?"

"The Lord giveth and the Lord taketh away."

Feodora got to her feet. "But you are not the Lord, Tom O'Connor. You're a miserable half-breed, and if there's ever a next time, I promise to take you with me."

Tom smiled, recognizing the familiar tone of her voice.

Feodora strode across the deck, taking firm steps. Then suddenly she spun around and came back to Tom, looking at him with her eyes narrowed. "God knows," she said, "I think you might actually try it. Try to kill Señor Salazar in cold blood. God knows he might actually do it. But that will never happen."

"It won't?"

Her mood changed abruptly and she was all smiles and gentleness. She kissed him on the cheek and said, "That's a job for a Spaniard, you see."

He stared after her, thinking that it was possible, but only possible, that he had been mistaken about the Spanish race. Maybe there was some good in them after all.

A short time later he was lying next to Nyo Boto. "Isn't life grand?" whispered Tom as he closed his eyes. "Even though your shirt stinks of mold, life is still grand."

"When the smell is gone," replied Boto, "I'll give the shirt away."

"But I thought you loved that shirt."

"I do."

Tom sighed. "I don't think I'll ever understand you."

The next day Tom was summoned to the captain's cabin. It was an unusually still day, with almost no wind. Even though the frigate was barely moving, the seamen took it in stride, since they were ahead of schedule. For the same reason, a number of minor repairs could now be made. The rigging could be inspected and the rudder cleaned. For that job they called on Tom, who was forever bragging about his diving ability.

In the cabin along with the captain were the first officer and Señor Salazar.

"The first officer thinks the rudder is sluggish." The captain was beaming. "So we thought it would be best if someone went down to give it a proper inspection. I've called for the carpenter so that O'Connor, the Irishman with the great talent for diving, can confer with him." The captain looked at the first officer, who scowled at Tom. After the episode with the miscalculated course, their relationship was less than amiable.

"Because you really are as good a swimmer as you claim, aren't you?" growled Muñeco.

Tom didn't have time to answer before there was a pounding on the door.

"Oh yes, the carpenter." The captain opened the door himself.

A man stepped inside. Tom felt as if time stood still. As if he had been abruptly placed at the end of a long gorge, and yet the distance wasn't enough to prevent him from seeing the man quite clearly. Suddenly he heard the wind in the sugarcane and the sound of the mill vanes turning. He felt the heat in the fields, the knot in his stomach, and his mind cracking in two.

But he was not in a gorge nor in a field of sugarcane but in the captain's cabin, where he was standing face-to-face with the summoned workman, who stared at him with his hand to his chin, as if to indicate his surprise, his joy, and his tremendous luck.

"Tom O'Connor," said the carpenter, taking a step closer. "We meet again."

Muñeco looked at him. "Do you know each other?"

The ship's carpenter didn't take his eyes off Tom, merely nodded. "Oh yes," he said. "You might say that. Isn't that right, Tombomba?"

Tom did not reply, just glanced from side to side, like a mouse looking for a hole in the woodwork.

Felix Salazar sensed that something unusual was going on, and he now turned to Tom. "Explain yourself, boy. How do you happen to know the carpenter?"

Tom fixed his eyes on Salazar, realizing that if he was going to get out of this situation, his only salvation would come from that quarter. "From my days on a plantation," said Tom in a low voice. "The carpenter is French and his name is Pierre, though he's called Lupo."

"And this Irish lad," shouted Pierre in a loud, quavering voice, "is being searched for all over Jamaica, even all over the Caribbean."

The silence that had descended over the sea slipped inside the cabin. A smile of anticipation spread over the first officer's face.

"I recommend," continued Pierre, "that the captain put this fellow in chains at once. When you gentlemen hear what Tom O'Connor has done, you won't want to have him walking around loose a moment longer."

Everyone's attention now rested on Tom, who quietly explained that he had acted only in self-defense.

Half an hour later he was still sitting in the captain's cabin, but with his hands behind his back, where a solid length of rope and a tight knot bound him to the chair. On Tom's left sat Felix Salazar, the first officer, the boatswain, and the surgeon, along with a colonel selected from the passenger list. To his right sat Lupo. In the middle, enthroned behind his desk, was the high judge, Captain Muñeco, who had taken time to change his clothes and wig. He rang a little bell and began the maritime inquiry by immediately giving the floor to the ship's carpenter, Pierre Augustin. The man stood up and bowed respectfully.

"Captain, sir," he said, "and honored gentlemen, my name is Pierre Emil Augustin, I am forty-six years old, born in Marseilles, and trained as a ship's carpenter. For the past five years and up until the day of departure for this good ship, I was employed on a sugar plantation in Jamaica by the name of Aron Hill. A place with a good reputation, known as a model farm that treated the blacks well. On the plantation I was employed as a bomba and supervised the work crews, or rather the slaves. My superior was a Dutchman by the name of Joop van den Arle, may God be with him. There were eight bombas all together, and we worked hard, from morning to night, because we knew that some of the slaves were planning to revolt. Especially one of them. His name was Kanuno. He was wild and rebellious and just waiting for the day when he could ram his hoe into a white man and set fire to the crops."

Lupo let his gaze move from one man to the other.

"But this black devil, this Kanuno, realized that he couldn't carry out his plan without help, because Aron Hill, as I mentioned, was a model farm, and we bombas kept close watch on him."

"Try to keep your story brief," said the captain.

Lupo nodded. "One day we discovered smoke in the southwestern corner of the fields. And even though we fought as hard as we could, the fire spread rapidly to most of the plantation. The fire had been set by one of Kanuno's cohorts, a man by the name of George. We seized Kanuno at once and chained him to a stake and then rode out to capture the arsonist. One of the white overseers was Tombomba, that red-haired Irish boy you see before you. And he was friends with this George. A slave lover of the worst kind. And a storyteller of the worst order, which I beg you gentlemen to remember when he is allowed to speak. Tombomba found George, but instead of seizing hold of him so he could be given his just punishment, Tom gave the slave a horse and then, under cover of the fire, he freed Kanuno."

Pierre let his gaze slide over the audience. "In less than twenty-four hours, half of Aron Hill had burned to the ground. Thirty slaves escaped, and many of them managed to plunder the main house. We started our search for Tom O'Connor, and my friend and colleague, Frans Brüggen, found him in Port Royal."

Pierre bowed his head and continued in a stifled voice.

"In a room of a filthy inn, this O'Connor cut the throat of old Frans, who bled to death in less than an hour. Master Joop and the other bombas pursued the murderer through half the city and finally caught up with him out at sea. Joop told him to surrender so that legal proceedings could be instigated, but Tom O'Connor shot and killed Joop van den Arle and then evaded his own fate on that bloodred sea. I can fully understand his desire to leave the Caribbean, and I understand why this murderer now wishes to be far away, fleeing even all the way to Spain. But it warms my old French heart to find that a higher justice exists, which will now give this murderer, this arsonist, this rebel what he deserves. I have nothing more to say, Captain, sir. May God be my witness." Lupo sat down, turning his back on Tom in disgust.

A fierce muttering started up among the men. Finally Muñeco asked Tom to speak.

After a brief moment to gather his thoughts, Tom told them about his time on the plantation. About his friendship with Sugar George and his wife, Ina. About the sale of their little daughter, and about the way Frans Brüggen and Joop van den Arle treated the blacks. He also began talking about his friendship with Sarah Briggs, but was interrupted by the captain, who wanted to know whether Tom had helped to set the fire. Yes or no!

"No, señor," replied Tom.

"A lie," shouted Lupo.

The captain told him to keep quiet. "Did you or did you not cut the throat of a white bomba?"

"In self-defense, señor. It was him or me."

"And did you shoot and kill this Dutchman, Joop van den Arle?"

"No, señor. He was shot by a Spanish officer. I have never owned a pistol."

"Lies, all lies," shouted Lupo. "We're looking at a double murderer and a . . ."

Captain Muñeco was on his feet. "This is a very serious matter," he said. "I'm going to ask four members of the crew to be in charge of the accused. They will take him below, to a holding cell. There he will stay until I have made my decision, in consultation with these gentlemen. If we should need more information, Pierre and the accused will be brought back here. Otherwise, the inquiry is over. The carpenter may go now."

The cell into which they locked Tom was about the size of the doghouse he had occupied at Aron Hill. There was a table, a cot, and a little narrow peephole—no more than a crack, really—that told him he was somewhere on the starboard side. Through the hole he could catch a glimpse of the sea, but nothing more. How long he had been in the cell, he didn't know, but dusk had started to fall by the time the first officer opened the door.

Outside stood the captain, Señor Salazar, and the portly colonel. The first officer read the verdict out loud. It was written in red ink on a piece of heavy paper and furnished with the captain's seal. "Seaman Tom O'Connor, who stands accused of two counts of murder, arson, and disloyal behavior toward his employer, is found—after a painstaking consideration by impartial men, none of whom has ever been convicted of a crime, along with the ship's captain, Señor Eduardo Rodrigo Muñeco—guilty of all charges. The verdict has been signed by those present and is an expression of their unanimous decision. Shortly before daybreak, a gallows will therefore be set up, and Tom O'Connor shall be hanged until he is dead."

After this pronouncement, the door was shut and locked.

Night fell, accompanied by a heavy fog. Tom sat at the narrow peephole, looking out on the blue-black ocean where the waves had been transformed into an endless sheet of iron. An hour ago he had had a visitor—his last. Feodora had been graciously granted permission to visit her brother, although only under the watchful eye of a prison guard.

They talked through the bars. Feo was grim, her gaze steadfast. They barely managed to slip their fingers between the bars to hold hands. Tom mostly wanted to talk about his mother, but Feo kept shifting the conversation to other things. She told him what a splendid brother he had been to her. What a splendid man she thought he had become. "Think about that, Tom—don't think about anything else. Your reputation will spread like rings in water."

He told her that he was worried about Nyo Boto and the fate that awaited him.

"Don't think about Boto," said Feo. "They're taking care of him."

It turned out that the captain and his wise men, after yet another consultation, had decided that Tom O'Connor's faithful esquire, the black boy whom everyone on board called Little Tom, would have to suffer the same fate as his master. But when Feodora saw that her attempts to save her brother had prompted nothing but irritation from Señor Salazar, she had thrown all her efforts into saving Boto, who had done no wrong.

At last Salazar admitted, "I may be able to save the black's life, but I can't prevent them from selling him at the next slave market. And it might cost me, since the captain is a greedy man. But I'll do it if you agree to marry me dutifully, Feodora."

Thus Feo was able to bring Tom the good news that Nyo Boto was not going to be hanged. "He's sitting in the hold, sewing," she said.

"Does he know what's going to happen to me?"

Feo nodded. "I told him. He took it well. He said he would name one of his sons after you."

Tom shook his head and pulled out his amulet. "I was thinking of giving this to you. A slave named Kanuno gave it to me. He said it would bring me luck." Tom smiled. "Maybe he was glad to get rid of it."

"Keep it, Tom," whispered Feo. "It's yours, proof of your courage."

"There's one more thing," murmured Tom, casting a glance at the guard. "Afterward, when . . . when I'm dead. What I want to say is that it would make me happy if you could arrange for me to have a proper sailor's burial. The priest doesn't have to say anything, but I'd like to be put into the sea. Will you take care of that, Feo?"

She didn't answer but disappeared from his field of vision and slid to the floor. Then she got back up, took his hand, and kissed it before the guard pulled her away.

"Farewell, Feodora," said Tom. "Live well."

He heard her screaming and cursing all the way to the upper deck, where it sounded as if a fierce scuffle took place.

Later that night Tom awoke to a pounding and hammering up on deck. It wasn't hard to figure out what the ship's carpenter was doing. Or with what zest and zeal he was making use of his tools.

It must be close to dawn, thought Tom. "Close," he said to himself, "very close. My sister is going to marry Father Innocent and I am going to be hanged. Do you hear me, Mother? I hope not. Worse fates could hardly be imagined for your children. But I want you to know that you're not to blame."

At that moment he caught sight of the little algae-colored gecko sitting on one of the beams in the ceiling.

"Oh, I see I have a fine guest," said Tom. "Can I do anything for you?"

"Well, what do you know?" said the lizard. "The very words I intended for you." Its forked tongue flicked in and out. The gecko crept closer. "The last time we spoke, he was more cocky."

Tom nodded. "You're right about that, you slimy lizard. Now you can have the whole thing for a pittance. What's a heart selling for these days?"

"Oh, but he has already given his heart away to a girl whose name he can't remember."

"You're a clever little fellow," said Tom. "But if you're not here to barter, then to what do I owe the honor?"

"Curiosity," the gecko said, smiling. "Death has followed in your foot-steps all your days, Tom O'Connor, right on your heels, you might say."

"Come closer, gecko," whispered Tom. "Let me whisper a secret in the tiny hole you use for hearing."

"Can a condemned man tell me anything I don't already know?"

"On death's stallion, a person gains a special perspective, old friend."

"Is that true?" murmured the lizard, as it crawled down to Tom.

"Now listen here." Tom suddenly stuck out his hand, grabbed the lizard by the stomach, and squeezed hard. The animal twisted and turned, blink-ing its eyes and spitting and raging. But no matter how it struggled, noth-ing did any good.

"Do you feel it now?" whispered Tom. "The embrace of Death, cold as ice, merciless and painful. What do you have for me at this moment, you cold-blooded reptile?"

"Let me go," groaned the gecko. "What pleasure can a condemned man take from another's pain?"

Tom laughed hoarsely. "Quite a lot, my slippery friend, quite a lot. You've always shown up whenever I was in the greatest need, or the most unhappy, or all alone. But did you ever offer me any help?"

"He was miserly whenever I proposed a sensible trade."

"Maybe you're right. Maybe I'm being too harsh. It occurs to me that all your days you've wanted to be anything but a lizard. Isn't that true?"

"Does it make any difference now?" gasped the gecko.

"Oh yes, it does," said Tom, "because I'm going to give you an astonishing insight. First as a bird, then as a fish."

"How will that happen?"

"Very easily." Tom stepped over to the narrow crack that faced the blue-black sea, feeling the gecko wriggling in his hand. "*Adios*, old friend," he said. "Fly like a bird, and if that fails you, then swim like a fish. At any rate, you won't be a gecko anymore."

He stuck his hand out. Heavy drops of fog dampened his skin.

"Yet another misdeed," gasped the animal.

Tom pulled his hand in and let the lizard go.

"Thank you, master," moaned the gecko, scurrying for the ceiling. "You'll never regret this, if it's the last thing you do."

But Tom wasn't listening. He was staring out at the gray fog of the night, where the outline of a ship had briefly appeared and then vanished. All was quiet except for the monotonous clacking of the rigging as it struck the masts and the gentle slap of the waves against the hull.

The shadow appeared again, this time taking on a more distinct shape. Gray and sinister it looked, like a ghost ship approaching the Spanish frigate.

"On the starboard side," murmured Tom, narrowing his eyes, "where we have no cannons."

She was somewhat smaller than the *Oceania* and moving very quietly because she was being rowed under the cover of fog. Not a soul was visible to Tom, and all of the sails were reefed. Not a sound could be heard except for the oars, which were placed in the water as delicately as spoons in a cup.

Tom looked up at the ceiling, but the gecko was gone. When he shifted his glance back to the sea, he could see the strange ship making ready to turn so she would come alongside.

And now it came. Something that made Tom's blood freeze and his heart skip two beats. For on the farthest mast, the mysterious sailing ship had hoisted a coal-black flag with a bright yellow skull and crossbones.

22 C. W. Bull

THE *OCEANIA* was literally caught napping. In fact, most of the crew were lying in their hammocks when the first cannonball burst through the starboard side and water began to pour in. The next direct hit struck the mainmast, and the third snapped the mizzen-topmast right in half.

From his cell Tom heard the tumult give way to panic. The first cannon salvos had spread terror among the passengers and crew who, at the sight of the black pirate flag, gave up any thought of defending the ship. Instead they tried to turn the *Oceania* around, but the two ships were now so close together that the pirates could leap straight onto the frigate, where they hooted and hollered, fired their pistols and carried on.

The smoke from the upper deck drifted in long fingers and finally reached Tom, who sat with his back against the wall, bursting with tension. The screams of the passengers quickly stopped, but the silence that replaced the commotion was, if possible, even worse. Tom took it for granted that the *Oceania* had surrendered without a fight. Helpless with rage, he pounded his fists against the door, cursing Captain Muñeco and his cowardly crew. He feared for his sister's fate and dreaded what was in store for the boy in the red shirt.

He heard the rattling of keys, and then the door opened.

"We've been boarded, Tom!"

He stared at Nyo Boto, who threw out his hands apologetically.

"As the mouse said while the barn burned, at least we won't die of the cold." Tom's voice was resigned. He edged his way out of the cell and asked what had become of the passengers.

"The pirates have hanged the first officer from your gallows and taken Muñeco prisoner. I took the keys out of the dead man's pocket."

"What about Feodora?"

"Still unmarried," murmured Boto. "Come with me; we can't stay here. This old ship is already listing so badly I'm afraid we're going to sink."

Tom didn't reply. He was looking at a tall rough man who had appeared on the stairway. The man was wearing striped pants and a blue shirt. He had a cutlass in one hand and a dagger in the other. His skin was dark, but he was not African, nor was he white. His profession, on the other hand, was not difficult to guess.

When the man caught sight of Tom and Boto, he took three steps down and waved his cutlass in front of their noses. "You two. Yes, you—the red-haired lad and the black in the red shirt. Get up here."

On the upper deck the pirates had herded the crew to one side and the passengers to the other. Señor Salazar was standing next to Feodora. The two were pale but composed. There were no wounded and no dead, except for the first officer, who would never again have to bother with navigation.

The women were crying and the children whimpering, but the crew stood in silence, making do with glaring at the pirates, about thirty in all, who had taken over the ship so quickly. Some of the bandits were up on the bridge, others were in the process of rummaging through the passengers' possessions, but most were on deck watching the crew.

Tom looked at the buccaneers and thought to himself that their reputation held true. They were colorful, rough, swaggering men. Their clothes were exotic-looking. Many wore gold earrings, bracelets, and bright neckerchiefs. In their breeches, threads of gold and silver shone, bearing witness to much successful plundering. The pirates' swords and cutlasses gleamed as if they had come straight from the smithy. There were no drunkards, no wooden legs. The capture of the ship had been carried out with precision.

They worked according to a plan; each man knew what his task was. One of them in particular attracted everyone's attention—a mountain of a man with a tiny pitch-black topknot on his head and a long, scraggly beard. His skin was yellow, his eyes were slanted, and he looked like he could hoist a barrel of water all on his own. The mere sight of this Mongol seemed enough to keep the crew in check.

Captain Muñeco had been bound and tied to a chair. His orange-colored wig was askew, and his lips were quavering. "Take whatever you like," he shouted, "but spare our lives."

"Yes," cried his men, "spare our lives."

"Silence," bellowed a tall, slender man wearing red clothing, shiny new boots, and a handsome purple hat. He was so obviously in charge, Tom guessed he was the captain of the pirate ship. He had a crooked nose, piercing eyes, and a huge scar that ran from his ear to his chin.

Various objects and belongings were now dragged out on deck, where the pirates had spread a gaudy cloth. There wasn't much loot, which seemed to disappoint them. They kicked at the candlesticks and drinking tankards, the old jewelry boxes and chests of linen.

"Take what we have," repeated Muñeco, but he was reduced to silence when the pirate with the scar plucked off his wig.

The topgallant sail was burning. Fiery shreds rained down, and the ship continued to list from the water she was taking on. We're sinking, thought Tom. Before long, the *Oceania* will be lying at the bottom of the sea.

Tom tried to catch Feodora's eye. She stood there calm, defiant, and ready for battle. Her cheeks blazed and her eyes were shooting fire. She was wearing a beautiful but very simple black dress with a white shawl. A little sprig of dried flowers adorned her hair. She didn't look like a bride but more like a girl who was assessing her fate, ready to take matters into her own hands should the opportunity arise.

The buccaneers walked among the passengers, stripping earrings and bracelets off the women and examining the men, staring into their mouths and feeling their bodies under their clothing. "Damned bunch of weaklings," they snarled, kicking at them.

The Mongol rummaged through the heap of valuables, spat into the air, and cast a menacing glance at Tom, who had stepped forward from the group of sailors and pirates. "Excuse me," said Tom, "but we're taking on water."

There was a moment of silence. The passengers, the crew, the pirates, and the children all stared in terror at Tom. "What was that I heard?" growled the pirate with the scar.

"I just said that we're taking on water," muttered Tom. "We might be able to save the ship if we act quickly."

Two more pirates came over. They stared in disbelief at each other and started to laugh. But the man with the scar didn't laugh. He seized Tom by the collar and flung him to the deck. "An example to the others," he declared. "The next one who feels like bleating will suffer the same fate as this ill-mannered lad." One of the other pirates handed the man his pistol. "I've never much cared for redheads," muttered the scarred man, aiming at Tom, who lay on his back less than six feet away.

"Only a savage would shoot an unarmed boy," said a voice.

Tom glanced from Feodora to the tall man. His snakelike scar had turned bright red. "It seems to me," the man said, "that I'm in need of two pistols." He went over to Feo, who held her head high and looked him right in the eye. "A savage," he muttered, shaking his head as he let the muzzle of the pistol slide around Feo's face. "A person would have to be either unbelievably stupid or awfully tired of life to call Indigo Moon a savage."

"I'm neither of those things," said Feo in a loud, clear voice. "But I do fear for my brother's life; his only crime was to say that . . ."

The man called Moon interrupted Feo by firing his pistol very close to her head. The passengers stood as if frozen, and many of the mothers thrust their small children out of sight.

"Now she has to choose," shouted Moon. "Is it going to be her or her brother who dies?"

"Only a moron would give a girl a choice like that." Feodora looked from Moon to Tom, who was still lying on the deck.

"She has chosen," bellowed Moon as he pressed pistol number two against Feo's forehead.

"The captain!" shouted a voice all of a sudden.

A narrow plank was slapped into place between the two ships. The pirates reacted by lining up in front of the crew, their sabers, cutlasses, and swords all at the ready. The man with the scar turned his back to Feo, planted his feet far apart, and shouted, "The crew bids you welcome on board, Captain."

Tom scuttled a few feet back and looked up at what had just appeared out of the haze. The man was six and a half feet tall, his clothes were pitch-black, and his boots brand-new. On his head he wore a three-cornered hat with a skull and crossbones made of silver. But what commanded the most attention was his enormous beard, which was plaited in dozens of tiny braids around his red lips. His eyes were big and black, and his coal-black eyebrows merged with his beard.

The pirate was chewing on a ragged and partially smoked cigar. He spat on the deck, then coughed and gnashed his teeth, suddenly convulsed with a terrible shivering fit. Without a word he stretched out his hand behind him toward a fat little man wearing a striped shirt. The little man was holding a round object with a white wick. It looked exactly like a grenade.

"Fire," growled the pirate captain, winking cheerfully at one of the female passengers, whereupon Moon struck a spark with a flint lighter and lit the fuse. The captain let his gaze slide over the passengers and crew. Then he strolled across the deck with a demented gleam in his big black eyes and stopped in front of Muñeco.

The sputtering fuse was no longer than the cork on a wine bottle, and yet the pirate was taking his own sweet time. From his lips came the sound of stifled chuckling. He looked around with a cunning smile and kissed Captain Muñeco on the forehead. Then he carefully placed the round object in the captain's lap and said, "*Adios.*"

The next moment there was a deafening boom. After the explosion, most of the deck was covered in clouds of smoke. Everyone stared at the remains of Muñeco's chair, on which there was a circular stain. The only things left of Eduardo Rodrigo Muñeco were his shoes.

The passengers gasped and crossed themselves. Some even fainted.

"A tradition," sighed the pirate captain with a shrug of his shoulders. Then he caught sight of Tom, who was still crawling around on deck. "Next time you'll stand up in the presence of C. W. Bull."

When Tom awoke he was lying on the middle deck along with ten other youths. Why he had fainted, he couldn't say, but after the encounter with the pirate captain, he had fainted dead away. He looked at Boto, who was sitting with his back against a barrel, mending a tear in a cloth doll.

"What happened?" whispered Tom.

"Oh, it's just a small rip," said Boto.

"Not that—with the ship and with us."

"Some were put into the water," replied Boto, "aboard rowboats. Most of the crew, I think."

"What about Feodora?"

"I can't really say. Maybe she left in the boats too; maybe they're going to burn the ship."

Tom got to his feet and realized that the wind had shifted and was gathering strength. The topgallant sail was gone, but the royal sail and mainsail were undamaged, as were the foresail and topsail.

"If only we could hoist the anchor," muttered Boto.

"It takes five men to bring that anchor up," said Tom.

"We could cut the anchor chain," said Boto.

"Why should we cut the anchor chain, Nyo Boto?"

"To turn the vessel around," said Boto. "If we can turn the vessel, we can attack him with our cannons. If we're lucky, that is."

Tom sighed. "Do you know who you're talking about, Nyo Boto? Do you know who boarded us?"

"I don't think I caught his name."

"His name is C. W. Bull," said Tom. "He's the worst, most bestial, most formidable pirate captain ever to sail the seven seas. His crew consists of cannibals, murderers, and escaped prisoners. He sold his soul to the very Devil. Bull is your worst nightmare, little man."

Nyo Boto nodded. "But for the time being he has saved your life." He sighed. "And now I'm going down to the capstan."

The confusion on board the *Oceania* had grown so great during the past few minutes that Tom and Boto had no trouble reaching the other deck, where the winch for the anchor chain was located. Boto found a hammer and chisel and gave them to Tom. "You worked for a blacksmith, didn't you?"

Tom nodded and with three blows he split the chain in half. It whistled around the capstan and vanished like a snake into the waters.

"The old ship is free now," said Boto and dashed up the stairs, where two pirates appeared, dragging the ship's carpenter and tossing him over the side. The Frenchman Pierre hadn't seemed to offer any resistance. On the contrary.

Tom stared down at the water, where the former bomba disappeared in a froth of bubbles. Boto gave Tom's shirt a tug as he passed on his way up to the quarterdeck, and Tom raced after him. "This will never work," he snarled.

Boto grabbed the wheel. "We'll lash it in place," he said, "and she'll turn on her own. Then we'll go down to the cannons and fire on him."

"You're out of your mind, Nyo Boto." Tom shook his head but began securing the wheel.

At that moment a voice said, "What the devil do you think you're doing, lad?"

Tom gave a start as he saw Indigo Moon come out of Muñeco's cabin.

"Is he thinking of going somewhere? Answer me when I speak to you."

Tom had noticed that the only pirates on Bull's ship who spoke English were this man and the captain himself; all the rest spoke Spanish or Portuguese.

"We were thinking," said Tom, as he gave Boto a defiant look, "of lashing the wheel in place, turning the vessel around, manning the cannons, and attacking Bull's ship broadside."

Moon's mouth fell open, and for a moment it looked as if he might have to lean on something to keep from losing his balance. Then he put a hand to his forehead. "You are truly headed for an early death. Fortunately, there's already a gallows on deck."

"It was actually intended for him," said Boto in a helpful tone.

The man stared in disbelief from Boto to Tom. "Is that so? And what had the red-haired boy done, if I might be allowed to ask?"

Tom said, "I was condemned for a mere trifle, Mr. Moon."

"Well, even the purest among us can wind up unlucky," grumbled the pirate. "But tell me what you were sentenced for. It will make the experience of hanging you all the more pleasant."

Tom cleared his throat and glared at Boto, who placed his arm around Tom's shoulders and said, "He set fire to a sugar plantation, killed two bombas, stole three horses, freed thirty slaves, and shot a Dutch overseer by the name of Joop van den Arle. He's also my best friend. His name is Tom O'Connor. He once worked for a blacksmith, and he's quite good with a sextant."

Nyo Boto stopped when the man pulled out his cutlass.

"And by the Devil, you're going to die, O'Connor," Moon snarled. "Aside from Bull's life story, I've never heard the likes of it."

"Allow me," said Tom quickly, "to take off this amulet, which I would like to give to your captain. It's worth a great deal of money at the market." Tom pulled Kanuno's amulet over his head and handed it to Moon, who looked at it suspiciously.

"The boy can give it to Bull himself," said Moon. "Because bad news often comes back to haunt the messenger." Moon took off his hat and scowled at Tom as he opened the door to Muñeco's cabin.

In addition to Bull, three other pirates were present, along with the second officer and the colonel from the passenger list, as well as Felix Salazar and his little scribe.

"We have a condemned man here who wants to give the captain a present," said Moon.

"Usher him in!" growled Bull.

Tom was pushed over to the desk where Bull was sitting with his feet up. His black eyes shone with malice, and his coal-black brows jumped up and down as he gnawed on his frayed cigar. For a moment Tom had trouble getting the words out. Standing so near to Bull, he could feel his throat closing up and his stomach knotting.

"Is the boy mute?" grumbled Bull.

Tom shook his head.

"He has something for you, Captain, sir," said Moon.

Bull gave Tom a piercing look. His gaze held disapproval, brutality, and two other things that Tom tried to name. One of them was pain. The other was a glint that in the best of cases might be interpreted as humor.

"An amulet from my paternal grandmother." Tom bowed.

Bull tore the amulet from Tom's hand and looked with disgust at the round stone. In the meantime Indigo Moon explained Tom's plans for the wheel. Bull did not react.

"And afterward," continued Moon, "this Irishman was actually going to man the cannons and attack us broadside. According to his own statement."

Now Tom had the captain's full attention. Silence filled the cabin. Several of the men shifted uneasily. Felix Salazar shook his head in resignation. Then the captain bellowed with laughter and tossed the amulet aside. He picked up his pistol and shot the scribe's hat off his head. After that, he lit his cigar and summoned Tom forward with the crook of his forefinger.

Tom reluctantly walked around the desk to stand close to the big man, who reeked of tobacco and a negligent regard for cleanliness.

"Hmmm," growled the captain, "a snippersnapper from Ireland, which has fostered so many drunkards and fools. Did the boy know that the most common cause of death in Dublin is an unintended shot to the mouth? These accidents happen whenever the Irish clean their teeth with their guns!"

Tom swallowed hard and watched Bull's gigantic head coming closer.

"I can see resistance in his sea-green eyes. The Devil take your grandmother's amulet. May the old hag rot in Hell."

"That happened long ago, Captain," said Tom, giving Bull a look of feigned bravery.

"What was it the monster said about his drunken grandmother?"

"That the woman was already cooking in the Devil's frying pan."

"The old shrew must have had just as brazen a mouth as her grandson."

"Even more brazen," said Tom, "for she was none other than Gráinne Ni Mháille."

With that, Bull had a tremendous coughing fit, followed by a terrible wheezing, which seemed to make his already testy mood even worse. So when the colonel, in a fit of commiseration, patted the captain on the back, Bull tore his pistols out of his belt and shot two holes in the stout man, who fell to the floor with a look of apology on his face. Bull paid him no mind but took a swig from the wine bottle, wiped his mouth, and admitted that he had a hell of a toothache. Then he caught sight of Tom again and swiftly pulled him close.

Tom had a good view of the rotten state of the tooth. Especially because Bull was breathing long and hard, right in his face.

"Ugly, isn't it?" Bull growled.

"Maybe it ought to be pulled," gasped Tom.

Bull let him go. "Gráinne Ni Mháille," he bellowed, "was the world's worst pirate, the most loathsome and the most cynical female privateer ever to sail the ocean. And now here I am, looking at her grandson, a little red-haired shit who has the extraordinary gall to speak disparagingly of Mrs. Brown. Who do you think you are, you little whelp?" Bull lifted Tom up by his hair.

"I don't even know the lady," Tom groaned, attempting to reach the floor with his toes.

"That lady," snarled Bull, "happens to be sitting in my upper jaw. And she has tormented and plagued her host for three years and nineteen days, refusing him solid food and the simple joy of torturing Spanish officers.

Mrs. Brown has kept C. W. awake day and night. What do you have to say in your defense, my boy?"

Tom, feeling half-strangled, remarked that he had nothing to do with the bad tooth. He was then tossed to the floor, where he landed at Señor Salazar's feet.

Salazar, in an attempt to ingratiate himself with Bull, gave Tom a kick and said that he was in complete agreement with the captain. He'd never known such impudence, and unfortunately it was true that Tom was a direct descendant of the dissolute Gráinne Ni Mháille.

Bull, who was in the process of gathering up the *Oceania* sea charts, froze and for a moment turned to look at Tom, still lying on the floor. "Señor," he said to Salazar, his voice now deadly sweet, "do you happen to know this boy?"

"Unfortunately all too well." Salazar drew himself up. "And I can only say that he is a wicked person with a long list of sins. It seems perfectly understandable that his paternal grandmother was the objectionable Gráinne Ni Mháille. May I say that I am at your disposal when it comes to finding the jewels and precious gems that the passengers and crew have undoubtedly stowed away."

"You are a most kind man, Mr. Salazar," snarled Bull. "I would almost call you a gentleman."

"Thank you, Mr. Bull." Salazar bowed his head.

Bull lit a new cigar and began puffing on it as he rolled his eyes, coughed and hawked, spat and cursed, then fixed Tom with a sallow gaze. "What do you have to say about this nice man, you who claim to be the grandson of the Devil's dam?"

"Señor Salazar," said Tom, "is certainly a fine man. He was formerly known as Father Innocent, but that was back when he was working for the Inquisition."

Bull spun on his heel. A big smile spread across his dark visage. "The Inquisition?" The captain walked over to Salazar, who closed his eyes and smiled modestly. "My compliments, señor," continued Bull. "All my days I've admired the Inquisition for its methods, which in thoroughness and refinement far exceed the capabilities of a privateer."

"The captain is much too modest," said Salazar, with a smirk.

Bull interrupted him by seizing hold of his collar, only to let go at once.

"Modesty, señor, is a virtue unknown to me. But people like us, who have devoted our lives to the world's creators—the dear Lord and his faithful henchman, the coal-black Satan—must have something in common, if only the joy in serving our masters. It's not every day that a person has the opportunity to appease the Church and simultaneously tickle the Devil under the chin. Would you do me and my ship the honor of dining with us this evening?"

Salazar stared at Bull, dumbfounded. "It would be an exquisite pleasure, Captain, sir."

"And so eloquent," said Bull as he lunged for Tom and flung him into the arms of Mr. Moon. "But this lad here," the captain spat with disgust, "will get no dinner. On the other hand, he will suffer the indignity of waiting on me and the pious father."

"And what about his friend?" asked Moon. "The red-haired boy had a slave with him."

"Give them our lackey uniforms to wear, the red ones with the gold buttons. Make them polish our silver service, and then bring the best wine in the house for our guest. We'll dine in my cabin." Bull turned to Salazar. "With your permission, I will withdraw to dress for dinner. I never eat wearing my work clothes. My men will look after you, pious father. *Bon appétit.*"

With these words Bull and his crew departed from the *Oceania*. By that time the rowboats were drifting around on the waves, filled to the bursting point with terrified people.

After the pirates had left, Tom picked up his amulet. Then he and Boto, the second officer, the cook, and three passengers set about sealing up the hole in the starboard side. An hour later all hands were ordered to the pumps to make the *Oceania* seaworthy again. And as the day waned, the vessel had righted itself and the rowboats had returned, anticipating that Bull would allow the *Oceania* to sail on its way, now that she had been stripped of all valuables.

And that was what happened. Shortly before the *Oceania* set her sails for the swiftest possible escape, Tom and Nyo Boto, Señor Salazar and his scribe, along with Feodora left the old tub and boarded the pirate ship, where they were received by three crew members. Immediately afterward the anchor was hauled up and the sails set. The man named Moon gave the orders, which were followed to the letter, and soon the *Oceania* was no more than a speck on the sea.

Feodora went over to Tom, who was standing at the port railing. "Out of the frying pan and into the fire," he said.

"But at least your death sentence has been postponed," she said. "So let's enjoy every minute."

Candles have been lit on Bull's ship. Six candleholders, each with seven candles, are burning on deck, forming a kind of passageway down to the captain's cabin. Tom and Boto have been commandeered by Bull's cook, a fat little man with breeches and a bare midriff. He's the one who shows them their servant clothes and explains their duties. He's a pleasant, jovial man who hums as he works. The galley smells wonderful, and Tom casts an envious eye at the big pot that the cook is sprinkling with thyme.

"*Voilà*," the cook says with a wave of his hand, "dinner is ready. And if you don't make fools of yourselves or otherwise annoy the captain, there may be hope for you yet."

"We'll do our best, Señor Cook," says Tom. "We've served as tasters on a sugar plantation, so we know all about how to behave at a dinner table."

"You can take the pot off the stove," mutters the cook.

Tom gives Boto a jab with his elbow as the two of them drag the pot off the fire. "It's true what they say," he whispers. "They really do have only nine fingers."

When Tom and Boto stepped inside the captain's cabin, Señor Salazar was already seated at the end of the table, about to tuck his napkin under his chin. The cabin afforded a spectacular view of the sunset. The whole western horizon was on fire, casting a magnificent glow across the bountiful table. Heaps of fresh fruit stood next to blue- and jade-colored wine carafes, and the newly polished silverware gleamed on the lace-trimmed damask tablecloth.

Bull had not yet appeared, so Tom had plenty of time to study the captain's private quarters, which consisted of two tastefully furnished rooms. In one of them was his bunk, hanging next to a table with a washbasin and pitcher. On a shelf lay a brush, a comb, a mirror, and a pen and ink along with the ship's log. The captain's desk was in almost perfect order. The telescopes were arranged according to size, as was the collection of diverse pistols, knives, daggers, and cutlasses. Everything sparkled, as if they were polished every two hours.

On the floor by the wall stood various paintings with subjects from distant parts of the world: women dancing, shepherds with their sheep, and angels with harps. The furniture was a mixture of styles but exquisite, and the tapestries glittered as if they had been sewn with threads of gold. Tom hadn't seen such beautiful furnishings since he had visited Mrs. Briggs. Feeling at ease, he lit the candles while Nyo Boto, with the air of an expert, straightened the heavy drapes.

They had laughed upon seeing each other clad in the red uniforms—until Tom happened to think about Feodora, who had been locked up in a cabin all alone.

"We'll take off as soon as there's an opportunity," Boto had said.

"Not without Feo. But otherwise you're right, and better today than tomorrow."

At last Bull appeared. He was wearing a deep-red jacket with black lapels, a chalk-white shirt with frills, and a pair of tight black breeches that were tied with silk ribbons just below the knee. His stockings were ivory-colored and just as new as his shiny shoes. His hair had been pulled back and gathered up in a silver clasp shaped like a skull. His beard was still damp from being washed.

The captain took his place in the big chair with the carved arms. He offered his guest some grapes which, as he said, were excellent for the digestion. The two men drank a toast, and Salazar praised the captain for his choice of wine.

"From Andalusia," said Bull. "I thought it might appeal to a Spanish palate. But let's eat, señor. I know that the cook has done his utmost." The captain clapped his hands. "Waiters!"

Tom carried the platter of lentils, meat, and olives over to Salazar, who did not hold back but filled his plate, once again thanking Bull for the invitation.

The captain showed more restraint, excusing himself by saying that his bad tooth was in a foul mood. "So tell me about the Inquisition." Bull rubbed his hands together. "You must have thousands of amusing stories up your sleeve."

Salazar washed down his food with some wine. "Satan never sleeps, as the saying goes."

"But the custom of burning people at the stake, surely you've given that up, haven't you?" Bull winked at the former inquisitor.

"Evil must be driven out with evil," replied Señor Salazar, helping himself to another piece of meat. "Are you a man of faith, Mr. Bull?"

Tom cast a sidelong glance at Bull, who was studying his glass with a sly expression. "Señor," he whispered as he leaned across the table, "you are looking at a man who has sold his soul to the Master who never sleeps."

Salazar stopped eating for a moment. "Surely you must be jesting, Captain, sir?"

Bull shook his head. "But I was well paid," he added.

Bull started plucking purple grapes from a big bunch on the table. There was a pause in the conversation, during which the insatiable Spaniard could be heard mumbling apologetic words about the inadequate meals he had been served on the *Oceania*. "A man prefers to eat meat," he said, reaching for the platter. "But tell me, Captain Bull, how does one go about selling his soul to the Master who never sleeps? It interests me, as a purely theoretical problem, of course."

Bull looked away, as if distracted, but then gave Salazar a demonic smile. "The same way that a priest consecrates his life to *his* Master," he replied.

"Does that mean," said Señor Salazar, "that the captain never listens to God?"

"Which god?" growled Bull.

"The one and only," replied Salazar, bowing his head.

"You mean the one who burns people alive?"

Salazar cleared his throat and held out his glass toward Tom, who with trembling hands filled it from the big carafe. Bull put his hand to his cheek and cursed Mrs. Brown.

"A toothache," said Salazar, "can be a torment."

"The pain keeps me awake," Bull said. "And in my profession a person always has to be alert."

"That's understandable," said Salazar.

The captain looked at Tom. "So he's the grandson of Gráinne."

"Yes, señor," said Tom.

"My name is Mr. Bull," the captain corrected him. "I'm an Englishman."
Tom bowed and apologized.

"And as an Englishman, I also know what happened to the old witch," Bull went on, studying Tom.

"She must have been hanged, wasn't she?" Salazar was sucking the marrow out of a bone.

Bull got up and stood behind Tom. "After pillaging and plundering the west coast of Ireland for twenty long years, she was granted amnesty and a pension by Queen Elizabeth in 1593. Women are extraordinary, aren't they, Mr. Inquisitor?"

Salazar wiped his glistening lips. "The English queen must have had her reasons."

"Perhaps," said Bull. "Who knows? Perhaps C. W. Bull will also receive a pension someday. What does the Irish lad think?" Bull twisted Tom's ear halfway around.

"I wouldn't count on it," groaned Tom.

"Can't you behave yourself?" scolded Salazar, adding that since he was betrothed to Tom's sister he felt like a kind of guardian to the boy, who had neither mother nor father.

Bull stared with glee from Tom to the inquisitor. "That's a big responsibility you've taken on, señor. Lads of his age"—Tom's ear was given another twist—"can be odious. But I assume that after all your years in the service of the Inquisition, you've gained a certain amount of practice when it comes to discipline."

Salazar hauled the last piece of meat off the platter. "If the donkey refuses to listen, it has to feel the whip, as the saying goes."

Bull switched to Tom's other ear. "I could imagine that in this case a flogging would not be sufficient. Tell me, you red-haired beast, how could a boy your age afford to buy a slave?"

"Oh, but it's not true at all that he bought the black." Salazar laughed loudly. "He pulled that slave out of the sea, like a half-dead herring. In fact, that's a story you might enjoy hearing, Captain. This red-haired fool actually traveled the world over looking for that little black cork, and spent two years of his life on the search, only to find the savage at the bottom of a Spanish galleon." Salazar laughed so hard that he got a piece of meat stuck in his throat.

Bull shot him a piercing look, but then joined in with the noisy outburst and ended up gnashing his teeth. "How ironic." He punched Tom on the cheek. "But tell me, how did you get him out of the Spaniards' custody, you watery-eyed monster?"

Tom cleared his throat. "I made them think that he had the plague, Captain, sir. Upon hearing that, they supplied us with an eight-man skiff and enough food and drink for several weeks."

"What a liar he is," said Bull, yanking on both Tom's ears. "But why go to all that trouble over a slave?"

"First of all," replied Tom, "Nyo Boto is not a slave anymore."

"He's not?"

"No, I gave him his freedom."

"Has the captain ever heard the likes of it?" Salazar laughed. "First he spends two years searching and finally finds his modest fortune, only to throw the whole thing overboard."

"Nyo Boto," said Tom, "comes from the Bissagos Islands. Maybe the captain has heard of those parts?"

Bull did not reply but went to get a bottle of rum. He pulled out the cork with his teeth and took a drink. "Go on," he said.

"At those islands," said Tom, looking at Boto, "my friend was seized as an ordinary slave by the Portuguese. What they didn't know was that he is the son of a king. When I heard about his origins, I was obsessed with the thought of taking him back, in the hopes of being rewarded by his father." Tom looked around uncertainly. "But my greed for gold," he added, "is no longer as great."

Salazar laughed and suppressed a belch. "And now the Devil has joined a monastery, if the captain will pardon the expression."

Bull had walked around the big table so that he now stood between Salazar and Tom. "Tell me," he said, "you who are the grandson of Gráinne, tell me about the greed for gold."

"It sits in a man's ring finger," whispered Tom, "in the middle joint."

After that remark something happened to the captain, who with a distracted expression went over to the big window and gazed out at the moonlight, which lay like a yellow cone on the calm sea. For a long time the only sound was the endless smacking of Salazar's lips and the surreptitious rumblings coming from his stomach.

"Tomorrow," said Bull, who was still standing with his back to the others, "this boy will be keelhauled. That's the only thing his kind has any respect for."

Señor Salazar shut his eyes halfway and smiled gratefully at the captain.

Bull turned around. "When a man, such as myself, has sold his soul to the Devil, he knows when he encounters a like-minded person."

"My soul wasn't sold," Tom objected. "It has never been for sale."

"Can you hear a flea bark?" exclaimed Salazar, making an effort to get to his feet.

"His kind are usually more compliant after a keelhauling," said Bull. "But now it's time for me to retire. It has been a long day, and I haven't had time to write in my logbook. *Buenas noches, señor.*"

"*Buenas noches,* Captain, sir." Salazar bowed. "I will withdraw now and join my scribe."

Bull, who was already standing in the doorway to his bedchamber, stopped and turned around. "Your scribe, señor? You won't be seeing him again."

"But he came on board with me." Salazar looked around uncertainly. "Where is he?"

C. W. Bull went over to the former inquisitor and gave him a bright look. "Señor," he said, "you have just eaten him!"

23   Indigo Moon

CAPTAIN BULL KEPT HIS WORD. Shortly after dawn Tom was rousted out of bed. He had spent the night on the middle deck, wrapped in an old Portuguese flag. The air was mild, with a light breeze from the east, which made the ship rock from side to side like a giant cradle. Before Tom and Boto had fallen asleep, Tom had praised their good luck.

"You think we're lucky, Tom?" Boto had sniffed at the flag fabric.

"In spite of everything, we have a warm and comfortable place to sleep and we're not lacking for anything. Yes, I think we're a couple of lucky rascals."

Boto replied that, based on his experience with both good and bad luck, it was difficult if not impossible for him to see how they were lucky.

Tom moved closer. "It seems to me that you've gotten used to your new status of freedom awfully quickly."

Boto said that all his days he had been good at adapting.

"But surely the fact that you're free doesn't mean you should always contradict me." Tom turned onto his side. "I'm the one who's going to be keelhauled, after all, not you. And if the person who's going to be keelhauled feels lucky and happy and lighthearted, then his good friend shouldn't argue. You have a lot to learn about friendship, Bibido."

"My name is Boto, Tom."

"I'll call you whatever I like," Tom snapped, "and right now I feel like being happy and optimistic and lighthearted. Take a look around—isn't it pleasant on this mild night?"

"Yes, but Portugal smells moldy."

"You do too. And remember one positive thing: they haven't killed us yet."

"No, that's true, Tom. They haven't killed us yet."

"Are you trying to be funny?"

"No, I'm trying to sleep."

"We also have our freedom." Tom smiled confidently. "In fact, we could jump into the sea whenever we like and swim away."

"Do you think that's a good idea?"

"I said if we feel like it. We're not locked up, are we?"

"We're not?"

"By the Devil, you're pigheaded. Have you completely forgotten that not long ago you were tied to a post among the rats and scorpions and leeches, without food or drink? And that I, Tom O'Connor, even a shorter time ago was less than five paces away from the gallows? And now we're lying here under God's open sky, free as birds, and when dawn comes . . ."

"We'll most likely be eaten," said Boto, adding that he preferred to be served with yams.

Tom sat up. "Boto, the two of us are not going to end up in the cooking pot. Listen here, we've done this before—escaping from a ship. Who says we can't do it again?"

"Should I pretend to have the plague?"

"No, you shouldn't pretend to have the plague. We have to . . . think about things and not have such a gloomy outlook. We're in a good situation."

"Well, maybe you're right," murmured Boto. "But I keep on thinking about that little scribe. The one that Salazar ate. He smelled so good sprinkled with thyme."

Tom stared at Boto's back.

"Maybe he tasted good too," Boto added. "I once ate a pangolin that we cooked with yams."

"Thanks a lot, Boto," grumbled Tom.

"Should I tell you about the boiled yams called fu-fu?"

Six hours later the big Mongol was leaning over them, holding the Portuguese flag. He waved his hand at them. Tom told Boto that this must mean they were supposed to get up.

"Do you speak English?" asked Tom.

No reaction.

"*Español?*"

Still no reaction.

"Maybe you can't talk at all?"

The Mongol grabbed hold of Tom's hair and sniffed it. His fat belly wiggled all over. At that moment Mr. Moon appeared, and he was not amused. He ordered Tom and Boto to the upper deck, where most of the crew had gathered, along with Feo, who was sitting on a chair. It was an unusually quiet day. Feodora didn't have to raise her voice when she asked what was about to happen.

"I have the feeling that I'm going to be punished." Tom looked around for Señor Salazar, who had not yet made an appearance.

But then Bull arrived and, judging by his expression, he hadn't slept very well. This was evident in the demeanor of his men, who were clearly familiar with his moods. Even the toughest-looking characters lowered their eyes as he passed. The cook, who was apparently the captain's personal servant, tiptoed behind him with a little brush, with which he diligently tried to clean Bull's jacket. Unfortunately it was one of those mornings when the captain did not wish to be brushed. Suddenly it flew over the side.

"That was the last brush," stammered the cook, and then slapped his hand to his mouth.

"Begone!" bellowed the captain. "Or he'll be keeping the brush company."

"But the captain himself said . . ." began the poor cook.

"What did I say?"

The cook glanced around for support from his companions. For some reason they all seemed preoccupied with something very important.

"That if there was so much as a scrap of lint . . ." whispered the cook.

Bull's expression changed, and he fixed his servant with an ominous look.

"A scrap of lint," he repeated. "Oh yes, that's true, we all have a purpose here in life. And besides making porridge that causes either constipation or diarrhea, he discharges the honorable duty of removing lint from his superiors. I had forgotten all about that. But now he's fired as a lint remover." The captain surveyed his men. "Is there anyone who'd like to take over the job?"

The pirates glanced at each other nervously and did their best to ignore

Bull who, with his hands behind his back, made a show of inspecting them. It was now evident why all their weapons, pants, jackets, and shoes were in such remarkably good order. And when Bull managed to find a shirt with a tiny green patch of mildew, he pulled the sinner out on deck and cut the shirt open from the man's collar to his waistband.

"Do I really have to repeat the ship's regulations every single morning?" shouted the captain as he sliced off the man's belt. "Does my good mood always have to be spoiled by this general lack of cleanliness? A dead rat knows more about the importance of cleanliness than this scum who, to top it all off, has the temerity to show up bare-assed in front of his captain."

"But you cut off my belt yourself, Captain, sir," muttered the man.

Bull stared at him in disbelief. "Is he claiming that C. W. Bull is responsible for his filthy body and his infested shirt?"

The pirate shook his head.

Bull went over to his first officer. The captain had been in an uncommonly bad mood, but now he turned downright malicious.

"Tell the men, Mr. Moon, who on board this ship is the only one privileged to be rotten through and through!"

The otherwise fearsome Indigo Moon replied in a shrill voice, "Mrs. Brown, Captain, sir. Mrs. Brown is the only one with that privilege."

Bull looked around and went back to the man who was still standing without pants or shirt. "Did he hear what the second-in-command said?"

The pirate nodded.

Bull put his hand to his cheek. "He can thank his Lord that right now the lady is taking a nap."

The captain went over to Tom. "It's not for the sake of entertainment that we sail under the black flag. That's why a man has to jump at any opportunity that comes along. So now we're going to have the pleasure of finding out what a green-eyed monster has learned from the Devil's dam. I have to assume that he has inherited at least something from Gráinne, who was surpassed in ugliness only by Lucifer himself." Bull twisted Tom's ear. "Since we're speaking of rottenness, let me tell you that she had no equal— except maybe that noblewoman who plagues my jaw so the carefree soul I was born with is singing its final verse." Bull bent down and looked Tom in the eye. "I see a defiant look on his face. Did he ever meet his detestable grandmother?"

Tom cleared his throat. "Only in my dreams, Captain, sir."

"In his dreams, he says. So tell this inquisitive crew how Gráinne looks in your dreams."

"Like a rotten tooth, Captain, sir."

For a moment it seemed as if Bull was going to explode. Then he let go of Tom's ear and lowered his voice to a hoarse whisper. He uttered only one word: "Keelhauling!"

Tom looked at Boto, who was perched on the starboard rail, inspecting his beloved buttons. He had no idea what a keelhauling was. Tom, on the other hand, knew very well. He stared at the two men who stepped forward, dragging a couple of long ropes. The thinner rope was used to bind Tom's arms and legs.

He stood like a mummy, unable to move.

"How long?" asked one of the men.

And Mr. Moon replied, "I'll tell you when it's enough."

He nodded to the semi-naked man who held the thick rope in his hands. From the port rail he yelled a woman's name, which was repeated by the rest of the crew, and then the man was in the water.

Feodora stood up and went over to Bull. "Is it permitted to ask what good all of this will do?"

Bull simply turned his back on her.

Feo walked over to Moon, but before she could open her mouth, he began shouting to the assembled men that the red-haired Irish boy had escaped the gallows, which was the punishment he had earned on land. Now he was faced with a keelhauling, which was the punishment he had earned at sea.

"What does this mean?" Feodora's voice was now less certain.

Moon smiled at his men. "It means that we will now give young O'Connor a rare but thorough insight into what it looks like beneath the keel of this proud vessel. And as tradition requires, every man will have a try at the rope, so it could take quite a while."

Feo nodded. "You want him to drown, is that it?"

"You never know what you're going to drag up after a keelhauling." Moon smiled and went over to the railing.

Another long minute passed before the man in the water resurfaced with the rope. Moon gave orders to haul the pirate on board. In the meantime

Feo looked at Tom. Neither of them said anything, mostly because there was nothing to say.

Tom was now dragged over to the starboard rail. The thick rope was bound around his ankles and under his armpits. On the opposite side of the ship stood Moon and two other men, one of them the Mongol, holding the line that would pull Tom around the keel. Indigo Moon raised his hand. "According to our laws," he shouted, "an offering must be made to the great God of the Sea before a keelhauling."

The pirates grinned and began shoving each other. Now the cook appeared with a big bloody pig's head. There was the sound of scattered applause. Moon pulled out his dagger and stuck a number of holes in the head before the cook was allowed to throw it overboard.

Tom cast a glance at Boto, who was looking straight back at him. Boto put his right hand to his chest and nodded somberly.

"Of course it can't be ruled out that the offering may end up in the wrong mouth," shouted Moon. "Sharks recognize no laws but their own."

The remark prompted a good deal of laughter and merry cheers that were cut short when Bull suddenly stirred.

"Give your family my greetings," the captain growled at Tom. "Say hello to Gráinne and tell her that you came from my ship."

"We'll meet again," whispered Tom, "if not before, then in Hell."

"What a devil of a mouth he has," grumbled the captain. "Throw him in."

There was a roar from the crew as Tom hit the water. Then everything fell silent.

It's dark underwater, but he very quickly gets himself oriented. He can feel the tug on his ankles and desperately wriggles his arms and legs. He realizes that he can't pull free. His body bangs against the belly of the ship. He is dangling like a weightless cocoon when there is another yank on the line. Tom stares at the keel, which is slowly approaching. Even though the situation is anything but pleasant, he can't help admiring the belly of the big ship, which floats, silent and secretive, covered with barnacles and seaweed that sways in the current.

Tom turns halfway around and is gashed by the shells embedded in the ship's hull. Tiny red clouds of blood rise up and drift away like spiny creatures. If there are sharks in the water, they will be summoned by this haze of blood.

For a long moment he lies still. Then he feels the first pressure in his lungs. They're taking their own sweet time up above; maybe it's their intention for him to die down here. All his life he has prepared himself for death by drowning. He has always known that shortly before a person drowns, in the seconds before the ocean takes over his body, he sees everything that is hidden from the living. This comforts him now, though not much. He stares at a serpentlike creature, a slender sea snake two feet long, heading right for him. The snake is yellow with a wavy pattern on its back. It has no eyes but is navigating by instinct. Tom feels the snake's mouth against his ear. It has two fork-shaped feelers on its head. They inspect his middle ear before the snake moves farther in. Tom tries to rotate on his own axis and feels the animal slipping inside his head. In a moment, he thinks, it will be behind my eyes, but for lack of anything better, it will turn back to my ear, where it will find a rare warmth. Enough for it to feel like spawning.

There is a yank on the rope, and now he's moving swiftly downward. He slams against the keel and for a moment forgets about his new lodger. He spins around, releases a bubble, and then presses his lips tightly. He's stuck.

They pull from above, but it only makes matters worse.

Tom twists and turns. He thinks about oxygen, about opening his mouth. His lungs are aching. He knows that now will come the pressure in his ears, the blood in his nose, and the pain in his temples. A black-and-white explosion splinters his vision. Pieces of debris, both big and small, swirl like feathers around his head. Nevis has broken apart, with its volcano, rain forest, monkeys, and inn. In a triangular scrap of the familiar world, Joop van den Arle drifts past along with Frans Brüggen and Señor López. Other figures attempt to materialize, and just as the image of Ramón the Pious takes shape, there is a yank on the rope.

He opens his eyes and meets the ocean's bubbles, releasing the last bit of air from his tormented body—hardly aware of the tugging on his feet as he is pulled around the keel.

He opens his mouth wide and utters his mother's name; he is just about to say Nyo Boto when the sky opens up. His lungs explode and his back rams the side of the ship. His ankles hurt. Water is gushing from his eyes, ears, nose, and mouth.

Now comes the sound of people yelling at each other. Feodora's voice. He catches a glimpse of Boto, and hears Moon shouting to his men.

Tom is lying on deck. Through a red fog he sees all the faces. He has the taste of blood in his mouth and a protracted pain that stretches from the back of his neck to his loins.

The rope is untied. The ocean continues to seep out of him. The last thing to slide out of his ear is not water but a long, slippery snake.

He gets to his feet, but his legs buckle under him. He throws up and falls onto his side. He sees Feo's face before him, but she is pulled away by Indigo Moon. Moon's lips are moving, and suddenly the sound comes through. "Looks like somebody has earned himself another turn."

Tom stares at the first officer, who makes way for Bull. His black eyes study Tom. "He must have the lungs of a dolphin," the captain growls.

"I say, let's give him another try, and then we'll see about that," shouts Moon, and the crew chimes in.

Bull's face is now very close to Tom's. "Another try. What do you say to that, O'Connor?"

Tom gasps for breath but doesn't have enough air to speak. Feodora does, however. She looks so small as she stands before Bull, who does his best to ignore her. But Feo wants his attention, and she grabs hold of his jacket. "If you absolutely must kill a defenseless boy and possess neither the guts nor the courage to fight a duel with him, then I think you really should keelhaul him one more time, Captain Bull."

The captain sighs in resignation. "I would hate to be the mother of these children," he groans.

The crew has begun chanting in unison, egged on by Moon, who is leading a rhythmic shout: "Keelhaul, keelhaul, keelhaul."

Suddenly Bull yanks Tom up from the deck and stares at him. Tom is dangling three feet above the planks, trying to say something that is incomprehensible. Bull has to speak loudly to be heard over the shouts of his men. "Are you trying to tell me something, you red-haired monster?"

Tom nods. The captain places his ear against Tom's lips.

"Take my ring finger," whispers Tom. "Take it, Bull. Make me a pirate. But do it now, before they tie me up again."

Bull glances around. "Does he know what he's saying?" The captain looks at Tom's hand.

"Yes. I know what I'm saying. Take my finger. Another trip under the keel will be the death of me."

"And what do I have to lose by his death?"

"Your pride, Captain," whispers Tom.

Bull stands with his legs wide apart, shaking his head. "There's a hell of a lot of Gráinne in the lad." His voice is low and surprised.

Indigo Moon comes over to him and asks what it's going to be. Bull shoves him away. "It's time for Laem Sing!" shouts the captain.

A roar goes up from the crew at once, and it sounds so full of anticipation that Tom has misgivings. But when he sees Moon's look of disapproval, he realizes that his sentence has been mitigated.

Laem Sing turned out to be the name of the big Mongol. Included among his many duties was the ritual performed whenever the ship took on new members. It was always carried out at sundown. Thus Tom gained an entire day in which to consider his situation.

The anchor was hauled up and all the sails were set. As far as Tom could tell, they were headed due west. The division of labor was clear. Mr. Moon was the first officer and second-in-command. Then came the boatswain, cook, second officer, and the sailors who manned the capstan, oars, pumps, and took care of the provisions. The rules were simple; everyone knew what he was supposed to do.

The ship was not large, but swift and compliant. The sailors who tended the sails worked under Moon's command. It was a pleasure to watch them turn the ship and make the best use of the wind, no matter what direction it came from. Nothing happened by chance; everything was planned down to the smallest detail. The galley was the cleanest Tom had ever seen. And if there were rats on board, they were well-hidden.

Feodora had been given her own little cabin. Tom had told her what had happened to the scribe, so that when Salazar finally appeared, she understood why he looked a bit green. He was shaking all over, and he told his betrothed that he had sacrificed to the sea all night long, but that he hoped this would be the last joke Bull would try to pull on them.

"There's one more left," murmured Boto. "It's called Laem Sing."

Salazar gave him a fierce look. "Laem Sing? Is that some kind of vicious entertainment?"

Tom shook his head. "That depends on how you look at it. In the captain's cabin there's a small cupboard with a lock and key. Behind the door are thirty-nine hooks, one for each pirate. And from every hook hangs a finger, each one bluer than the last."

"What kind of madness is this?" gasped Salazar, looking from Tom to Feo.

"Madness," muttered Tom, "yes, maybe so. But before the day is over I will be freed of an old vice, for they say that in the middle joint of a sailor's ring finger sits his greed for gold. If it's removed, the captain will have peace on his vessel."

"What a loathsome superstition."

Tom shrugged his shoulders. "We'll soon see, my lord inquisitor."

Three hours later a galleon came into view. Bull appeared on the quarterdeck and studied the unknown ship in his spyglass.

"A Spaniard," growled Moon. "Two cannons astern and six on each side. Slave ship from Africa."

"Let her pass," grumbled Bull. "Too many cannons."

"The men will be disappointed," Moon observed.

"Perhaps he didn't hear what I said."

"We could take a vote." Moon smiled.

Bull looked at him. "I think," he said in a low voice, "that it's time for me to take leave of Mrs. Brown. And we'll let the Spaniard pass."

"The captain will regret this," snarled Moon.

Bull stared at him, and from the looks the captain exchanged with his first officer, it was clear that their relationship was balanced on the edge of a knife.

"If you're having a hard time hearing, Mr. Moon," said Bull, "there's help to be had. As the first officer knows, besides being the captain I'm also the ship's surgeon, whose duty it is to treat acute and chronic problems alike. And when it comes to the sense of hearing, Doctor Bull is a real expert. One more word out of you, Moon, and I guarantee you I'll employ my skills without hesitation."

At that moment Tom and Boto were in the galley. They had fallen into conversation with the cook, who suffered from homesickness. Tom told him that it could be cured with cinnamon bark and a touch of nutmeg. Unfortunately, they didn't have either. Instead, Tom sat down on a water barrel and recounted the first chapter about Ramón the Pious, who was the world's biggest liar and born in Cádiz. The cook poured them some beer and breathlessly followed the story, and before Tom was done with the first chapter, eight men were sitting around the cook's table, listening to the tale of the untrustworthy boatswain and his remarkable fate.

Later, when Tom was alone with the cook, he learned about the feud between Mr. Moon and Captain Bull—a two-man war that threatened to split the vessel apart. "Every night," said the cook, "we expect one of them to die in his bunk, and the way things stand, it could be either one of them. Half of the crew belongs to Bull, but just as many favor Moon. The problem is that Mrs. Brown has ended up making more decisions than the captain, who lies in his cabin all day long, groaning in agony. His mood shifts like the breeze—first he's munificent, then he's in a vile temper—but each time she's the one who decides. And that can only lead to trouble."

"Whose side are you on, cook?" asked Tom.

"I usually vote for the captain," sighed the cook, "but Moon has threatened me twice, so I don't know. I think he's going to take over the ship before long. Heaven have mercy on us."

The acrid smell of tar hovers over the upper deck. A table and chair have been placed in front of the stairs up to the bridge. The ship has dropped anchor and is rocking in the flaming sea of sunset. Tom is standing with Nyo Boto and Feo. Indigo Moon gazes at Tom with an expression both cautionary and searching.

Now the captain appears. He is dressed in his finest. In one hand he holds a piece of paper with a seal. He asks for silence and then gives the paper to Moon, the only one among Bull's crew who can read.

The rules of initiation are simple. The man swears eternal loyalty to the brotherhood and takes a solemn oath. Then he places his right hand on the table and splays his fingers.

Tom steps forward. He casts an uneasy glance at the knife and wooden club that are ready for use. Moon takes Tom's hand and nods to the Mongol, who places the knife blade against the base of Tom's ring finger.

"Do you swear eternal loyalty to the ship's crew and captain?" intones the first officer.

"Yes, I swear eternal loyalty." Tom bows his head.

The gentle ripple of the waves is heard. Mr. Moon nods to the Mongol, who raises the club above his head and slams it down on the blade, which chops off the finger with one blow. Tom stares at his severed finger. He feels no pain, feels nothing at all.

The crew starts murmuring, and a few applaud. In the meantime Laem Sing dips his brush in the pot of hot tar. Moon puts a spoon between Tom's teeth. "Now the fun starts," he says.

Tom stares at the Mongol, who is holding the tar brush. Then he looks at the open wound that has begun to bleed. Laem Sing mutters something and presses the tar against the wound.

White lightning slices through Tom's brain. The pain from his finger settles in his knees, and for a moment he almost faints. Then he opens his eyes wide and swings his left hand. His fist strikes the Mongol on the jaw.

For a second the giant doesn't seem to notice the blow. Then he sails backward six feet, but Tom flies right after him. Blind with pain, he picks up the club and raises it to strike, though he never makes it that far. He is overpowered by Moon and two of his men, who throw Tom to the deck and hold him there so the cook can pour a little rum down his throat.

Tom stares up at the sky, which has turned lime-green with orange-colored clouds. A hideous face is staring down at him. All colors vanish and only the milky-white iris remains. "Zamora," he whispers, "leave me alone. Let me go." He blinks and notices that he's freezing and sweating at the same time. Zamora's eyes turn black, and she now has a beard all over her face.

Bull is leaning over Tom. "Welcome aboard," he growls.

Many hours later he is lying under the Portuguese flag, listening to the rigging and the distant sounds of chattering birds. Feodora is sitting with his head in her lap; his face is ashen.

"What are you thinking about?" she asks.

Tom lies still for a moment without answering. Then he says, "I'm thinking about a plan that I have. It came to me underwater when I saw the blue mussels clinging to the hull and traveling all around the world absolutely free. Even a mussel has a plan for its life."

Feo shakes her head and smiles. "And what are you dreaming about, Nyo Boto?"

"I'm dreaming about a freshly slaughtered pangolin and boiled yams," says Boto. "The tailor who lives in our village is a very good cook. I want to be a tailor when I have my own house."

Tom looks up at Feo. They smile at each other.

"What do you want to be, Feo, when you have your own house?" asks Boto as he takes off his shirt and folds it up, as if it were new and very expensive.

She gives him a dreamy look. "When I have my own house, I want to be a shepherd," she says. "But right now I'm as tired as anyone could possibly be."

"Me too," sighs Boto, gazing at his keelhauled friend, who is getting some color back in his cheeks.

Tom stares up at the sky. "Now I'm a pirate," he whispers, "just as it was foretold."

24 ⊙ Orion's Belt

HE IS STANDING IN THE CAPTAIN'S CABIN. The ship is quiet. For six days they have been waiting for wind and, as always, the waiting time has taken its toll on the men, but on this ship it has led to war. There is a shortage of water and food, but it's the shortage of plunder during the past few weeks that has had the worst effect on the crew. They haven't yet taken up arms, but it won't be long now.

They're situated south of the Tropic of Cancer, at twenty degrees latitude and fifty degrees longitude—in other words, in the middle of the Atlantic with oceans of water on all sides. While they wait, there isn't much to keep the men busy, aside from tending to their weapons. They sharpen their knives, making sparks fly, and every cutlass gleams as bright as a mirror. Pistols are cleaned and the powder kept dry.

Moon's men have withdrawn to the hold, where they're huddled around the first officer. What they're talking about is anybody's guess, but judging by the looks they give Captain Bull's men, there can be no doubt about their intentions. As the cook has told Tom: "Storms and mutiny don't go together. It's when the wind dies down that sailors whet their knives."

Tom has used the time to teach Bull the alphabet. He had been on board now for three weeks and thought the captain was making progress. Tom knew that the ability to read was part of the reason for the war between Bull and Moon. The captain couldn't stand the thought that Moon was able to do something that he couldn't.

At first Bull claimed that of course he could read—he had simply forgotten a couple of the letters.

"Are you thinking of the ones from *A* to *Z*?" asked his teacher.

"There's no damn reason to get so cocky," shouted his difficult pupil. "There are limits to what I'll put up with."

"Well, what does it say here, Captain, sir?"

Tom pointed to a sentence he had written himself, which said: *I am picking a pomegranate.*

Bull hemmed and hawed, growled and gnashed his teeth, but got no farther than *I.*

Tom concluded that Bull still had a long way to go, but that in spite of his squabbling, the captain was an energetic and promising pupil. As he said to Tom, "I want to be better than Moon, who's always showing off with his letters. And he wrote things in my logbook that only he can understand."

Tom agreed that it certainly was important to be able to read.

"The pen," groaned Bull, "is the weapon of the future."

As for Salazar, he had recovered enough that he had chosen sides in the feud. He now belonged to Mr. Moon's men and walked around carrying a knife. He refused to speak to Tom, who spent so much of his time in Bull's cabin that he was regarded as one of the captain's supporters. The same was true of Feodora Dolores Vasgues, who managed to keep her head above water even when the men tried to get their hands on her. Feo's ability to elude any problem did have its limits, however. One evening when Indigo Moon made a clumsy attempt to embrace her in the moonlight, he felt a dagger under his left armpit.

"Did you know, Mr. Moon," said Feo, "that human beings have a vein in their armpits that is so big that a single cut can completely drain away a man's blood? There is no doctor, no medicine, and no bandage that can stanch an open wound in the armpit."

Moon had retreated, but not without warning Feo that her time would come. "When the captain by the name of Mrs. Brown no longer plagues this ship, everything will be quite different, and then the girl's days will be numbered. You can consider that a promise, señorita."

That same night Feo said to Tom, "It's only a matter of hours before all Hell breaks loose. Maybe it would be best if Bull surrendered without a fight."

"That will never happen," Tom replied.

"No. They'll fight to the last man. What are you going to do about it?"

"I told you, I've got a plan," said Tom, "but I need a little more time."

"For what?"

"Trust takes time."

The next day brought no change in the wind situation. On the other hand, the first officer made his move: he took control of the ship's last barrel of water. If Bull wanted any water, he would have to go down and get it for himself. But he would never come out of the dark hold alive.

Tom now knew that he must act. His plan would have to be put into effect at once, or else mutiny would destroy everything.

Bull was the only person who refused to acknowledge the threat posed by Moon. His joy at being able to read had apparently clouded his good sense. With a triumphant look in his eyes he shouted, "I . . . am picking . . . a . . . pomegranate."

"Very good, Captain," said Tom. "Very good."

"That's right." Bull put his hands on his hips. "I can read. And better than anyone else on this ship. There's not a man south of the Tropic of Cancer who reads better than I do. But now I'm going to lie down because my tooth is in a foul mood."

"Can you also read this ship?" asked Tom.

"I can spell ship! *S-H-I-B!*"

Feo went over to the captain. "Ship is spelled with a *p*. Can you also spell *sundown*? Because everyone knows that before sundown this ship will have a new captain."

"What the devil is she talking about?" Bull pulled out his pistols but then put one hand to his cheek. With a stifled growl he backed over to the stairs and disappeared.

Tom took that as a clear omen. "Are you ready, Boto?"

Nyo Boto, who was mending the Portuguese flag, put down his needle and thread. "Yes, I'm ready."

Tom opened the door to the captain's cabin. "Good afternoon, Captain, sir." True to form whenever his tooth was bothering him, the captain was soothing the pain with a tankard of rum.

"The lessons are canceled," growled Bull. "Can't you see that I have a meeting with Mrs. Brown?"

Tom nodded to Boto, who shut the door.

"Captain, sir," Tom said, "I once worked for a blacksmith."

"Doesn't interest me. Hand me the white rum. It's more effective than the brown."

"And at the smithy," continued Tom, "I learned all sorts of different things."

"Is the boy going to leave or should I use him for target practice?"

Tom pulled a pair of pincers out of his pocket. At the sight of them, Bull's eyes froze.

"That's why, Captain, sir . . ."

"Is he deaf in both ears? I said begone!"

"It will only take a minute."

"Maybe I should call for Laem Sing so he can rip the arms off both of you."

Tom put the pincers on the desk and moved the bottle of rum out of Bull's reach. "First Officer Moon," said Tom, "is sitting down in the hold, as everyone knows. But before we get any wind, yes, even before the cook serves the last ration of lentils, this ship will be sailing under a different flag. And the captain's name will be Moon. Why? Because the former captain spends all his time holding meetings with Mrs. Brown. That's why that rotten tooth has to come out, and it has to be now!"

Bull didn't reply but fixed his gaze on Tom. Then his expression changed and he grinned slyly.

"Does he really think I haven't made plans? Does he think that Bull is so stupid that he hasn't taken any precautions? The barrel that Mr. Moon is sitting there nursing contains nothing but seawater. The cook and Laem Sing emptied it last night. The drinking water is stored in the galley. But Mr. Moon doesn't know that. And in front of the stairs leading to the hold is Mrs. Brown's mother-in-law, which is the biggest cannon I have, and she has a thirteen-pound cannonball in her throat. So when Moon and his men discover that they're pouring the Atlantic Ocean into their mouths and come charging up the stairs for freshwater, they'll be staring into the maw of Mrs. Brown's mean-spirited mother-in-law."

"And how do you think the first officer will react to that, Captain, sir?" Tom looked out at the dark-blue sky, where a low-hanging cloud bank in the shape of a coral reef was building on the western horizon.

"He'll piss in his pants," bellowed Bull, "because Moon knows better than anyone that a cannonball of that size could send him all the way to Madeira." The captain rubbed his hands together with a gleeful look.

"He also knows," murmured Tom as he walked over to the window, "that you would never dream of firing a cannon belowdecks."

"I wouldn't?"

Tom shook his head. "Of course you'd have the pleasure of seeing Mr. Moon soar all the way to Madeira, but the hole he flew out of would also be as big as Spain." Tom leaned against the desk. "The ship would sink before you had time to say *pomegranate*. So that wouldn't be a wise captain's plan."

"Whose plan would it be, then?" shouted Bull, fingering his pistols.

"Mrs. Brown's. That rotten old hag has spread from the root of your tooth to your mouth to your skull and from there into your brain. And if you don't get rid of this misery, you'll be playing a card game with the crocodiles before midnight."

Bull's eyes flashed and he growled like a bear. "I can feel the rage coming," he bellowed.

"I can feel the night coming," Tom whispered, "along with Indigo Moon."

The captain's lips quivered urgently, but not a sound emerged. He looked in desperation from side to side and ended up scowling at the pincers. "How did the Irish devil plan to carry it out?"

Tom sat down on the edge of the desk and crossed one leg over the other. "Like we did at the smithy on Jamaica, where we followed a simple but effective procedure. To prevent the patient from injuring himself, we would tie his hands and feet to a chair."

"Not on your life!" roared Bull.

Tom looked up at the ceiling. "I remember an Arab who needed to have a crooked eyetooth pulled from his lower jaw."

"The Devil take Arabia," whimpered Bull.

"Unfortunately, the blacksmith forgot to tie up the patient. So when the tooth came out, the Arab grabbed his scimitar and chopped off the head of his servant and the arm of my master who, with his remaining hand, grabbed his sledgehammer and smashed the brains out of the patient. All that trouble for nothing. Forgetfulness," added Tom as he tied a rope around Bull's wrists, "is in truth a nasty thing.

"Are you comfortable?" asked Tom.

"I'm not comfortable at all, damn it. Untie me. I've changed my mind."

"No, you haven't changed your mind. Now, moving on to the next point. My assistant, Nyo Boto, had the foresight to carve this fine block of wood."

"What does that have to do with me?"

"It's carved to fit in your little mouth, Captain, sir. You see, you put it between your teeth, so there's no risk of you biting your tongue in half—or even worse, biting off my fingers."

"May the Devil strike me with lightning if I'm going to put any wooden block in my mouth."

"But first a drop of rum, Captain." Tom poured rum into a green mug. Bull looked at the bottle with anticipation. "No operation without a drop of rum." Tom emptied the mug.

Bull stared at him in disbelief. "What in hell, you spawn of Lucifer? Are you going to stand there and swill it down without offering me any?"

"It's important for the patient to remain scrupulously sober. Open up!" Tom wriggled the wooden block between Bull's teeth.

Now his jaws were wide open.

"So far, so good, Captain, sir."

A flood of incomprehensible sounds came from Bull, but Tom chose to ignore them. Instead he pulled Bull's pistol out of his belt and stuck the tip of the muzzle into his open mouth.

"Whthdvlryudoon?" roared Bull.

Tom looked at Boto. "Do you understand what the captain is saying?" he asked.

Nyo Boto nodded. "I think he's saying: what the devil are you doing?"

Tom looked at Bull. "Is that what you're saying, Captain?"

Bull nodded vigorously.

"Fine, now listen here. We Irish usually shoot off the rotten tooth. That way we get the whole thing."

The captain vehemently rolled his eyes. He yelled something unintelligible.

"Yes, but before you get too riled," said Tom, "there are a few little things that we have to make clear. As far as I can see, you're sitting here with a pistol between your teeth, your hands and feet are tied, and standing behind you is my friend holding a cutlass, which with one swing could slice your noggin right off."

Bull didn't reply as he stared furiously at Tom, who continued.

"Let's be frank. I'm holding your life in the palm of my hand. I know that you've sold your soul to the Master who never sleeps. Now the question is: what do you have left to trade? Do you have anything at all that might tempt a grandson of Gráinne Ni Mháille? A boy whose left forefinger is trembling with anticipation on the trigger?"

Bull desperately tossed his head.

"I think the captain is trying to say something," said Boto.

Tom nodded. He removed the block from between Bull's teeth and pulled out the pistol. "You wanted to say something, Captain, sir?"

"I'll have the both of you chopped to bits! Piece by piece! And broiled! Broiled and eaten like suckling pigs before the night is over. I will, damn it all, I'll . . . I'll . . ."

"You won't be having dinner at all," said Tom, "because you'll be lying in the belly of a shark."

Bull gnashed his teeth and rolled his eyes.

"But the question is whether we should make a deal," said Tom.

"What is it you want, you green-eyed spawn of a walleyed harpie?"

"The course," said Tom.

"The what?"

"Change the course, Bull. Sail us to the Bissagos Islands."

The captain looked from Tom to Boto and back again. "Has insanity broken out here?"

"Is that how it feels, Captain, sir?"

"Does he realize how far it is to those islands?"

"Not in actual miles, but I believe it takes four weeks in good weather."

Tom cast a confident glance at Boto, who nodded and said, "If we're lucky."

"Does he really think," growled Bull, "that the crew, including Indigo Moon, would remain docile for four weeks? Doesn't he realize that these men couldn't give a damn about the Bissagos Islands? They would chop off your feet and pull the skin off your ankles like stockings."

"Kindle their greed," said Tom. "Promise them gold and green forests."

Bull looked away and shook his head.

"Think, Captain Bull," said Tom. "Think big."

The captain changed expression and scowled up at Tom with a cunning smile. "What makes him think I won't cut off his ears as soon as I have the chance?"

"Isn't a promise a promise?" asked Tom. "And a man a man?"

"You have a devil of a lot to learn from the school of life," roared Bull.

"That's true," said Tom, "but the question is whether you and I have a deal."

"A man doesn't make a deal with a pistol at his head," fumed the captain.

"Then when does he?" asked Tom. "Isn't it before the cold eyes of the shark that a man clasps his hands? Isn't it on the edge of the abyss that a man sells his soul to the Master who never sleeps?"

"Your tongue was forged in the bellows of Hell," growled Bull. "But so be it. All right! Yes! Now get me out of these chains."

"Does that mean we have a deal, Captain Bull?"

"Until it suits me to break it."

Tom cocked the pistol. "Your courage is impressive," he said, "but time is running out. I can see that you're not to be trusted. But I'll give you one last chance. Do we or do we not have a deal? You just have to nod. Otherwise your eyes will end up in the back of your head."

"He speaks with his grandmother's voice," snapped the captain.

"You're quite right about that, Captain. Just imagine what Gráinne would have done in this situation."

Bull's eyes went blank. "May her corpse rot in Hell," he groaned. "But so be it, you devil. Untie me. Satan has gotten his way."

Tom smiled. "No deal is good," he whispered, "unless it's good for both parties. So I assume that this deal has an amendment that says that before sunup we will have keelhauled Indigo Moon and promised his friends more of the same unless they behave themselves and comply with the oath of the severed finger."

Bull's face brightened. "With the greatest pleasure."

"Then that's how it will be." Tom nodded to Boto, who put the wooden block back in the captain's mouth, whereupon Tom picked up the pincers, grabbed hold of the tooth, set his boot against the chair, and gave a hard yank.

The next minute Bull was lying in one corner of the cabin and Tom was in the other.

Nyo Boto stared from the captain's bloody mouth to Tom, who was still holding the pincers. They were clamped around a brown eyetooth with a long peg-shaped root.

"Say good-bye to Mrs. Brown," said Tom. "She's on her way out."

The ship is drifting quietly in the black night. The sails are reefed, but the anchor has been hauled up. Most of the crew has gathered on the quarterdeck. All eyes are directed at the western horizon, where a gray cloud bank has started to form. The older men speak of low pressure, others talk about a hurricane, but most of them are silent.

All rancor has been forgotten. Indigo Moon has even gone to see the captain to hear what they should do about the approaching storm, and Bull has told him that he will leave the decision to the bullet he carries in his leg, which never fails when it comes to determining the force of a storm. With brisk steps he comes out to speak with his crew, who are gathered on deck.

"Your captain," he thunders, "has no intention of letting a little wind destroy his good mood."

The men scowl at each other and listen to Bull's account of his fortunate leave-taking with Mrs. Brown. He goes up to each and every man so the pirates can see the hole where she once lived.

"The lady is now in a jar of seawater," explains Bull, "which will embalm that rotten tooth for all eternity. A chosen few may have the honor of an audience with the deceased—simply put in a request." The captain gives his men an inviting look.

Now Moon steps forward. The gravity of the situation overcomes his hostility toward the captain. With a gloomy look he points toward the sea. "We have more important matters to think about," he says gruffly.

"What could be more important?" Bull turns his back on the first officer.

"Our lives," snaps Moon.

Tom gazes out at the sky and the sea, which have merged into a grayish-black horizon. Suddenly he feels an icy shiver race through his body. For once he agrees with the first officer. "Captain," he says, pointing up at the dark night sky, "what would you call that constellation you can see near the heavenly equator?"

Bull doesn't have to get out his telescope. "Three stars," he mutters.

"There's no question—it's what the Spaniards call *el cinturón de Orion*— Orion's Belt."

Tom nods and shifts his eyes to the horizon, where the cloud bank has taken the shape of a gigantic grayish-black cocoon.

Nyo Boto comes over to him. They give each other a somber look and feel the first portent of what is to come: the previously calm surface of the sea has taken on a rippled pattern. And now the riggings begin to sway. The timbers creak, and soon they can hear the underwater grumbling of the rudder moving in the current.

"Have you ever seen a cloud like that before?" asks Boto.

Tom shakes his head. "Never, but I've been warned about Orion's Belt."

Feodora joins them. "Is that the storm over there in the distance?"

"That," growls the captain, putting a hand on his thigh, "is not a storm but a hurricane, and she measures a hundred English miles across. Right now she's far off, but she won't stay there for long."

Indigo Moon comes down from the quarterdeck. "Has the captain figured it out yet?"

Bull glowers at him and lets his eyes slide over his crew, sizing them up. "Men," he shouts, "the bullet in my leg tells me we're in store for a hurricane."

"And it will strike before midnight," adds Moon.

"I know that." Bull gives his first officer a stern look. "And I also know what it means for this vessel and for every life it holds."

The otherwise-hardened sailors cast anxious looks at each other, and the cook starts to whimper.

Bull stares at his first officer with a malicious smile. "What does Mr. Moon suggest we do in this situation? What advice would you give your captain? That we start rowing? Or that we fold our hands in an attack of piety and pray to the merciful God?"

The captain looks around at his men, who have formed a circle around him and Moon. "We've all seen it," says Bull, "and we can all put a name to it. We know its course and can already feel its power. We can lash and tie, seal and caulk, pray to Allah and God and Muhammad and to the Master who never sleeps. Each man can do as he likes. When it comes to hurricanes, a man has to obey. But we can also empty the last bottle of rum and turn our faces to the west and hope that it will all go quickly."

There is a moment of silence.

Then Feodora says, "Is that all you have to say to your men, Captain Bull?"

"Captain?" bellows Bull, turning his face toward the wind. "I am no longer captain of this ship. The captain is coming from out there, and he is a vicious master. I've seen hurricanes the size of continents, and they leave only splinters behind."

"It's God's punishment," screams Salazar, putting his hands over his face.

Moon leaps up onto a crate. "Listen to me, men—there's still time if we do things right. Because we have demons on board. Birds of ill omen. A hurricane does not come of its own accord, and if we get rid of the demons, the storm will take a different course and spare this ship. Your captain proposes that you make yourselves blind with drink. His good sense must have been lodged in that rotten tooth. But I say: string up the demons, string them up one by one, and we will be spared."

The eyes of the crew turn spontaneously toward Tom, Nyo Boto, and Feodora.

At that second Tom knew that the prophecy about Orion's Belt was true. But he also remembered something else Zamora had said, about choosing your own course, being your own captain, and not drifting with the current.

Some of Moon's men had already drawn their knives; the mood was wicked and tense. Moon kept his eyes on the crew but pointed at Tom. "I say, let's make the storm a sacrificial gift."

The men nodded.

"Let's give the hurricane a sacrifice for each star burning in Orion's Belt."

Tom looked up at the three stars that formed the hazy constellation. Was it really possible to read in the stars that he would die as a bird of ill omen? That Orion's Belt would signify his death? Or was it merely a portent?

"Let the lass with the sharp tongue be the first." Indigo Moon pulled Feo over to the railing and enlisted the help of three of his men. "When she's gone," shouted Moon, "it will be her brother's turn, the boy who breathes through gills, who was born to a lineage with horns on their brows.

As soon as the sea has received him and his sister and the little black Satan, then the ship will have nothing more to fear. As sure as my name is Indigo Moon."

Tom looked at Boto, who stared at him expectantly.

"Great sea," intoned the first officer, "kindly receive our offerings; hear the prayers of these men for a merciful wind." Moon twisted Feo's arm behind her back and shoved her against the railing.

In two strides Tom was standing at Bull's side. "Do you also believe in demons and birds of ill omen, Captain, sir? Do you believe a red-haired boy from Nevis and his haughty sister, along with a skinny little lad from Africa, could summon up a storm like the one that's on its way?"

"I believe that a man should save his own hide and get up when the privy is burning." Bull gave Tom a warning glance.

Tom clenched his teeth and seized the captain's pistol, which he placed at Bull's temple as he stepped into the circle of men. "Hail Hippocrates," Tom said in a low voice as he cocked the trigger. "For the best friend of disease is the sailor's superstition. God's will has nothing to do with fever, and the plague is something that you get from rats. Hurricanes come from the sea, not from people." Tom paused, then turned abruptly and placed the pistol against the forehead of First Officer Moon and pulled the trigger.

When the roar of the shot faded, Moon lay dead at Tom's feet.

"What you have just witnessed," whispered Tom, "was not God's will or the Devil's or the ocean's—it was mine." He raised his voice. "I am Tom O'Connor," he shouted, "grandson of Gráinne Ni Mháille. I am wanted all over the Caribbean because I kill and I set fires, I free slaves and I steal horses. They have tried to drown me, shoot me, stab me, and hang me. I have been whipped, robbed, rolled, and keelhauled. They have taken my last penny, my best knife, and one of my fingers, but Tom O'Connor is still standing. And if any of you would like to follow the example of First Officer Moon, step forward. If not, then I suggest that we stand together, shoulder to shoulder, and keep this ship afloat for as long as we can."

Tom set his jaw. "Let the first rat leave the ship, but let the captain be the last, as it should be."

The pirates looked at each other. One of them nodded, several others clenched their fists and kicked at the first officer. The murmuring among the men rose to a shout. Soon they were all shaking hands, forgetting old grudges. Bull was once again in high spirits, giving the necessary orders to fulfill the duties of a doomed man.

The swells were now so violent that the ship was pitching up and down.

"This is how it sounds at the ends of the Earth, you red-haired O'Connor," bellowed the captain.

"Yes," replied Tom, "but before death arrives, there is still life."

They were standing on the quarterdeck where the blasts of wind threatened to hurl them over the railing. Hammering and pounding came from the yards and riggings, and everything that wasn't lashed down slid from side to side, from stem to stern.

Bull grabbed hold of Tom's collar. "The Devil takes care of his own." He smiled crookedly.

"That's what they say," replied Tom.

"In another life," continued the captain, "I could have taught this red-haired Satan all sorts of things about life at sea."

"Yes, and who knows, maybe you would have finally learned to spell *pomegranate*."

"Impudent to the last. He must indeed have served at Satan's court." Bull lifted Tom off the deck. "I had a rotten tooth," the captain muttered. "I don't have it anymore. I also had a ship. Soon that too will be gone. Gold, ivory, jewels, and candlesticks, everything that was meant to ensure a comfortable old age for Charles Winston Bull. All of this I now give back to the sea, for the Master who never sleeps is on his way to collect his payment. I can feel it in my bones and in the bullet that is gnawing at my leg. But they say that a condemned man should be granted his last wish."

Bull put Tom down. "One last wish before the long darkness. Shouldn't Providence grant an old pirate a last wish before his ship is smashed to bits?"

"What is your wish, Bull?" Tom asked quietly.

Bull put his hands around Tom's neck and lowered his voice to a whisper. His mouth was serious but his eyes were smiling. "I wish that this green-eyed sailor will survive the storm and keep on tormenting the world until he dies of old age."

Tom looked at the black hole where the ring finger of his right hand used to be. "Thank you, Captain," he said. "Thank you for your wish."

"But wishing for it isn't enough to make it happen." Bull scowled at the sea. "I can feel it in my leg: death in the shape of wind is on its way. Go below to your sister, lad. I think you must have things to talk about."

Feodora had found a sheltered spot on the middle deck where she was sitting with big Laem Sing and Nyo Boto. She had put all of her possessions in a little bag, and she looked at Tom with an expression that was firm and determined.

He nodded, realizing that she understood the situation. "Is this where we're going to sit?" he asked.

"Yes," replied Feo, "this is where we're going to sit."

"Are you scared?"

She nodded.

Tom took her hand. "It will go quickly, so quickly that we'll hardly feel it."

"I'm just sorry that I never got to see the world," she said.

"Maybe, maybe there's a life after this one."

"Do you think so, Tom O'Connor?"

He looked into her hopeful eyes and gave her his best lie. "Yes," he said, "I think there is, Feo."

The hurricane struck Bull's ship around midnight.

But before the storm reached the ship, a wave ten times the height of the masts rose up. Beneath a sky sprinkled with fire and ashes, the ocean opened its mighty jaws, in the midst of which the mother of all ships looked like a rowboat.

Tom stared at Feo as he clutched Boto's hand. They shut their eyes. For a moment they were weightless and stripped of all fear. For one long terrible moment every living thing held its breath.

Then the wave slammed down with all its might and splintered the upper deck, where planks, nails, tacks, and fixtures exploded in a howling, hammering inferno. Sails, rigging, timbers, and yards were crushed like kindling, carrying the first sailors overboard.

Tom saw big Laem Sing hanging horizontally in the air, borne by floods of water that tried to flush him into the sea. Nyo Boto was gone. But Feodora was still there, caught like a fly in a net woven from the lines that had saved her from drowning.

Tom was hurled below and was now sitting with his back against the galley door. He was trying to call for Feo when the next wave struck the ship, splintering the bowsprit. He clung to the door, which had been torn off.

Three figures whirled past, carried by the flood that was raging over most of the midship. One of them was the lifeless Salazar, whose pallid face disappeared in the gray-green waters that were assaulting the ship from all sides.

The mainmast was still standing as the hurricane plowed over the ship's stern, shattering it to bits in seconds. The sailors in the captain's cabin were flung three hundred feet into the air before they vanished like rag dolls in the foaming swirl of the great storm, which sucked in everything only to spit it all out again just as quickly.

Laem Sing was gone, Nyo Boto was gone, and when Tom once again got his head above water, he saw that the net that had held Feo on board had disappeared from the deck. All that remained of the ship were the lower deck and the base of the masts, along with a few barrels and a couple of loose oars.

In the surging sea drifted a jumble of planks, timbers, shreds of sail, and drowned sailors. The hurricane slowly moved on with a hoarse, thundering roar that yanked up the keel so that it stood for a moment like a gray-green wall; then it struck the waves with a deafening crash and disappeared.

He is hanging on to a board that was once one of the ship's ribs. Moonlight casts a deathlike sheen over the rolling sea that is gradually returning to calm. The pirate ship and its crew have been scattered to all the winds.

For hours he drifts on the sea, convinced that he has been deserted by all living things—that in this mass grave there is no hope to be found, and he has no desire to watch any more faces float past. He looks up at the cold oval of the moon and asks if this is the moment when he should let go, or whether Ramón the Pious is going to appear, disguised as a seahorse, and rescue him one last time.

But the moon doesn't answer, and Tom's hands are now so stiff with cramps that they refuse to obey. During the hours until dawn only the stiffness in his limbs keeps him above water.

• • •

The sea is quiet now. Above the surface of the water drifts a thick fog. He can feel a heavy pain in his stomach, as if he had swallowed a granite rock. Listlessly he watches his fingers slide down from the board, and in despair he calls out his mother's name. He feels the sea in his mouth, gasps, blinks his eyes, swallows water, and discovers . . . that he is standing on the ocean floor.

For a moment he lets the current carry him, flailing his arms wildly, and then he stretches out his legs and feels the rippled sandy bottom. He looks up at the fog, where the rays of the sun are gaining force. He turns around in the shallow water and meets the hazy image of a palm-dotted shore, a lagoon with coconut trees and now the sound of parrots, cackling birds, and the gentle trickling of a stream. On a rock sits a lone pelican, preening itself.

Tom crawls ashore on all fours, throws himself onto the flat beach, and looks up into the bright, blue sky. He hears the familiar thud of a coconut striking the sand. It makes him smile, and then he falls asleep until the heat of the midday sun awakens him.

25 Gianlucca from Portofino

HE DRANK LIKE AN ANIMAL, filling his belly from the trickling stream, and then he threw it all up. He staggered around, stopped, and tore off his shirt. Then he moved on, attempting to form some impression of the world in which he had landed. By the time the sun disappeared behind the jungle, he had found nothing but coconuts and empty bird nests.

Under cover of darkness he made his way to the edge of the forest and discovered a hollow where he lay down to sleep, clasping in one hand the old amulet he had been given in a previous life by a slave whose name he no longer remembered.

The next morning he woke with an empty heart. He walked to the beach and stared out at the ocean, certain that the world had vanished. All that remained were the sky, the sea, and this little island. "After the end of the world," he whispered, "the only thing left will be a single island and on this island will live only one person as witness to a time when humans occupied the Earth, which was lush and bountiful and teeming with life."

He had dreamed that he was a volcano, a conical mountain clothed in the colors of gloom. Out of the volcano's mouth came mango-colored lava, a long sticky river of vomit, bile, blood, and entrails. Everything had to come out so that in the end he would be nothing but an extinct and ice-cold cone. In his dream the faces were hardened by the smoldering Earth: Feo, Boto, Bull, and Indigo Moon.

He had woken in the middle of the night and stared out at the iron-blue sea that now held these souls, feeding its fish with their flesh. He had buried his fingers in the sand, picked up a handful, and watched it slide through his fingers. He had never been quick to shed tears, which apparently came from a place deep inside him. They had fallen onto the lines of his palm—the lines that formed a secret pattern depicting his life. On one palm he had a scar, a scar that intersected the will of destiny, a lava-red cut that sliced across the first draft of fate.

He had whispered his sister's name and had fallen asleep with the image of Nyo Boto in his mind.

Now, at daybreak, he felt heavy-headed from the dream and hollow with grief, but he pulled himself together and moved on, searching aimlessly. Twice he crossed his own tracks. He fell to the ground, burying his hands in the sand, and then looked at his fingers, which were black with ash.

Ash!

He repeated the word, tasted it, and washed his hands in the dry, silvery powder. He smeared his face with it and felt a gurgle of laughter in his throat. Because the ash was still warm. He got to his feet and ran over to the edge of the forest, shouting at the top of his lungs. "I'm here, I'm here." And to himself he added, "Whoever you are."

He stayed near the fire pit until the rains came and then he sought shelter under the foliage, where he waited until the downpour stopped.

The face hovered among the waxy leaves that formed the undergrowth of the forest. Tom sat for a long time, staring at the face, convinced that his imagination must be playing a trick on him, that it was a trick of the leaves and the sunlight. But the longer he stared, the more certain he was, because in the middle of the green were a nose, mouth, and eyes. The skin was the same color as algae, and the hair, which hung in long thin wisps, was as gray as the ash he had rubbed on his face.

We're watching each other, thought Tom. Maybe he's just as scared as I am, but I'll show him that I'm not afraid of anything. That I've been dead so many times that it would take much more than this to frighten me.

"Did you hear what I said?" he yelled.

The pale eyes widened, and the soft toothless mouth formed a slightly demented smile that gave way to a soundless chuckling.

Tom moved the heavy leaves aside and looked the man over. He was short, almost a head shorter than Tom. Except for a filthy loincloth, he was naked. There was something trusting about him, like a child. And when Tom introduced himself, the little man took his hand and swung his arm, as if he wanted to dance.

Idiot, thought Tom. I'm stranded on an island with an idiot. "Do you speak Spanish?" he asked. "English? Portuguese?"

The man didn't reply but pulled Tom down to the shore where he pointed at the sea, the forest, and the sandy beach, as if to show him around. It was impossible to guess his age, as if many years of solitude had erased all trace.

"Tom," said Tom, putting his hand on his chest, "my name is Tom O'Connor."

The man nodded like an impatient child. "*Io pòvero me,*" he said, bowing his head.

"I don't understand," muttered Tom.

"*Io pòvero me,*" sighed the man.

Tom nodded and patted him on the back, then pointed at the fire pit. "Is that yours?" he asked.

"Er . . ." said the man, "*si, si.*"

Tom knew the word *si* and repeated it. This amused the man, who said, "Portofino."

"Your name is Portofino?" said Tom.

The man took Tom's hand and placed it on top of his head. "Gianlucca," he said sadly.

"Gianlucca? Is your name Gianlucca?" asked Tom.

"*Si,* Gianlucca." The man nodded and tugged at Tom, laughing as he ran.

Maybe this is a game, thought Tom. Maybe I'll end up an idiot on this island too.

They ran for ten minutes or so before Tom decided that he didn't feel like playing anymore. But the little man insisted. Tom told himself that if he turned his back on his new friend, he would be turning his back on half the world.

Gianlucca had stopped near a cove. He pointed at something that was sloshing around at the water's edge, half covered with sand. The shape lay on its back with one leg bent and its arms spread out.

Tom felt the hair on his neck stand up as he leaned over Feodora and carefully brushed the sand from her face. Her lips were the color of purple grapes. Her skin looked like fish meat. He gathered her into his arms but was immediately rebuked by little Gianlucca, who laid Feo back down on the shore, grabbed her ankles, and pushed her legs up like a frog's.

The water that burbled out of Feo's mouth was black and thick. This amused Gianlucca, who kept on pumping.

Tom stared at Feo, uncertain whether this treatment was a good idea or not. But when Feo gave a slight cough, Gianlucca clapped his hands and looked with glee at Tom, who breathed hard, tensed every fiber on his body, and then bellowed his gratitude.

Maybe that was what finally made her look up.

They're sitting close together, almost like one body, rocking back and forth, paying no attention to the fact that they're actually a trio, since the little man from the forest has nestled close to them. Slowly the warmth returns to Feo's body, her blood starts to flow, and her breathing grows steady.

"Is it just you and me?" she whispers.

"And Gianlucca," replies Tom, not knowing whether to laugh or cry.

Feo gazes out at the water and starts talking in a monotone. About the shipwreck, the hurricane, and death in the water. "Salazar," she says. "I saw him for a brief second before he drifted out to sea. He was looking straight at me, trying to say something. He looked like a young man."

Tom pulls her close, but Feo wants to tell her story. "I should have drowned," she says, giving Tom a piercing look.

"Me too," he mutters.

"No, that's not what I mean. I was lying on the lid of a barrel, and suddenly something rammed into me. I lost my grip and went under. The last thing I saw was bubbles."

"But you were washed up onshore," says Tom. "And besides, does it really matter now?"

"I was much too far out." Feo pulls free. "There's something that doesn't fit."

"But what, Feo? What are you thinking?"

She looks at him. "I think someone must have dragged me up onto the beach."

They're sitting around the fire. Gianlucca has put a few small fish on a spear, and they eat them with gusto. The fish taste like mackerel, and Tom smiles cheerfully at Feo, who now looks more like herself.

The little man with the long hair jumps around, uttering sounds that are probably meant to be a song.

"Idiocy," says Tom.

"No," says Feo, "loneliness."

Afterward they lie close together like three spoons, with Gianlucca in the middle, because that's the way he wants it. Tom looks for Orion's Belt but can't spot the constellation. He takes that as a good sign.

"And besides," says Feo suddenly, "besides, I was much too far from the coast."

Tom looks at her. "I thought you were asleep."

She sits up. "Someone pulled me to shore. There's no other explanation."

"Forget about it." Tom closes his eyes and thinks gratefully about the fish he has eaten. He falls asleep seeing its scales and tasting its meat.

Around midnight he wakes up because someone is shaking him.

The night was black and moonless. A faint light came from the sea, which always held on to a remnant of daylight. Tom looked at Feo, who was huddled up like a frightened little monkey, staring into the darkness. She was holding a stick in one hand. "Feo," whispered Tom.

She shushed him. "Somebody's out there."

He looked around but couldn't see anyone.

"In the forest." Feo gave a toss of her head. "I heard them a minute ago."

"Is there more than one?"

"No idea. But I don't think they've seen us yet. Otherwise they would have come out."

Tom turned over onto his stomach, thinking that they were well hidden if someone were to come from the forest side.

For a long time they heard only the waves striking the beach; then there was a rustling. As they ducked down, they caught sight of a shape, half animal and half human, wandering among the trees. It was hard to make out the contours of the silhouette. The creature had two legs, four arms, and a swollen, stunted torso. Whatever it was, it was groaning loudly. Suddenly, it stopped, as if to orient itself, then bent down and dropped its burden. The big body became two. So it wasn't an animal after all.

Tom looked at Feodora, who was on her feet. She struck at the shrubbery with her stick. The sound reached the shape, which stopped in mid-stride. With an effort it gathered up its burden and stepped out of the forest's darkness.

It changed from a black monster into a shabby, ragged man with a big black beard. He was wearing a pair of tattered pants and a shirt with no sleeves.

"Bull," whispered Tom and then stared at the figure the captain had now placed on the ground.

"He broke both legs," growled Bull and sank down next to Nyo Boto, who, with a wan little smile, looked from Tom to Feo.

The canoe was long, narrow, and well-built. As far as they could tell, it was not the result of Gianlucca's handiwork. He didn't show much interest in it either, but tried to explain that it had appeared on its own. They had been on the island for three weeks. They lacked for nothing because Gianlucca was a generous host, who enjoyed taking care of his guests. They spoke no more about the shipwreck, since the story made the captain depressed. Feo had found out that Bull had gathered her up from the remains of a barrel that had been floating like a nutshell on the heaving seas. He had put her down next to Boto, whose legs had been crushed in the hurricane. They had gotten separated in the surf, but before Boto disappeared too, Bull had lashed him to his back. As if to excuse his charity, he said that the boy was worth something, after all, according to that liar Tom O'Connor. The rest was just speculation.

Feodora had examined Boto's legs, which hung from his body like two lifeless posts. He had no pain, and after a closer inspection they agreed to make two splints in the hope that the bones would knit back together on their own.

Boto himself was full of confidence about the future. When they found the canoe, he told them that he had had a good deal of experience with that type of vessel.

After two more weeks they started talking about leaving. Tom and Bull had carved some pieces of wood into what passed for paddles, and they had repaired the damage to the canoe. Based on the starry sky, they had a relatively clear idea of their location.

"Approximately ten degrees north of the equator," said Bull.

Tom guessed the longitude.

"Is that far from Nevis?" asked Boto.

Tom told him not to worry about anything.

Bull spent his days down on the beach, staring at the horizon. As time passed, he became more and more withdrawn. When they spoke to him, he would reply in monosyllables, evidently wishing to be left alone. But one day he took Tom aside and said that the time had come.

"What are you thinking about?" asked Tom, even though he knew quite well what the captain was considering.

Bull nodded toward the canoe. "It's not impossible," he said. "I've been mulling it over, and it's not impossible."

"But in that little boat?" asked Tom.

"If we really are where we think we are," said Bull, "then we're not far from a well-used sailing route. Many Portuguese sail this way when they're heading home from the colonies. If we're lucky, we'll run into one of their ships."

"Yes," said Tom, "if we're lucky. You're starting to sound like Boto."

"Another week and I'll start to sound like Gianlucca from Portofino."

The canoe is rocking on the waves, loaded with freshwater poured into a barrel, which was the only wreckage they had found from Bull's ship. There is also a pile of dried fish and a few root vegetables that Feo has wrapped in palm leaves.

It's late at night, and the yellow crescent moon is high overhead in the pitch-black night sky. On the beach sits Gianlucca, who refuses to leave. He won't go voluntarily. He laughs and waves and rattles off a string of sentences in the language they don't understand.

"Idiot," grumbles Bull.

"No," says Tom, "lonely."

Nyo Boto is lying in the bottom of the boat, watching Feo grab hold of a paddle. Bull is sitting in the stern because he's the one who will steer. They have decided on a course that is due north. According to their calculations, they have enough water for five days. What will happen after that, they haven't discussed. There are a number of things they haven't discussed. But when Tom looks into his sister's eyes and studies Bull's determined efforts, he understands the situation. Once the decision was made, no more words were necessary.

They wave to Gianlucca, who runs along the shore like a child. Boto is still wearing his red shirt. The smell of mold is gone, but now it has no sleeves.

They paddle steadily and calmly, with a quickly developed sense of teamwork. The chill of the night does them good. Each has agreed to paddle as long as his strength holds out, to sleep in shifts, and to rest during the midday heat.

Tom watches the coast disappear and wonders about the hand that has thus far spared him. Is it still there? Is there any meaning to this life, or is each person left to his own devices and the caprices of the moon? He thinks about Sugar George and Ina and about their daughter, little Sunday. About Ramón, Albert and Bruno, Señor López, and Mrs. Briggs. They wander through his mind like a procession of hazy images on their way toward the farthest point of land where the sparks from a bonfire dance in the night. Soon the ashes are scattered to the winds. It's all inside me, he thinks, and will never disappear.

He opens his hands and stares down at the ingenious network of lines. A sea chart that was created when he opened his hand for the first time, that irrevocably marked out his fate.

Tonight I will grant you perfect recall.

Those were her words, on that night in September. And he has remembered every word. He looks up at the misty stars. He feels Feo's eyes on him. She smiles. Nyo Boto looks at him too. And also smiles.

What are they up to?

Maybe they're not up to anything. Maybe they're just smiling.

I love them, thinks Tom. And I never want to be parted from them again. That's how it is. He nods to them and doesn't need to say a word.

On the second day he starts telling the story about Ramón from Cádiz.

"Is it a good story?" growls Bull, who's paddling like a galley slave.

"You'll have to decide that for yourself, Captain."

"What does a good story need to have?" asks Feodora.

"I want a story about gold, precious gems, and silk stockings," grumbles Bull.

Tom raises his voice. "The captain will get his wish, because the story about Ramón and his friend Bibido does indeed concern gold and precious gems. I'm not so sure about silk stockings. But once upon a time there was a boy who was the son of an Irish fisherman, who had unfortunately died of fever. Each night this spirited lad would set out to sea to search for wreckage so he could support his mother and his Spanish half sister. And the boy was a natural at navigation. He was as smart as a whip, familiar with the ocean and the newest ideas of astronomy, because he had studied with Copernicus and that's how he knew that the center of the universe resides in the sun and that ships that sail far enough will one fine day come back around to the place where they started from.

"Then one night, which more or less resembled all the rest, this Irish rascal became the owner of half a slave whom he had pulled out of the sea after a violent shipwreck. But listen closely now, because this slave was not just an ordinary slave; he was the son of a king, a prince from the Bissagos Islands. Bibido was his name, and he was worth his weight in gold. Doesn't that sound like a good story?"

"It certainly does," replied Feo.

"How much did he weigh?" grumbled Bull.

Tom smiled and resumed his story, which continued all the way up to the plantation on Jamaica but went no further. Around midnight Feodora caught sight of a hazy but constant apparition, and toward dawn it grew clearer and clearer until finally it was transformed into a three-masted galleon.

Bull is standing up in the canoe, which threatens to tip over.

"Portuguese," he says hoarsely, "just as I said."

"We're saved, Boto." Tom stretches his hand down to the boy in the bottom of the boat.

They paddle like maniacs, but the closer they get, the less certain they are of their luck.

"The sails are hanging in a strange way." Bull puts up his hand to shade his eyes from the sun.

"What do you make of it?" asks Feo.

Bull spits over the gunwale. "Either the first officer is drunk, or it's a ghost ship."

26 São Miguel

THE SHIP HAD NOT DROPPED ANCHOR but was drifting in the wind, on no set course and with no one steering. The sails were in good shape, and there was no sign in the rigging or timbers that she had been through a battle.

Tom suggested that they paddle around the prow, and when they rounded the bowsprit, Bull put their shared suspicions into words. If there had been plague on board, it was conceivable that the passengers and crew would have abandoned the ship, which was now drifting around like a floating tomb.

Tom was just about to say that he was prepared to climb up to take a closer look, when Feo caught sight of a child staring at them from the starboard side. They could see a topknot of hair, two frightened eyes, and part of a nose.

They paddled closer. Tom called out to the child, but the boy didn't react, and when Bull, in a fit of irritation, bellowed at him in English, he vanished.

Feo advised Bull to keep to the background, which unleashed a lengthy argument, but then a young woman appeared. She had the boy in her arms, and he pointed down at the canoe. Behind them stood a girl about ten years old.

"Hello, up there," shouted Feodora. "Do you speak Spanish?"

The woman hesitated, then nodded.

Feo introduced herself and explained that they had been shipwrecked, and that they wished to come aboard.

The woman glanced from side to side but didn't respond.

"Are you deaf?" yelled Bull.

The woman disappeared.

Feo glared at Bull, shaking her head. "Haven't you ever been a child, Captain Bull?"

"No, I was born as I am. With hide and hair."

Feo shouted into his face, "But haven't you ever been scared, Captain? Haven't you ever been alone, so terribly alone that you . . . that you . . ." She had tears in her eyes. "I have," she added.

At that moment the little girl reappeared.

Tom shouted that they came with peaceful intentions.

"That's right, we're the four apostles," barked Bull, glaring at Feo.

She nodded. "Someday," she said, "someday I'm going to shoot your hat off, Bull. Maybe I'll miss. Maybe I'll aim too low. We'll have to see."

Bull asked Tom whether all the women in his family were scornful and hot-tempered.

Now an elderly man appeared. He said a great deal in Portuguese and raised his arms toward the sky as he wailed his distress.

"It's just the usual," said Bull. "The Portuguese are always complaining about something."

"As far as I can tell, there's been a mutiny," said Feodora. "The Spanish crew revolted against the Portuguese captain."

"Of all people, I detest Spaniards the most." Bull smiled at Feo.

"Is there anyone you don't detest, Captain?"

Tom intervened, realizing that a discussion about Spaniards might quickly develop.

"How long have you been drifting around like this?" he called.

The old man shook his head in resignation and continued wailing.

Feo translated as best she could. "They were on their way to Bahia with slaves for the coffee plantations. I can't understand the rest."

Now the girl's mother joined the conversation, and the sound of her voice attracted even more women. Finally almost fifty passengers were standing there, women and children and old men, quarreling over who should do the talking. When they couldn't come to an agreement, they started speaking all at once.

The ship had headed out six months earlier, setting course for the São Jorge al-Mina, where three hundred slaves had been purchased, to be sold when they reached Bahia. But on the way across the Atlantic, sickness had broken out, and the blacks had died like flies. For that reason they changed course and went to Hispaniola, where new slaves were bought. When they got as far as Trinidad, trouble erupted over wages. Now that the voyage had been altered and extended for several weeks, the crew refused to work without an increase in pay. The whole thing ended in mutiny. To make matters worse, a disagreement arose, which finally erupted into all-out war among the Portuguese, Spaniards, officers, and passengers. Ten days ago the last able-bodied man had died of his bullet wounds. Now there remained only women and children and a handful of old men, but no one to steer the ship.

"Do you have water?" asked Tom.

From above the answer came that they had plenty of water.

Bull stroked his beard. "Then let's board her."

"My dear Captain." Feo spoke in her most angelic-sounding voice. "Maybe we should change our style a bit."

"Whose style?"

"Yours, Captain, sir. These people have been frightened out of their wits. They've been through terrifying experiences."

"Exactly. They're ripe for the plucking."

Feodora attempted a strained smile. "Would it be too much to ask you to use a name other than C. W. Bull? Considering your fame, that is. There's no getting around the fact that you're quite famous."

"That I am," growled Bull, "although most of the witnesses are dead."

Tom intervened. "I suggest that we leave everything to Bull. After all, he's the oldest and most experienced. I'm sure he'll think of something that will placate the passengers."

The captain snickered and turned away from Feo, who said she was certain he would.

"We're extremely lucky," continued Tom, "to be given such a splendid ship, and all we have to do is climb on board. So why fight over trifles?"

"There are fifty terrified people up there," whispered Feo. "And if that man," she pointed at Bull, "acts the way he usually does, we risk being sent back to the canoe with bullets in our foreheads."

Bull stared at her. "I can feel the rage coming," he roared. "You're looking at someone who has never done anything but capture ships."

Feo smiled acidly. "That's what I mean. We're not here to capture, Bull. We're here as guests and thus should behave like guests."

Tom took his arm. "Captain, sir, let's take one thing at a time. First the ship, then the introductions. Are we agreed on that? Good."

Tom turned to face the crowd of people who had been following the discussion with great interest. "Hello, up there," he shouted, "may I be permitted to congratulate you?"

They looked at each other.

"It's your good fortune to have run into one of the greatest captains on the seven seas."

"*The* greatest," growled Bull.

"The greatest of all," said Tom, pointing to Bull. "I myself have been trained as a first officer, and I offer to take you wherever you wish."

The passengers withdrew to discuss the proposal. A moment later a tall old man appeared. "We thank you," he said, "but can you tell us how far we are from the mainland?"

"Ten days' journey," replied Tom in a firm voice.

The man conferred with his fellow passengers. "In that case," he said, "we invite you aboard."

Minutes later a rope ladder was tossed over the side. Tom clambered on board first. Behind him came Bull with Boto on his back, followed by Feodora, who stepped on deck like a queen.

"Permit me," she said, smiling, "permit me to introduce ourselves." She smoothed down her crumpled dress and patted her hair. "My name is Feodora Dolores Vasgues. I am a full-blooded Spaniard, but grew up on Nevis. This is my half brother, Tom O'Connor, and the black boy is a freed slave by the name of Nyo Boto. He's from the Bissagos Islands. The older gentleman with the black beard is Captain Charles Winston Bullerick from England. We thank you for your hospitality and promise to do everything we can to comply with your wishes. Both O'Connor and Bullerick are experienced seamen. In spite of his youth, Tom has been a second officer in the Spanish navy, and Mr. Bullerick has been the captain of a . . . a spice ship from the West Indies Company."

Feodora stopped there and received a long, warm round of applause from the people gathered on deck.

Tom smiled and cast a sidelong glance at Bull, who was staring at Feo as he chewed on his knuckle.

"We thank you for those introductions," said the old man. "This is in truth good news—finally we have experienced men on board. We hope that we can be of assistance so that Captain Bullerick can set the ship on the proper course as quickly as possible."

"To begin with," said Tom, "it would be good if we had a look at the provisions at once. Then we need to divide you up into work teams. I assume that you're the only survivors?"

"We have gotten rid of the dead," said an elderly woman.

"Very sensible," said Tom.

"But some of the blacks have probably died since the last time we were down in the hold. We don't like going down there."

Bull winked at Tom. Out of the corner of his mouth he said that if they played their cards right, a hold full of slaves could be quite lucrative.

"Folks," said Tom in a loud, clear voice, "shall we ask the captain to go to the quarterdeck so we can get this ship under way?"

The suggestion was met with more applause.

Afterward Tom and Feo went around shaking hands, and Bull was surrounded by the older boys, who wanted to know if he had ever run into pirates on his voyages carrying spices.

"A couple of times," he replied cryptically.

"What did you do, Captain Bullerick?"

Bull gnashed his teeth and rolled his eyes. "I skinned them alive."

This reply unleashed loud laughter, and one of the boys exclaimed that in his view Señor Bullerick looked like a real pirate captain himself.

The comment mollified Bull, who without further invitation made his way to the galley, where he found two bottles of rum and stuck them in his pockets.

That turned out to be a breach of the ship's rules. An older woman explained sternly that all the passengers were against liquor.

"All the better," growled Bull.

"We would therefore appreciate it if you show the same type of restraint, señor. For rum was created by the Devil."

"We don't disagree about that, dear lady." Bull took a healthy swig.

"We've seen enough of drunken sailors, and a befuddled captain can't steer a ship," continued the woman.

"Shall we wager on that?" Bull wiped his mouth and gave a tentative tug on the rigging.

The woman had now been joined by three like-minded passengers. "We demand that you refrain from drink," said one of them.

Bull took a comb out of his pocket. "Allow me," he said, "to show you ladies this modest object used for tending to the hair. What do you ladies think it was made from?"

Tom shot the captain a warning look, but Bull turned his back. One of the women guessed that the comb was made of bone.

"Correct," said Bull. "I carved it myself in my spare time."

The woman studied the comb and praised the captain for his skillful handiwork.

"A bone from Countess Olga's hip socket," said Bull, giving the ladies a smile.

And with that, the subject of liquor was closed.

The rest was hard work. They needed hands at the capstan and sails, and people in the galley. A watch schedule had to be set up, and last but not least they needed someone to take care of the blacks. Everyone obeyed orders, happy to have something to do.

The captain's big cabin, which had been used for the children, now had only one occupant, who was glad to help himself to the cigars, pistols, and additional furnishings the cabin provided. But there were other excellent cabins, and Feo was assigned to one that she shared with three other girls.

Tom and Nyo Boto had another cabin to themselves.

Feodora turned out to be good at getting people moving, either with sewing or playing games, and after they managed to isolate Bull so he went only to the quarterdeck or to the captain's cabin, the worst danger was over.

Tom was the first to go below. There was almost no light and the stench was unbearable. The slaves lay like sardines in a barrel, with shackles around their ankles. There were men, women, and children, about a hundred in all. Some of them were frightened and weeping; others lay dozing. Many of them were dead.

During the first night Tom and Bull threw thirty-one bodies into the sea. Reluctantly Tom counted each and every one.

"Is it necessary to count them?" growled the captain. "Isn't it bad enough as it is?"

"It's important to know that they were here," murmured Tom. "We can at least give them a number."

Bull didn't answer, but when the last slave was gone, he took Tom by the scruff of the neck and muttered that this damn well wasn't a job for a lad his age.

"I can manage," replied Tom.

"That's what I mean," said the captain, and he walked off with a gloomy face.

On the fourth day they had wind in their sails. That was the day that Feo suggested they let the slave children come up on deck. Tom watched the first gaunt youngsters, frightened and despondent, stand and stare up at the enormous sails. The children blinked at the sun and padded after Feo, hampered by their shackles. Most of them had been without fluids for so long that they could hardly even hold a cup.

The rest of the passengers kept their distance or walked away in contempt. They thought the slaves should stay in the hold.

"The blacks belong to the shipping company," said one man. "I hope you understand that, young lady."

"That's why we should treat them properly," replied Feo. She was standing between a group of passengers and the cluster of black children.

"But they don't belong on deck with the whites," said one woman.

"We've taken a vote," the man continued, "and you'll have to comply with the results, Miss."

But Feo won support from an unexpected quarter when Bull came down from the quarterdeck. He was barefoot and wore only pants and a ragged shirt. His hair stuck out in all directions, and the look in his black eyes indicated that he had just woken up. "What the devil is all this commotion?" he shouted. "A man can't get a wink of sleep."

The passenger held out a piece of paper with a handwritten list of regulations for the ship and its cargo. "Here are the rules for the slaves," said the man, "and this was signed by the owners of the shipping company. What are you going to do about it, Captain?"

"That's simple," replied Bull, and set the paper on fire.

But that didn't solve the problem. On the contrary. The next day it was announced that the passengers refused to share their freshwater with the slaves. "We have tolerated the blacks coming up on deck, but we won't share our water with them," said the Spanish-speaking man.

Feo explained to him that if the children didn't get water, they would die.

"They're slaves," the man replied.

"Señor," she said politely, "I'll give these children my ration. Are you satisfied?"

Her comment cooled tempers, but only because Tom and Boto also shared their portions.

But freshwater alone wasn't enough, and on the tenth day they had to bid farewell to two more children who had not survived the night. Tom could see that the work was taking its toll on Feo. Day by day she grew paler and more exhausted. She had to divide up the porridge and water under the cover of night, and each day listen to more and more complaints.

They were sitting in Tom's cabin. He had just calculated their position and was pleased that they were on course. It was a starry night and everything was peaceful.

"You should allow yourself more sleep," he said.

"And you should allow yourself a little less wine," Feo retorted.

"An officer needs a certain ration." He pointed to Bull, who had collapsed with an acute attack of dizziness.

"Why is it so hot here?" she asked.

"Because we're in the middle of the world," replied Tom. "We're sailing right on the equator."

Feo wiped her face with a little white cloth.

"We're going to be short on water, you know," he said. "You're squandering it."

"When were you last down in the hold? Do you realize how unbearable it is down there?"

"You're worn out, Feo. Get a couple of the girls to help you."

"They won't have anything to do with the slaves. They refuse. But listen to me, Tom. There's actually a black girl who speaks English. I'm going to ask if we can let her give me a hand. Good Lord, what harm could it do?"

"You want to take off her shackles, is that what you're saying?"

Feodora gave him a somber look. "Yes, I want to take off her shackles."

Tom unrolled a sea chart and pointed at six black specks on the great ocean. "These are islands," he said. "São Miguel is one of them. We should reach it within a couple of days. According to the shipping company's old logbook, it's a Portuguese colony. We can take on freshwater and fruit there. Doesn't that sound good?"

"You say that you once worked for a blacksmith," she said.

"So?"

"Can't you cut the shackles off the girl that I mentioned?"

"We'll just have more problems," sighed Tom.

"Leave that to me."

"Damn it, Feo, we'll reach the islands in a couple of days. Can't you wait?"

"In a couple of days we'll lose two more! Look at me, Tom. I have to have some help."

"I don't know of anybody as stubborn as you." Tom swung his legs off the bunk and went to get a hammer and chisel.

Feo and the black girl stood in the passageway in front of the galley. The slave was wearing a dress that was much too big for her frail body. Tom bent down and with a single blow cut the shackles from her thin ankles.

The girl did not look at him or Feo, just stood there with her head bowed, weak and dazed.

"Where did she learn to speak English?" asked Tom.

Feo turned the girl around. "She's not very informative, but take a look at this." Feo held the lantern up to the girl's left shoulder, where a brand had been burned into her skin.

Tom gasped and, without thinking, took a step back. "Mr. Briggs's seal."

The girl raised her eyes to his.

Tom cautiously placed his hand against her cheek, which had once been round and soft. "It can't be possible." He turned his back to his sister and stood with his face to the wall.

"What's going on, Tom?" Feo asked.

He wiped his eyes and squinted at the girl, who hadn't moved. "I know her," he said, "and she knows me. Don't you?"

The girl wet her lips. "Tombomba," she whispered.

The name made Tom fall apart. He looked at her thin ankles, scarred from the heavy chains.

Feo begged him to explain.

"Her name is Sunday Morning. She's the daughter of George and Ina."

He is standing in the dark, looking at the sleeping Boto. It's an hour after Feodora put little Sunday Morning to bed in her own bunk. They've talked about it over the flickering light of a candle, he and Feo. And now, as he stands beside Nyo Boto, the decision is irrevocable.

"Do it, Tom," Feo had told him, "but do it soon."

"Even if it costs me my life," he whispers into the night.

Two days later they had São Miguel in sight. The islands appeared on the horizon like a hazy mirage.

"We'll be there sometime this morning," said Bull, gnawing on a dry cigar stump.

Tom shut the door to Bull's cabin. The time had come. "Bull," he said, "I want to be completely honest with you."

"What a pleasant change." The captain poured himself a glass of rum.

Tom nodded. "First of all, why the hell would you want to go to Bahia anyway?"

"To put the passengers ashore and sell the blacks," growled Bull. "No use sailing without getting paid."

Tom looked him in the eye. "The slaves don't belong to us," he said, "just as the ship doesn't belong to us. But since I know that those sorts of things don't matter to you, let me point out another problem that will be unavoidable when we reach Bahia. There will be representatives from the shipping company at the dock. And as is the custom when big ships put in to port, there will be crowds of people. It would be strange, not to mention unthinkable, if one of them didn't recognize the infamous Captain C. W. Bull. What do we do then, Captain, sir? I'm sorry to be so blunt, but I can already see the gallows."

"In that regard," snarled Bull, "we have nothing to discuss."

"I agree completely, but nevertheless what should we do? It'll be too late when the noose is around your neck."

Bull emptied his glass. "May I remind him that all my days I've been used to a certain amount of trouble, and I've always managed to get off. I don't sail without being paid. Your sister has done nothing but feed the blacks, and I've accepted that because the price for nothing but skin and bones is very low."

Tom placed the palms of his hands flat on the table. "Think, Captain," he whispered. "Think big."

"I've never done anything else."

"I'm glad to hear it, because it's true what they say, you know: God didn't give a big man big hands just so he could pick nuts."

"Now you're talking. I can feel the lice fleeing."

Bull gnawed on his cigar stump and gave Tom a reproving look. Yet Tom felt as if he had made an impression.

"I've been asking myself, why give up this marvelous ship? I've seen you up there on the quarterdeck. There is no better captain on the seven seas. You suit each other like the emperor and his castle."

"Oh, sing, liar, go ahead and sing. Let the shit fly, as the donkey said while it grazed in the field of peas."

Tom smiled and lowered his voice. "Why settle for silver when you could have gold?"

Bull arched his brows. "That wouldn't be like me."

"No, it wouldn't."

"But where is all this gold the Irish cur is singing about?"

"Right in front of our noses, Bull, right in front of our noses."

"The Devil take me, he's just like his hideous grandmother. When she arrived in Hell, the Devil turned green with envy."

"Captain, I'm talking about the prince from the Bissagos Islands."

Bull flung his cigar away. "As if I want to hear that old story again."

"A person never gets tired of hearing about gold."

"Words never made a poor man rich—any thief can tell you that."

"I've told you before, the boy is worth his weight in pure gold."

"You'll have to do better than that."

"His father is a king."

Bull snickered. "I suppose the tailor told you that himself?"

Tom shook his head. "I heard it from a man by the name of Ramón."

"Oh yes." Bull slapped his forehead. "The sneaky fellow from Cádiz— I'd forgotten all about him. Your instructor in lying and conniving."

"The biggest liar Spain has ever fostered," admitted Tom. "But who knows the truth better than a liar?"

Bull leaned forward with a menacing look. "Sweet rum turns bitter with that kind of prattle."

"Captain, sir." Tom perched on the edge of the desk. "I wholeheartedly believe that a man gets only one big chance here in life. If he passes it up, he loses himself. Ramón from Cádiz was such a man. He was truly dejected, down at the heels, and in debt. But I'm not. I was once given a letter of reference by a distinguished lady for whom I read aloud from the Book of Psalms."

"Dear God," howled Bull, "now the Devil himself has joined the monastery!"

"She herself said that Tom O'Connor was untainted. Look at me, Bull. Because that's what I am. Untainted! And when we stood on deck two weeks ago and had to throw one life after another into the sea, that's when I knew that the two of us were cast from the same mold."

"He certainly has a damned high opinion of himself. After Bull was made, they destroyed the mold."

"You have greatness in you, Bull."

The captain slammed his hand against the desk. "Now they're laughing in Hell," he shouted. "Who do you think you're talking to, boy? I've skinned more Spaniards than there are herring in the sea. In my wake lies an entire armada, and I'm wanted in seven countries. There are even governors who would give their right arms to be the one who goes down in history as the man who hanged Charles Winston Bull. So don't come here and pretend to tell me anything."

"In other words, you're rotten through and through, is that what you're saying, Captain?"

"I can feel the rage coming."

"Let me tell you about a ring, Mr. Bull. Not a ring made of gold or precious gems, but a gray and insignificant little ring. You've seen it on Boto's finger, but not long ago it sat in his throat, sewn on with fishing line. That ring is proof enough for me. That ring testifies to his royal status."

Bull stuck his face close to Tom's. "I don't care if he's the Pope in Rome."

Tom smiled. "The Pope in Rome / Has an empty dome. / On him the biggest lump / Is his paunch and his rump."

The rhyme amused Bull, who graciously allowed Tom to fill his glass.

"I'll give you a share of the boy," said Tom. "I'll give you exactly half."

"In return for what?"

"For seizing the ship." Tom clapped his hands and gave the captain an eager look. "Take it, Bull! Leave the passengers behind on São Miguel. We've seen enough of them. And if there's any trouble, give them one broadside! Show them who you are. The great, the proud, the invincible Captain C. W. Bull. The hero of every boy and the terror of every mother. Take this ship, turn the wheel, and set sail for the Bissagos Islands, where the fortune is just waiting to be plucked. I guarantee, no, I promise on my mother's grave, that you will never regret it."

Bull said nothing and found a new cigar, which he began to gnaw on.

Tom made use of the pause. "What did you dream about as a child, Captain Bull?"

Bull's eyes lit up. "About capturing ships."

"You dreamed about gold, Captain. Oceans of gold."

"How can he know what repulsive little Charlie from Bristol dreamed about? I wanted to capture ships and fight to the last man. Be captain of my own galleon, master of my own life. Bull was not born to serve anybody."

"Exactly, Bull, exactly. You're crude all the way through, and you only go after the biggest prize."

"Does he think I'm an idiot? Doesn't he think I can hear his sly tongue?"

"Take the ship, Bull. Take the ship and get the fortune that's waiting off the coast of Africa."

"We're going to Bahia, and that's final."

"Then I'll do it myself," whispered Tom.

"Over my dead body," growled Bull.

Tom unfolded a sea chart. "That's not impossible," he said softly.

"Not so fast, my red-haired friend." Bull was standing with a pistol in his hand. The cigar stump moved from side to side between his black teeth.

Tom looked up. "But Mr. Bull, would you really shoot an unarmed boy?"

"I saw what he did to Indigo Moon. He may be hot-tempered, but deep inside he's as cold as a shark. Maybe the time has come for us to find a place for the untainted Tom O'Connor. A place behind lock and key."

"My sister will flay you alive, Bull."

"She would make a good figurehead, if he understands what I mean."

"I thought we were friends. I thought we stood shoulder to shoulder. I was the one, after all, who got rid of Mrs. Brown for you."

"All of it," bellowed the captain.

"All of it, Bull?"

"I want all of it, not half. The honor can go to the red-haired boy, but the gold stays with Bull. Otherwise the little Boto man will never see his home again, as sure as my name is C. W. Bull."

Tom straightened up. "Captain Bull," he said, "you have my word as a man of honor. All of the fortune will be yours."

"Did he say a man of honor?"

"Then take my word as a thief, damn it all, if that will make you happy."

Bull leaned forward and lowered his voice. "Can you write it down, you apostle of Lucifer?"

"Of course. I almost forgot that you can read now."

A minute later the document was completed. Tom extended his hand. The captain shook it.

"To the Bissagos Islands," said Tom.

"To the Bissagos Islands."

27 Prince Abebe's Ring

THE CRESCENT MOON HANGS LOW over the islands of São Miguel. The wind in the palms hums a melody about the sea, for that is where it comes from. In the sand lie ripe coconuts, downy as infants.

Birds cross the moon like the strokes of a brush, and from the jungle comes the shrill call of a trumpeter bird. Then silence returns, settling over the low houses along the slumbering coast.

On the beach are the seven skiffs that for a time have granted the passengers solid ground under their feet. The Portuguese are sleeping soundly at the big inn. The day was spent taking on freshwater so that the ship could set course for the mainland in the morning.

That's the plan. That's what Captain Bull has told his passengers.

But at this late hour ten black hands and two white ones are working at the galleon's capstan, which slowly but surely is weighing anchor. Afterward Tom distributes freshwater to his new crew.

The slaves drink in silence. They don't speak to each other, merely stare at the scars made by their shackles—and at the hand that split the chains.

They're standing on the upper deck, and the mood is strained. The slaves watch the formidable captain, who has told them to be as quiet as mice. They have just emerged from the cargo hold and do not yet trust their new status. One of the young men actually tries to jump overboard, but Feo manages to stop him. The fellow is shaking all over and his fear is about to infect the whole group.

Tom looks at the shore and nods to Bull who, in a mixture of Spanish, English, and Portuguese, explains that they have decided to set sail. But his words seem to make no impression.

Sunday Morning points out a woman who was the one keeping up everyone's courage during the most difficult times. She is tall and slender, quite young but with the composure of an older woman. She is holding an infant who was born on the galleon, with Feo acting as midwife. Only three hours ago she came to the bridge and made Tom take the baby in his arms.

"It's a little girl." Tom smiles at Bull, who is standing at the wheel.

"Yes, I can see that," the captain says gruffly.

Feo goes over to him. "The question is whether this little girl is going to be put in shackles like her mother. What do you think, Bull?"

"Can't you see that I'm on duty here?"

"Have you ever tried to hold such a tiny baby, Captain Bull?"

"Isn't that what women are for?"

"But what about the shackles, Bull? The girl obviously wasn't born with them on."

At that moment Boto appears. He has sewn a shift for the child, made from the Portuguese flag.

"I suppose she's going to end up wearing a bonnet too." Bull snickers and spits on the deck.

"I think there's actually enough material left for a bonnet," murmurs Boto.

Bull stares off into space. "Then maybe there's enough for a skullcap for the first officer," he grumbles. "It would suit his red hair."

Tom smiles. "But I don't think we'll need any shackles."

Feodora takes the infant and goes back to the hold to the child's mother. That night all of the slaves' chains are tossed into the sea.

The new mother asks Feodora whether Tom O'Connor has bought their freedom. Feo goes over to her. "It's a long way home," she says, "and if we don't work together and do as the captain says, we'll never get out of this bay."

"Is he our new master?" The woman points at Bull.

"Just say yes," mutters the captain, adding that the truth, in limited quantities, never hurt anybody.

Nyo Boto comes tottering out on deck. He looks from Bull to the group of blacks and then starts speaking, as quietly and calmly as always. It sounds as if he has begun telling a long story.

Tom glances at Bull, who narrows his eyes and asks him what's going on.

"Boto is telling them a story about the prince's ring," says Tom. "About how he became a slave. And about how he was set free. He's also telling them that Tom O'Connor is his best friend."

"I suppose he's not going to mention who saved his life when his black legs were crushed to kindling," growls Bull, swaggering a bit.

In the meantime Feodora has poured a tankard of rum, which she hands to Bull. "The story Boto is telling is as long as the voyage to Africa, and if we have to wait until dawn for him to reach the end, then we'll wait until dawn. Because we're not going anywhere without the slaves' help. Apart from the fact that they're not slaves anymore."

"Is the spawn going to teach the fish now?" Bull hitches up his belt.

"It was just a reminder."

The captain leans down. "When you threw the shackles into the deep, the ship's fortune vanished," he growls. "The Devil take me if it was part of the deal that the blacks were supposed to go free. I won't stand for it, O'Connor. You've foisted many things on me, but Bull is not going to stand for this. The deal was for the Bissagos Islands and that's all. The blacks will be sold as soon as we reach the next harbor."

Feo crosses her arms. "There's something I have to tell you, Captain Bull."

Tom sighs and shuts his eyes. In the meantime Feo says that Bull must have forgotten that he is no longer the captain of a pirate ship, and that there are no slaves on this galleon.

"Does she see this?" Bull aims his pistol at Feo.

Tom asks quietly if he might say something, but Bull ignores him.

"One more word out of this Spanish finch, and we'll be using her as a telescope. When I say that the blacks will be sold, then they're going to be sold, damn it. Is that understood, Miss Vasgues?"

"Say yes, Feo," whispers Tom. "Do as I say, just for once, otherwise we'll never get out of here."

Feo looks at the captain with a furious smile. "Not on your life! We can't ask the people to work day and night so that you, Bull, can collect your fortune, only to sell them at the nearest harbor. When I was little I had a tendency to give things away and then demand to have them back later. That was an unforgivable habit. I realize that now. So I'm not cutting the shackles off these people and then putting them back on later."

Bull cocks the hammer of his pistol.

At that moment Boto appears. He's holding some sort of hair clasp in his hand. The clasp doesn't look like much, and the primitive teeth have been worn crooked.

"What the hell is that supposed to be?" Bull waves his pistol in annoyance.

"It's a gift," says Boto, "from those people over there." He cocks his head toward the group of blacks who are watching Bull with wide eyes. "They want to thank the captain for giving them their freedom."

"Unfortunately, I don't think the captain wants their gift," says Feo. "Aside from the fact that the clasp is old and worn, it's Bull's plan that we should work these people for the rest of the voyage and then sell them at the nearest marketplace."

Nyo Boto nods in his customary way and starts tottering back to the group of slaves.

"Where does he think he's going?" bellows the captain.

Boto turns around and replies that he's just going to give back the clasp.

"He'll do nothing of the kind, damn it all. Instead he's going to . . . I will . . . give me that clasp, you crippled hunchback."

The captain tears the clasp out of Boto's hand.

The slaves look startled. "I think you're supposed to put it in your hair," explains Boto.

"I'm not going to put any damn thing in my hair."

The woman with the little baby hands her child to Feo and comes over to Bull. She looks a bit scared, but she takes the clasp, gathers up Bull's hair, and fastens it.

The captain stands as rigid as a stick and stares, dumbfounded, at the woman. A breeze rustles the mainsail and tugs gently at the rigging. The woman takes her baby back from Feo and snuggles it against her shoulder.

Bull glances sideways at Tom. "Is he standing there laughing at my expense?"

"Certainly not, Captain, sir."

Bull glares from Tom to Feo and from Feo to Boto. His eyes are alert.

He is breathing in short little gasps and shifting his feet. "Isn't this old tub ever going to put out to sea?" he roars.

The slaves flinch.

Tom picks up the bottle of rum. "Yes, it is," he says, "but first we're going to drink a toast to the ship. Then we're going to toast the captain. I seem to recall that the captain has had to put up with a rebellious crew before, hasn't he?"

Bull looks at him with wide eyes. "You must be joking," he thunders. "I won't soon forget those devils that I gathered up in Port Royal last winter. Murderers and thieves, the whole lot of them."

Feo takes the captain's arm. "Tell me about it, Bull," she says in a silky voice. "It would be nice, for a change, to hear a story from real life."

"Let me start from the beginning," he growls, "for the world has never seen the likes of that rabble. There was only one thing they understood, and that was the taste of the whip. But does she think I managed to break them?"

"Let me guess." Feo pauses for effect. "Yes, I do believe you did, Captain. By God, I think you probably managed to transform those murderers and bandits into first-class pirates. What an achievement. It makes me quite dizzy."

"Yes, well, I'm nobody's fool," says Bull with a smile, and then he goes on to tell them how, in a moment of inspiration, he thought up the idea of chopping off the fingers of his men.

An hour later the galleon heads out with all sails set. The wind is from the south and the course is clear. The ship plows through the waves. Along the railing stand the black youths, cheering as the water is hurled in salty sprays over the deck. In the galley the women are working with Feo and Boto, who at dawn totters up to the bridge with the captain's first meal on the free galleon.

Bull looks at the bowl of food. "What's that supposed to be?"

"It's fu-fu," says Boto.

One day follows another.

The captain issues orders to his new crew. Tom shows them how to climb the uppermost yards, how to set the sails and navigate, and how to measure their speed and make best use of the wind. The men turn out to be fast learners and good seamen.

Weeks give way to months, and one morning Tom rouses Nyo Boto out of the hammock that he has made for himself.

As always when Tom shows up to wake him, Boto is already alert. This continues to be a mystery to Tom, but on this morning he has other things to think about. He helps Boto up to the bridge and hands him the telescope.

"Look carefully," whispers Tom, "because they're still very small, but they really are there. The captain showed them to me before he went to bed."

But Nyo Boto ignores the telescope and gazes out to sea with his naked eye. "I can see them," he says. "I saw them before I woke up. The Bissagos Islands."

Tom leans against the big wheel, watching Boto, who totters down the stairs and positions himself at the port railing. Then Tom goes down to join him. "With the wind we now have," he says, "you'll be home before sundown."

"I know," says Boto. For the first time in all the days Tom has known him, Boto looks a little uncertain.

"I understand," whispers Tom, "I understand how you feel, Boto. I felt the same way when I finally saw Nevis."

Nyo Boto leans the back of his head against the timber. "The closer we get," he says, "the greater the distance between us, Tom. I can feel it in my stomach. Every night I've lain in bed, listening to the rigging and the water against the bow, telling me that it will soon all be over. I've asked Sunday to stay with me, and she said that she will. I haven't asked you, Tom, because you belong somewhere else."

"I hardly know where I belong," murmurs Tom.

"There are some people who belong in between," says Boto.

Tom looks out at the sea and nods. "Tell me about your islands."

"There is a fort," Boto explains, tilting his head back, "with cannons. No slave ship will ever come into the bay to take us away. But beyond the fort lie the villages and fields, the pens with our animals, and the big house where the king lives with his family. He and his men are the ones who built the fort. He protects us. He will never forget the night when the Portuguese ship *Santa Helena* sent sailors and soldiers to the islands. They pretended to come in friendship. Happily we rowed out to the ship, where they put us in chains."

"They took his son," whispers Tom.

Boto nods. "Yes, they took the prince."

"But now you have come home," says Tom. "And one day you will succeed your father as king."

Nyo Boto looks at the little gray ring on his finger. "I remember when we lay in the cargo hold. They had divided us up according to age. I lay next to him. I thought that as long as we had him with us, nothing bad would happen. But day by day he began to fade, until one night he was gone. I took the ring off his finger and promised him that I would bring it back to the islands. Early the next morning the crew came to get the dead. They dragged him out by his feet. Maybe that was what caused all the commotion."

"Who are you talking about?" asked Tom.

"I'm talking about the king's son, Prince Abebe."

Boto looked at Tom. "My father is a fisherman," he said quietly. "But a very good fisherman. He has his own boat and every morning he goes out to the fishing spots with my brothers."

Nyo Boto took Tom's hand and shrugged. "I'm not Prince Abebe, Tom. I'm just Nyo Boto."

Tom sat lost in his own thoughts for a moment. Then he nodded, as if he had known all along. At the same time he felt an unfamiliar warmth behind his eyes. He pressed a kiss on Boto's forehead and started to laugh. He laughed through his tears and saw a little smile spread across Nyo Boto's brown face, a cautious little smile preceding a great and heavy solemnity.

"The Devil take me if you're not the world's biggest liar," said Tom.

"No," replied Boto, "you are, Tom."

They are sitting in Gianlucca's canoe. Bull, Feodora, Sunday, Tom, and Nyo Boto. It's evening and the shadows lie like sharks' teeth over the wide bay where five seaworthy vessels of a different type are on their way toward them. In each canoe sit four men, and all of them are carrying guns. On the shore can be seen a large group of people, also men. But according to Boto, that is normal.

"We shall soon see," thunders Bull, dipping his paddle in the water.

As they approach the native canoes, they are hailed in a language that Tom doesn't recognize. With an effort Boto gets to his feet and answers the men in his own language. Soon all the canoes have come alongside Gianlucca's boat, which doesn't look like much next to the others.

The men point their pistols at Bull. Boto leans forward and hands one of them the little gray ring. This prompts an agitated murmuring. A couple of men fire their guns into the air. Tom doesn't understand what they're saying, but he hears the name Abebe repeated over and over again.

Bull gives him a wink and raises his eyebrows in anticipation.

Now there is a great deal of activity on shore, where the news has spread like wildfire. Women and children, old and young, storm toward the water, and at last he appears. The king of the Bissagos Islands. A short stocky man wearing a white coat. He has a gold chain around his neck and a yellow straw hat on his head. At his arrival everyone falls silent.

Tom helps Boto out of the boat and watches him totter up to the old man; he bows and hands him the ring. The king speaks to a group of men, who study Boto's ring. Then the king takes the gray ring and holds it over his head. His gesture unleashes a jubilant roar from everyone around him.

Tom looks at Feodora. From far off comes the sound of deep, thundering drums, reverberating across the bay.

"We can damn well hope that they're not cannibals," grumbles Bull.

"If they are," says Feo, "maybe you could get a job as a cook, Captain Bull."

The king and his retinue are on their way up to the fort. Behind them follow the villagers in small groups, dancing.

"Have they forgotten about us?" mutters Feo.

"No," says Tom, pointing to two men coming toward them.

In Spanish one of them says, "Welcome to our islands."

They were given lodgings in three small huts. Basins of freshwater were brought so they could tidy up. Afterward they were escorted down to a clearing in the forest where a long table had been set up with places for fifty people. They were seated not far from the king, who greeted each of them and said something that sounded like a warm thank you.

The dinner went on for hours, and in addition to the many courses served, the guests were treated to entertainment—dancing and singing—which was interrupted only by speeches that Tom, Feo, and Bull could not understand.

Bull whispered to Tom that it probably hadn't been such a bad idea after all to bring his son home. As far as Bull could tell, the king appeared to be a very wealthy man. On the whole, the captain was in splendid spirits, displaying a ravenous appetite and an impressive thirst.

Tom spent most of his time watching Nyo Boto. He was seated between a woman and a man who, unlike all of the others, were not wearing jewelry or fine clothes. The man and the woman ate very little, drank almost nothing, and in general looked rather ill at ease.

Feo leaned close to Tom. "It's strange that Boto isn't sitting next to his father," she said.

Tom sighed. "There's a reason for that. But you'll have to be patient."

The king was the first to leave the table, and after his departure, the dinner broke up. Bull, slightly tipsy, allowed himself to be escorted to his hut. He shouted to Tom that as far as the gold was concerned, he was prepared to wait until morning.

Soon after, Tom was lying on his pallet, looking up at the straw-covered ceiling. Feo had come to visit him and was sitting on the floor. The village was now very quiet. Except for a dog barking at the moon, the only sound was the breeze rustling.

"What are you thinking about?" asked Feo.

"Nothing," replied Tom.

"You're lying."

"Yes, I'm lying. Because I'm the world's biggest liar."

"How does somebody get to be the world's biggest liar?"

"It just takes a little imagination," said Tom, "and one other thing."

"Tell me what it is, you Irish half-breed." Feo smiled.

"It requires that you know the truth."

"If you're so clever, then maybe you know why Nyo Boto wasn't sitting with his father?"

Tom hesitated. "But he was."

Feodora got up and stood next to Tom for a long time. "What exactly are you saying?"

"I'm saying that Prince Abebe is dead, and that Nyo Boto is the son of a fisherman."

Feo looked at Tom in disbelief. "Do you mean to tell me that you've traveled halfway around the world to bring the son of a fisherman back to his family?"

"Something like that," Tom said softly.

"What an achievement, Tom O'Connor, what a magnificent achievement. Will the world ever learn to understand an Irishman? And now here he lies in the Bissagos Islands without a penny to his name, just as poor as when he was scrubbing tables at the inn back on Nevis. What a miserable half-breed you are."

Tom smiled to himself. "What does a Spaniard know about heroes?" he muttered and fell asleep.

The next day Tom stood in the village secretly watching Nyo Boto, who was sewing buttons on to a new shirt. He was sitting with an older man who had apparently been trained as a tailor. They were deeply absorbed in their work and paid no attention to anything else.

Perhaps that's what convinced Tom that it was time. There were still a few details that had to be taken care of; for instance, he had yet to tell Bull that he probably shouldn't expect quite as much gold as he had been hoping for. Most of the former slaves had decided to stay on the islands, but a few of them had chosen to remain with the ship.

Tom was on his way to tend to Gianlucca's old canoe when he ran into Sunday Morning. Maybe their meeting was not by chance, maybe she had followed him, because suddenly she was standing on the path, smiling with embarrassment.

Tom glanced at Bull, who was walking around the canoe, making it ready.

"I'm glad to hear that you're going to stay on these islands with Nyo Boto's family," said Tom.

The girl smiled and nodded shyly, then asked whether Tom thought he would ever go back to Jamaica.

"Of course I'll go back to Jamaica," replied Tom.

"Maybe," said Sunday, "maybe one day you'll meet my mother and father again."

Tom took her hand. "Of course I will. I promise."

Sunday backed away, stretched out her arm, and threw him a kiss. Then she spun on her heel and flew off, like a butterfly.

Tom turned around to Bull, who was standing right behind him.

"What did the little girl want?" asked the captain.

"To say good-bye," muttered Tom, recalling his time at Aron Hill when the taster had told stories to the kitchen staff about his days fishing for sharks. Some of the stories had been close to the truth, and some of them had been utter lies. But they were all swallowed whole by little Sunday Morning, who had such faith in life.

Suddenly Tom put his arms around the captain and held on tightly.

"What the devil?" growled Bull. "What's the meaning of this?"

"It's not what you think," whispered Tom, burying his face in Bull's chest. "But sometimes a person has to stand . . . with his arms like this."

"Is that so?"

"Yes," said Tom, "that's so." Tom took a deep breath and patted Bull on the chest. "All right," he said, "now I'm fine. Now they're all gone and will live only in my memory. Sunday Morning, Sugar George, Ina, Joop, poor Mrs. Briggs, and Fanny. Not to mention Ramón the Pious." Tom sighed. "In truth, flesh and blood turn to ashes and rise up again as tall tales. Some of them have already been erased, like the ripples on the seafloor."

"Not me," growled Bull, pinching Tom's cheek.

"No, not you, Bull. And I'm glad about that. Do you have any children, Captain, sir?"

"It's possible."

"Don't you ever think about them?"

"Never! I detest children."

"Really? Why?"

Bull stuck his big dark face close to Tom's. "Because children have the unforgivable habit of growing up."

Tom smiled. "Not you, Bull. No matter how fierce you may be, there's still a remnant of innocence in you."

"Is that right?"

"Yes, that's right."

Bull smiled. "So I'm not completely rotten through and through?"

Tom tugged at his ear. "We'll see."

"Yes, because there's one small detail that we need to talk about," said the captain. "I thought we might discuss it over a drink in my cabin. The prince has mentioned our outstanding business matter to His Highness, hasn't he?"

"His what?"

"The king, Tom, the king." Bull smiled expectantly. "I'm talking about the fortune, of course."

Tom cleared his throat. "Oh yes, the fortune," he said. "I forgot all about that."

A short while later they were sitting in Bull's cabin, and the captain was pouring the drinks. They toasted each other and tossed down the rum.

"That's the way a pirate drinks," snarled Bull. "I'm shivering with anticipation and can hardly feel the bullet in my thigh. But Tom, tell your old friend about the gold. I tossed and turned all night. Your spiritual godfather has barely slept a wink."

Tom cleared his throat. "Let me start by telling you about this Ramón, who strangely enough was nicknamed the Pious. He was just as careless with mammon as he was with the truth. On the other hand, he had a heart of gold. As you do too, Captain, or my name isn't O'Connor. A richer man the world has never known."

The captain laughed loudly and held his clenched fist in front of Tom's face. "You're a thief, you Irish lad. If I didn't know better, I'd say it sounds like he's telling me that there wasn't a damn shilling in sight. Such poor taste would make the bullets fly and the funeral bells ring."

Tom gave the captain a wan smile. "Maybe we should partake of another drink, Captain, sir."

They toasted each other.

"Yes, because I can feel my whole body shivering with anticipation." Bull rolled his eyes.

"Anticipation, Bull?"

"I'm talking about the house I'm going to build with the generous reward. It will have fifteen gilded halls, a sparkling mirror room, fourteen privies, and a kitchen just like my old galley, which smelled of fresh thyme and cooked wenches. I'll have four balconies, one for each corner of the Earth, all with a view of the ocean. For Bull's palace will be built on an island, chosen for its heavy surf, its rocky cliffs, and its punctual but generous tides, which every day will leave behind something from the sea. What are trifles to the ocean are riches for a man, and my house will bulge with all sorts of wreckage, and it will be more beautiful and splendid than the sultan's palace. Look, people will say, that's where the richest man in town lives, C. W. Bull. What majesty. He has a chest with three hundred pistols, one for every rascal he ever shot, and in the study there's a cupboard with forty blue-black fingers, to remind him of his loyal cohorts who served on the proud ship that flew Bull's flag. In the garden will grow lemon and olive trees, and at the southern corner of the house will stand a flowering fruit tree with the sweetest pomegranates. Yes, I can see it all now, and the sight makes me almost sentimental."

"What a dream, Captain, sir," said Tom, clasping his hands in front of his chest. "What a marvelous vision. You're a real poet."

Bull leaned back and said that plenty of good poetry can be hidden inside a solid bout of drinking.

Tom sighed and glanced up at the ceiling. "You're so right about that, Captain, sir. But tell me, have you ever heard the story about the green pelican?"

Bull narrowed his eyes. "To hell with that mangy fowl," he snarled. "Let's talk about the gold instead." The captain rubbed his hands together with glee.

"Believe me, Mr. Bull," said Tom, "there are more important things in life than that base metal. People say, you know, that no matter how much gold the Pope may have stashed away in the Vatican cellars, his church craves still more, for as we all know, greed is a bottomless pit."

Tom reached out for the bottle but Bull shoved it aside and grabbed his cutlass, swinging it like a pendulum under Tom's chin.

Instead of flinching, Tom moved closer to the big captain and looked him deep in the eye. "Captain Bull," he whispered, "you, who have sailed the seven seas and flayed more cadets than there are rats in the Spanish armada, is it true that you sold your soul to the Devil?"

"For half a pot of drinking water and a dead rooster. Soul, heart, and conscience. They all disappeared one October night in the year of Our

Lord 1627. For I was at the ends of the Earth, and out there you can't be stingy, let me tell you."

Tom flung his arms wide. "Captain Bull," he said, "at this moment I am offering to give you back what you lost. Your pure soul, your untainted conscience, your fearless pride. The child in you will reawaken."

"Sing to me, you liar, sing. Tell the reborn man how this miracle could happen."

Tom lowered his eyes. "It's quite simple, Captain. Give me your hand and I will release you."

"Release me, he says? From what?"

"From your greed. Because any fool knows that greed makes a man blind. But it's only one finger, and you'll still have nine left to do good deeds. Laem Sing was his name, wasn't it? Yes, that's right. Afterward we'll give the severed ring finger to the sharks, whose simple lives remind me so much of yours."

"What the hell? Is he comparing me to a flounder?"

"On the other hand," continued Tom, "you'll be a whole man afterward, with your heart, your pride, and a conscience as pure as the first baby tooth. Because if truth be told . . ." Tom paused for effect before he went on. "If truth be told, Nyo Boto is no more a prince than you or I; he's the son of a fisherman."

Bull stared straight ahead, dumbfounded, but then he leaped up and swung his cutlass.

"I knew it," he bellowed. "The gold is gone. I won't get a tuppence for my trouble, and yet he has the impudence to want to make me an invalid. There went the palace and the garden with the pomegranates, while I'm left with nothing but the memory of forty blue-black sausage fingers and half a pot of rum. But I'll make you eat your words, you Irish bastard."

The captain sat down at his desk and pulled Tom close. "It's going to cost you, O'Connor, it's going to cost you your sick tongue. No man under the sun makes a fool of C. W. Bull. The last one who tried is now running an inn for sticklebacks south of the Tropic of Cancer, three miles down. If he knows what I mean."

"I'm getting tired of admiring your regard for the English language, Captain, sir," said Tom. "I myself will have to settle for a few brief words.

What's it going to be? Finger number forty-one or a plug between your legs?"

Bull's expression opened like a fan. "Is he adding insult to injury?"

"Not at all, Captain, sir, but under the desk I'm holding my dagger, and it's pointed right at the Captain's genitals. I've always kept my knife sharp, and with a single cut I could sever whatever pleasure the Captain takes in standing up to urinate."

"How dare you, boy? The Devil must have been present when you issued from your mother's womb."

"Not as far as I know, but there were seven crocodiles on the wharf, if that means anything to you. I think it was an omen of a hot-tempered nature and a reckless regard for other people's lives and well-being. So. Let go of my collar, drop your cutlass, and say something nice that will soothe my irritable mood."

"You red-haired monster, you watery-eyed rabble, may your father's arms grow shorter and shorter and his rump begin to itch."

Tom pressed a sharp point against the captain's crotch. "Well, that's certainly not what I had in mind," he said with a sigh.

"I don't trust him any farther than I can throw him," sneered Bull.

"That was exactly the sentiment of a bomba at Aron Hill and a first officer named Moon." Tom closed one eye. "If you know what I mean."

A moment passed, and the cutlass fell to the floor. Bull released his hold on Tom's collar.

"So now the only thing left is the soothing words," said Tom.

The captain rolled his head and gnashed his teeth. "Unfortunately, I'm a little out of practice when it comes to sweet words. We had a rather different way of talking on my merry ship, as he may recall."

Tom shrugged apologetically. "As the bald man said when he found a comb: what do I care? And let's not forget who bestowed on you the alphabet and the pleasures of reading."

"What pleasure will I get from being able to spell pomegranate if my member is lying on the floor? Oh, you Irish demon, there's a cobra inside your jaws."

"Flattery will get you nowhere, and my patience is running out like the last grains in the ship's hourglass."

Bull glanced around furiously but then looked down at his crotch and his expression changed. A reluctant smile spread across his big mouth.

"Upon closer consideration," he growled, "we've spent a good many hours together that might be called pleasant. My whole crew of sober men could have testified that I have never harmed so much as a hair on the boy's head, even though his tongue has often sparked my desire to rip it right out. And let's not forget that shrew of a sister who was foisted on me. A lass that came into this world when Satan mated laziness with impudence. And yet I never allowed it to ruin my good spirits. No, old Bull turned a deaf ear and suppressed his desire to make belts out of her back. My innate modesty almost forbids me to add that I also kept that skinny slave alive, even though the crew, especially when we were becalmed and the days dragged, would have liked to have a go at him."

"You just saved one testicle," said Tom, "but I would think you could do better than that."

"I can feel the rage coming," roared Bull, as he kicked the desk, which slammed against the wall.

In less than a second he had seized his cutlass and raised it overhead, only to stop cold. In disbelief he stared at what Tom was holding in his hands and what had been threatening his life. The pen was red and the feather was broken in two places.

"What in hell? Is he threatening me with a pen?"

Tom stretched out his arms. "It's the weapon of the future," he said, "and I am now your loyal servant and slave. You can do with me as you please. I'm as poor as a church mouse, homeless and orphaned, and thus with nothing left to lose."

"He's going to end up in Hell."

"Well, then we'll see each other again," said Tom, bowing his head.

At that moment a shot whistled through the air. The bullet tore off the captain's three-cornered hat, which landed on the floor of the cabin with a hole in the middle.

In the doorway stood Feodora, holding a pistol in each hand. "Next time," she said, "I'll take better aim. That's a promise." She put down the pistols and took the speechless Bull by the hand. "But let's not fight over trifles. We've been invited to dinner with Boto's family. I thought I might comb the Captain's hair and delouse his beard for the occasion."

· · ·

They're sitting at the long table belonging to fisherman Boto, who is presiding at one end. His nine children are seated according to age. There are many songs and a great deal of laughter. Even though Bull claims that the wine is watery and there isn't enough of it, the mood is festive. The celebration goes on until the moon rises, yellow and warm, behind the silhouette of the Portuguese galleon anchored out in the bay.

Tom, Bull, and Feodora are standing next to Nyo Boto on the beach, where the canoe has been made ready for departure. It's a quiet evening with almost no wind. The gentle waves strike the shore like the even breaths of someone sleeping. Boto gives the captain a necklace made of shells strung on fishing line and arranged by color.

"Am I supposed to put this bit of tinsel around my neck?" grumbles Bull.

"It will bring you good fortune," Boto answers, adding, "if you're lucky." Then he gives Feo a strap made of crocodile hide and a tortoiseshell clasp.

Feo smiles and hugs Boto, whispering something in his ear. She walks over to the captain, who is pulling the canoe into the water.

Only Tom remains. The distance between him and Nyo Boto is a mere four feet. All he has to do is stretch out his hand. But he doesn't move.

Boto's expression is steady and inquisitive, calm and a little melancholy.

Tom has known that this moment would arrive and has prepared himself for it, yet the words refuse to come, as if they are chained inside his throat. He takes a deep breath and helplessly flings out his arms. He hears singing in the darkness, coming from all sides, and now he sees the first torches, glittering like fireflies on the mountain slopes. The whole village is on the move, men and women, young and old. Their torches merge like a long luminous river on its way to the sea.

By the time they reach the shore, the song has acquired words. It makes Tom's skin prickle. But only when the first torchbearers are standing behind Nyo Boto, is it possible to see how many there are. And only when they stop singing and silence descends, does Boto take two steps forward and reach for Tom's hand.

Tom tries to smile but gives up and looks at the knot formed by his hand and Boto's. "Live well, Nyo Boto," whispers Tom. "Live well, my best friend."

Nyo Boto gives Tom his red shirt and slips a little gray ring on Tom's finger.

At that instant the torches are put out. All that remains is the slapping of the waves in the moonlight.

The slender canoe glides toward the big ship. In the bow sits Captain Bull, in the middle Feodora Dolores Vasgues. Tom is paddling. "Let me tell you about El Casto Josephine," he says.

Bull turns around, "Sing, you liar, sing," he bellows, "but I would rather hear about the sneak from Cádiz, the one who called himself the Pious."

"Yes, but Captain, sir," says Tom, "they were one and the same person. If we're going to have that story, then it's best we start at the beginning. You see, the story begins on a dark and stormy night in the year of Our Lord 1639 . . . ."

Tom's voice disappears into the sound of the waves, returns for a brief moment carried on the breeze, and then vanishes.

Epilogue

THREE YEARS LATER Tom O'Connor returned to Nevis and continued to run the inn in his mother's name. Tom remained on the island until the morning when he collapsed in his skiff, at the age of eighty-three. And if it were not for the names that had once been carved into the thwart in awkward, childish letters, old Tom O'Connor would never have been brought home from the sea. He was placed in the ground next to his mother beneath the olive and lemon trees, which grew at the south end of the inn.

Tom O'Connor left behind a wife and two children, a son and a daughter. The son, TomBoto, was born to him and his one and only wife, who came from Jamaica, while Annabelle was the girl that his wife brought with her to the marriage.

As an adult, Feodora Dolores Vasgues traveled to Spain and from there to England, living out the rest of her days on the remote cliffs of the Scottish highlands, where she raised sheep. She never married but established a school for orphaned children.

Sugar George and Ina were reunited on Saint Christopher Island and lived there the rest of their days.

The fate of C. W. Bull is unknown, though it's claimed that he lived to be as old as Methuselah, and he may well be alive today.